ALSO BY MARY DI MICHELE

FICTION

Under My Skin

POETRY

Debriefing the Rose

Stranger in You

Luminous Emergencies

Necessary Sugar

Mimosa and Other Poems

TENOR OF LOVE

MARY DI MICHELE

A TOUCHSTONE BOOK
PUBLISHED BY SIMON & SCHUSTER
NEW YORK   LONDON   TORONTO   SYDNEY

For my father, Vincenzo Di Michele—
and for those who love and do not love opera

Touchstone
Rockefeller Center
1230 Avenue of the Americas
New York, NY 10020

Published simultaneously in Canada by Penguin Canada

TOUCHSTONE and colophon are registered trademarks
of Simon & Schuster, Inc.

For information regarding special discounts for bulk purchases,
please contact Simon & Schuster Special Sales at 1-800-456-6798
or business@simonandschuster.com

Quote on page 295 is from *Letters of the Younger Pliny,* translated by Betty Rodice.
Penguin Classics, 1963. Reprinted with permission.

Manufactured in the United States of America

1   3   5   7   9   10   8   6   4   2

LIBRARY OF CONGRESS CATALOGING IN PUBLICATION DATA
Di Michele, Mary.
Tenor of love / Mary Di Michele.
p.   cm.
"A Touchstone book."
1. Caruso, Enrico, 1873–1921—Fiction. 2. Tenors (Singers)—Fiction.
3. Singers—Fiction. 4. Opera—Fiction. 5. Italy—Fiction. I. Title.
PR9199.3.D498T46 2005   813'.54—dc22   2004058908

ISBN 0-7432-6692-7

AUGUST 3, 1921

At the central train station, a lone traveler, a woman, steps off the overnight train from the north. Her face is hidden by a veil—a mantilla of midnight lace. She wears a long black gown. Her dress, the fullness and length of the skirt, the corset, look like a costume from another era. As she walks, the clacking of her heels echoes through the station.

In the predawn, in the precious coolness of first light in August, there's not a cab to be seen outside the station. But she doesn't need one; it's a single kilometer to her destination. And she knows this city. For ten years she once lived here, for ten years she sang opera on its central stage. But that was some time ago, and she has not returned. Only he could make her come back to Naples. Before the world adulated the tenor Enrico Caruso, she loved him.

She is a traveler without luggage; she only carries a drawstring purse, its woven handle wrapped around her wrist. She makes her way slowly across Piazza Garibaldi, and then turns onto the *corso* towards the bay, to the boulevard of grand hotels by the waterfront. As she walks her foot catches on the hem of her long skirt and she stumbles. She reaches out to air, there is nothing to keep her from falling, but the reaching out balances her, and she rights herself. She does not fall onto the dirty, litter-strewn street.

Turning onto the marine road, she does not glance behind her to the sinister beauty of the volcano, nor to the side at the bay, at the familiar flashing blue horizon. She doesn't need to look at the sea when she can smell it. There is a brisk wind tugging at her veil that carries with it the sting of salt along with the smell of kelp and decaying fish. Her legs feel leaden yet she walks steadily on.

As the sun rises the air thins, and the light looks like thinned milk to her now, blue in its hue. There's nobody on the street except for long shadows (long shadows cast by nobody). She continues to look neither to the right nor to the left. The long skirt hides her steps. She might be a puppet on wheels inching ahead, drawn along by some invisible wire.

She approaches the Hotel Vesuvio; she sees the gleaming brass of its doors. Then she looks up to the suites. The windows are blank faces. Enrico Caruso's body lies somewhere within. Long queues to view the body are expected to snake around the doors of the grand hotel, and to wind through the surrounding streets.

Now that Caruso is dead, she herself feels like a ghost. She stops by the main entrance and imagines what the interior of the hotel might be like at that hour. She imagines it as half dormant, the night clerk at the reception desk dozing over a newspaper, his face with an orange cast from the lamp burning at his side. And if she is a ghost, she will not be seen, she will not be questioned until she gets to heaven's gate.

Who is she? Now that he is dead, who besides her sister, Ada, remembers? If Dante were to make a second voyage into the underworld, he might see them there, the tenor and the two sisters, in one of those burning circles in hell, bound together forever in lust and jealousy. In the inferno she would be compelled to confess.

She pushes through the door and it is as she has envisioned it. The desk clerk does not look up from his paper. Like a cat, she walks on her toes, soundlessly across the marble floor. As if her grief requires stealth. She steps into the elevator and presses the button for the seventh, the uppermost floor. Inside the elevator the walls seem to close in on her. She sees them padded with silk, as the airless container that is a coffin. With a jerking motion, the elevator starts to move, but the sensation is strange, she's not sure if she is ascending or falling into some abyss. So it is with relief that at last the doors slide open, drawn open by invisible hands, this mechanism seems mysterious to her, the stuff of fairy tales, and she steps into a hall of shining darkness where the floors and polished brass fixtures glow in orange-red incandescence.

At the door of the royal suite, again she hesitates. But, separated from him now as she is only by the thickness of a door, how can she stop there? What does she have to fear—that the widow's tears might drown out her own? She raises her fist to knock. She must knock several times before she gets a response, steeling herself each time to try again.

At last a servant answers her knock, and she is relieved because she knows him, that gentle man has been in Caruso's service for decades.

"Signora." He bows graciously, but he does not smile. It is not a time for smiles.

She doesn't have to ask him; Martino knows why she is there. He beckons to her to follow him. It's a good time to come. Martino whispers that they're all sleeping, she need not fear encountering the wife.

The suite is gloomy. In the half-light they do not see the pale figure seeming to float down the hall. But Dorothy Caruso sees them.

IT IS ABSOLUTELY still in the household, nothing, nobody, is stirring. Dorothy's eyes flutter open. Though the shutters keep out the light, they are not firmly shut, they bulge out in the wind and she can see bands of blue light where they gape open at the top. A new day is dawning, and she will get up from her bed and put on the same blue dress she cast off onto the chair the night before.

Three years, what is it to remember three short years of marriage? It replays in her mind in the space of a few hours. Like a reel of film it has been playing and replaying to its snapping conclusion behind her closed but sleepless eyes throughout the night as she has been trying to remember it all. She must write it down before it is entirely lost. This is the story that is her life, her life with him, Enrico Caruso, and there will be no other story for her. But even now, it seems as if she can only grasp at small moments, her memories a series of anecdotes, little scenes like insects preserved in amber. Strung together they might make a beaded necklace—not a biography.

But, if she can lie in bed with her eyes closed and not sleep, Dorothy wonders, might Enrico be similarly lying in his bed, not really dead? Perhaps he is playing one of his jokes on her. How he loves to joke! Perhaps he is testing her, to see if she loves him. She loves him.

If she goes to his room now and sees his eyelids flutter then she will rejoice that his death is merely a bad dream. Yes, maybe just a joke, maybe just a bad dream, so she will go now to Enrico and ask him if he would like some coffee. Of course she won't disturb him if he wants to sleep later, he's been so ill. He needs his rest or they would not be sleeping separately, but if he would like coffee in bed, she'll bring it to him, just the way he likes it, black espresso without sugar. She'll make it without bothering the servants. Let them sleep, since they can. That way she will have a few moments alone with him as she sips at the bitter cup that only tastes good when she's with him.

Dorothy dresses. She moves about the suite very softly. The baby, Gloria, is sleeping in the adjoining room. She turns in her sleep, makes little snuffling noises, and then quiets. Dorothy bends over the crib and kisses her cheek. Blonde curls form an aura around the sleeping child's face.

Submerged as she is in grief, Dorothy feels as if she is floating down the hall towards Enrico's room. Four chairs are set up around his bedroom door with people sleeping in them. The coarse fat man is his brother, the two tender young men, one fair, one dark, are his sons, and the white-haired woman, his step-mother. Careful not to brush against and disturb the sleepers, Dorothy eases the door open.

The master bedroom has been turned into a shrine. Candles burn all around his bed. White flowers, so many he seems to be resting on a bed made up entirely of flowers, echo his pallor, their petals glowing in the candlelight. They have removed his pajamas and dressed him in a tuxedo. How could he possibly get any sleep in that outfit? Dorothy's throat constricts as she swallows the cry surging up to her lips. She stops by the foot of the bed, then slowly backs out of the room. She cannot wake him after all. She cannot touch him, not with the smell of death all around.

As she closes the bedroom door behind her, she hears a knock, the front door of the suite opening, and then some whispering. All his family is here, sleeping on chairs, Dorothy cannot imagine who would visit at such an hour. As she walks down the hall, two figures approach. It is Martino, leading a strange woman, a dark figure dressed as if for the operatic stage. Dorothy knows the story of Enrico's first love. This woman, she thinks, must be Ada Giachetti, the mother of his sons.

BOOK ONE

Rina

LITTLE SISTER

*In quella parte del libro de la mia memoria dinanzi
a la quale poco si potrebbe leggere, si torva una rubrica
la quale dice: Incipit vita nova.*

*In that part of the book of my memory before which little can be
deciphered, there is a rubric that reads: Here the new life begins.*
—DANTE, *LA VITA NUOVA*

I

Every summer my family would escape the heat and the crowds of Firenze and move to Livorno where we had an apartment on the uppermost floor of a building on Viale Regina Margarita. Poplars shaded our home there, singing sotto voce in the marine breezes. The scent of pinewood, tamarisk, and lime trees blended with the salt in the air.

It was early in July, nearly noon, when a young man presented himself at the door. In 1897 I was barely seventeen; I was sixteen and counting the days. The poplars shone so brightly that morning they were themselves green suns. Their leaves shivered in the heat and wind, the light in them rippled. The foliage seemed to move in waves so the street became a high sea, a sea not blue like the Ligurian, but verdant.

Only Mamma was home when he knocked. He came with a letter of introduction from Leopoldo Mugnone, the Sicilian conductor and composer who had helped launch my sister Ada's singing career. When the young Enrico Caruso asked Mamma if she could recommend a *pensione* for him to stay, she felt sorry for him and offered our spare room to this stranger carrying his things in a cardboard suitcase.

That morning Ada was rehearsing at the Goldini, while I was shopping at the farmers' market. Mamma had a craving for artichokes and I had gone to fetch some. I filled a sack with those thorny green roses. The prickles are on the head, surrounding the heart, and the choke is at the center. Roses don't threaten their own beauty; they keep their thorns on the stem. The artichoke is not a mistress, but a wife swathed in a chastity belt. Mother had been planning to stuff and stew the artichokes for dinner, but the tenor's unexpected arrival changed all that.

It must have been stepping out of the brightness of the afternoon and into the cool dimness of the house that made everything seem so dark, so altered. I smelled him before I saw him. His scent was a murky music composed of musk and wood, and yes, also some kitchen smells. It was more than the slick air of his brilliantine and the must of stale clothes that I sensed. It was the odor of cooking oil and of Sicilian olives spiced with garlic and chilies. It was a smell of eating in bed, not the invalid's, but the lover's.

The bag of artichokes dropped out of my hands. The loose heads rolled freely, bloodlessly, as if from the clean execution of the guillotine. I scrambled after them, gathering them up in my skirt.

"Signorina." At the sound of his voice I looked up and it was then I saw him for the first time, the view of his face from below. I was on my knees. He was smiling, and although he had already begun to laugh, from the angle that I saw him his face seemed grave and his eyes were obscured by deep shadows.

"Signorina," he repeated, and when he spoke the syllables resonated as if I were being called to worship by a golden bell. I say worship, but the voice had body, not just spirit. Maybe I had tasted something like it; maybe it was like cream, cream when it is whipped, the volume filled with sweetness. I felt a weakness in my stomach and in my knees. I felt a fluttering in my knickers as if a moth, asleep for sixteen years, had suddenly burst through its cocoon and was beating its wings against my bottom.

"Mamma" was the only word that escaped my lips. It was the voice of a doll you have to shake to make her talk.

I went running into the kitchen, the artichokes bunched up in my skirt, not aware that I was exposing myself. He followed closely. I turned and saw his grin and that his eyes were fixed on the lace of my bloomers. I dropped the artichokes again and that was the end of having them for dinner.

To THANK US for our hospitality, the *napoletano* insisted on taking us all out for dinner. He used the money the theater had advanced to him for lodging. We went to a trattoria nearby, nothing fancy, but where the food was always good.

The young man, Enrico Caruso, seated himself between Ada and me, but his chair was turned towards her and his thin frame angled her way. As soon as he saw Ada he seemed to forget me, and I began to watch as if from offstage, as if from the wings.

We were seated in the patio garden, so Ada was careful to stay in the shade of the awning. The tenor was a thin man, as dark as Ada was fair. His darkness might have affected an air of melancholy, but his eyes, his mouth, were mobile with lines of laughter. Laughter was a kind of light in his face; it shone even in the shade. I watched him watching her and tried to see what drew him to her. What was her allure? At twenty-four, Ada was a woman with a body ripe from having given birth the year before. Her complexion was creamy white, moist and glowing. She wore her hair pinned up at the back and combed away from her pale face, framed and softened by wispy curling tendrils. Her hair was the ashen color of wheat after the fields have been razed. Her eyes were chameleons; at times they were the color of seawater in the shallows where yellow sand makes it look green as a pasture, at other times they were the blue of ocean as on the horizon between sea and sky. Her eyes were green that day. In spite of the Neapolitan's gawking at her, Ada studied the menu as if unaware of his attention. You couldn't see her eyes then, just the eyelids, so finely veined they seemed purple, and the thick dusky lashes.

Mother ordered a simple dish, *spaghetti alla marinara,* and I chose what she chose, but Ada ordered the most expensive dish on the menu, *vitello,* stewed in Marsala and served in a cream sauce, and then dessert.

Ada led the conversation. "Verdi is divine, but he's old now, his music is getting tired. While this new composer, this Puccini, well, for me, he is a god among gods. His melodies make me throb when I sing them." She stretched out her white neck and touched it as she spoke as if to point to where the arias had pushed her heart into her throat. Ada was generous to this southern young man with her opinions, spreading out the wings of her beauty and her growing reputation. Ada already saw herself as a diva.

"Mugnone praised your beauty and your singing, signora. When the maestro showed me your photo, he wagged his finger at me and warned me not to fall in love with you."

"Do you think it's a good likeness?"

"If I may say so without offense, signora—it pales. Your complexion requires a portrait artist—nothing less than an artist will do to capture it."

"And how is that scoundrel? Does he miss me?"

"Miss you? Signora, they all pine for you, from the musicians to the stagehands. They say there is nobody like you! My poor head has been filled with visions of your beauty."

Miss her, I wished that we could miss her a little. What chance would I have with this man when my sister had him enthralled even before he met her?

Caruso took a sip of his wine, as well as a few sips of mineral water, and then continued with his Sicilian story. "Yes, Mugnone is a good and generous man. When the company closed for the season, he knew I needed to keep working and got this summer engagement in Livorno for me. But, let me tell you, I had quite a trial by fire on his stage.

"It's true that I like a little wine, but I never allow myself to get drunk. Our Neapolitan wines are light, like water. I can drink a couple of glasses and I'm refreshed, relaxed, ready to perform. But those Sicilian wines! They're closer to liquor than table wine. By the time I realized this I was drunk, and on my usual two tumblers with dinner.

"*Lucia di Lammermoor* was the production that night. Luckily the tipsy man knows no fear, but when I went to sing my role as

Edgardo, I slurred the lines: *'sorte dalla Scozia'* sounded like *'volpe dalla Scozia.'* I was jeered off the stage. After that I was ready to quit, to leave Sicily forever. Mugnone brought in another tenor to take my place. But, imagine this, the audience wouldn't accept a substitute, and he had to call me back because they kept shouting for the little drunken singer; they kept calling for me as the 'fox of Scotland.'

When the waiter came round to our table to pour more wine for us, the young tenor placed his hand over his glass and shook his head. With a wide smile, he said, "No, *grazie.*"

2

Living with my sister was like being blinded by sunlight. Before Ada's brilliance, that dizzy dancing of light on water, I felt dimmed. But I can't say I always minded when the intensity made me, for the sake of so much pleasure, squint. Ada was always the primary light, the dazzling one. The best I could do was to reflect her. Like the day moon, flattened, almost invisible in the depth of blue sky; the white of my face and the white of the fair-weather clouds were the same. My beauty was in harmonizing. Who, what man, would ever notice that? Perhaps someday a poet, dreamily looking up, might spot me. But most men were not poets, so I remained, because of my sister, a seventeen-year-old spinster.

Though Ada was now a married woman and a mother, she had abandoned her family to stay with us in Livorno. Nominally, it was just for the season: "My career demands it," Ada proclaimed. After they had married, Gino, her husband, whom she had met on the operatic stage, gave up his singing to work in the bank. But Ada wasn't prepared to give anything up; she kept performing publicly even when her pregnant belly began to show. One evening, from my seat in the audience, I saw the baby kick during an aria. I'm certain that if there had been a single birth staged among all those deaths in grand opera, my sister might have shown the audience the real thing.

Ada left her son to be the leading lady with the local opera company. When wet nurses can be hired for a few *soldini*, a woman with a purse needn't be tied down; she could keep her own big breasts firmly tucked inside her corset. If the child wanted his mother, he would have had to go to the opera to catch her dying as Verdi's Violetta or Puccini's Mimì on the stage of the Teatro Goldini. The poor child, his mother was lost to him. It was drama—it was role-playing that Ada really loved. The role of mamma that was not sung was not for her.

NOBODY EVER OVERLOOKED ADA, least of all the young Neapolitan tenor, Rico, as he urged us to call him. It was closer to his baptismal name, Errico. But "Enrico" sounded more like the name of a star, so he had changed it. Our aspiring star, Rico, became solemn when Ada ("sleepyhead," she called herself!) walked in, all primped and powdered as if even the family dining room were a stage set to showcase her beauty. Ada expected to be looked at; she rarely deigned to look at you. She kept her eyes lowered. They were heavily lidded, obscured by long lashes darkened with castor oil to make them seem even longer. Even as she kissed Papa good morning and sat beside him, her eyes stayed half closed, as if she were still in a dream—a dream about herself.

Even though Ada hardly glanced Rico's way, as soon as she made her entrance, Signor Napoli's mouth would drop open—

no longer to eat, but to gape. Though he had been joking while tearing thick slices of bread, soaking the crusty chunks in his bowl of steaming coffee and milk, slurping up heaping spoonfuls, the frothy milk forming a white scum on his black mustache, though he had been animated and partaking of the meal while talking to me or Papa, it all stopped then so that he could watch and listen to Ada. Rico would hang on to her every gesture; he seemed to be reading her desperately, as a singer might study an unfamiliar score, a new libretto, hoping for a starring role for himself. But when I spoke of Rico to Ada, she always dismissed him as the "little man, the pipsqueak."

"ADINA, ADETTA, ADETINA, ADELLA, ADELLINA ..." Every morning I had to listen to my father's variations on my sister's name, that unending string of endearments. There weren't enough syllables, not enough diminutives, in our language, not nearly enough variety in our phonetics, to express his delight in once again finding his firstborn child at the breakfast table.

"*Il sole si siede alla nostra tavola.*" The sun, the sun was sitting to table with us! Such extravagant phrases, yet my father was not a cavalier in the royal guards, but a civil servant in the national treasury. Still, his eyes were a blue so bright that when they turned to look at you it was like being placed in the limelight.

"Good morning, Papa."

"Good morning, Rina," he would answer. Apparently my name in itself was good enough for me.

For hours I have watched a man stroking a cat with such tenderness when that same man would disdain even to offer the lightest touch to his companion, his so-called lover. How Ada behaved at breakfast reminds me of that. It was on Papa that she lavished all her attention. She spoiled the older man in front of the young one. She catered to Papa's every need, as if he were the child: tucking in the napkin around his neck for him, offering to cool the hot sop of his breakfast, blowing on the spoon, her full lips puckered.

How a daughter indulges her father, how a lover strokes a cat, these are thinly coded signs, easily read. I was barely seventeen, but compared to Rico, I thought myself not the half as naive. At least not when it came to my sister.

"Would you like a little more hot milk in your coffee, Papa, or how about another sweet bun?" Ada coaxed.

Mother had already left for mass. We never saw her first thing in the morning, but we always found evidence of her attention in the table laid out for us with fresh bread and milk. I would make the espresso. My mother was a saint, and I wanted to be like her because I loved her. I was not myself so devout. I couldn't get up at first light to accompany her to church. But there were masses later in the morning on Sundays; I would go with her then. While Mamma practiced her faith daily, praying for hours on her knees, first at mass, then performing her novenas, I was a weekend Catholic.

Mamma wouldn't be back until we had finished eating, and then, even though past satiety, I would sit with her and drink more coffee while she broke her Communion fast. When she was done, we would clear the table together. I was my mother's daughter while Ada was my father's; that's how it worked in our family. My mother loved the Son of God, *Gesu Cristo,* while my father loved his mistress, Teresa.

PRAISE HAD BEEN THE RIGHT first note to strike with Ada, but Rico kept hitting all the wrong ones. None of us had ever heard him sing before. So when they started rehearsals, and our tenor sang at half voice, Ada feared she was doomed to play with a nobody. She despised him.

"He's no Scottish fox, he's a Neapolitan mouse, a thin-lipped rodent with no voice, with no range!" she complained.

Rico's singing practice was to save his voice for performances before an audience; at rehearsals he didn't use his full powers, but this was not generally known in the company. The impresario kept this secret because it was a privilege he feared that others might demand. How was he ever to judge the readiness of the production if they all decided to follow this Neapolitan's example?

So Ada was not impressed by the southern tenor.

"This, this is what you offer me as a leading man, this, this ... *tenorino!*" She stamped her foot and demanded that he be fired.

"But he sang in Sicily like you! And with great success!" The comparison only infuriated her more.

"*Tenorino!*" Ada spat out the word as she recounted for me all the details of her argument with the manager. "The *napoletano* thinks he's a singer, but his breath is too short for bel canto. Send that nobody back to Napoli—and the slum that spawned him!"

But in spite of her protests, the impresario had insisted on honoring Caruso's contract. There was nothing to be done, so the little tenor became the object of her scorn. That, I suppose, even if it were unwitting, was a stroke of genius on her part. It seems passion has no hotter fire than that fueled by a woman's scorn.

ONE NIGHT when I was half asleep, Ada came into my bedroom and sat on the edge of my bed. And she talked to me then the way she used to, before she married, before she became a signora and that abyss that gapes between married woman and virgin, between knowledge and innocence, opened between us.

"What if we shut down in the middle of the season because of that pipsqueak? My husband will expect me to come home—he'll read the disastrous reviews and immediately let the wet nurse go! *'Basta,'* I can just hear him now, 'for the sake of Lelio, for the sake of our son, even if you care little enough for me, your husband …' He is jealous, Rina—he is jealous of my talent. He quit the stage because the reviews stung him, not because of duty, as he would have the world believe. The critics all lauded my charms, my voice, and on his performance, their silence was deafening. So do you know what he wants now, what he's planning to do? I know he'd like nothing better than to shut me up in that bank vault with him. Is there music in a safe, Rina? What clerks call notes is the rustling and stacking, the sorting of paper money—to an artist these are just scratching sounds. The kind rats make! I will die, Rina, I will die if I have to go back to such a life!"

While she was complaining about Gino, all I could think of was Rico. "His speaking voice is an angel's—it scales upward, it soars; it has the softness of wings, not like feathers, but like what's underneath them, like the down—how could he possibly sing badly?"

"What? Who? Gino? *Parli di Gino?*"

"No, not Botti, not your husband—I mean Rico."

"You can't be serious! Rico? Do you mean Caruso, the tenor who sings as southern flies buzz? All wind, and precious little of it too. Ah, you like him—that little Neapolitan nobody. You like him so much you have no sympathy for your sister!"

"He likes you!"

"What do I care if the man likes me? What's his smile to me when my singing career is at stake? If the company has to shut down because of him—because of his failure—we will all be tarred from the same pot. There may be no next role—no next contract!" She started to weep then. "What is my life worth if I can't sing?"

I could think of no words to comfort my sister. Opera was Ada's passion, her lifeblood. She lived for the many small deaths of the stage. In opera, you could count on the soprano's cough to turn out to be consumptive. Somebody always has to die onstage, die or marry; that's the only difference between a comedy and a tragedy as far as the world knows.

She calmed herself, her tone shifting from sorrow to anger again. "Rina, since you like this man so much, *va bene,* then marry him! And make him get a job in a bank. Do me, yourself, and bel canto a big favor—make him withdraw from my *La Traviata* at once!"

3

Without my friends, summers were lonely in Livorno. But like any student not fully dedicated to her studies, I found it a relief to get away from the textbooks. Though I loved poetry, subjects like mathematics, Latin, and Greek bored me. That year I had completed intermediate level at school, and the relief would be permanent unless I continued with music studies as my father urged me to. I enjoyed music, but I didn't have the discipline or the desire for a career in it. Music was the *zabaione,* the sweet and frothy dessert in life's feast. The first and primary course was always the family; a husband and children was what I planned for. I had had enough of studying. I wanted suitors, and now that I'd found one in Rico, I dreamed of nothing else.

My father was on assignment a lot for the national treasury and traveled all over the country. He had seen the world and had picked up progressive ideas. He believed that daughters should be as cultivated, as accomplished, as sons. He didn't want us stuck in Old Country ways—my mother's ways. For Mother, the Church was the savior, but for Father, it was a big part of the problem. Ada was the model he held up to me, the rising star of opera. But what I envied was her husband, her child, not her career.

Mother was the one from a once-wealthy family. She inherited property, the palazzo in Firenze, and a bit of money, but we had to rely on Father's salary to live. It was my mother who first taught me to play the piano, as her mother had taught her. I still remember the touch of Mamma's hands guiding my small ones on the keys, so patient with my many blunders. If I loved music, it was because of her hands; I could not touch piano keys without remembering the warmth of them cupped over mine. Music might have been as abstract as mathematics to me if it had not been for my mother's piano lessons.

I had watched and listened as she taught Ada before me, Ada who hardly ever made a blunder. But Mother later turned away from music to religion. Anything that distracted from God and from family had become a sin. I don't know when or why this change in her occurred. Did she blame herself for Ada's neglect of family for a singing career? Mother complained that opera was not pure music because it was sullied by the stage and shameful stories. But that hadn't deterred Ada. And what scandalized Mamma made Papa proud.

THAT SUMMER IN LIVORNO everyone in the household had a position except me. I was the daughter-in-waiting and what I was waiting for was a husband. And now he had a name: Enrico Caruso. Rico and Ada would be at the theater nearly every day, Father had his business affairs, and Mother her prayers, so I would have been bored beyond redemption except that I was in love and those hours alone were filled with my fantasies.

From our apartment it was a short walk to the waterfront. Mornings I would climb the old fortress and look at the blue-green water, the Ligurian Sea where the English Romantic poet had drowned. From the lookout, I could watch the fishermen struggling with their nets. Then I would wander on the beach for hours, picking up shells to listen for the verses trapped inside. I'd take my shoes off and let the foam of the waves lick my feet, then suck at my toes as the water withdrew again. What would a man's mouth, a man's tongue, feel like? Would it be rough as a cat's? Cold like the surf's?

I spent every morning on the beach, but I whiled away afternoons in the apartment and out of the sun. Then I occupied myself with indoor games: I was a girl, playing house, and I used to pretend Rico and I were already married. Didn't I send out his clothes to be laundered; didn't I place the folded garments neatly into his dresser; didn't I touch even his underthings?

When nobody was home I would go into his bedroom, not by stealth, but by what I imagined as marital duty. His bed was always made, military style. The bedspread was not pulled over the pillows, but tucked under them. I touched the pillowcase. The linen was cool, not, as I had hoped, still warm from his sleeping head. Taking the pillow to my nose and sniffing the cloth, I caught whiffs of the lanolin of his hair oil.

On the nightstand, there was a photograph, its face turned towards the bed, as if placed there to watch over the sleeper. It was a death portrait of a woman. The eyes were like his, black and round, dark yet luminous, though the look in hers seemed as melancholy as his was merry. A prayer card, the image of the Madonna of Pompeii, frayed at its edges, was tucked into a corner of the frame.

I couldn't help myself; I had to snoop around while I had the chance. I looked for letters, for a journal, for any form of writing that might open what was in his heart to me. In the drawer of the nightstand there was a note from his brother in the army, asking for money. Rico had doodled in the margin a scene from an opera where the singing was performed by thousand-lire bills, except for a smaller one, which, in spite of being marked as a mere fifty lire, filled the biggest balloon with its voice. In the wastebasket I saw a scrunched-up piece of paper. I took it out and smoothed it down to read. The script of the letter was smeared, but my fear of a romantic rival made me struggle to read every word.

Caro Giovanni,

I'll send money as soon as I can. You don't have to remind me every time you write that you are sacrificing yourself for me in the army. Better you than me, because what good is a tenor as a soldier? You know I have no talent for such things. I only have one talent and that's to sing. One day I'll make it all worth your while. Be careful with that gun, it has a hair trigger. I almost shot my foot off cleaning it one time.

Your loving brother,

Rico

4

That summer was the time I remember our family as happiest. Even Mamma, whose increasing religious devotion was turning her into a dour woman, her soft full lips constantly pressed into a thin and disapproving line, even she softened again and opened herself to giggling with me in the kitchen. She was teaching me to cook and I was her curious, eager student. As I worked I thought of him, my future husband, the one I dreamed of, Rico, our Neapolitan tenor. Making pasta, I would get flour in my hair and eyes from handling the dough. Rolling out sheets of it and then cutting it into squares, I would spoon the filling of ricotta, spinach, and egg onto the layers, and then fold the pasta into the shape of babies' bottoms, pinching and sealing the tortellini. To me they looked like babies' bottoms, but the legend was that a cook had a vision of Venus and created tortellini in the shape of her navel.

I was pleasing my mother by my new interest in domestic tasks. This assured her that I had not been corrupted like Ada by love of opera. Mamma feared that she might have raised both her daughters as prima donnas.

THOUGH LIFE ITSELF that summer seemed occasion enough for celebration, we marked every day as if it were some saint's holiday, and each meal we prepared as a feast. We all liked to eat, but none of us had the appetite of our young guest.

"I'm hungry tonight; I think I'm hungry for all the nights I've been hungry. Even though I am stuffed, it's as if I'm still empty inside; it's as if there's a hole in my stomach. Maybe this hole is the hole that the music pushes through."

"Surely you needn't fear hunger again. When Mugnone recommends you that means success in this country." Mamma refilled his bowl.

Rico capped his mountain of pasta with cheese.

"*È così buono.*" He was a thin man, "thin as an anchovy" he said of himself, yet he tucked into such a big second helping.

"Only the fat he will store from our meals will keep this *tenorino* from starving to death on his talents!" Ada hissed in my ear.

I left the table to help Mamma serve the espresso and dessert. When I returned, carrying the sputtering coffee pot, I saw a kind of comic pantomime: Rico's head was turned towards Ada, Ada's was turned towards Papa, while Papa concentrated on the bits of meat still clinging to the bone of his pork chop, gnawing at it as if he had been infected with the younger man's appetite.

For dessert Mamma had made a special dish in Rico's honor. It was a cake laced with Marsala and crowned with custard and fruit called *zuppa inglese* that, in spite of the English in its name, was invented in Naples.

First, I poured the coffee for Rico; he was our guest. The delight with which he responded to every gesture of courtesy touched me. Then I poured the next cup for Mamma, but she passed the cup immediately to Papa. Then I took his empty cup and tried again to serve her. This she passed to Ada, who did not refuse it. Again I took one of the two remaining empty cups and filled it. That one I set firmly before my mother.

"*Per piacere, Mamma, prendi questa tassa.*" I am the only one Mamma will not defer to. I'm used to the dregs from the bottom of the pot, the gritty taste of grounds, bitter, but also sweet when spoonfuls of sugar are added. Sugar is the cure, a little sugar or a lot, to cut the harshness of the leavings. When will we be first, Mamma, when will women like us be first? In heaven—that's what she believed.

None of this really bothered me then, as I said this was the time I remember as happiest, the season when to Ada—indeed, to the world—Rico was a nobody, while to me he was music itself. He was birdsong—he was flowers—if flowers can be used to describe a man. Only they could approach the textures in a voice that was somehow both airy and densely rich. Think of orchids, think of night bloomers opening only for the moon, such beauty unfurling in mystery and darkness. Think of ferns—though delicate as fans, in tropical rain forests they grow as mighty as trees.

I was in love for the first and last time in my life. And the only language of love I knew was the language of poetry written by men to describe women. Is there any other? The rose may be Dante's, but the fern, the fern is mine. I hope it is mine.

RESTLESS, AT NIGHT I would accidentally touch myself while dreaming of him. The first time was an accident. It must have been my ignorance of men that made me imagine his skin as an extension of my own, as smooth, and the belly round and hairless, my fingers lingered in a territory both familiar and strange.

5

On Tuesdays the opera house was closed—no performances, no rehearsals. I planned a picnic, wanting only Rico to come, but I had to invite my sister as well. At first Ada had said yes, but then she backed out at the last moment. I was glad that didn't stop my fun because my mother seemed to think of Rico as family, and did not insist on a chaperone. And as for my father, as I have said, he was an educated man with progressive ideas. Ada and I were treated like sons insofar as Father allowed us the kind of freedom that was scandalous to neighbors, but mostly envied by my friends at school.

With a basket filled with good things to eat, bread and pecorino cheese, fruit and a bottle of red wine, we set out for the countryside on bicycles. Rico balanced the basket on the handle-bars of his bike, a rusty old thing he had fished out of the garbage somewhere.

We kept a leisurely pace. Under different circumstances I might have welcomed a race, the flush, the exhilaration of speed, on the road and in the blood, the heart mistaking itself for a prisoner, knocking forcefully in the chest, that sealed chamber without a door, but in Rico's presence I wanted to stay fresh, sweet. My great-est fear that day was not the road, not its dust, nor the stray stones that might play hazard with my wheels, but my menstrual flow, the mess and smell of it. Though I had doubled the rags I was wearing, I felt its flow in hot gushes. I feared to find the back of my skirt, the bicycle seat, red, wet, and sticky with my shame.

IN THE METEOROLOGICAL RECORDS for Tuscany, there is perhaps no note on the perfection of that morning. Let me record it here for posterity. Although it was only a little after ten in the morning, the cicadas were already shrilling the high heat. The sun was a lemon on fire; there was a citrus sharpness, some-thing refreshing in its heat.

The road we took ran parallel to the shore. There were fields ripening red, openly bleeding with poppies by the roadside.

There were hills rising to the east, dense with dark pinewoods. Wind blew briskly from the sea and added a salty sting to the air. As we pedaled along we could see the seascape, bands of bright blue through clearings in the woods to the west. It was good to feel the sea breeze on my face. It was like the caress of a fan, and I was a woman who lowered hers and exposed her lips, naked and burning.

WE FOUND A SPOT secluded from the main road where we could see the shore and the water, the blue of the Ligurian Sea merging with azure at the horizon. It was seamless—sky and sea formed one continuous sphere as in some prehistoric time, before God separated the elements. From where we sat there was no evidence of man, of modern time; not a sail could be seen. The water was flat and shining; it might have been fathoms deep, or merely knee-deep. There was little surf. All I could make out was some white foam along the shore like a border of ecru lace on a woman's shirt. It seemed that we had stepped onto a pristine planet, into a garden there. We might have been Eve and Adam.

We laid out our picnic lunch near the entrance to a grove of oaks. Rico sat with his back braced against the trunk of one of the trees. He picked up acorns lying around the camp and shot them randomly into the woods. While he rested, I laid out the food on a cloth, checkered red and white.

We drank wine directly from the bottle. That seemed to me our first kiss, when he drank, tilting the bottle back high, as if it were empty, not full, then passed it over to me and I drank. I put it to my lips, the glass mouth where his lips had just been, and while I lingered, he started to eat. Breaking a large chunk off the loaf of bread, Rico held up the piece to heaven as if it were a sacramental offering. Then he sniffed the moist center. He buried his face in the hunk before he tore off a morsel with his teeth.

"Bread too has its music." He placed the remainder of the loaf against my ear. "Listen, Rina, can you hear it? The slapping of hands, the slow way that yeast makes melody, it rises in the dough and into a symphony. Listen to the overture. It's in the air—it's captured in the pockets of air in the bread. Here are the stanzas of song; here too is the silence—when the singer stops."

I strained to hear the mysterious music he described, but I heard nothing, only the rustling sound my hair made as the loaf brushed against it. But when I pressed the bread harder against my ear I made out something like the sea you hear in a shell, but throbbing.

The next kiss was different. All the wine had been drunk, the food mostly devoured. I can still feel that kiss, the real one. I can still taste it on my lips when I try to lick dryness away and I sample my own blood, the sweet salt of it. The first kiss was not what I had imagined, not like what I practiced in bed on my own hand, after whispering, "Rico, Rico, *ti amo*." That hand was small and plump, smooth and coolly moist from applying cold cream. That was a child's gesture; that was a child's hand.

A couple of crows, perched in a nearby tree, seemed to run a conversation parallel to ours. They spoke only as we spoke, they paused to listen as we listened.

"Vieni qua ... vieni caaaw caaaw." My hair was long and woven into a single thick braid, tied at the back. Rico grabbed my braid and pulled me gently towards him as one tugs a shy and reluctant puppy by a leash. Imagine his breath and my breath forming one single deep breathing, his face and my face so close we bump noses.

Then he whispered something, something I couldn't make out; I heard instead flapping sounds as the birds above shook out their wings.

"*Rina … Rina … signo … rina …* " It seemed he sang my name, the tenor I had yet to hear sing. But his speaking voice was more interesting to me than any song.

"*Rina … Rina … signo … rina …* " He played with my name again, followed by some words I couldn't make out, and then he sharply nipped at my ear.

The crows cawed; it seemed they knew me too.

Our faces were so close that when I tried to look at Rico my eyes crossed. I saw a double image; I saw the two faces of my lover, but I didn't know how to read either one of them. So I closed my eyes and it was then he kissed me again, his mouth pressed very hard against mine this time. So forcefully, it was closer to a punch than a caress. His mouth opened wide and it seemed he might swallow the entire lower half of my face. Then his tongue pushed its way between my puckered lips. As if a snake had entered my mouth, not one of our stringy Italian vipers, but some Amazonian monster as thick as my arm, as if to kiss meant to eat—or to be eaten. I had to push him away to get my breath back. And he let me.

"What was that—what you did?"

"That was a lover's kiss, Rina, *piccolina*." He crooked his little finger in a come-hither gesture. "*Vieni qui …* nobody will see."

The crows echoed our words, but perhaps it is arrogant, if all too human, to think so; they may have had matters of their own to discuss that day. Though I hesitated briefly, I found myself too soon falling into his arms, my lips parted. When his tongue traced the inside of my mouth the feeling I had always attributed to the divine during Communion, that sublime tingling I sensed when peeling back the Sacred Host from where it clung to the roof of my mouth, I felt then with him—that ecstasy and awe.

The thrusting motion of his tongue threatened to push through into my very brain—into the seat of all pleasure. But it was a sensation so intense it might have been pain. It seemed I was stepping out of myself and into a zone of transformation, of metamorphosis, to inhabit a new body. As in the myths, I expected my arms to become laurel, my belly to turn into a bird's nest.

But my legs were still just my legs when Rico touched them. His hand was in my skirt, his fingers had pushed my bloomers up, and he was stroking the inside of my thigh. It might have been virtue or it might have been the thought of the sodden, smelly rags between my legs that gave me the strength to push him away.

"No, Rico, please, no. You must speak to Papa first. I love you, but … you know I—until we're betrothed—until we're married we can't do more than kissing." *Love,* I said the word so easily, I said it without realizing that it is not the first thing that a man wants to hear from a woman. The crows cawed along with my stuttering little speech.

I was taught that sex must be sacred not to be a sin. It had been almost a scandal when Ada married; the neighbors counted the months to the birth of her son and counted short. Mamma did extra penance as if it were her fault. So, it seemed the right thing to do that day, to make Rico wait for my body.

"You know I have no money now. I cannot speak to your father until I make a debut at La Scala, until I make my career. But after my success there, when my future will be assured, I will beg him for your sweet hand. Come, *picina,* another kiss. If you love me as you say you do, you won't deny me."

"If you love me," he said, and there was no doubt of that, I loved him. He *would* ask for my hand after he succeeded in Milan. Soon, his success would surely be soon.

When he kissed me the third time I learned more about my mouth, how the lover runs his tongue over your teeth, then slips again into the arched cathedral dome of the mouth. You cannot pray unless you go inside.

Without my mother's novenas I might have been lost that day as his hand went up my skirt again, this time to my waist, to pull my bloomers down. When he paused at my hips, this gave me the moment I needed to come to my senses. I pushed him away again, and I jumped to my feet. Some instinct told me not to run. To straighten my bloomers, I had to reach under my skirt. Rico watched me the whole time—I dared not guess what he was thinking as I struggled to adjust my underwear without lifting my skirt.

Then I made myself busy packing up the remains of our picnic. I took what was left of the bread, broke it into bits, and threw them onto the ground for the crows. Slowly they spiraled down to us and had their own picnic with our leftovers.

"Don't be mad. Let me carry the basket, Rina." When he spoke I was relieved. I expected him to be the angry one. "*Ascolti,* Rina, *picina.* It's lack of money, not lack of love, that keeps me from marrying you."

"But … I can wait. Oh, I will wait for you, Rico! I love you with all my heart. If the Madonna would give me a second heart, a simple pump, I would tear this one right out of my chest and give it to you. It stays in my breast because I do not want to die, because I do not ever want to be parted from you. You must know—you must believe me—I would do anything for you!" I imagined love to be like Dante's love for Beatrice, that passion and purity were one, scripted in longing and celestial distances.

And it was true that I would have done anything for him, even though, that afternoon, I wouldn't perform the act I knew then only as a mortal sin. I withheld my body. It was only my body, not my heart. But what's a heart without a body? Something sacred, like the scapular with the image of Christ's heart, bleeding with its crown of thorns, imprinted on felt. My mother told me to wear it around my neck, under my shirt, and if I were really devout, to sleep with it on. You don't offer such a thing to a lover.

I believed he would marry me. I thought that by my promising to wait for him, he would wait for me too.

6

As I raved to Mamma about what a wonderful man Rico was, so warm, so kind, so full of spirit, a *simpatico,* one who, even though he had very little money, was open and generous with all, one who would share his last crumb with a bird just for singing in the meadow, she stopped me with a raised finger:

"*Attenzione, Rina, è veramente simpatico e gentile*—but you must remember that he is still a man."

"But, Mamma, I could hardly forget that!"

"*Allora …*" She shook her head, closed her eyes.

"And Papa, isn't he a man?" I quickly interjected. With that I thought I had won.

"*È vero.*" Drawing her lips into a fine line with the truth of it, she refused to say anything more.

I HAD YET to hear Rico sing, unless you count his humming early in the morning something from Verdi as he made his way to the toilet on the roof. I was excited when he sent us all tickets for his first performance in *La Traviata*. Ada always expected us to get them for ourselves. I had seen Ada perform many times; our father was perhaps her most devoted fan. I was bored with that. Each opening night would find us all in front-row seats to add to, if not actually lead, the applause. That night I wasn't at the opera for her. I was there praying for Rico's success so that soon, all the sooner, we might marry and live happily together.

At the theater we were seated in a reserved box. I sat in the middle, separating my mother and father. Father had rolled his copy of the program and, like me, was surveying the audience, dressed in their silks and jewels, seated in the gallery below us. Mother sat quietly, the program held flat between her palms like a Sunday missal, the words so familiar she no longer needed to read them. In the summer heat, the hall exuded scents: tobacco, perfume, and sweltering skin.

The curtains rose to a drama in which my sister and Rico played the parts of lovers. *Misterioso,* love was mysterious; *croce e delizia al cor,* love was pain, delicious pain. Of that I was easily persuaded, I knew from the tightness in my chest as I listened to Rico sing, the sharply intense pleasure of it. If I loved his speaking voice as much as I loved music, still I was not prepared for the thrill of his singing. And the mouth with which he sang, the tongue that I had tasted, were tasted anew in rhapsodic song.

I was swept away by the pathos of the drama. Ada and Rico, the principals in the production, were my intimates, but onstage they were larger than life. In the third act of *La Traviata,* when all the violins vibrated with the sound of yearning, Ada's Violetta turned to Rico's Alfredo and sang to him with her dying breath. I think it might have been then that my sister began to die too as she fell deeply in love with her leading man. I think that now, though at the time I only thought that it was very fine acting on her part. Tears welled up in my eyes.

"WITHOUT HIS FULL VOICE, he was like a flower without a scent." It seemed even my sister was reduced to flower imagery to describe him. "But when he sang for performance, it was round and rich, it was caramel in its sweetness, liquid in its texture. As it soared as a bird soars, it also had depth, like clear spring water rising from a well—bubbling up from the cavernous darkness, yet filled with air and light. I felt his voice enter me; it made me shudder; it filled me to the brim—to the brim."

It was apparent that Ada had forgotten her husband some time ago. But that she would turn her attention to my fiancé, when she herself had ordered me to marry the *tenorino,* felt like a betrayal.

THE REVIEWS WERE VERY GOOD and they favored Ada. *Il Trovatore* described her as "an artist to her very soul … She infuses all the sentiment, grace, perfumed, sweet melancholy that the delicate creature requires!" Even the very few who doubted Ada's singing ability acknowledged that she was a remarkable actress.

As for Rico, he was not yet the Caruso; his performance was cited in the *Gazzetta Livornese* as deserving praise, "a voice and method that have become very good." Nobody was obviously complaining; in spite of Ada's fears about her *tenorino,* the show would go on. So in the beginning, although she overshadowed him, Rico proved himself good enough to sing with her. He had begun to create roles, but he had not yet created himself.

7

Ada wanted Rico to get the part of Rodolfo in Giacomo Puccini's new opera, *La Bohème.* She already had the role of Mimì. This was an opera that, in spite of the hissing on opening night and the bad reviews that followed, was playing to packed houses all over Italy, and its word-of-mouth success was already moving quickly all over the world. To keep Rico singing by her side, Ada had to approach the manager again. And there she was, stamping her foot at him, the same scene with a twist—this time she insisted on keeping the Neapolitan as her leading man.

"I tell you, Signora Botti, it's beyond my control! Ricordi keeps an iron-fisted hold to the rights to all Puccini compositions. He will not allow just anyone—particularly not an unknown tenor under contract to a rival house—to sing the operas he publishes. The Neapolitan would have to get permission, a signature from Puccini himself, for Ricordi to agree to it."

Rico also approached the manager and begged for the role. Just for the opportunity to prove his worth, our tenor foolishly offered to sing for free. The man raised his eyebrows at that; he slowly shook his head, shrugged, and spread out his hands, palms up, in a gesture of helplessness. Then he repeated that Rico must get Puccini's written permission.

It was Ada's idea that Rico make the short trip to Torre del Lago where Puccini lived and audition for the composer. Every morning, for two weeks, she coached him in the role. If her husband was expecting her home during the break in the season, he was disappointed. Did he think she was hard-hearted, neglecting their baby son? Or did he write it off as the egotism of the artist, as her obsession? It was egotism, yes, the artistic kind, but vanity too, the female kind. She wasn't prepared to leave her new conquest behind. Love is a glove; love is a gauntlet. It had been thrown down, and it had been picked up.

$\mathscr{S}$INGING $\mathscr{L}$ESSONS

Here with a Loaf of Bread beneath the Bough,
A Flask of Wine, a Book of Verse—and Thou
Beside me singing in the Wilderness
—EDWARD FITZGERALD, *THE RUBÁIYÁT OF OMAR KHAYYÁM*

I

We were becoming known in town as the house of song, with
two of the leading performers in the Teatro Goldini's summer
repertoire under one roof. In the morning, on waking, Ada
would open the window, draw back the shutters, and sing in full
voice to the street below. Luckily for our neighbors, she was not
an early riser. And even luckier for herself, our suite was on the
top floor of the building or she might have found herself victim
of the chamber pots—emptied onto her head to shut her up.
But Ada had a fan club to satisfy, a circle of young men, smoking
cigarettes as they kept vigil by our balcony.

The singing lessons had begun, and for nearly two weeks we
spent every morning indoors. I stopped going to the beach
because, with Rico rehearsing at home, I preferred to stay and
listen to him sing. Such beautiful summer mornings they were,

when gardens beckoned to be strolled in and birds made music all of their own. But it wasn't all sweetness, there was noise too, that was the music of the port: ships and their horns from the distance, and below our windows, carriages rolling by over cobbled streets, the squeak and grind of the wheels, the knife sharpener and his bell, the hawkers shouting their wares. Might the clomping of horse hooves be mistaken for indolent applause? For whom did the streets clap—for the birds in the trees, or for the tenor rehearsing in the drawing room of the Giachetti residence?

Those were long and intimate hours of which I was the silent witness. The soprano was the teacher, seated at the piano, ivory fingers at the ivory keys, the tenor, hovering by her side, occasionally bending over her, inhaling her perfume as he scanned the sheet music, peering at the notes, peering at her nipples, which were prominent, pushing against the light muslin of her gown. Those were long and intimate hours while I sat in the corner, using my needlework as a disguise.

"It is not enough to sing it, the role must be lived!" That was Ada's method; that was Ada's style, and that's where he learned it.

"You think to sing Rodolfo I must write a play, then burn the manuscript, my only copy, just to keep warm?"

"You must imagine what it is to be cold and to be hungry. Let the hurt open up in you—if you dare to feel it—then the chest will expand. You must sing through it, through deprivation, through the chill of unheated winter attics, through the thread-bare coat, the unrecognized work, and the loss of love. Make the wound your larynx!"

"I think I understand you. You want me to forget that it's summer, forget my breakfast, the coffee, the milk steaming in the bowl, and the bread that I ate barely an hour ago. 'Imagine,' you say, but I only need to remember, remember thin soup and stale bread soaked in water to make it palatable, remember that saint, my mother, resting at last because she is dead. This Rodolfo is privileged to have paper and ink to write with—to have pages to burn! But since I have tasted life here, maybe I can understand that too."

"Sing the pain, yes, sing it with all your heart!"

Then Rico began the aria at half voice as he had for rehearsals at the theater until Ada, in frustration, turned a light melody into a storm, pounding the keys in cacophonous thunder.

"I can't hear you! I can't hear you!" she shrieked.

"This is how it will sound." To appease her, he sang a few bars in full voice, *"Aspetti, signorina, le dico con due parole ..."* in that voice that was like revelation, like light in the sky parting dark clouds. "Trust me, Ada. I have to spare my throat. Vergine, my teacher, dismissed it as reedy; he said that it was a bit of wind whistling outside the window. But if I build the song slowly—I'll try to explain—it's like the charcoal sketch, the study that the artist does before he paints the fresco in all its colors."

"Va bene. If you insist, it's a charcoal sketch. For that we need precision. We need to connect the lines of the poetry with the music, the feeling. The song is not just in your mouth. It's here." She made a fist, pushing against her stomach, caving it in, forcing her full breasts higher. "And it's here." She moved the fist to her left breast and made a knocking motion. "Then it runs through here." She threw her head back, her white neck exposed. "It moves through here"—she stroked the curvature of her throat— "and then out here." Her fingers traced the outline of her parted lips. "And it must all be connected."

SEATED BY THE WINDOW, embroidering a tablecloth for my
trousseau, I had my threads, their vivid colors, lined up on the
ledge. I was working on a floral design, stitching the roses in red
and the forget-me-nots in blue. I was imagining our monographs
joined, *RG* and *EC: RG-C*. I liked to imagine that Rico needed
me there during his lessons, that my presence made a difference
to him. It was for him that I stayed. In the afternoons the heat
drives you into the house anyway, but in the mornings—only
love could have kept me inside. For love, I might have been
happy even as a seamstress, if I could have been his seamstress.

Every so often he would turn to me and ask me what I thought.

"Do you agree with this sister of yours? Am I holding back the
feeling? Don't say yes or no right away, first let me explain what
I'm trying to do. I tamp down the emotion—like coffee grinds
in the espresso pot—so that with the heat of the action, with the
rising steam, the song pushes through in a jet. Jet is the power
and jet is the rich dark color of the coffee. But what Ada wants
is the feeling all the way through like sugar in a cake, while
what I want is climax."

I liked the way he was speaking of Ada in the third person, as
if only the two of us were in the room, but how was I to
comment on *climax*? I probably knew more about music than
Rico, who only had an elementary school education, but I was
puzzled by the terms of his analogy. I thought he was talking
about coffee, I thought he was talking about music.

"Why do you bother to ask her? She knows nothing. She's
a baby."

"She's more than a baby. She's filling out."

Ada gave him a look with narrowed eyes. "Do you want to
learn this song or do you want to argue over the moon?"

Rico began to sing the aria again, *"Che gelida manina ... "* As he sang I watched my own hand holding the needle. In the lyrics the hand of the seamstress is small and cold. It might have been my own, that hand in the song, over which the tenor's voice lavished such poetry, such tenderness, *"È una notte di luna, e qui la luna l'abbiamo vicina ... "* Even in such muted tones I felt something swell then knot in my chest. His singing changed the very nature of song for me. It was no longer dessert; it had become Communion wafer, and his body was the sacred body I sought there. I wanted his tongue again in my mouth. I vowed that if I could not have the man, if I could not have true love, I would fill my mouth with its songs. I would hold the notes in my lungs like breath from an opium pipe so that I might be utterly altered.

Birds were singing outside in a kind of chorus for Rico. They held nothing back from their music. It seemed they burned as hotly, their little bodies, for song as for flight.

As soon as Ada pronounced Rico ready, he set off for the Puccini estate. The composer's home was on the shores of a large lake. Torre del Lago lay near Viareggio, directly north of Livorno. The distance on the map was not great, but it involved a change of trains in Pisa. Rico was sure to get hungry along the way and so I prepared a lunch for him of some panini with mortadella, some fruit and fennel, which he accepted readily enough. In thanks, he gave me a little kiss on the forehead. His lips felt hot. Then, laughing, he pinched my cheek and asked me to wish him luck. But when Ada stepped into the room, he put the lunch bag down to embrace her. Bowing deeply, he took Ada's hand, a hand studded with rings, *"Ecco, la maestra—è la più bella donna nel universo!"* and kissed it. The most beautiful woman in the universe!—that covered a lot of territory, a lot of other women. Gratitude is a virtue in a man. I thought he might have been a little less grateful to her.

And the meal I had prepared for him remained on the shelf in the parlor; brown paper bag, brown wood, and brown paneling, camouflaged or forgotten there.

2

Evening came, the withering of light, and by night Rico still did not return from Torre del Lago. I tried not to worry. But all that time I listened for him, for his whistling steps. I heard gulls pierce the night sky with their cries; I heard the wind in the poplars like the whispering of a restless audience. I kept going out onto the balcony, hoping to catch sight of him. After the sun had set, all bloody reds and roses, the air had cooled, but I had a heat in me that would not dissipate. I watched the moon rise, so close, I saw that its mouth was shaped for the round notes of the dirge and I feared for him. What would be worse—failure or robbers, maybe even murderers, on the road? I knew I would answer one way, and Ada, perhaps even Rico himself, would answer another way.

I hardly slept that night. The next morning, I welcomed making more coffee when Mamma returned from her prayers. And Ada joined us then.

"Calm yourself," Ada ordered. "It's a good sign he's not back yet. If Rico pleased Puccini, the Maestro might very well have insisted that he stay overnight." But nobody had said anything.

It was a day as long as any I had ever known. The hours passed with a child's feeling of time, protracted, with an intimate sense of the infinite, but with no idea of tomorrow.

And Rico did not return that day, he did not return until late that night. It was well past ten when he came home humming the aria in a jaunty tempo and sporting a note of approval, signed by the distinguished composer, in his jacket pocket. He gave Mother a duck he had shot that morning while hunting with the great man. The head dropped limply out of the sack, blood on its bill; the dark feathers glinted emerald and topaz in the lamplight.

With a flourish, Rico pulled out the note and placed it on the table.

"I would like to have this framed, but I'm sure the manager will just pocket it for himself."

Now even Father was impressed. Although he himself had heard Rico sing many times that summer, it required another, more elevated, judgment for him to fully appreciate the superb qualities of our tenor's voice. Before Puccini's approval, it seemed as if half the world had been deaf.

"Show it to him, but make sure you keep it," Papa insisted. "Puccini's recommendation will open many doors for you. It's cash, it's like gold in your hand."

Echoing him, we chanted, repeating in intervals, comically, as in a Rossini chorus: "Keep it—keep it—you must keep it for yourself."

IN SPITE OF THE LATE HOUR, I made espresso and we all gathered around to hear the details of what had happened.

"Tell us all about it," Ada and I chimed in unison.

Demitasse in hand, we listened to Rico's story of his adventure.

"It's two kilometers from the town to his villa," he began. "That's not far to walk, but it's a dirt road. You all saw how I had made myself very presentable when I left here, but by the time I arrived at his gate, my shoes were white with dust. My jacket was grimy from the train ride, and I reeked. The gate was locked, and when I rattled it in frustration, big black dogs rushed at me, howling. I was happy enough then that what barred me from entering the estate also prevented them from tearing me apart.

"I waited outside the walls of Villa Puccini for a long time, but no one came to the gate. There was no bell to ring, nor any other means I could see for me to announce my presence. And I didn't have so much as a slice of salami to appease the hounds. Eventually, though, the dogs got bored and wandered off. I stood there with my lengthening shadow, hoping someone from the house would look out before dark.

"Although I could squeeze my face between the bars, it brought me no closer to meeting Puccini than the length of my nose. Desperate from the endless waiting, I decided to scale the wall. It was three meters of gray stone. Climbing up was easier than looking down to jump. I lowered myself, hanging by my fingertips, and then let myself drop. Luckily, it was springy loam and grass below, so I did not hurt myself, but I felt a tear at the back of my trousers. The mosquitoes found it sooner than I did. Fear of the dogs returning made me hurry to the house.

"By then it was late in the day, the churches were ringing the Angelus. I had climbed ramparts to meet the Maestro, I had faced the hounds of hell—why should an oak door give me pause? Not even the rip in my backside was going to stop me. I knew my Rodolfo would please even a musical genius. I gripped the heavy brass knocker from the jaws of its lion and rapped at the door.

"Puccini had become my god; I guess I hoped to walk in as into a church. But there was no response, so I rapped louder, longer. If that lion had had teeth, he might have lost a few because of my knocking. Finally, a woman answered the door. She was tall, with erect posture and high, full breasts—and she knew how to carry them. She had the carriage of a queen, but she was wearing an apron. After looking me up and down, she very curtly asked me what I wanted.

"I told her, 'To see the Maestro, signora, please. It's very important that I meet with him.' Savory smells of roasting meat drifted towards me. I hadn't eaten lunch. As the soul responds to incense, to bells, the odors made my stomach wake up. I had to swallow hard, moisten my lips, before I could reply to her next question. 'Is he expecting you?' I answered yes, a simple lie, and she believed me. '*Va bene,* it's almost suppertime. You can be the one to interrupt his work and tell him so.' She led me to a room in another wing of the house and briskly walked away.

"Imagine, genius could be found on the other side of that ordinary wooden door. Even such a regal woman—she was Elvira, his mistress—did not dare disturb him. And so there I was waiting again in front of a closed door. I put my ear against the wood and listened. I heard a piano and fragments of some melody, then I heard crashing stops, and behind it all, the crackling sound of a fire. Drawing on all my courage, during a moment of pause in the music, I knocked loudly.

"'What is it this time? It'd better be important, my pigeon, or you'll join the birds in the gun room!'

"'No, no, it's not the pigeon. It's me.'

"'*Me!* And who, may I ask, is this "me"?'

"My name was most likely unknown to him so it was useless to give it. In sudden inspiration I sang my response, '*So-no po-eta!*'

"At that he laughed, 'Ah, another bohemian! I suppose you want to join our club?' I was still standing behind the closed door. 'Come in, come in, what are you waiting for?' He continued laughing and there was something melodic even in his laughter.

"The room I walked into was stifling hot. Who in the heat of summer piles wood onto the fireplace and makes the fire blaze hotly except for cooking? The windows were sealed shut and genius was seated at the piano. He wore a hat, riding boots, and a coat jacket with the collar turned up. He looked like one of his own characters, one of the starving artists from *La Bohème*, bundled for winter.

"'Maestro, I must apologize in advance—the high C at the end of the song gives me some difficulty.'

"'It is as difficult as it is beautiful, but not absolutely necessary. I put the high C there in my dream, in my ideal of how the song might soar, but you can hit it a little lower if you like. What I really despise is the tenor who'd sacrifice the whole aria in order to reach that note.'

"I found it hard even to breathe in the room. How was I to sing in it? Yet sing I did for him, the aria so tenderly that it brought the chill of the garret to my spine. I shivered even in that inferno.

"In the middle of the song, Puccini stopped playing. Wheeling his stool around, he turned to me. Shivering himself, he spoke in hushed tones.

"'Who sent you to me? God?'

"'No, Maestro,' I replied. 'It was an angel, the soprano, Signora Ada Giachetti-Botti.'

"And as he wrote out his endorsement for me he invited me to stay overnight.

"'You must join me in a hunt. In the morning we'll slink among the reeds. The ducks are timid as virgins, but that won't stop us from bagging them.' He jumped then from the piano stool and strode out of the room.

"I followed as best I could. Puccini is a physical giant too; I had to run two steps for every one he walked.

"'This is my other room. At the piano there's creation, but here, there's—recreation.'

"Guns lined the walls of the room in glass display cases. In one corner there were rows of rubber boots in many styles. A yellow pair glistened wet as lemons after rain; and except for their enormous size, they seemed girlish. Puccini took out one of the guns and stroked the barrel with his index finger as if it were a woman. Her inner thigh.

"'Splendid, splendid, that you're here.' He aimed at some imaginary target between my eyes; then smiling, he lowered the weapon. 'We'll take the boat out in the predawn and shake all the pretty little birds out of their beds.'

"The room had the air of a cathedral whose incense was gunpowder. Puccini's shrine was stocked, not with statues, but with the work of the taxidermist. There were many wild birds mounted on sawed-off branches or uprooted trunks of trees. One poor creature, a rust-colored hawk, had its wings spread out as in flight. Somehow hunter had been taken in the hunt. Still its glassy eye seemed trained on me.

"'There are no singers among them, I hope,' I said.

"'No, no singers except when they complain. Sopranos when they're squawkers. I'd shoot more than one of them if it were legal. Here my birds are well placed, don't you think?' He chucked one under its chin, stroked its beak. Turning to me again he seemed to read my face. 'Ah, you are a tenor with a tender heart, I can see that, my little Neapolitan, *theo doros,* my gift from God. Tomorrow morning be sure to leave your tenderness at the door.' He cracked the rifle open and loaded it. Each bullet, as big as a songbird's head, gleamed silver in his hand.

"'Hardness wants to bury itself in softness. As it is in sex, so it is in sport, in shooting.' He turned to me once more, playfully aiming the gun at my head again. 'I believe aesthetic laws follow the natural ones.'

"This time I stepped quickly to the side.

"Puccini wanted to show me the boat, so we stepped out into the evening air. Outdoors it wasn't any cooler than in the house. The air buzzed with insects. That evening, Lake Massaciuccoli was like an immense marsh without a breeze. It smelled of the slime of stagnant waters. We walked along the dock where the rotting wood creaked beneath our weight.

"The boat, a simple rowboat, was half hidden among the reeds, whose velvety heads gathered darkness around them like old women with their shawls. The frogs were beginning their evensong. They formed a chorus, all baritones, hoarse from over-rehearsing at full voice, and not a star among them.

"We stepped onto a gazebo built right on the water to attend the concert.

"'Listen to that cacophony! You can be sure that is not what inspires my music,' Puccini laughed. 'The French are right to eat them. Their legs are a delicacy, you know—they taste like breast of chicken.'

"From our lookout we could see the tower that gave the town its name, a column of darkness. It could see us. And the stars were just blinking into view, one by one.

"'This lake is really a lagoon. In daylight you can see the Mediterranean although you might not recognize it.' Then he pointed and said, 'Look over there at that expanse to the west, where the blue has become dark as China ink. See, over there, yes, but you must look farther.' He gestured vigorously towards the setting sun. 'Tell me, my little tenor, what can you see?'

"'Ah, what I see now—and much closer than I ever imagined—are the steps of La Scala, and beyond that I can see the lights of America.'"

THE CLOCK CHIMED MIDNIGHT, twelve sonorous strokes, signaling us out of Rico's story and back into the dining room, where we continued to sit in silence. When I finally got up to clear the table, rattling the cups, the spell was broken.

"I'm tired," Mamma said. "And no wonder, it's very late. How will I get up in time for mass?" It wasn't too late for Papa—he went out for a stroll to the piazza to have a drink and smoke at a bar.

Ada left the room immediately after, followed so closely by Rico she must have felt his breath burning at her nape. With her hair worn up, the delicate curves at the back of her throat were exposed. Rico followed like a devoted dog at the heels of his mistress, a dog expecting some choice tidbit.

"Buona notte!" I called after him. I had the sugar bowl, the coffee pot in my hands.

He half turned to me and smiled, *"Buona notte,"* but continued after Ada. If Rico must thank Ada for his success, would it take him farther away from me rather than bring him closer? I washed out the espresso pot with a feeling of dread. The grinds are coarse and have a slightly burnt smell. I watched the few that I rinsed out from the filter cone swirl and sink down the drain. After that night I began finding his bed unmade, but not slept in, because when I sniffed the sheets they still smelled of laundry soap.

3

My innocence, my virginity, what I believed to be my strength, my advantage—was my weakness. And for the assurances of propriety I denied the evidence of my eyes, my nose. I believed my sister, a married woman and a mother, could not be a rival for Rico's love. I was wrong. It was the right thing to do, or so I had been taught, to deny him my body, to stay virtuous until the wedding night. That was the only way I knew to find a man and keep him as a husband. I was wrong. If I had asked my mother for advice, she would have confirmed what I thought, she would have quoted from that catechism I had been made to memorize.

Things had changed between Rico and me. He began to act like an uncle; he would tweak my nose and pretend he had pulled it off, showing his thumb through his fist as evidence of his catch.

"You don't need such a pretty little nose, Rina, *signo-rina!* Let me keep it as a souvenir." He was after my nose, he who already had my heart.

There was no more tongue in his kisses. He would peck at my cheek, or barely brush my forehead with his lips. He would kiss the tip of my nose and treat me like a little girl.

I could not compete with Ada, not once she began to use her body to entrap him. I was finished. I was as good as forgotten. *Who buys an ass, when you've got one who'll carry you on her back-side for free?* I have overheard the *contadini,* bending over their labor in the fields and laughing together, talk that way. When sex is involved, I have come to understand that men are more pragmatic than most women. And Ada's body was his in spite of her marriage to another man. She had never asked *him* to wait.

Their affair became an open secret in our household. Even I, blind with love, had to see it. There were no more late and dramatic entrances made by Ada at breakfast. With Rico in tow, she began to arrive promptly for all our meals. Since this had been his habit, perhaps I should say "with Ada in tow," except that she still made her entrance like a diva and he followed her.

Our house had become a house of sin. Papa went away for days on end. It was August, the month of holidays, and there could be no pretense that he was on the road for the treasury. If an emergency arose, we all knew, without his telling us, where to reach him—in Rome, at the apartment he maintained for his mistress, Teresa.

Mamma had taken to wearing black, as if she were in mourning for the family's moral life.

"It's my fault. I brought scandal into this house when I opened the door to a southerner."

Mamma retreated more and more from family life. She no longer joined us at breakfast. Every morning, as if it were Lent, the time for penance, she could be found on her knees at mass.

Her room was next to Ada's. Did she hear what I heard when I crept down the hall in the middle of the night to listen at my sister's door? From Rico's room there was not so much as a snuffling sound anymore, while from my sister's room I could hear heavy snoring, or sometimes something worse—the rhythmic creak, creak, creaking of the bedsprings. Slipping into her room one morning when she was at the theater, I found what I could only naively guess to be a burst balloon. I picked it up; it felt sticky and smelled of dead fish.

During evening meals, the only time we were likely to be gathered together, Mamma stopped speaking at all anymore. She ate with her head bowed, her lips moving more often in prayer than in chewing. Her rosary beads clinked in her lap. When Papa returned and ate with us, he was there in body but not in spirit. Neither Ada's gossip about the theater nor Rico's jokes distracted him from the clock he watched as he ate. Nothing seemed to dampen the romantic couple's spirits. It was clear to me that their lively talk at dinner was not for the family, but for each other.

4

"Remember our picnic? Wasn't it fun? Why don't we go again? I can pack special treats. There's a Neapolitan who has a stall at the market and he bakes little pizzas that will make your stomach sing."

Rico seemed tempted. His eyes lingered on my lips.

"Yes. That would be fun." But then he turned to Ada: "What do you think of *picina*'s idea? Shall we go?"

Ada gave me a look. When she narrowed her eyes, their blue had a cutting edge; when she spoke, it was to Rico.

"No, *caro,* I have an appointment with my hairdresser tomorrow morning. And you know I get sunstroke so easily. But make my little sister happy. If she likes picnics so much, take her!"

THE NEXT DAY the angel of weather was on my side. The sky was like a bolt of luminescent silk, unfurled, the sun a halo of blazing light.

Once again, with our lunch basket balanced on the handlebars of his bicycle, Rico took the lead. Following a mere bike length behind, I was close enough to whisper to him and to be heard, yet the gap between us seemed great.

What had I hoped to accomplish that afternoon with Rico? To lie down in tall grass and lose myself to the ticking of insects in their music created by the rubbing of legs? Arthropod legs!

How best to reconstruct the unidentified, unidentifiable longings I felt? What virgin, do you suppose, really hopes or schemes for sex? The neophyte dreams of the moment before and the moment after; his arms embracing her, then his arms holding, not letting her go. My desire was a child's desire: to be engulfed in the warmth of the larger body.

And like the child that I was I challenged Rico to a race just for the fun of it. As he cycled a bit ahead of me, the basket posed a handicap. That balanced things out, I thought. But for some there's no fun in any contest, there's only competition. Rico was like that. At first he just laughed, but when I shot in front, he began to pedal in earnest. He was the man and he had to win. But he needed both hands on the handlebars to speed. By leaning forward and holding down the basket with his chin, he managed this feat. I looked back frequently to make sure he stayed in sight. He couldn't see me, nor could he see where he was going, with his face buried in that basket. He charged ahead like a bull.

When I saw what looked like a good spot for our picnic, I turned into the woods, calling out to Rico to follow. It was the beech trees that drew me, their pale, naked-looking torsos.

The woods were cool. And the stillness slowed me, soothed my flushed face, and eased my hammering heart. I left my bicycle against the trunk of one of those trees and plopped myself down to wait. There I arranged my skirt in artful folds, hoping that Rico would rumple them.

If I had been the one carrying the basket, he might not have found me there, holding such a pose. I would have been laying out our lunch, because this doing nothing but waiting, this arranging of myself instead of the food, was much harder. I took off my hat, untied the thick braid of my hair so that it fell in soft flowing waves across my shoulders and down my back. Chestnut, the hue of the fruit of that tree, my hair was dark brown and red in its gloss.

Grunting with effort, panting, Rico came thrashing through the grove. He jumped off the bike without slowing properly to a stop and it kept rolling until it crashed into a tree. The bike fell flat on its side, but its wheels continued spinning. Rico laughed, he laughed like a cock crowing, a laughter of beginnings, not endings. Though he had let the bike go, he still held on to the picnic basket. Placing it between us, he sat down beside me under my tree.

"Where are you? I can't see your face behind all that hair!" As you push back a curtain to spy on your neighbor, he pulled back the hair from one side of my face. "Ah, there you are again; I haven't lost you after all!" Then he turned his attention to the food. "This racing has given me an appetite." Opening the picnic basket, he pulled out bread, some spiced Sicilian olives, cheese, prosciutto, and wine. "Where's the pizza?"

"No, not on Tuesdays, I forgot."

"This is good. This is even better. A loaf of bread, wine—what more could we want?"

"'*Tu—cantando nel deserto del nulla.*'"

"No, not me. I'm heading for La Scala."

"It's a poem."

"A poem? Whose? Is it Dante's?"

"No. No matter, it's stupid. It's a translation of a translation."

"If it's poetry, it's not stupid—it's essential. Think, what would opera be without the libretto?"

"But when words are sung, they don't mean the same thing, they don't have the same effect. In the lyrics for *La Bohème,* *'arrosto freddo'* and *'io ti amo'* seem to have the same power to move us. Yet we don't expect deep emotion or delicate beauty from antipasto. But sing 'cold cuts' or 'I love you' on Puccini's stage and suddenly there is such yearning in every syllable of every word, regardless of what they mean, that it makes us weep."

"Maybe Puccini was hungry when he wrote that. To a starving man, a prosciutto might look almost as good as his sweetheart. Maybe even better."

I laughed.

"*Picina,* you are so pretty when you laugh, almost as pretty as when you argue with me."

"As pretty as Ada?"

"Ada is not pretty. She … she is … magnificent—like a queen, like someone you could not hope to touch."

"You think she's beautiful but that I'm only pretty—you think she's a queen and that I'm just a child!"

"No, no. What's this? Are you jealous, *picina?*"

I refused to say anything more. I pouted.

As if to comfort me, he put his arms around me. In his embrace I felt myself melt. When he kissed me, my mouth opened fully to receive him, but the smell of my sister's perfume on his clothes made me push him away.

"I know you're not a baby. You open your mouth like a woman."

"For you. Remember—it was you who taught me how."

"Ah, well, let's practice a little more then."

"Have you talked to Papa?"

"Tell me why should I talk to your father?"

"About us …"

"It's not so simple as in the Bible, you know. In life, in a career, it's not just ask and you shall get."

"But you promised! You're successful now!"

"I'm just beginning."

"No, don't wait for La Scala. Marry me now, Rico. But if you must go there first, I promise I'll wait for you. I'll wait for you forever!"

"You think forever is until the day after tomorrow, don't you?"

"No. I love you, only you. I'll love you forever." I pointed to my left breast. He placed his hand over it, cupped and stroked my bodice.

"Your forever is soft, smooth. I can cup your forever in my hand. I can squeeze it a little to see what it's made of, and it's firm, like good bread. I could eat it. Or when I'm old and have no more teeth, I could gum and suck on it with perhaps even greater pleasure. Yes, it's good. Can I see what it looks like? Release that sweet bird from its cage."

I felt his touch as a burning. A strange vertigo overcame me. He touched only my chest, but I felt the heat everywhere.

"As soon as we marry …"

"I'm not ready to marry. I'm waiting too—not for someone, but for something. For La Scala, for America, for the world to recognize me."

"Papa would never forbid our marriage because of money, not if he knows how much I love you. Tonight I'll tell him so myself!"

"No! Don't do that! There are complications you're too young to understand."

"What complications? Don't you love me, Rico?"

"No! I mean … yes, I love you, *picina,* from the first moment I saw you—you dropped the artichokes and it seemed golden apples rolled by my feet. But Ada … Ada … it's Ada I adore!"

He reached to embrace me, his face, crinkled in concern, guessing how much he had hurt me, but I leapt to my feet. My bicycle was nearby and I grabbed it and pedaled away from him. But there was only one place for me to go, and that was home to where my sister, my rival, also lived.

He didn't follow me. When, late that afternoon, he returned to Livorno, the picnic basket was empty.

THE HOLIDAYS WERE OVER. They ended when I got back to the apartment and found Ada waiting for me.

"It didn't go as you expected—your little picnic?"

Through eyes burning with the tears I was holding back, I glared at my sister with all the hatred I could muster. Then she changed her tone to patronizing sympathy.

"You're young, *sorellina,* your heart will mend, while I, I've met my true match in this tenor."

What was a "true match" for her was true love for me. I couldn't stand to stay in Livorno and watch Rico adore her. I packed my bags. My half-crazed despair moved my mother to pity and she sent a telegram to Felicia, our housekeeper, asking her to meet me at the central station.

Felicia was a second mother to us. "What could be more secure?" I asked, and my mother had to agree.

5

In summertime, my hometown, Firenze—which the English call Florence—is always milling with tourists. They crowd the cathedrals, not praying, but sightseeing. Foreigners mob the galleries, not to appreciate the master works of art, but to visit the souvenir shops and purchase postcard images of them. They stroll about town, making their useless umbrellas useful as walking sticks. Even in the unbearable August heat, Englishmen continue to wear their tweed jackets. They must be a cold and bloodless race, with too much rain in their veins.

Our palazzo was on Via dei Serragli, in an area known as the Artisans' Quarter. The vast, drab stone medieval church, Santa Maria Del Carmine, is nearby and draws crowds of sightseers throughout the season. I couldn't step out my door and walk to the piazza without wading through the thick of them.

What was I to do with my life now that I had lost my true love? I did not want to marry anybody else. So the spinster must find a career. I remembered my vow that if I couldn't have the man that I loved, then I would fill myself with his music. I enrolled at the Istituto Musicale the way a noblewoman in another age might have entered a convent to live a life of learning and devotion. If music became my church, it was another I really worshiped there—Enrico Caruso.

What kind of person would engage in an art out of envy or the need to be loved? And require a stage to express their feelings—hidden, forbidden feelings? Who would use opera, music, as a personal code, or as a cheap form of catharsis? Perhaps all these reasons meant that I was not a true artist. I was a jealous sister and I was an abandoned lover who had enrolled at the institute for music where Ada had studied before me. My ambition was not pure, it was not for the art of bel canto itself, but to challenge my sister on the operatic stage and then, what was even closer to my heart's desire, displace her as the soprano at Caruso's, at my Rico's, side. Call me an amateur if you like, but I was never a dilettante.

I did not think of Rico and Ada as I crossed the river by way of the Ponte alla Carraia, hardly pausing to look at the waters, the churning currents, below my feet. The river had purpose, it had drive, while I sleepwalked my way to the lessons each morning, floating along, bumping into foreigners or, worse, the vendors who catered to them and cursed me if I happened between them and their dupes. I did not think of Rico and Ada during the singing lessons, raising my chin as I vocalized as if to lift up the notes, when the truth was the opposite, when it was music itself propping me up. I did not think of them when I made mistakes and Maestro Ceccherini, who had taught the world-famous Eva and Luisa Tetrazzini before me, rapped my fingers in class with a pointer even though Rico and Ada and their infernal coupling were what I knew to be mistakes, errors in my life. I did not think of them when I chose to eat in the kitchen with Felicia rather than eat alone in the dining room; she didn't mind if I kept my books by my side at the table, she didn't require conversation, nor did she object to my constant humming. No, I didn't need to think of them when I could smell them; the odor of their bedsheets invaded me at night, that smell of candy dropped on a beach, sticky sweet encrusted with salt.

With my family in Livorno, there was nothing to distract me from music. And Firenze hardly seemed my home anymore, teeming as it was with strangers conversing in languages I didn't understand, so much so that it began to feel as if I were the foreigner, the stranger, speaking a minority tongue in my own country. So when I wasn't at the institute, I stayed at home with Felicia. She was a simple woman—she had a quality, invisibility, acquired, I suppose, from a lifetime spent as a servant, that did not alleviate my loneliness. It didn't seem possible to disturb her, so if she heard throughout the night the restless rehearsals of a ghost—that ghost was myself on the piano playing a moonlight sonata in the darkness—she never mentioned it.

My sleep was fitful, my dreams upsetting. I would dream of the creak, creak, creaking sounds of the bed in Livorno and wake to cries, to shrieks which might have been a baby's or a cat's. Untangling myself from the clammy sheets, I would go to the window overlooking the garden and look for the moon. With the first rays of the sun breaching the horizon, the moon was the color of an apricot, a fruit bruised from too much handling.

The air felt almost cold on my damp skin. Dizzy from exhaustion, I would remain at the window, hip half propped on the ledge, to listen to what remained of the night. The house was absolute stillness. If Felicia was snoring softly in her bedroom, I could not hear her, not over the gurgling, splashing sound of water, rising and falling from the fountain where the speech of Orpheus was a cyclic and fecund flow from his marble mouth. Like his—I thought I must train my voice like his and allow music to flow through me rather than merely from me. Our Orpheus was the poet before he met the Maenads; his limbs were intact, his robe still untouched. He was the bard just returned from his descent into Hades, after the turning around and loss of his beloved for the second, more bitter time. His lyre was held low; it idled at his hip. There were marble tears on his cheeks, wet and glistening with the spray sent up by the fountain. *"Che farò senza Euri-di-ce, Euri-di-ce,"* I imagined hearing the strains from the aria he inspired Gluck to write.

Alternately bright then dim, the moon appeared to swing through clouds in a dance of many veils.

Silence too is composed of sound, sound and interval, defining each other as life is demarcated by death, as death by birth. We would not know death except for the millions of beats of the human heart; we would not hear the silence. The word death came readily to my mouth then. I thought I could be safely in love with it, that death would not despise me because I was not yet old. What I called death in my youth was not what I face with aging, the death that takes you by the hand and tugs you along, reminiscing, until the end of the journey. No, it was not so slow and chatty a figure. Death had panache then—it was self-expression as self-immolation, the way the young and other immortals conceive it. That summer in Firenze I dreamed an end to my life because I could not imagine an end to my love.

Directly below my bedroom window was the courtyard with its granite flagstones reflecting the bluish cast of gas lamplight. Jumping didn't seem dangerous. I expected broken bones, not death, from such a gesture. I needed a tower or a cliff with rocks and a raging sea below. Lacking a suitable stage, I balked at the act. And then the chill that in time crept into my bones made me close the window on all that and put on my robe and go to the piano where I played the melodies from the many tragic stories of opera. If I suffered as my heroines did, nevertheless, I did not die, I simply sang on through the night.

6

In September, when Mamma and Papa came back to Firenze, Ada was not with them. She had returned to Fiume and her husband's family there. My father was proud that the music institute had admitted me into their advanced program with a full scholarship. Maestro Ceccherini himself had agreed to supervise my training. He remembered instructing my sister. I was grateful for the award though I loathed being compared to Ada.

When my friends also returned from their summer villas and began calling on me, I did not welcome their calls. Nor would I accept invitations to go out. No, this aria must be learned, perfected, the intonation in the second verse particularly difficult. No, the blessed Virgin would have to celebrate her feast day without me. I was still flesh, but I was determined to model myself as in a fairy tale, as a golden bird, worthy of singing for an emperor. Nothing as natural as a nightingale could ever satisfy bel canto.

"You should write to your sister in Fiume, tell her of your progress at the school. She'll be proud that you've followed in her footsteps."

But all I dreamed of was erasing those steps, stomping out every trace, of inverting things, of making her my shadow, my cadet.

7

As the weather cooled, the crowds of foreigners also thinned and the city was returned to the Italians. Lessons and long hours of practice, the structure of my studies and the discipline sustained me. Life settled into a familiar routine with Father on the road for the treasury and Mother full-time at her prayers now that she had Felicia to take care of the household duties. I would drink my coffee alone in the mornings. When Mother returned from mass I would already be gone to school. I allowed myself no thoughts on the way that could not be represented in musical notation. I made progress, I won praise from Maestro Ceccherini, and so his pointer began to serve as a baton, it no longer came crashing across my fingers because of a flat note. I did well and I wanted to do better, and the choice of singing that had been a kind of retreat from life, from the wounds of love, became, in truth, my life. It seemed that if I had not truly chosen music, then it had chosen me.

Then my peace was disrupted. It was nearly suppertime and we were all home that evening when there was a knock at our door. Felicia answered and when I heard his voice, the sound of music mixed with laughter, I ran to him. I told Felicia that I would take care of our guest and she went back to the kitchen. Rico was grimy from his trip on the train, but that didn't stop me from hugging him.

"How wonderful to see you! Supper's almost ready, won't you join us?"

He lamented that it had been standing-room only on the train and with all the windows open because of the heat he had become filthy. There was a film of dust, that black and sticky residue from the burning of coal, on his clothes and on his cardboard suitcase. I took the suitcase from him; it weighed next to nothing and contained all his worldly goods. Then I offered him a clean towel so he could wash up before dinner.

Later, when Rico joined us at the table, his face was ruddy from scrubbing. He accepted a glass of red wine from Papa, but it was water he drank first. There were tall glasses filled to the brim and clinking with ice when you raised them to drink. Moisture beaded on the outside of the glasses, as if they were so full that water seeped from the sides.

Over dinner, Rico gave us an account of his troubles.

"After the Goldini settled with me, I found myself poorer than before I started singing there. When I left Mugnone's company I had money to spare. But now I'm stuck—and there's no one I know in Milan, even if I had enough for a ticket to get to the north. I had just enough to come here. There were some music students on board with me, in a corner of the aisle, behind the door to the next compartment; they opened their instruments and began to play. I suggested they play an aria for me and I sang. The train was full of tourists—they were the seated ones who got up and filled the hat the cellist had put out for donations. We shared the pot and so I have the price of a ticket to Milan now, but not nearly enough to set myself up in the city, at least not until I get paid there. I still need fifty lire. I need a room and I need clothes to present myself at the Lirico. You know the Goldini held me to my bargain and only paid me fifteen lire a performance."

Papa was indignant. "That wily snake! The impresario took advantage of you—of your innocence and your ambition. Such talent, such candor, should be encouraged, not exploited! You had Puccini's written approval—he took no risk at all! And he made you pay for it, young man, pay for your own success. It's an outrage!"

The injustice of the young man's plight truly upset Papa. He gladly gave Rico the fifty lire he needed, as well as an invitation to stay again as a guest in our home.

I KNEW NOTHING of money, or of what it might mean to go hungry, or to have to pose for photographers draped in bedding because your single shirt is in the wash. Rico had a home in Naples, a stepmother who adored him there. Why hadn't he gone home? Why did he choose to stay with us? Although before each performance Rico had to pray for help from his Madonnas or he dared not sing, he still did not return to Naples, the city of shrines to his female trinity composed of the Virgin Mary in her manifestation as the Madonna of Pompeii and the two women who raised him. Anna Baldini, his saintly mother, had died when he was still a boy, and Maria Castaldi, his stepmother, who favored Rico as if he were her own son, was the only living Madonna among them. He included her in his prayers, but he did not return to her. She had to content herself with the occasional letter and lire from him. So I persuaded myself that I might be the reason why Rico stopped and stayed in Firenze rather than continuing his journey home. I knew nothing of the cost of train tickets or the mix of a man's pride with his gratitude.

IF MY DISCIPLINE, my devotion, and the long hours I spent at the piano changed during Rico's stay with us, it was only to intensify. However, the music I played became Rico's music, for Rico's roles, the ones he was learning for his debut in Milan. Of course, I would often sing as well—as soprano to his tenor—in the duets he needed to master, so my voice continued to be trained. In the mornings I went to the institute, I came home for lunch, and then all afternoon I played the piano for him, and often long hours into the evening. I would have gladly continued as Rico's shadow and merely mouthed the songs; to stay with him, I would have gladly existed as his echo.

Mine was not Ada's role, I was not his teacher, or his lover, I was merely his accompanist. I didn't go to his bed, nor did I invite him into mine. This restraint was good for my mother's nerves, if not for mine. The vertical bar etched between her brows smoothed to a wrinkle. She slept later; she joined us for breakfast and ate good bread with us, not just holy wafer in the company of priests and statues. Papa was staying at home again. A shroud was lifted from our family life and the sackcloth of sin and penance stored away. Such music and laughter rang out from our house that those who knew us, and even strangers, would stop in the street to marvel and listen.

8

They say that the golden age cannot be recovered, that the gates of Eden, our first paradise, are sealed against us, but those eight days in Firenze at the end of the summer of 1897 both belie and confirm that for me. Ours was the music of the spheres, we sang as angels sing in the firmament. It is written that Jesus said that angels have no sex. They are no sex. This was perhaps what also made us perfect then, and our music heavenly.

We loved each other as innocents. Touch was a hug, a tweak of the nose, a tousling of the hair on my head. My fingers were dedicated to the ivory keys of the piano as to a rosary. His hands I studied as they opened in dramatic gestures for a song. They were not a gentleman's hands, but rough ones, callused from physical labor. Over the summer they had begun to acquire some polish; the nails were trimmed now and buffed to shining. Half-moons could be seen rising, nacreous, from every nail. Rico drummed the digits on the ebony of the piano top as if he were drilling for the tempo. If I lost my place in the score, he could lead me back in an instant. It is believed by many that a young girl never has a sense of her own place, wherever it might be, home, school, church, or family. But that was of no great matter to me because it was his place I wanted to find, it was beside him that I needed to stand.

But this idyllic time ended the day I opened the door to the mailman and accepted a perfumed letter from Fiume for Rico. I recognized the seal, and the scent was hers, that heady mix of flowers, amber, and musk. Without opening the letter, in fact barely glancing at the envelope, he slipped it into the inside pocket of his jacket.

"Aren't you going to read it?"

"What?"

"You know, the letter. Who is it from?"

"No—it's nobody. It's more important to continue rehearsing. The letter can wait."

We had been together, as one, for eight days, but suddenly I felt myself shut out. Rico was lying. His excitement, his sudden discomfort in his own skin, gave him away. He fidgeted and hopped about as he again attempted to sing the tragic aria we had been rehearsing that day. He kept touching his jacket pocket and feeling for the letter.

When he finished the song, Rico called for a break. He said that he had to rest. He shut himself in his room. In my mind I followed him. In my mind I imagined the envelope as my sister's white throat and I watched as, with a blade, he ripped it open. I couldn't read the writing, blinded as I was by all the blood. Later, when I went to his door to call him in for the evening meal,

I paused, listening before I knocked. I heard light snores; I had to rap loudly and call out several times to wake him.

At dinner he was his usual lighthearted self. More laughter than bread was broken at that meal. He toasted Felicia for the spaghetti cooked nearly as well as it is in the south! Because in our family we saw the *napoletani* as underdogs (once you've discovered one that you could trust, that is), nobody was offended. We all laughed.

Then, assuming a solemn air, Rico raised his glass again and turned to my father: "To your generosity, sir. I hope to repay it soon."

"To Papa!" I joined the toast to my father who had welcomed the tenor back into our home.

Twilight descended while we ate, not darkness yet but blue light, air thickening, acquiring the look of water. The wine was done, but the fine speeches were not. Rico had one more thing to say to us.

"It is with regret that I must leave you all. I'm heading north tomorrow because I have been offered a small contract and, as you know, I need the money."

I knew that he would be going to Milan, yet I did not feel prepared for him to leave so soon.

It was to be the last dinner together, the end of an era for us, and the beginning of another.

AFTER SUPPER, Rico suggested we take a stroll to the piazza for some gelato. But as for the sticky sweetness of lemon ice on the tongue, that was a pleasure for another time. If it was to be our last evening together, then I wanted to be alone with him. I suggested we sit in the garden; the cool spray from the fountain would disguise any tears that might escape from me.

It was my habit to sit there, and with the long light of summer evenings to see by, I would embroider flowers on the linens for my trousseau among the real flowers of the garden. It was dusk, but habit made me take my embroidery with me anyway.

Rico gave up ice cream to be with me. "It's not what you do, it's the company you keep that counts," he said.

I will always cherish those words. Later, when Rico was the famous Caruso, and I would read the critics of the world, how they all tried, in language, to describe the qualities of his voice— how they all tried and failed with their superlatives to come close to the beauty—the tone of that phrase, those words from near the end of summer, so long ago in Firenze, that sentence spoken, not sung, came back to me, and once more my ear was stroked as if by a rose.

"*Va bene*. We'll sit in the garden, but put that needle away! Those days in Livorno when Ada worked to undo Vergine's bad teaching, and you sat by the window, you looked like a little girl playing with rainbow-colored threads."

"Well, I'm not a little girl. I'm a young woman and Mamma says it's important that I work on my trousseau. When I make my marriage bed, it will look like a field of flowers."

"It's for your trousseau! Ah, you expect to marry soon, do you? Well, let's see what lies ahead. Let me look into my crystal ball." He pulled out his handkerchief and swiped at air cupped in his hand in a circular motion. "That's better, the glass was gathering dust, but now I can see far into the future." He darkened, deepened his voice for prophesy. "Out of the fog comes a man, and yes, there's a woman on his arm, and that woman is you—it's you, Rina, and looking magnificent, with a broad-brimmed hat tilted to one side and jewels sparkling from your ears and from every finger. You are like a goddess to radiate light in such fog! What else is there—I think I see something more—but what is it? It's a strange vehicle, no horses, but it moves anyway. It follows slowly beside you and your husband as you stroll along, and you are walking, not because you have to walk, but because you like doing it for a little while. It's for your health! You walk to take the air, and if it's cold, that's no problem because you're wearing furs." Rico looked up at me; in the gloaming his smile was the sun's last stand. "Oh, and with this fellow you won't need a trousseau, Rina. He isn't looking for a dowry. He's rich. He'll buy you everything you need and anything you want. So put that needlework away—or else I'll have to find something interesting to do with my hands. Like this!" He tickled me.

I shrieked, running around the fountain as he chased after me.

"*Basta,* help, help!" So much laughter took my breath away. "Please, please, stop! Oh, Rico, I could be so happy here with you!"

"Aren't you happy now, *picina*?"

"No ... I mean, yes—with you here I'm very happy. Because I love you, I really love you!"

"Thank you."

"*Thank you?*"

"Yes, I know—I mean, I love you too, Rina, but ..."

"You love me, you do? Why must you go away, then—and so soon? Won't you stay with us a little longer?"

"I have to go. Try to understand, Rina, I have nothing to offer a young woman like you. Not even my life is my own anymore. I owe my brother Giovanni, who went to military service in my place, years of my life. I owe Vergine, that good-for-nothing teacher of mine in Napoli, a percentage of every contract. Now I even owe your father fifty lire—and that's the part of my debt to him that can be measured! How could I, with any dignity, with any sense of decency or gratitude, for that matter, dare to claim you, his youngest daughter, for my own?"

Our relationship was on a higher plane, or so I consoled myself. We enjoyed friendship, not lust, but a pure love. This, our higher love, would be the true love that would hold him. His relationship with Ada was adulterous, a thing of scandal and sex, and doomed to end badly. Love always wants to believe; like a bird it can live on crumbs.

The next morning he walked out our front door into a morning of brilliant sun. The cicadas were already shrilling. He walked out carrying his cardboard suitcase, swinging it lightly as he walked. I wanted to accompany him, but I had a lesson scheduled with my maestro, and Rico insisted I go to the class. I thought he was taking the train to Milan. But if I had gone to the station, I would have seen him buy a ticket for Trieste instead.

9

We did not learn of Rico's true whereabouts until Gino Botti, Ada's husband, wrote to Papa. I did not recognize the handwriting when I gave the letter to him that evening. It was Ada who generally conveyed all the news of their family to us in her own letters; she missed us all, she said, although her letters were addressed to Papa. A letter from Gino was a rare thing.

"What's this?" Papa frowned at the letter. "Why is Botti writing to me? It's bound to be some business affair, no doubt advice on how to invest the extra money we don't have." He seemed reluctant to open it, bored as he was by his son-in-law tenor turned accountant. After dinner, while Felicia was serving coffee, I watched Father slit the letter open in a distracted manner. But as he read it, he turned red in the face.

"What's this?" he said again, but this time breathless with fury. "This can't be true!"

Mother picked up on his alarm: "Something's happened to Ada! To Lelio! Please, God, say that it isn't so!"

Father crumpled up the letter and threw it onto the floor. "He writes filth. I won't have it at my table!"

"But what is it, Papa, what's the matter?"

"Gino claims that Ada is having an affair with the Neapolitan tenor. Our Rico is not in Milan after all, but singing at the Comunale in Fiume. Gino writes that their relationship is a public scandal."

Papa refused to believe the gossip, while I did not *want* to believe it. But Mother thought it prudent that we investigate the charge, and I was sent to visit Ada, to find out the truth of the matter. Whether my mission was to appease the in-laws or support my sister was unclear to me. But if Rico were really in Fiume, I had a mission of my own, and that was to rescue him from the clutches of my sister.

IO

Fiume, what had become to my mind Ada's city, was a port on the Adriatic Sea, in the far northeast of Italy, bordering on Slovenia. At seventeen, I had never been on such a long journey on my own. At the station my father spoke to one of his contacts there to ensure my comfort and safety. Because of all the traveling Papa did for the treasury, he was well connected with the railroad and its officials.

It was such a slow train—my heart beat faster than its wheels turned. It was a milk train that stopped at every village—at every henhouse, it seemed to me. The train's wheels kept spinning without ever seeming to arrive. And I was anxious to do so even though I dreaded what I would find there. Was Rico's parting tenderness a sham? Was he there with my sister in Fiume, and not in Milan?

My first-class compartment, empty except for myself most of the way, was unbearably stuffy. The rocking of the locomotive was too jolting to be lulling. I felt my body, my stomach, heaving as if at sea. I had hardly slept the night before, but I couldn't sleep on the train even though I kept my eyes shut for hours contemplating the variegated darkness behind my eyelids. It was pink and more so, fuchsine in spots of intense color. A phantasmagoria took the shape of Rico, then Ada, then the two of them entwined. These visions might have been a form of clairvoyance. If so, it was Cassandra's kind, that gift for prophesy but not for persuasion. Even I refused to believe what the images revealed.

As we passed through a tunnel, the rose-colored images became black. When I opened my eyes again we were passing through hills, trellised by vineyards, and green-gold with the harvest of grapes.

The constant motion, the dream visions, made me dizzy. There was a sour burning in my throat as fluids backed up from my stomach; my lunch or that poisoned stew of suspicion, jealousy, and desire that I kept stirring was about to choke me. The look of my half-eaten sandwich revolted me; the white fat border of the prosciutto was sweating oil, the red of the meat taking on the color and consistency of coagulated blood. Just the sight of it compelled me to throw it out the window. Suddenly, I could breathe more freely. After that I was able to doze, but my dreams were like my waking visions: Rico and Ada, Ada and Rico. The rhythmic creaking and swaying of the train was the motion of their bed.

When I changed trains in Bologna, getting the line to Trieste in the northeast, I moved into a sleeping compartment. It was extravagant to pay for a sleeper when I could not sleep, but it eased my mother's worries about my traveling alone so far. I was perfectly safe, and I could lock myself in.

THE NEXT DAY the real woman, not the phantom of my imagination, not the straw figure I would have readily cast onto the heap of burning chairs at *carnevale,* was waiting for me at the station. I saw Ada before she saw me. I recognized the regal turning of her head from side to side, not as if she were looking for someone, but as if she were being looked at—the queen acknowledging her admiring throng. Gazing into a crowd as if into a mirror. Still, when our eyes met, the widening, the brightening of recognition in her blue-green eyes, her laughing smile, gave me my true sister back for a moment. I remembered that same softening of her lips when she would find me in our games of hide-and-seek where I, *sorellina,* was always It. I used to have to wait forever to be found. Where had she been looking for me? I marveled at her silence and stealth, until I inverted the game and went to look for her.

Through the keyhole of her bedroom I watched my sister, seated at her vanity, manicure her nails, pluck and shape her eyebrows, putter among her cosmetics. Powder rose in a cloud from her puff before it was patted onto her nose. Turning her head from side to side, she surveyed her face in profile. As if it belonged to a stranger, some beautiful stranger.

My cramped body was hard to straighten when, bored at last, she glanced at the clock, and only then—forever had been nearly an hour—did Ada come looking for me. As rock sunk into soil, my knees felt implanted into the ceramic tile where I knelt. I couldn't move.

ON THE PLATFORM in Fiume we embraced as equals now that I had grown to her height. But she patted my cheek as if I were still a child.

"Is this my little sister? Are you really a woman now? And wearing heels?"

"I'll be a woman when I'm married."

"There's time enough for that. Don't let the relatives pressure you—they all think there's nothing else that a woman's made for!"

"But, but … you're married!"

"Yes! Because I listened to them! But you don't have to." She looked at my face and her tone changed from irritation to tenderness. "Oh, my little sister, I can see that you're tired."

Ada called the driver to take my bag. He helped us both into the carriage and we rode with the curtains drawn. Even in the light filtered through muslin, Ada's face seemed to glow. Her complexion was always protected with lotions and hats so that her skin was milky white. But that day the color in her cheeks was ruddy, whether from health or fever, I couldn't tell.

Glancing furtively out at the driver, Ada whispered in my ear— as if he could hear anything she might have to say to me over the squeaking, grinding of wheels, the clomping of hooves over cobblestones, the cries of vendors, the anxious pitch of mothers calling to their children, the babble, the noise that was an Italian town at the turn of the century. In those days it was raucous with more voices than motors, more animals than engines, but it was a cacophony nonetheless. Above the din of local traffic came the sound of the whistle blowing as the locomotive pulled out of the station.

"You'll never guess who's here." Ada's breath smelled of sweet mint. Her whisper frothed like meringue, more air than substance.

So it was true! The sweetness of her whispering turned poisonous. I played along with her guessing game with as much bravado as I could muster.

"Oh, but I can. It's Rico, isn't it? In fact, that's why I've come. There's talk. Your husband wrote to Papa about it."

"What! That sniveling coward—*cornuto,* if ever there was one who deserves to be! Gino's not a man—he's a whiner. He's afraid I'll leave him for good this time."

"Is it true, then, that you have a lover? Is it … is he …?"

"The world is my lover. I'm on the stage. I'm admired. For that my husband burns! Well, let him, I say, let him burn to a cinder for all I care."

"He wrote that Rico … that you …"

"Rico? He named him? And you believe it, I suppose—you believe that I've betrayed my husband?"

I did not want to believe what I thought I knew. "If he deserves it …"

"He does, he does—but look, we've arrived. Here's the house. Smile sweetly for my mother-in-law, coo for the baby, let's pretend this is a normal family visit, and not an inquisition."

II

I did as I was told. The baby was plump as a peach, with golden curls on his head as downy as the fuzz on that fruit. When Ada took him from Signora Botti to hand him over to me, he cried. I was afraid of his tears. I knew what it was supposed to look like, the Madonna with her child, but unlike statues, the baby squirmed. Bawling, he thrashed his arms about.

"You don't hold a baby like a sack of sugar!" Signora Botti scolded, then in somewhat softer tones she consoled her grandson: "*Poverino,* you must be hungry now. Don't cry. I'll take care of you when that worthless mother of yours won't do anything about it."

In her black-clad arms, the baby stopped thrashing about. Grasping for her breasts, gumming her bodice, he alternated angry cries with desperate sucking sounds. His *nonna* gave the baby her finger to suck on and took him to the wet nurse.

"That's the way it always is with her—nobody else knows what a mother should do—I can't get it right no matter what I do. And that son of mine is a real Botti! Just like his father, his heart is in his stomach. Lelio loves best the peasant woman who feeds him."

ADA SHOWED ME to my room.

"Rest now, after dinner we'll go for a walk, you and I. Alone. I have a secret, an important secret, to tell you. But not in this house where even the walls have ears."

I had difficulty stilling the motion of the train, it had stayed with me, in my bones, rattling, or it was the house itself that jerked and swayed. Although Ada's tantalizing promise to tell me a secret excited me, exhaustion and dizziness forced me to lie down on the bed. The mattress was very soft in the middle; I felt myself sinking into the space that had been shaped by another's body. The coolness of the room was welcome, as well as the shuttered dark. But I wasn't sleepy, not with Rico somewhere close by and perhaps part of Ada's secret. In the dim light I tried to read from a book I found on the night table, poems by the young poet Gabriele d'Annunzio. His images enthralled me: the *lunar dawn*, the moon as a *philter*, and stars that wept yet were *adamantine*, intractable. The page had the texture, the clarity of a woman's skin; the poet's woman was *infinite in her nudity*. And his songs were timeless, though he called them his *children*, and he disciplined them—like horses, with a strong hand. Nor was the poet burdened, as was my sister, with a mother-in-law who knew better how to care for them. But I was young like the poet then and seduced by his images, nor was my idea of children any less romantic than his; I too knew nothing about nursing and dirty nappies.

The atmosphere at dinner was strained. *Nonna* insisted on keeping her grandson on her lap the whole time. The baby had already eaten, he busied himself grabbing and throwing cutlery to the floor. Gino, to whom the baby bore no resemblance, not with his dark hair and burly features, hardly spoke throughout the meal except to ask for more wine. Breaking bread, he frowned, raising a glass to his lips, he frowned, looking into the liquid, its darkness suggesting some sort of depth, all four centimeters of it, he frowned. When coffee was served, he took his cup to his study. With a satchel under his arm and a folded newspaper, he left the table.

"Work and more work. My son is a model employee. They say he will be appointed director of the bank soon." This was spoken with some authority by Gino's father since he owned the bank. He was a short bald man with sagging skin around his neck, which gave his head the aspect of a cheese, a *caciocavallo*.

12

After dinner Ada's mother-in-law took the child for a nap while the men returned to the bank. The sun was too hot and so we put off our walk until the evening. The food, all that pasta and roasted meat, had made me drowsy and I had to go and lie down again. Like the baby, I needed a nap.

So it wasn't until nearly sunset that Ada and I went out for our walk. We strolled, not to the piazza, as one would expect, but into the fringes of the town, stopping in a lane where the stucco facades of buildings, long rows of three-storied tenements, dropped crumbling mounds of white dust onto the beaten earth and gravel of the road. Barefoot boys played in the street, two groups of them competing to kick a weather-beaten ball. The runny noses, the scruffy faces, the blackened feet and crusty knees did not make it look very attractive to raise children.

A few of the boys jeered at us, but some of the bigger boys whistled.

"Keep your diapers on!" my sister scoffed. Then they started throwing stones at us. Our shrieks brought someone running out of the building.

At first I only saw the back of his head as he chased after the urchins. But when I heard his voice, when I heard that laugh which might have been mistaken for some percussion instrument,

I knew it was Rico. Along with the joy of seeing him again came pain. What was he doing in Fiume? Why had he lied? I did not know whether I was more hurt than angry.

He was running after the boys, shouting at them all the while, "*Mascalzoni!*" And they, crying out in mock terror, all scampered off in different directions. When, laughing and flushed, Rico turned back, they called out to him, "Over here! Come get me! Here! Over here!"

From the merry look in Rico's eye I guessed that this was not the first time he had given chase to those brats.

"They're devils, those boys, but they've got spirit!" he laughed. After mopping his forehead with a handkerchief, he turned to me. "Rina, *bambina*, won't you give me a hug?" It was good to feel his arms around me, to breathe in the salty sweetness of sweat along with eau de cologne. But then, without asking, he embraced my sister.

"*Cara,*" he called her. "This is a very happy day for me because here we're all together again."

"I thought you were in Milan." I said that with acid on my tongue.

"Ah yes, I'm there—but not just yet." He was unabashed at being caught in his lie. "You see, your sister found me some work. I'm filling in for the tenor at the Comunale for a few performances. It's Rodolfo again, what could be better? Let's go now, those boys will get bored with each other and may return to taunt us at any moment."

THE LIGHT WAS DIMMING as we walked; the dusk was a poet coating the texture of things with layers of beautiful obscurity. Even gravel had the look of velvet. White flowers glowed ghostly while others, the darkly colored blossoms, were swallowed in shadow. The landscape became invisible except to the nose. And the scent of those flowers was a kind of Braille through which rose could be read.

We walked into the cemetery where the faces in the photographs of the dead, their crosses and saints carved in stone, some illuminated by candles, those tended daily and not forgotten, watched us pass. As for the others, the more numerous, we were as blind to them as they were to us, their names, their faces, unreadable in the night.

We stopped to rest by a grove of trees. Moonlight shimmered, made everything seem ethereal. Our bodies were plated in silver, a strange alchemy translating us from organic to metallic.

The cemetery was vast, the graves encroaching on land reserved for a park. Rico shook out a large linen handkerchief and spread it out on the ground. The air smelled of freshly mown grass, sweetened by chamomile and clover. Bowing, with an extravagant flourish, he offered the seat to Ada. Then he squatted beside her. I was the only one still standing. Because they were seated, it seemed as if they were my audience, as if they were expecting to hear, if not singing, then speeches or sermons from me. The stage was set; it was time to say what I had been sent to say.

"Ada's husband wrote to Papa—he calls it a scandal. Not that he names the man, except as the *napoletano*." I said this in a rush. That was the easy part, fulfilling the role of messenger. The hard part was what followed, the lie I told to try to find out the truth. "But I told Papa that it couldn't be true—that it couldn't be you, Rico! I told Papa that it must be all lies because you are engaged to me!"

Brushing away something, then gathering her skirt in more closely, Ada remained silent.

"It's me you love, isn't it?" The silence was too pregnant with what I might not want to hear. "Tell me! Tell her now that you love me!"

Rico shook his head helplessly. "Yes, this love is strong. It feels like family. I love you, Rina—truly—and Ada, Ada—not even King Solomon proposed such a difficult choice!"

"But she's already married. You can't choose her. You don't need King Solomon's wisdom to figure that out!" But if he was the king, I guess Ada and I were the two feuding mothers. The baby, I suppose, was his heart.

"My husband is a Philistine. He's a pig!" Ada cried.

"How is a man to choose between an angel and a goddess?"

"What! There's been no talk of choosing in my bed—only vows of eternal love! Is my sister then going to slip in with us between the sheets?"

"His love for me is more than lust!" I declared.

Rico jumped up and began to pace, tearing at his hair and his clothes.

"I can't, I can't choose. It's killing me to try—to even think of it!" Then suddenly he pulled something out of his jacket pocket. I could not make out what it was in the dim light. He waved it around above his head and moonlight glinted off a gun.

"It's killing me," he repeated, "and with this gun I'm going to finish the job!" Then he aimed the revolver at his temple. I heard Ada gasp, while I was so stricken with fear I could hardly breathe. I was paralyzed. And he seemed paralyzed too, waiting for I know not what, for the music of the aria to begin? Or was he still trying to decide, and among three women now, Ada, myself—and Lady Death?

Then I heard the trigger cock, and that sprung me into action. I threw myself at Rico, grabbing his arm in an attempt to wrest the pistol away from him. Ada just shrieked. As we struggled for the gun, it went off, shooting into the air above us. The explosion seemed deafening at such close range. The bullet flew up into the trees. It didn't hit anything. The bullet soared to the moon for all we knew. And that night the moon was a Janus figure, its face half in light and half in shadow.

Staggering as if he had been shot, Rico dropped to the ground where Ada embraced him, covering his face and head with little kisses. In truth, he was no more wounded than I was.

The gun had been knocked to the ground. Gingerly, I picked it up and examined it. It was no larger than my hand and lightweight as a child's toy. Still I felt myself recoil at what might have happened, and I dropped the gun.

"No, it's too terrible. Forget me and go with her. Go." In the battle for his heart, it was I who surrendered.

13

I should have left then; my decision had been made. I was packing the suitcase I had unpacked earlier that day when, without knocking, Ada entered my room. I kept packing. The extra care I then took to fold my clothes into the desired creases was the only change that might have betrayed that I was aware of her presence.

She cleared her throat to get my attention: "Rina, *sorellina*." She cooed the endearment, little sister, so tenderly. When does a snake sound like a pigeon? "You're so brave!"

We would always be sisters, so because of blood I turned to her, because of blood I listened.

"What you did in the cemetery was really brave."

"Thank you. Now kindly let me finish packing—I want to go home."

"If you must, Rina, but before you go I'd like to talk to you, I'd like to explain something. I don't care what Gino thinks, nor the world, for that matter, but you, you—please understand, oh, Rina, please—I've finally met the man for me. Other men, they're just toys, I tire of them quickly. But Rico, he is my Adam. It feels as if I've never known another man!"

Why is it that when women talk of their love they become entangled in myths, in clichés? Why, when we love, do we believe it's the first time for the world, that nobody has ever loved before? And, in spite of that conviction, we end up using the same words, the same stories, using the same lies, as our ancestors. We continue to want the same things: for the heavens to weep with us, for the stars to burn out like lamps whose oil cannot be refilled when he leaves our bed, for the mountains to move to the city, to the country, where he lives. We continue to want the same and incompatible things: passion and motherhood.

Who can tell people apart when the language they use is identical? My sister and I sang the same tune, read from the same libretto.

"I love him too, you know. I love him more! It's not fair, Ada, I saw him first. It's wicked of you to take him from me."

"Ah, but he saw me first, didn't he? My portrait. Even before he boarded the train in Palermo for Livorno, he told me that he was already in love with me."

Though we were sisters, we were not alike and this was

perhaps the central difference between us: I saw, she was seen, I loved, but she was loved.

"I want to marry him and you know you can't! What will you do? Leave your husband? You know you can't do that without losing your son—especially with your mother-in-law in charge of the nursery."

"Lelio is every inch a Botti. I can't find myself in him."

"But, Ada, I don't understand, he's still your baby! What will you do? The Church will never allow divorce in Italy. You know you can't live with Rico without living in mortal sin." I could not imagine then that ordinary life could be lived outside the bonds of Church law.

"Sin is what they call love when it's bigger than the dowry. And the children born are branded as bastards."

"Bastards?"

"Duty is dry as dust, but this"—she touched her belly, rested her hand there tenderly—"this time I feel the swelling, not as flesh, but as song."

So that was her secret—she was expecting Rico's child.

"Who knows?"

"Nobody. Just you now."

"That scene in the cemetery could have been avoided. Why, in heaven's name, didn't you say something to stop it?"

At that she began to laugh.

"It was just a little joke, Rina. The pistol was a prop from *Forza del Destino*. It was loaded with blanks."

I didn't laugh. That made her triumph complete, I suppose— she was going to have Rico's child, but she wasn't using the baby to keep him. What was hurt more, my vanity or my love? But sometimes they're hard to separate, easy to mix up.

So I unpacked again, she helped me, and I stayed. Without hesitation I stayed, not for my sister's sake, but because this child might have been my child. I stayed because this child *should* have been my child.

14

Ada no longer left the house without me. If I had been sent by my family to assuage Gino's fears, acting as her constant companion, I did that. But it might have been better for him to fear his fears.

It seemed as if, for the Botti family's purposes, I had become her chaperone; in actuality, I was her accomplice. Mrs. Botti was pleased, remarking on Ada's heightened color, the glow in her skin, the brightness in her eyes, *"Vi fà bene."* She actually encouraged us to go for those long evening strolls into a countryside lit only by fireflies and stars. There is a green glow to the insect bodies which might also be true of the stars—to know, we need to get close enough to really see them, close enough to catch and cup them in our hands.

We would walk together, Rico in the middle, an arm around each of our waists. It was almost enough just to be close to him. I laced myself tighter and tighter. I blamed the corset for my difficulties in breathing, not my lungs, not the heart in my throat, choking me with desire. I was impaled on the pin of the voyeur. I had to watch Rico love my sister—as if such love could be enjoyed vicariously. Not the carnal act, we were not so depraved, but the romance of courtship. Still, it looked like happiness from the outside. There was so much laughter that it brought us all to tears!

It wasn't because the evenings were getting so much cooler but because Rico had gone to Milan that our excursions into the countryside ended. We would only walk the few paces to the piazza and back. Ada could no longer be persuaded to walk more than that, but she would agree to sit in a café. Sipping her coffee with her little finger raised, she would peek out from under the wide brim of her straw hat to see who was watching. Her eyes and skin continued to glow, a look as full of moisture and light as a rose after rain, a white rose. But soon there was another and more telltale sign of her pregnancy: she began to put on weight and her belly grew, both tubular and round, a ripening melon draped in crepe de chine.

When the pregnancy became obvious to all, Ada announced it to her mother-in-law, who was delighted although she scolded because she had not been told sooner. When his mother announced it over dinner, then Gino knew too.

"Do you suppose this child will look more like me?" was Gino's sardonic response.

"What's the matter with you!" Signora Botti chastised. "What's running through those veins of yours, my son? Blood? Or is it silver? Forget the bank for a minute—this is your family. Your wife is pregnant, this is cause for celebration."

In my dreams the baby appeared as a miniature Rico, as an infant with a full head of black hair, with his broad hands and blunt fingers, with his dark eyes, their incongruous sparkle of diamond in the depth, with his intelligent and laughing face, with his strong white teeth and wide mouth, open and crying the high C which came more easily to the son than the father.

I was helping the lovers exchange letters. Rico's had to be addressed to me when they came to the house. I would make a show of it for Mrs. Botti and open the letter in front of her. Then I would go to my room and read it before I had to give it over to Ada. She couldn't ask for it until we were alone. Rico was writing to Ada daily, begging her to join him in Milan.

Carissima Ada, my goddess, my queen,

Days I keep busy with rehearsals, nights with performance. I am perfecting my voice—fame is near. I enclose the review of my performance in L'Arlesiama. When I sang the romanza "Il Lamento di Frederico," the audience rose to its feet in thunderous applause. I know that I will sing on the stage of La Scala soon! I dream of nothing else now—in this, of course, I speak only of the singing career. Those are the dreams of the head. But the dreams of the body are all of you. When will you come to Milan and live with me?

   I kiss you here where I have drawn the lips. Kiss me back.

Yours forever,

Rico

P.S. By the way, tell Rina I remember her, and thank her for helping us.

I was disappointed to find myself only mentioned in postscript.

Ada gave me her letters written in response to him to address and mail. The writing on the envelopes had to be in my hand. She would watch me write out his address and would make sure I sealed the letter in front of her. But if she was called away, it was easy enough to tear the letter open, read it, and then re-address and seal another envelope. Nobody would know the difference.

Dear Heart,

My life is hell here in the house. If it were not for singing, I would be weeping all the time. Gino, believe me, is no longer my husband in any way but in name. He looks at me and at my growing belly with contempt. We have not slept in the same bed in more than a year. I do not have to tell him that the child is not his, he must already know. Still he says nothing. If he could, I know he would not come home. He would sleep in the bank.

My mother-in-law thinks I'm carrying another Botti so I'm in her good graces again. But now she wants to forbid me the stage. Hah! As if she or anybody else could! I will sing until the end of the season or be damned.

Darling Rico, you beg me to come to you. Don't think that I don't want to, don't long to come to you, but how can I live with you in your tiny room, as you describe it, and give birth to our child there? The burden would be too great for you! The art must never take second place, not even to our love. If I hinder you now, your heart will cool to me, I know. I stay in Fiume, not for myself, but only to make it easier for you. First you must establish yourself, gain the reputation as a singer you deserve, then, and I believe very soon, we will be together in Milan.

The paper scorched my mouth where you had drawn your lips with such ardor. I kiss you back. I burn you too.

Ada

And so the duet of disguised letters continued with my help until Ada was in her eighth month of pregnancy and Rico returned to Fiume for a short engagement at the Comunale. He was a stand-in for the principal tenor, and happy to do so when it meant singing with Ada in *La Bohème, La Traviata,* and *Mefistofele*. There was my sister onstage with Rico and visibly pregnant with his child. The tenderness her condition elicited from his voice was of such exquisite sweetness that the audience, that even Rico himself, was moved to tears by his singing. The only person who remained unmoved, indeed irritated and afraid, was the manager who may have feared a messy birthing scene on his stage.

15

Then it was another summer again when sopranos and tenors must give way to the chorus of insects. The opera season ended in Fiume. Who do you suppose was the more reluctant to leave the Comunale: Rico to go back to Milan, or Ada to exchange the manager for a midwife? My sister and I both abandoned the Botti household then and returned home to Firenze. Ada wanted Mamma with her during the birth of her second child, even if it meant leaving her firstborn behind. Moreover, with her child by Rico soon to arrive, Ada wanted to tell her husband the truth. This, she thought, could best be done by post in a note, which, this time, she showed to me before sending.

Caro Gino,

Don't blame me. Remember it was you who changed our love when you took up with the bank. I was made for art, you know, and not for such a bourgeois existence. I must leave you or die in my soul. I insist on a separation. There is no other way.

Ada

"WHAT ABOUT LELIO?"

"You know he's lost to me now. If I thought I could have taken him with me, I would have. Before he becomes all Botti!"

Gino didn't write back, he came in person to speak to his wife. My sister was surprised and distressed to see him. Though she maintained her composure, her stiffness gave her away, at least to me. She showed her husband into the drawing room as you might receive a merchant or a creditor. It seemed that she knew how to manage him, how to set the tone for their encounter, and he followed her complaisantly enough, his hat in his hand. She did not invite him to sit down and she herself remained standing. Leaning heavily on the mantel because of the strain of her weight late in the pregnancy, her fingers showed her tension. Her hands were alabaster; she wore a ring on almost every finger, one of which was Gino's, the white gold and diamond-encrusted wedding band, another of which was Rico's, the tiny topaz one. Her skin had the same sheen as the porcelain figures, the shepherd and shepherdess, madrigals in fire-glazed clay—earth rendered as moon, white and luminous on the mantel. She was rearranging these figurines, brushing off imaginary dust with one of the cream-colored linen hankies she kept tucked in her sleeve. She did not look at him. She waited for him to speak.

I had feared how Gino might react to a letter as curt as the one Ada had written to him. My place in this scene was observing all this from behind the screen painted with the figure of Dante. I looked through his eyes where, many years before, I had made some slits.

"I'm here to take you back to Fiume. You are my wife, or have you forgotten? Must it be written in a libretto for you to remember your role?" His sarcasm was not likely to win back my sister's heart.

"I *was* your wife. That's all in the past. It's done." She spoke firmly, without a trace of emotion.

There is a physical law I'm sure that makes ice speak to fire, so Ada's coolness sparked Gino's rage.

"No, we are married. It is not done until death! I have the right to make you come home." He was snarling by this point, with fists clenched at his side.

"Your right is the cuckold's." She placed her hand on her big belly. "This child is not yours!"

Cuckold, that word, then the explosion. Gino began, not to shout as you might expect from a man, but to scream. The pitch revealed his operatic training. But the blow that followed was not a singer's, but a boxer's; he punched her belly hard and knocked Ada down, bringing the porcelain figures crashing around her.

Gino's face was twisted with rage. He continued kicking at Ada's belly as she lay moaning on the floor while I tried to pull him away. Did I leave something out? I knocked down the screen in my haste to reach my sister. I feared for the baby as much as I feared for her. When my own scream came, out of helplessness and desperation, it ran the full range of octaves. Was it my voice or a careless hand in the struggle that caused the crystal wineglasses, which were to be part of my trousseau, to shatter? He stopped kicking my sister. This was perhaps the high point of my fledgling singing career.

I was crouched by the unconscious Ada, pulling at her arm in an attempt to rouse her, when Felicia and Mamma came rushing into the room. They joined the shrieking when they saw that tableau of blood and broken china. In her fall, Ada had cut herself. The wound was minor, but the effect of the blood, the lifeless woman, and the writhing movements from her belly was appalling.

Felicia was sent back to get some smelling salts while Mamma tied a strip of cloth she tore from the hem of her petticoat around Ada's cut hand to stop the bleeding. Mamma stroked her belly, murmuring, ministering to it as if it were another wounded presence in the room. I stayed crouched on the floor to gather up the broken pieces of porcelain. A fragment of the head, the half face of the shepherdess, pale and bordered by ashen-colored curls, I held in my open palm; I scrutinized the piece as if it could make sense of the scene for me. In the end it was not my wounded sister but the shattered doll that made me cry.

Gino had stopped shouting profanities. He sat in a chair weeping, a ragged sobbing into his hands.

"Assassino," was the only word my mother spoke to him.

Then Papa entered the room along with Felicia with the smelling salts. In the presence of another man, Gino stopped crying and rose from his chair.

"Step aside," Papa commanded.

Anxious to revive Ada, we were all crowded around her, making it hard for any of us to breathe, let alone the victim. But the smelling salts revived her. She coughed and pushed them away. Only when Ada responded to Papa's string of endearing names, "Adina, Adetta, Adellina …" with *"babbo mio,"* did he turn to Gino again and order him to leave.

"But I'm here to take my wife home." He had pulled himself together again and remembered his rights.

"Are you deaf? You're not welcome here. My daughter has asked for a separation. Leave this house at once!"

"Your daughter is a slut."

"Then you are a bloody cuckold and a fool. Announce that to the world if you like! But I tell you—and don't make me repeat this—you have no more business here in my family!"

So my sister's marriage came to an end—or should have. But there is no divorce in Italy. The Catholic Church legislates on these matters, and run as it is by celibate priests, it's not likely to change in a hundred years. What do they know of the hell that is marriage when it's gone bad?

ADA MOVED IN with Rico. She became married to him in all ways except in the law. On July 2, 1898, in Milano, their first son was born. Only the birth of the baby forced Ada to take a rest from the stage for a few months. It was Rico who registered the birth at city hall. He named the boy Rodolfo, in honor of his first big success in the Puccini role.

Where Ada's name should have appeared on the birth certificate, *"n.n.,"* for the Latin *noto nono,* mother unknown, was stamped. Ada could not be named on the birth certificate or the child would have been legally Botti's. And so my sister was erased from the public record for the birth of her second child. What's more, she lost Lelio. Gino forbade her to ever see him again. Ada seemed easily resigned to losing her firstborn child. With such laws, perhaps it's not surprising that Ada acted as if her children belonged not to her, but to her men.

16

Important artists did not live in rooming houses filled with the smell of frying onions and garlic. Not in Milano. Not if your ambition was to sing at Teatro alla Scala. Not if your singing was of any importance, that is. On the stage, playing *La Bohème,* it was fashionable to be a starving artist, but in society it was shameful.

Papa pawned the silver and I sacrificed my gold medallion of the Madonna along with the linens that I had embroidered for my trousseau. These treasures I sold off without regret. Because I could no longer dream of a life with Rico, I had abandoned the idea of marriage altogether. And so we raised enough money to set Ada and Rico up at a respectable address on Via Velasco. There they resided and without a lira to spare after paying the inflated rent.

Milano, that so-called second Rome, was dirtier. Although the king did not live there, nor was the pope nearby, Milan was nevertheless a sort of capital—a capital of opera and industry. It teemed with workers rather than tourists. Tourists passed through; they rightly preferred the clean water and air of Lake Como in the Alps just to the north.

During the 1898 season, Enrico Caruso would continue to perform in the city under contract to the Teatro Lirico. It was a good company, but it was not La Scala, and like every other singer in Italy, Caruso's ambition was to perform at the queen of all opera houses. But here in Milan he had come closer to fulfilling it. When he walked along Via Verdi, he could see the doors of La Scala, and they seemed to be beckoning to him.

When Mamma left for Milan to help care for Ada and the new baby, she took me along. Nobody, not even my apparently indomitable sister, could sing opera and nurse an infant at the same time, and so their household income had been drastically reduced. They could not afford servants then; they needed us.

That summer, Ada had to watch Rico leave for Livorno to sing without her. She didn't take it well, not singing, being left behind in the heat of the city. Her milk began to dry up. Fofò's feedings had to be supplemented with a bottle. Any of us could have done that, but he preferred me. As he drank the fresh goat's milk, he would pull at my ear, a soothing, rhythmic stroking that sent me into a trance of my own. Sensuous musings bathed in sunshine and green pastures. Through the warm body in my arms, the eager sucking sounds, I could conjure the father. Even though he was just a baby, not the man, and his head could fit into the palm of my hand, he was Rico's son. His skin was silk with dew on it, sprinkled with sweet-smelling talc. Fofò's dreams were milk dreams, I imagined, creamy, abundant, and white.

With this infant in my arms I did not want one of my own. I wanted him and I wanted his father. I felt serene with Fofò sleeping in my lap and I didn't want to budge from this reverie, sweet, sweet reverie. I didn't leave him until Mamma or Ada came into the room.

"What? Are you both asleep, then? Put the child down in his crib. He'll rest better that way."

Mamma might linger with me, singing a lullaby to the sleeping child, but Ada never did. I never heard the singer sing for her son. She took the infant to the nursery and put him to bed with the same efficiency with which she cleared the room of his nappies and toys.

TIME THAT SUMMER was measured by the baby's needs. The pendulum of the clock had been replaced by his feedings, the gongs of the passing hours by his cries. We took turns in the night; we napped during the day. We enjoyed promenades along the boulevards, through the park, Fofò in a carriage decorated with satin ribbons. Strangers stopped to admire the baby. The rocking motion of the carriage kept him happy, but if he started to fuss, Ada would push the carriage while I, walking alongside, gave him my knuckle to suck.

One day became another until, with the August feast days, Rico returned to us. Then the center became diffused again, as two males, the patriarch and the son, demanded attention.

17

In November the world premiere of *Fedora* at the Teatro Lirico marked the turning point in Rico's career. Although he was just a short-order replacement for the role of Loris, and not much was expected of him, he triumphed in the part.

With the words *"lo fà doro,"* the critics hailed his Midas touch.

But Ada criticized. Ada pushed him to do better. "You have to work harder, your voice is still too short. It went well enough in *Fedora* because so much of the singing is *parlato*. But when the piano was playing onstage in the second act, your voice could hardly compete."

"You know more than the critics, I suppose."

"I heard that Verdi was in the audience and that he was not impressed."

"Well, he's an old man. Maybe he's gone deaf!"

"Singing is not shouting."

"But when the song needs power—"

"Then you must draw your breath from the diaphragm so you don't have to shout. That way you won't lose your voice. Nor will you have to save it during rehearsals. Learn from Fofò—remember how he could cry all night long? That's because his crying's not from the throat. Babies breathe from their bellies. Look at him when he's sleeping, at how he breathes, and you'll see what I'm saying. His whole body is in his breathing—like a bellows."

And so she continued to instruct Rico when he might have preferred to enjoy his success.

THE OPERA'S THEMES, with its undertones of nihilism, rebellion, with its secret police, were timely. It was a big hit and went on to be staged in London a few years later with Mugnone conducting. And although Caruso still had to wait two more years to make his debut at La Scala, he never again wanted for money. After his success in *Fedora,* the contracts never stopped coming.

Then we became a comfortable household in truth, not one hiding behind a scrimped facade. As soon as Ada was able to hire a wet nurse, she accepted singing engagements again. She went off to Turin. And after that there was lots of money. Before she and Rico departed together for a tour in Russia, they hired a housekeeper as well. With Papa working at the central office, based in his Rome apartment, Mamma and I were all Fofò had of family while his parents gallivanted across continents.

While on tour Rico wrote regularly, letters addressed to the baby, as if Fofò who could not yet speak could already read. This was Rico's teasing way. I knew that this time the letters were really meant for me. I would read them out loud to Fofò even though he didn't understand a word. He would chortle and grab the paper out of my hand and put it in his mouth. Mamma would sit and knit as she listened.

Caro Fofò,

What a great success we are here in St. Petersburg! Yesterday we were invited to the palace to be presented to the tsar, Nicholas II. We waited a long time for him in a very grand room. It was dark and somber because of the wood all around the walls. Even the ceiling was finished in wood. There was a fireplace in one corner, burning hotly, and your mamma and I waited near it trying to warm up. Russia is a country colder than you can ever imagine in Italy. The fireplace was faced with marble, but the chimney seemed to be made of wood, and I wondered if it would soon catch fire. But I didn't care so much because I was frozen. I thought then that burning up might feel good.

Finally a grand door opened and a servant led us into the tsar's working study. The room was filled with books and paintings and many desks and tables, not just one. If the emperor gets tired, there's a big divan against one wall where he can take a nap. But what I liked best was the smoking gear, all kinds of fancy cigarette holders, loaded with jewels. Let me tell you I have fallen in love with the Russian cigarette. I will smoke no other, and I must smoke now or I am too nervous to perform!

We were presented to the tsar. I made a nice bow, and when I straightened up to look at the great man, I had to keep looking up

*because he was so tall. He is an emperor, a ruler of millions. I
expected nobility, the broad brow, the erect bearing, but I did not
imagine such kindly eyes and their blue-violet of chicory. He gave
us gifts, your mother a Fabergé egg, and me gold cufflinks encrusted
with diamonds. We are very proud to be honored so much by
royalty. You must be proud too of your parents.*

*Tell Aunt Rina that she must take good care of you, and not
spoil you too much. Your nonna I don't have to tell because she
knows how to raise a child.*

Your mamma and I love and miss you,

Papa

Ada would write to us as well, sometimes to me, sometimes
to Mother. She knew babies; she didn't imagine that Fofò could
understand her letters even in jest.

Cara Rina,

*I am so happy to be on an international tour, to be acclaimed as a
star! I really have my life back, my art, my true life. Now that I
am myself again, I take this opportunity to advise you, as an older
sister should. I am pleased that you have been studying singing, but
let me warn you, and learn from my experience. The choices we are
given as women in our society are impossible. If we want a career,
we are denied love, a family. Though Gino offered to support my
singing, as soon as I gave birth to Lelio he wanted everything to
change, to become "normal" as he called it. He tolerated my
performing at the Comunale only because it was nearby. Though*

he balked at the engagement in Livorno, our family was there and I could insist on my right to visit. He made me limit my career to the local, when clearly I was made for the world! Most men will want you to stay at home and take care of the children, Rina, whatever it is they promise you before you marry them. This time I know that it will be different because Rico is a real artist and a true match for me. The stage is our marriage bed. But such unions, such men, are rare!

I know that Rico wrote to tell you about our visit to the tsar! I am enjoying myself here. Ah, these Russian men, they are not reticent! They adore me. They wait for me by the backstage entrance with bouquets of flowers. They want to take me out for moonlight rides along the shores of the Neva—the river is pure ice now, I think we could even ride on it! Of course, I don't go. But it's good that Rico sees the attention. He's a little piqued, of course, as he should be. Never let a man take you for granted. If he does, he'll start looking around himself, and you don't want that. Let him be the jealous one!

Your loving sister,

Ada

P.S. Give the baby a squeeze for me. Unlike his father, I know he's too young to understand letters!

MONTHS PASSED as they toured the Russian continent by train. When the couple finally returned, their pockets were full of money. They showed off their fabulous gifts from the tsar. Rico wore the cufflinks every day, while Ada placed the Fabergé egg on the mantel in the parlor where visitors would be sure to admire it.

Rico and Ada had become more than a couple, they were a duo, and if Fofò connected them together through their bodies, opera united them in their souls. I felt shut out. The only way for me to join them was to become like them, an opera singer. I expected music to transport me and transform me into that dazzling diva whose singing casts a spell on all who listen to her. The concern Ada expressed for me in her letter renewed family feeling, big sister was looking out for me, her little sister, and offering to guide me along the path on which she herself had floundered in her life, if not in her art. But my own goals were not so conflicted. She warned me that love would stop me when it was love itself that had started me, and love for the same man who she believed would not hold her back. Was it such a great leap from loving a singer to loving singing itself? Not for me, it was one and the same feeling. And so I found a teacher in Milan and resumed my operatic training.

In those rare hours when I was home alone, I would practice for my own pleasure. To sing made me ache very pleasantly. It had sweetness, the taste of candy in the mouth that just makes you hungry for more. Through music I could, without embarrassment, ask the world to love me. I was singing in this way one afternoon in the spring of 1899 when the doorbell rang.

"I am sorry, Signor Caruso is not at home." There were many calls for him.

"Ah yes, this is Caruso's house."

"And you are?"

"I beg your pardon, signorina. Forgive me for not introducing myself at once. Here is my card. My name is Monari, I am an impresario."

"But Signor Caruso is not at home. Would you like to leave this for him?"

The man raised his hat and made a slight bow, more like a nod really. He was so thin that his clothes hung as if draped on a wooden hanger, as if air rather than flesh occupied his jacket. Though his hair was darker than charcoal and his skin muddy in tone, his eyes were pale green and, in contrast, startling.

"Before I go, signorina, can you tell me who that was singing? I must know. It is my only reason for calling."

"But that was me, signore. I was practicing. In Milan they love the opera so much that none of our neighbors ever complains." Afraid he might think me vain, I added, "We are a singing household, you know. Even the baby will run the scales at any hour."

But he did not laugh. "Why practice, signorina, when you can sing on the stage? I've been scouring the city for a voice like yours! I can offer you a contract right now, to sing in *Carmen* for me in Zara. What would you say to that?"

I clapped my hands together in delight. I imagined myself becoming equal to my sister—a voice, a name. I imagined myself on the stage singing in a duet and, in the guise of art, making love to Rico. All this imagining must have taken some time; I heard alarm in the impresario's voice.

"Signorina, signorina, what do you say to my offer?" I turned to him and looked into his cat eyes, pale eyes of the black cat, his face crinkled up in the half-pleading, half-mocking of a suitor rather than a manager. "Tell me you'll sing for me, tell me you'll make your professional debut on my stage."

"This is so thrilling—my first role and in a real theater!"

"I have a standard contract right here in my briefcase. Would you look it over? If you sign, you'll not regret it, I promise you."

"Ah, but I cannot. My father must sign it. And he's not here in Milan with us. You see, I'm still a minor. I need permission from my parents. Could you come back later when my mother will be home?"

Monari promised to return that very evening. With new hope and renewed delight, I went back to my practicing. I riffled through the sheet music collection looking for an aria from *Carmen*. Rico had copied some of the pages by hand, and with such precision that they seemed finer than the printed material. In allegretto moderato I tested the lyric "L'Amour est un Oiseau":

L'amour est enfant de Bohème,
Il n'a jamais, jamais connu de loi,
Si tu ne m'aimes pas, je t'aime;
Mais si je t'aime, prends garde à toi!

I affected the coy posing of a coquette, I sang to my many admirers: the furniture, the books, dusty from not being read, the pendulum clock, generous with the rhythmic ticking of its applause (before the aria was over, before it had even begun), the curtains, their tulle restless in the breeze, the fickle, feckless Fabergé egg.

LATER THAT AFTERNOON, when the family returned, they found me singing and, as I danced about the room, shaking the imagined ruffles of my skirt. Rico laughed and immediately joined me in play-acting. He became my partner in the gypsy dance.

"Children, children!" my mother appealed, despairing of the fate of the furniture so newly acquired and at such cost. But we ignored her and continued to trace wide circles in our dance, knocking things about, until, breathless with laughter, we collapsed onto the couch. Then Fofò began to cry.

"Here"—Ada handed the child over to me—"you made him cry, now you calm him." If Fofò ever recalled his mother's touch after she had returned to the stage, it was when she delivered him from one set of arms to another set also not hers. She would pick the infant up from carriage or crib by cupping him under his arms. Swinging, in a wide arc, she held him away from her body. The child would hang in mid-air; he would simply hang there, as if from hooks rather than hands, poultry at the butcher's, and when the child found himself in an embrace, it was always in someone else's arms. There were never any stains on Ada's clothes from his spitting up. Still, her figure was maternal, even if she had stopped nursing. She looked as if she were made for babies, many babies. Her body was all curves, with the soft look of a sofa on which a man longs to sleep.

"He's just hungry." Fofò was sucking on a blue satin rose appliqué on my bodice. Mamma brought me his bottle. I tested the temperature of the milk on my wrist. "It's perfect, drink this, *angelino*." The infant had been alternately gumming the cloth and making little angry cries when no milk came. "It's a shame, even though they're so pretty, they're dry, they're not real flowers, there's not a drop of dew to be had from them. This is what you want. This will make you happy." But he wouldn't take the bottle; he wanted the breast. He didn't like being weaned. So I unbuttoned the top of my gown. The sight of my nipple made him open his mouth wide and so I slipped the rubber one in. He sucked greedily on the bottle, his small fist clinging to my naked breast. Rico watched me, his dark eyes strangely altered, not saying a word.

I hadn't yet told them about Monari and his offer. Not until Fofò was back in his crib and soundly asleep did I get an opportunity.

As the housekeeper served coffee and biscotti, I recounted my story.

"I want to tell everybody something—something very exciting!"

Ada poured sugar into her coffee until it formed a snowy cap in her cup. When she stirred, it turned into syrup; it was so thick her spoon could have stayed upright.

"What are you staring at?"

"I'm not staring. I'm waiting for you to pay attention."

"Well, what could be so exciting? Don't tell me you've found a *fidanzato* among the Milanese. They're such cold fish. I think they must be German, not Italian."

"No, no, no! Not a suitor! A manager, an impresario. I've been offered an engagement—to sing in a production of *Carmen* in Zara!"

"And who, may I ask, is this impresario who recruits children? He must be a madman—or an impostor!"

"Oh, you're just jealous because he asked me—not you!"

"Jealous? What, did you say jealous, for Zara? You must be joking. But you can be sure he came to see me, not you. Why, you're a baby, you're not a voice yet—you're just a student."

"Well, he liked what he heard! It wasn't you, but it was more than good enough for him!"

"Enough of this bickering. Were they always like this, Mamma Giachetti, always at each other's throats? In my family, we were so glad to survive, my brother and I from among the nineteen born to my poor suffering mother, that we have always clung to one another."

Mamma shook her head sadly. "No, this is new." She did not add, *and it is because of you,* if she thought it as I did. "Rina, who is this man? What kind of man comes to a house and visits when a young girl is home alone? I hope you didn't let him in!"

"Mamma, I did nothing wrong. Look—he gave me his card."

She took it, fingered more than read its heavily embossed gold letters, and passed it on to Rico.

"This is what happened. It's not as if I auditioned for the man! I was practicing and he said that he was walking by when he heard me. He called it a 'miracle.' He said it was 'a voice from heaven.' I want to sing. I must sing on the stage. When he comes back, you'll say yes, won't you? You'll let me go to Sicily and make my career? Please, dearest Mamma, please, I beg you!"

Then Rico spoke. "The stage is not suitable for a young girl. As the man of the house, I am head of the family now and responsible for you. For your own protection, no, you can't go."

The man I had once hoped would be my husband was now assuming the role of my father and that appalled me.

"You!" I spat out the pronoun. "You're not my father! What are you then? You're not even my sister's husband, yet you want to order me around! What makes you think you can deny me my dream?" What had become my dream because of him!

"But, Rina, you don't know what's out there—the dangers! You're young—you're innocent! You can't imagine how there are men in the world, men who think girls in the opera are just there for the plucking."

"But it's not for you to decide! Tell him, Mamma, please tell him!"

"Rina, listen to me now, child, listen to your mother. Rico's right. There are serious dangers even if only to your reputation.

A young girl, unmarried, alone in a strange city, and without her family—it's unthinkable!"

"But, Mamma, it's my future now. I will die if I cannot sing— if you don't let me go, it will break my heart and I will die because of it. I will die!" Sobbing, I fell into my mother's arms. Young and romantic as I was, death came easily to my lips, and the tears were the best way I knew to win over my mother. But they were real tears because I feared that to miss out on Zara would be to miss out on ever becoming someone whom Rico would notice.

Mamma tried to console me by telling me that there would be other opportunities. But I refused to be consoled. I refused to wait for an uncertain future when the future had arrived at the doorstep. I withdrew myself from my mother's arms. I dried my eyes with my handkerchief and gathered my resolve. I pressed my lips together and no longer asked, I announced:

"I'm going—I don't care what any of you say. If I have to run away, I will, but I'm going to make my debut in Zara. I'll gamble my reputation if I have to. Look at this family, look at you, Rico and Ada, if you're supposed to be my role models, then you should be supporting me in this." At that moment I hated him, the man who demanded my obedience, not my love.

But Ada had heard me and broke into the argument.

"Rico, stop playing the patriarch and listen to her. Maybe she's old enough. It takes courage to gamble everything for art. If she's made for singing, you know you won't be able to stop her. And it's a respectable company, it's not as if she's joining a troupe of gypsies!" She turned to me in what might have been grudging respect. "You are my sister after all," she said.

"I think she's too young, but she's mule-headed, this one!" Rico pretended to wash his hands. "Let her go, but I won't be responsible for her." He spoke as if I were no longer in the room, as if I had already left for Sicily.

Ada's support made a difference. And in the face of my determination, Mamma agreed to sign the contract, but on condition that she accompany me and live with me in Zara. Although I disguised it, I was relieved that she wished to go with me. It was clear that I had dramatic talent to convince them so easily, because I was actually afraid to go out on my own.

WHEN MONARI RETURNED that evening, he was welcomed warmly. Tempers had calmed and we were all at ease. His fawning civility was exactly the sort that Ada liked. He paid her a pretty compliment.

"Ah, you must be the sister of this miracle—and such beauty too!" With a deep bow, he brought her hand to his lips.

Rico looked over the contract and Mamma signed after he had declared that it was satisfactory.

18

That spring I left Milan no longer a child, no longer a student, but a young woman—with a contract to sing on a professional stage as proof. I was still angry with Rico that he had tried to stop me. Even if his fears for me and my reputation were sincere, I still saw it as hypocrisy. But really it was Italy's hypocrisy too. Our society valued the art of singing, even elevated the soprano to the status of diva in the theater, although back in her hotel room that very same woman would be judged a whore. No woman in that era could have a career in our country—certainly not on the stage—and be thought entirely honest. What was honest in a woman could only be that she should pledge herself in marriage.

A young woman living in a small apartment in a strange city, even with her mother, walked the tightrope of respectability. I wasn't married, the best protection for a young singer, but when I went home, my mother was there waiting. There was nothing to feed the gossips. Mamma spent her days knitting caps, sweaters, and booties for Fofò. When she had finished them, she would send the woolens by post to Milan. Because babies grow so quickly, she kept busy knitting clothes for him.

I was given the role of Micaela, the innocent young girl in the drama, the mother's choice for her son, Don José—not his— while the leading role of Carmen was played by a more experienced singer, a mezzo-soprano, called Signora Campodonico. She was called Signora although there was no signore to be seen.

The night of my debut I was so terrified I could hardly speak, let alone sing. My mother, my guardian and emotional support, was only one face in a theater of a thousand strangers. A face, in my panic, I couldn't find when I made the mistake of peeking at the audience before the curtain went up. I developed a knot in my throat; it was so tight that it was painful even to swallow. How was I to sing?

"Come. Follow me—this way, into my dressing room. I know exactly what you need!" Signora Campodonico took pity on me and offered some of her medicine for opening-night jitters. She poured me a drink from a large green glass bottle being chilled in a bucket of ice.

"It works like a charm every time. They say that the secret is in the bubbles, in the air trapped there. This drink expands your lungs at the same time as it calms your nerves."

So I picked up this trick for managing stage fright. Several glasses of champagne before the performance and I was so calm I was floating. My singing that night had the clarity, the volume, of that effervescent wine. The crowd, clamorous for an encore, cheered as they clapped, and after taking my bow, I repeated the *romanza*. That night it was a mystery to me how the audience, not I, became the more intoxicated.

They didn't know what to make of me, those men I had been warned against, aficionados of opera and its women. They came with their flowers. They followed me with roving eyes as I moved across the stage. Their hands, once the bouquets had been flung at me, would have liked to rove too, but I didn't linger backstage or go to the parties. I went straight home to my mother. But this did not discourage all my suitors. Some continued to send their posies, their poetry, and their proposals. I hid these notes from Mamma. I didn't want her to be upset or suspicious. They didn't mean much to me since they were not from Rico. I wasn't tempted, but I was flattered to have the attention of so many men. I was the new soprano with the company and I was much younger than Campodonico—I didn't forget that. And it all stayed harmless enough because, with my mother nearby, it was easy to keep them all at a safe distance.

19

Success brings success. Now we were all three singers in the family. At the end of the season in Zara I moved back to Milan, but not back in with the Caruso family on the Via Velasco. In the six months of my absence, I had not forgiven Rico. I was angry, and with an anger made sharper by my unrequited love for him. Besides, I didn't need to live with them, I had earnings and I expected to earn a lot more, so I rented a small apartment of my own. Mamma continued to live with me to satisfy appearances.

It was Ada who sought to reconcile us. We were barely settled in our new quarters when her letter arrived.

Cara Rina,

Congratulations on your success in Zara. Rico and I are very proud of you. But you know Rico's not likely to say he was wrong. In that he is like all men. Don't wait for an apology from him, it's not in the cards. But his affection for you is unchanged. We miss you and wish you would live with us again.

Ah, Fofò is growing so much you almost wouldn't recognize him. Though he calls me Mamma, he remembers you and wants his mammina too! How can you deprive him of his aunt? And Mamma? Shouldn't you think of her? You know she wants to be here with us. Don't be selfish, Rina, it's not like you. You have always been the good girl in the family. The role of being difficult, as you know, belongs to me!

Your loving sister,

Ada

A VISIT WAS ARRANGED for one afternoon when Rico would be at rehearsal. If I had missed Rico, I persuaded myself that I had missed Fofò more. I missed the smell of milk and talc; I remembered him as a small round soft infant gurgling in my lap. I had always been free to love the boy; Ada had always encouraged me to do so. She was the kind of mother who looked relieved when she saw her child in another's arms.

That day Ada greeted us dressed in a fabulous gown of the sheerest white linen that only enhanced the creaminess of her skin. If she was a mother, she looked like the mother of an angel, holding Fofò with his blond curls and the cherub roundness of his face. He didn't shy away from me; he came readily into my arms. We stayed for coffee and managed to talk away the afternoon. I had planned to stay for only an hour, but instead lingered until Rico was due home. The boy was sitting on my lap when Rico came into the room. Fofò was excited at the sight of his father. Rising from my seat, I put him down. He toddled away from me and into his papa's arms. This gave me a moment to compose myself. But how could I be reticent, how could I stay cool, try to be cold, when I heard Rico's voice? He laughed as he embraced his son and then tossed him into the air just to hear him squeal with delight. My knees felt weak, so I sat down again.

"*Babbo,* more!" Fofò never tired of the game before his father did.

"All right, my sweet boy, that's enough for now. Your aunt is here! I haven't seen her in what feels like a century. You must let me say hello to her."

Though I felt frozen in place, when he took my hand I rose and stepped into his embrace. He kissed me on both cheeks.

"You're home again with us. This makes everything perfect."

One visit was all it took to break my resolve to live separately. It was better for Mamma to be enveloped in the warmth and bustle of family life. This is what I told myself.

20

If success brings success, and more engagements than you can accept, such triumphs will keep the family fed—but not together. Rico was becoming Caruso, the golden voice, that prince among tenors. Tours meant long voyages by boat or train, months of traveling, seasons of separation, of silence. Sailing away for Buenos Aires in April of 1900, he wouldn't arrive until May. No letters could be sent or received by him while he was on board ship, though he rode with a cargo of them. He had to land first. Only then would daily postcards from Rico begin to arrive. But as soon as he departed, Ada started writing anyway. I imagined a trail of ships, following his own, carrying her postcards to him. She would write one in the morning:

Caro Rico,

Why do you leave me for so long? You must return as soon as you can! There is not even music in Milan without you.

I pine for you already.

Ada

And though it was impossible, still impatient to hear from him she would write two or three more in the afternoon. But that didn't make the mail arrive any faster. Rico must have received dozens of postcards at a time from her, all part of the same shipment.

When she finally received his first postcard from Buenos Aires, it said:

Conchiglietta, my little sea shell,

I heard you singing in the sea throughout the whole voyage. Be patient, my heart, in twelve weeks I'll come back to you. Wait for me!

Your loving Rico

But what comfort was that when it took a month-long voyage just to say so?

Though they could not satisfy her, still she waited impatiently for the next letter or postcard, for those flimsy messages that were all she could have of his love when he was so far away.

And she lamented, "But these letters must pass through many strange lands and hands before they can reach me. What is left of his touch on the paper then? I grasp the card, but all I can feel is the grasping of my own fingers! And in my letters to him, what is left of me in them? Can he smell my perfume? Or is it only the cargo hold and the dankness of sea water permeating the paper? I think my letters are special, but they get buried in huge sacks with innumerable others, strangers' emotions leaching into mine. I cannot touch him, he cannot touch me, and the words we write are like a veil, a gown, that even on the wedding night can't be peeled off."

With Rico on the other side of the world, Ada could no longer contain her restlessness. For her, it was always far better to act than to pine. She wasn't going to stay home without him and so she accepted a tour in Chile—even farther away than Argentina, a country on the other side of the South American continent. Because Rico objected to Ada's traveling alone, a spot was found for me with her company. He had been the first to leave for South America; we sailed two months later. And Fofò became his grandmother's child.

21

You can look at a globe, a model of the earth, and spin it with the push of a finger and your eye can encompass the whole in no time at all. Your fingers can move from Genoa to Santiago in an instant. You can take in those distances reduced to centimeters in a glance, but it takes a month and more by ship. The earth is not a painted ball with dots for cities and blue paint for ocean, with lines of latitude and longitude parceling it up. The real ocean is too big for our eyes and the earth cannot be encompassed in our hands.

If you spend too much time on deck during a sea voyage, the monotony of seeing becomes a kind of blindness. Waves move into waves, and there is no frame to this picture, no shore, but only the sway and heave of water, the surge and spume. Days, then weeks, then a month passed and we had yet to arrive anywhere. For all I knew, this voyage might take a lifetime.

At night I could be found on deck, watching the moon rise, its face turning almost imperceptibly to the other side as we sailed past the equator, and farther into the Southern Hemisphere. With no land in sight, the heavenly bodies were the only markers, the only view. I watched them change. I watched stars expire. In the heavens the dying stars were the moving ones, quickly burning out in a trail of incandescent dust, like moths immolated in their own light. I watched those stars drop into the distant horizon with no heat, without even the sputter of sparks from a fire. Glittering, the still ones seemed to be there on display, like the crown jewels—without the king himself.

These vigils I kept alone as Ada slept below in our cabin.

"Wake me up when we're in Chile!" she repeated every night. As if you could arrive at the ends of the earth in the course of a night's sleep.

"Not before?" The comic absurdity made me want to tease her.

"No, not a fraction of a second before!"

And so it was, this ritual to deny time, every night for the thousand and one nights of story time. When I would bend over her to kiss her cheek, the soft curls of her hair, unbound, would tickle my face. As soon as she tucked the sheets under her chin, she seemed to fall asleep. My older sister looked like the younger one to me then.

From the staleness of the cabin air, the medicinal cedar smell, I would move to the sharp salt coolness of the night above. Leaning against the railing, with my eyes wide open, I dreamed the dark hours away. There was nothing to see; the sea water was opaque although the waves seemed to glisten at times with stars of their own, or with moonlight, as if the light in them was also in liquid form, as a silver oil cresting.

There was also a kind of phosphorescence I would see lapping against the sides of the ship. It seemed to be mother-of-pearl as a fluid matrix. From such ethereal substance the sea must form its shells to send to the shore, each carrying its unfathomable song. I was a singer now and it seemed to me that the universe might be ordered by the rules of music. From the infinite, there emanated a sound of humming, but whose?

Only the voices of sailors, rum-thickened, calling out the change in watch, would break my trance, bring me back to the human realm and the kind of time that can be measured by clocks.

DURING THE CROSSING through the Strait of Magellan, nobody slept, not even Ada. Not when the sea rose in mountains of black water around us.

"Rina, if I told you to wake me up when we reach Chile, I still meant before I'm dead. Where are we? Is this hell? Santa Maria, forgive me for my sins!"

The ship was lurching so much that I had stumbled and rolled most of the way back to our cabin. I regretted having dined that night; my regret was filling the bucket and spilling over. I prayed for even a moment of calm to clean myself up, but things just got worse and I was pitched from one side of the compartment to the other.

"Hang on, hang on!" I shrieked, although I was the one being thrown about. Our beds were simple bunks, units built into the wall. I grasped one of the bars of the frame and hung on until my hands burned and I lost my grip and was once again thrown across the room. Ada secured herself on the bed by wedging herself against the back wall, holding on to the bar at the head of the bunk, and hooking her feet around the bar at the other end. When I managed to crawl back to the bunks, she gave me a hand and I climbed in with her. We rode out that storm in each other's arms.

THERE WAS NO WAY to tell time in the dark. The hours—or was it days?—stretched out before us like the sea itself, seemingly interminable. Nothing could be seen through the porthole. We could not tell if it was day or still night. We could not tell whether we were still on the sea—or under it. To stay in the room was to be shaken, but to venture onto the deck would have been suicide. We would have been swept overboard. So we stayed below, huddled inside that cell, floating in an aquarium of air. I imagined sharks circling, circling.

If, during that part of the voyage, there was a glimmer of daylight, it was masked by the storm. From what I had read about the region there was land to the south of us, the island of Tierra del Fuego. But if the native campfires that gave the island its name were still burning along the shore, we could not see them. With danger of crashing into rocks at any moment, we crossed the five hundred kilometers of channel. Ada and I vowed then that if we got through this time, if we survived the passage through the Strait of Magellan once, we would not undertake to survive it a second time.

WITH KNEES OF JELLY and legs of rubber, we disembarked at the Chilean port city of Valparaiso. Our faces were livid, our gowns were encrusted with yellow; we kissed the ground in gratitude, and then we kissed each other. The adventure we had shared, the suffering, had drawn us closer although it was still impossible to share what was deepest in our hearts: Rico. Envy, my envy, made it impossible. I couldn't forget that Ada was the prima donna in his heart.

22

If I recalled the taste of Rico's kiss whenever I looked at Ada's lips, I suppose I could not have loved, nor hated, my sister more than

I did then, on the other side of the continent from him, with no links by rail over the Andes, only mule trails and treacherous heights. Though death, the threat of death by water, had strengthened the bonds between us, the rivalry for Rico, and life, life on the road, loosened the tie again. We had been booked for four months in a tour of the country's three major cities, Santiago, Valparaiso, and Concepción. Ada sang the female leads in *Mefistofele, Mignon, Andrea Chénier, La Bohème,* and *Aida,* while I took the secondary roles. Imagine me singing Musetta to Ada's Mimì, if you can.

We had sailed from Italy in June and managed to arrive just in time for our debut there. It was mid-July in Santiago, but in the Southern Hemisphere July is like January. And though the sea moderated—Chile is a country of coastlines and we were never very far from the Pacific—it moderated with dampness. With the chill of Milan winter still in my bones, I felt cheated to have to endure another one like it.

When we were in hotel rooms or comfortably traveling by train, and no longer clinging to each other to keep from being smashed against the walls of the tossing ship, when I was the only one afraid in that untamed country, Ada forgot she was my older sister. There were men with Italian names in Chile following the Gran Compagnia Lirica Italiana, pursuing the troupe for the women who sang in the company, but she just laughed at my fears of those men and their importuning ways.

This was the time of the Yukon Gold Rush. The men back from prospecting in the wilds of Alaska spent freely, fists full of gold, drinking and gambling at the many casinos and saloons. Others, the many adventurers heading to Alaska, all stopped in Santiago after rounding Cape Horn, to win or steal the new-found riches of the miners, before continuing on. The gold was in the rivers, you could just scoop it up with your hat, or so the stories went, and it made many crazy with greed.

The men in Chile wore guns at their hips. In the theaters, in the streets, the guns outnumbered the women. For this part of our adventure Ada stayed awake, coiffed, perfumed, laced, while I retreated to the hotel, to my bed there, where I took a bromide and slept.

ADA WAS NEVER ONE to turn back flowers or invitations to dine. When I asked her to speak for me, to step in and stop the improper advances of a man who refused to understand my *no* (although it's the same word in Spanish as in Italian), she just laughed.

"I left the diapers in Milan. What's wrong with sharing a meal with a man? He's not going to eat you! What's the harm in a flower? An artist is open. An artist allows herself to be admired."

Such were her various responses to me. If Rico could have seen her then, he would have known that he had chosen badly.

"Rina, are you my sister? You're such a prig. An artist knows she must take risks. I thought you knew that."

"Is that your idea of an artist, then? A prostitute?" I was appalled.

"Some think that's always true of women in the theater! Remember, that's why we're traveling together, little sister, as insurance for the family honor. Let them judge us, I say—but on the stage—and by our talent alone!"

"My life is not an opera—nor would I wish it to be!" I protested.

"Such a distinction is for amateurs. If I'm alive when I'm not onstage singing, people have to remind me!"

"I don't understand. I like singing as much as anyone, but ..."
Ada silenced me then.

"Like? I can see that the stage is not for you. Those lullabies you sang for Fofò, that's your real métier, but bel canto is not for the nursery, it's not for soothing an infant, it's not for lulling him to sleep. You think love and the question of a woman's honor can be found in a catechism with its rote responses—but it can't."

That horrific passage through the strait was still too much with me to think of turning back. Cursing my sister and not a certain gentleman, I dropped the flowers he sent me into the garbage. Irrepressible beauty, the bouquet filled the wastebasket as if it were a vase placed on the floor. Such a curious sight, it captivated me. I had to succumb to those flowers. My nose ferreted for a rose, but the roses seemed to have no scent, or the waxy, solemn odor of lily, its memories of altars, of death and resurrection, overwhelmed the sweeter, more delicate perfume.

THAT NIGHT, when I got back to the hotel room, I wasn't tired. I felt restless. Burning every candle, along with the oil lamp, I paced the perimeters of the small room, one in the many hotels that served as rest stops, not home, for us on our tour. I circled the two beds, the single then the double, as if I were caged, as if I were not a willing prisoner. I felt bereft, lonely. My sister thought me priggish. Something tightened and then gnawed at my stomach like hunger, strange noises coming from my body. And there were other sounds, like footsteps in a haunted house, creaking, then the slamming sounds of doors.

Another knocking sound came from outside, along with a voice on the other side of the door. When I opened it, just a crack to see who was there, a black leather boot slipped in and jammed it. I could not call it forced entry because I had answered his knock. I had opened the door to my man of the flowers. His scent was dark with its tones of wood and ambergris, heady, and at war with the sickly sweetness of coconut oil slicking his hair. Where he lived I could not guess, for he was there, backstage, sending his bouquets, in each city where our company performed.

"I am your servant, signorina, your admirer, your slave, and your fool. You have nothing to fear unless you fear the gifts of a devotee to a goddess. Please, let me in." A silver box tied in gold thread, chocolates, and the jade-colored glass of a wine bottle, champagne, with these tokens he pushed his way in. I was weak, I was hungry, and I no longer tried to stop him.

IN THE EARLY HOURS of the morning or very late at night, however these subtleties are measured, Ada returned to the hotel. The birds were creating a cacophony, like an orchestra tuning up, half quarrel, half music. She found me still awake, sitting in an armchair, crying in the unlit room. The double bed was in shambles, the sheets smeared and sticky with blood. I could not lie down on it.

Ada went to the window and threw the drapes open. It was light enough to see, but Ada lit a lamp anyway, held it up high to examine the bed. My sister is a witch, I thought. She knows without my telling her.

With the sunrise, the moon sets. Apparently delayed by the branches of some nearby trees, the moon stalled; her light was dimming like a lantern left on overnight, its illumination imperceptible in the morning light. Ada placed the burning oil lamp by the window where it could mimic the moon, wasting its light.

"Nobody can call you a baby anymore."

I broke out into fresh sobs.

"This is not a matter for crying, but for celebrating. It's natural, Rina, it's the thing that men do for which women are judged. But I say to hell in a burning basket with that!"

"But … but … it's different for you. You are … were … you are married."

Ada found the box of chocolates and stuffed several pieces into her mouth.

"And he doesn't want to marry you—that Chilean of yours?" This was said very slowly, thickly, because of the sticky caramel gumming up her mouth. Waiting for my response, she sucked at her teeth.

"He can't. He's already married!" My sobs, which had been punctuated by hiccups, turned into sniffling.

"I suppose he only told you afterwards, after the vows of eternal love—after the tango in the sheets."

The bitterness of the truth—and Ada's surprising clairvoyance—calmed me. It seemed that she understood these things and that she would know what to do.

"You must remember this, Rina, men are all devils. If you like devils, there's no harm in them—not if you're a devil yourself, that is."

"So is that it? And what about love?"

"What about it?"

"Is there no hope? And what should I do now?"

"There's just one thing: we have to do something about these bloody sheets. It's unwise to upset the chambermaid and set her tongue wagging."

Ada took some of the rags we used for our periods and with a little water from the decanter she sopped and rubbed at the sheets. It caused a fresh bleeding.

"When the *margherita* sees these and takes them to the laundry, she won't suspect it's anything more than some monthly mishap. Nobody in the whole of this South American continent is going to guess a woman might still be a virgin at nineteen."

It was a relief to have Ada just take over. I wanted to trust her, I wanted to feel safe, so I blocked the image of the smile on her face as, raised lamp in hand, Ada had examined the bed. She might have been the man himself, the charlatan who deflowered me, with that look of a conqueror in her eyes.

23

To avoid the horrors we knew by sea, we risked avalanches and outlaws by crossing the continent overland, through the Andes to Argentina. We took a train from Santiago to the first mountain range—that was easy enough, even comfortable. But from there it was a three-day journey, riding on the backs of mules, over the mountains to the Argentine rail line that would take us east to Buenos Aires, to a ship there sailing for home.

The Andes is a mountain range born out of lava and ice. The trails were deserted, the paths narrow and shaky. We had a guide to lead and protect us but he was an old *mestizo,* so wizened that it seemed we were following no man at all but a leather hat and thick woolen poncho. He claimed that, in 1835, as a young man, a boy really, he had helped the English scientist Charles Darwin cross over these mountains. Although it was 1900, we more than half believed him. He looked as old as the last century itself. Most Europeans would have taken to their beds at his age, not ridden mules into the mountains.

"That Darwin is a godless man. He claims that we're descended from monkeys. You should have pushed him over—into the chasm below," I said.

The guide's face was so lined I could not make out his expression when, after a long pause, he responded, "I like monkeys—you can have the part of myself that's descended from Europeans." His name was Carlo; he had an Italian father.

It had been spring at sea level, but in the mountains it was winter. Our water bottles froze. We had to wait to camp and make a fire and heat the bottles before we could drink again. Carlo showed no sign of discomfort, but Ada and I both trembled with cold and with fear. We wrapped woolen shawls over our coats and still we were cold. Riding on the back of the mule, sidesaddle as propriety dictated, made me feel more like the burden than the rider.

There were trees along the way and then there were no more trees. There were patches of grass as prickly as cactus, or so we found out when we stopped to rest. The only other living things we saw were these strange camel-like creatures, small camels without humps, vicunas, Carlo called them. They fed on that spiky grass, a diet of thorns. But these graceful creatures, their oval ears raised for listening as attentively as at a concert, they too disappeared when we reached the snow line. It seemed that we had ridden into some polar region then, glaciers towered above us, iced the trail, and the slopes dropped into the abyss. Or so it seemed, as we climbed up and up. It became hard to breathe; worse, I could see no bottom. There were clouds of mist above us and clouds of mist below. Even our breath came out as icy vapor.

OUR RETURN TO MILAN via the port of Buenos Aires was a feat, both physical and critical. It had been a lot easier to impress the reviewers. Throughout our Chilean tour, the newspapers had carried raves about Ada's performances. She had created a furor wherever she sang. "There has not been anyone here to equal her either as a singer or an artist," one paper wrote about her performance in *Mefistofele*. Her Aida was declared "a true revelation of art." In *La Bohème* she was called "the most sublime Mimì, without rival for the impetus of passion, the color of phrasing, and the spontaneity of accent … the supreme attraction of that opera." The critics wrote as if she sang alone onstage. There was no mention of me, the Musetta, in this notice. I smarted in her shadow, both on the stage and off; Ada was a scene-stealer as well as a man-stealer. Those audiences and critics marveled at her, responding as if they had never heard a European woman sing before. I can still see the crowds jumping to their feet, I can almost hear the clapping and the shouting, "brava, brava!"—an old word in the New World.

24

We had been away for six months, but that was nearly half a lifetime for Fofò. He no longer knew his mother, nor me, his aunt, although at least he paused, swaying slightly on his plump legs, the dimpled knees, when I called his name. But when Ada bent to embrace him, he bolted away, hiding his face in the wide black skirt of his *nonna*.

"Silly, silly boy!" Mamma chided. "There's nothing to be afraid of. It's your own mamma trying to kiss you! And the other woman, that's your aunt Rina. They've finally come home from South America. Don't you know them?"

The boy shook his head, blond curls bouncing as he continued to cling to his grandmother. It wasn't until Rico came in with our bags that Fofò stopped hiding.

"It's your mother!" Rico teased. "You should be happy! You should be crowing!" He proceeded to imitate a rooster, with musical *coco-ricos* and much flapping of his arms. Then Fofò forgot his tears and laughed, clapping his hands together in a sticky toddler's applause, a standing ovation to his father. With laughter came courage and so the child allowed himself to be hugged by Ada and me.

THOUGH HIS SON KISSED ME, the father did not. Rico had been waiting for us at the central station. Our train had been delayed, and while he waited Rico had occupied himself sketching. With nothing more than a few napkins from a cart that sold panini, he had created a gallery of caricatures. Oily stains from prosciutto caused the ink to smear in spots.

I saw him first, but it was Ada who ran into his open arms. The kisses, the cries, the drama of the voices trained for the stage, even in that hall of reunions attracted some attention. I watched. I felt like a superfluous character in a play without an author— afloat—longing to be rewritten.

When Ada finally let Rico go and I moved forward to embrace him, he stepped back. But when I insisted and reached out to him, he did take my hand in his. Though he smiled, he smiled a sad, crooked half-smile.

"I can see you've grown up without my help," was all he said before he turned away to get a porter for our luggage.

25

Shortly after our return from the South American tour, my life as a fallen woman became confirmed. I did not have that marriage license, that license for licentiousness that had been Ada's ticket to freedom all along. What I hadn't realized was that even before our boat docked in Italy, Ada had betrayed me in a letter to Rico, a letter that he offered to Mamma as proof that I could not be trusted alone with my family's honor. She turned it over to me, demanding an explanation.

Carissimo Rico,

It seems you were right about Rina and the stage all along. And she has now lost that innocence you cherish so much. Not even my presence has prevented her fall. Regrettably, I was already asleep in the adjoining room when her suitor arrived. Did he wait until he saw my light was snuffed out? Did they conspire together on this? I'll never know for sure, but I was sound asleep when it happened, I heard nothing.
Rina did not know that the rascal was already married. I would have told her if she had asked me, I would have guessed immediately.

But Rina thought she had found herself a fidanzato. These Chileans have such importuning ways, but as for me, you know that I am used to being admired. It doesn't go to my head. Or make me act foolishly. But I think we should forgive the poor girl—after all she is so young! And bel canto can work like a drug in the blood, and if you're not wary, it can make you do in life the things you have acted out onstage. Please don't blame her, and don't tell Mamma about this. Let's keep it between ourselves.

I miss you and long for you, as ever, your,

Ada

So this explained Rico's coolness towards me. He was disappointed in his virgin sister. It seemed that he had been right—*forever* for a young woman and for romance was two or three years at most. But was I really expected to wait for the man who impregnated my married sister?

The polite distance that had grown between us was worse than indifference—it chilled me. I was no longer innocent. It only took a single act in a South American scene for me to be judged by my own family as a Carmen, a gypsy harlot. But if I was a fallen woman, at least that made me a free one. It was easier to make decisions, to leave now that I no longer had a reputation to protect. When I was offered a contract at the San Carlo in Naples, it gave me the chance I needed to break away.

Again there were protests about my leaving, and the loudest came from Rico himself. Last December, flushed from his first success at La Scala, he had made his debut at the San Carlo and been booed off the stage there. He warned me about fickle Neapolitan audiences.

"How can you think of performing there, after what happened to me? They're barbarians! If I ever go to that wretched city again, it'll only be to eat spaghetti—not to sing!" That was the vow he had made when he returned to Milan.

But I thought that if I could succeed where even he failed, then he would have to respect me again. With or without permission, I was going, and alone this time. Because my virtue had been compromised in Santiago, my mother would have had me wear sackcloth for the rest of my life or join a convent. But I had seen the world and was now a woman in every way. I was no longer afraid to leave home. While the household slept I packed a bag and then boarded a train for Napoli.

Tu Sei Pagliaccio

Ed un amore ch'era febbre e follia!

And a love that was fever and folly!
—LEONCAVALLO, *I PAGLIACCI*

I

It was *carnevale,* the day of feasting and carousing before the days of fasting and prayer of the Lenten season. Naples, that city of heat, of con artists and clowns, was cool under a spring rain. What did I have to fear? I asked myself, trembling as I descended from the train. I was an independent woman with money in my pockets, money I had earned myself, and I would be earning more of it at the San Carlo.

Waiting for me on the platform was a representative from the opera company. With a raised arm, he waved my telegram in the air to call attention to himself in the crowd. Roberto De Sanno, the impresario for the San Carlo, was a tall man who, though he dressed most fashionably, seemed to disappear in his clothes. You recalled the suit, not the man. What I remember best is the white carnation in the buttonhole of his lapel. He, who had not come with flowers to greet me, offered me his carnation. Before putting it behind my ear, I brought it to my nose, but it had no scent. His suit was a light gray and striped, but the stripes were so fine that they too, like the man, seemed half mirage. He wore white silk gloves, which he removed to take my hand. His bow was conventional but his lips did not kiss—to my astonishment, they sucked at the tips of my fingers. Then he offered me his arm as he escorted me to my hotel.

ONLY A FEW MONTHS after Rico's failure, I stepped onto the same stage and triumphed. Did my success at the San Carlo add salt to his wound? I so wanted to spite him then. My joy was complete when Roberto asked me to stay on as prima donna in the company—and in his heart.

ALAS, MY RESENTMENT had not stopped my love. After all, Ada was to blame for his cooling towards me; she had betrayed me twice over. There I was in Naples, the city that had given birth to Rico. Everywhere I looked I was reminded of him. I saw the contours of his face in that landscape. I imagined traces of him in the air I breathed, his native air. I saw him in the vistas of the bay, in that blur of blue, in the shimmering aura of heat haze, I saw him in the purple shadows of the volcano, I saw him wherever there was beauty and panorama. But I knew that my visions would not materialize into the real man. I was in exile from him now. Rico was proud; he never forgave a humiliation. I could not dream that Caruso would sing with me at the San Carlo. True to his vow, he would never perform in Naples again.

THERE WERE THE OTHER MEN who passed through my life like water at the mouth of a river and into the sea. They left no trace. But Roberto was more than that to me. I lived with him for a time. Not only was my lover in charge at the opera house, but he also organized the London seasons of Italian opera and so helped make me an international star.

Though I shared my bed with Roberto, I continued to pine for Rico and I stayed true to that love—in my fashion. I needed men—what woman alone in Italy then didn't need their protection?—but I did not marry them. And if I did not marry, if I still dreamed of Rico, who could blame me when that man was the king of tenors himself and I was an aspiring soprano? I could not forget him; it seemed his fame conspired against it. Who could forget when the name Caruso was on everybody's lips in Italy, and then the world?

All my strong emotions, my only emotions, were acted out on the stage, written by somebody else. Nothing else seemed real. It was an afterlife of shadows, a long sleep, a waiting.

2

That sleep descended on my heart for what seemed like a hundred years, though in real life it was just three. When I woke up again it was in another country, in England. The Royal Opera Company had offered me the role of Mimì in *La Bohème*. And the tenor was the man I had been waiting for—I was to sing with Rico at last.

The day I went to meet the company at Covent Garden for the first time, all I could think about was Rico! I did not know if it was rainy or cool outside, I knew clouds covered the sky and made the sun a stranger. I walked through something like mist, but the mist was in my eyes, as I made my way to the theater. I carried but did not need an umbrella; I swung it like a cane as I hurried to my fate. There were worse things to fear than getting a little wet. I did not know how Rico would receive me.

As I entered the theater I could hear many voices talking all at once. I listened for, but could not make out, the golden one among the babel. I dropped the umbrella into a stand and walked towards the voices. I moved with great care, as if I were carrying something precious and very fragile, something perhaps about to break and be lost for good.

The company was gathered on the stage where Caruso was the center of attention. He was being introduced all around by the manager, and as I joined them, I was presented to him too—as if I needed an introduction. Caruso greeted me cordially, but with coolness in his voice, like a glass served with more ice than water for your thirst.

"Caruso doesn't know me, but has Rico forgotten his little sister?" At this he laughed, and everything was natural again between us.

I was twenty-four that fall, the age my sister had been when she sang Mimì to his Rodolfo. That day my singing was astonishing. I sang with all the ardor and drama I had learned from Ada on the South American tour, with all the technique Ceccherini had drummed into me, with all the polish of my years at the San Carlo, and with all the fervor the dream of singing by his side had inspired in me.

I was in London without Roberto. Rico was there without Ada. After the rehearsal, we went off together to eat at an Italian restaurant in nearby Soho—alone again after so long.

THAT NIGHT, when we left the restaurant, it seemed that we stepped into fog. We made our way back to our hotels through a fog so dense we could see only as far as our hands could stretch.

From the mist a stranger emerged who seemed to know us. He greeted us as Signor Caruso and *la signora*. Rico smiled and nodded to the gentleman, but he said nothing. I had been mistaken for my sister. Then Rico took my hand in his. Though we both wore gloves, the feel of my silk ones sliding against his leather burns in my memory.

"Where are your artichokes now?"

"Still in my lap, but without the thorns. The heart's still there, but the choke's gone. Anybody can eat."

"Anybody?"

"Anybody who's you."

In the darkness, through the fog, returning to the hotel was more like a swim than a walk. Nostalgia was part of that atmosphere, fluid, filmy, yet tugging with enough force to pull us back to that summer long ago, to the kitchen in Livorno, to the unknown tenor from the south, and the tragic waste of it all, the artichokes scattering every which way.

We walked and walked, but it seemed as if we would never arrive, nor perhaps did we wish to, not when we knew it meant parting from each other. But then arrive we did at my hotel, the Radisson. He would have to continue on to his own room at the Waldorf.

We said good night, *"Buona notte, buona notte,"* but then Rico took my arm and pulled me away from the lighted entrance. "Stay. Not just yet. Stay with me while I smoke a cigarette." The brief bright flare of his match, and I could see his face in shadow and light, the Neapolitan face of a Caravaggio. Rico smoked, breathing in so deeply and then exhaling it seemed that the marvelous source of the fog that night was his mouth.

Sixteen notes in a baritone song, Big Ben rang in the night, then, with twelve bongs, signaled the beginning of a new day, another cycle in clockwork time. And we had yet to go to sleep. Years of unrequited love for him kept me by his side in the penetrating damp of a London fog. I wasn't cold. My love was ablaze in my body. But what was it that kept Rico by my side in the chill and wet of English weather after all those years of loving my sister, this man whose greatest fear was catching a cold or a sore throat? Were we finally ripe enough for each other?

He finished the cigarette, dropped it to the ground, and crushed the glowing ember underfoot. He felt his pockets for more cigarettes, but his case was empty. We stood there together in silence for some time, with no more excuse to linger. Big Ben sounded once more, the somber single note of the quarter hour.

"Good night, Rina. It hurts to say it when it means goodbye." He bent to kiss my cheek.

"No, not this time. I won't let you go." I turned my face up and offered him my open mouth.

3

When I returned to Naples, the longing I felt for Rico was more than that familiar and dull ache; it had become sharp, searing, fueled now by carnal knowledge, not just my fantasy. Consolation, what I had found in my relationship with Roberto, I just couldn't stomach anymore; as if my bread were baked with sawdust instead of flour, it could not be swallowed.

I lived for Rico's letters to me from America even though they promised me nothing. They acknowledged nothing. He wrote like an uncle. It was a pattern in our relationship, yet one I had moved beyond.

Cara Rina,

I was so happy when in London we at long last mended our quarrel and things are now as they should have been all along. The season at the Metropolitan will be over soon and I will be free to return to Italy. Last year I bought a magnificent estate near Signa. I named it Bellosguardo because of the beautiful views there. Ada is waiting for me with the children. I have a new son, he is named Enrico Caruso like me, a big name for such a small boy!

You know it's time to end your quarrel with Ada too and return to the family. Come visit us this summer. If you say yes, I will ask Ada to have a room prepared for you. I miss you and I know that she misses you too.

Rico

Another child with Ada! Could he have gone any farther from me, or made himself any less accessible? It seemed to me then that a child was nature's contract between a man and woman, and greater than that of any court whether of state or church. This made Rico twice married to my sister. If he wrote to me as if he had given me nothing more than brotherly kisses, perhaps he felt some shame. I felt the sting of it myself. But my desire was greater than my shame. I looked for something between the lines in the letter, for something I might have missed in the message. And how should things have been all along?

I had to see him again. I had to find out.

BELLOSGUARDO WAS IN THE HILLS on the outskirts of Firenze. On my first visit there from Naples in the summer of 1905, my sister welcomed me warmly. When I went to embrace her, I found myself approaching a mirror image. Her face seemed to cloud with my breath. Our roles were reversed; it was she now who reflected me. For the first time in my life I felt more than equal to her.

Ada's trophies, her triumphs now, were the house and her children. And the house was palatial, more like a museum than a home. Our footsteps echoed as in a vault, a bank vault. The heat of summer did not penetrate the thick stone walls, the marble floors. Although the myriad lights of the chandelier above us shone with the brilliance of the sun, it did not radiate any warmth. It was light refracted through ice.

There were portraits in oil, the severe faces of aristocrats, ancestors belonging to the house, mounted on the walls all around. As in their lifetimes they had embodied wealth, property, so in this afterlife they had become commodities, transferred with the deed of sale.

A servant brought the children down to see me and Ada presented Fofò, dressed formally in a checked suit, a blue silk tie choking him. He squirmed in these clothes. Like his hair which, slicked down, rose up in a stubborn cowlick at the back, he could not easily be controlled. I almost did not recognize my nephew; he had grown from a baby into a boy, seven years old.

The second boy was born in the fall of 1904—shortly after the time Rico and I had been reunited in London. I felt again that pang of guilt and shame. Did Rico feel that too? Where was he?

Ada called the baby Mimmi. He had been baptized Enrico Caruso Junior, but it was clearly too weighty a name for such a delicate-looking child. His soft curls formed a kind of aura around his head. Because of the white linen-and-lace pinafore he wore, along with his timid way of hiding behind his mother's skirt, he might easily have been mistaken for a girl. Using a large silk handkerchief, I lured him away from the shelter of Ada's dress with a game of peek-a-boo. Then he smiled at me for the first time. I continued to play the game until he was laughing and no longer afraid of me.

After Ada showed off her sons, I let her see my scrapbook of press clippings. "Rina Giachetti, international star of the first rank" was pasted on the opening page because, when compiling the work, I chose to narrate the progress of my career backwards.

Envy, jealousy, had been my lot; Ada didn't reveal any. "You're my sister. Opera's in our blood," she said, nodding appreciatively at my success.

She had scrapbooks of her own locked away in a drawer that she retrieved to show me. Her last clipping was from the *Gazzetta dei Teatri*, dated November 22, 1900.

"When Rico and I sang *Tosca* together in Bologna at the Comunale, the reviews singled me out and just lumped him in with the baritone as noteworthy. It irked him." She offered me the article to read for myself. "We haven't sung together since then. Rico forced me to retire. Before Mimmi, I had two other pregnancies—you know me, I sang anyway, and since I hadn't had problems before, why should pregnancy have stopped me then from performing? But I lost the last two babies, and with the second miscarriage the bleeding wouldn't stop. Rina, I came close to death. Rico was so distraught that he made me promise to quit the stage. He blamed my singing! He did not want to lose me. It's because he loves me so much that he asked me to stop. He said that he wanted me safe at home with the children."

"Ah, what a home it is! Is there a woman alive who would complain?" I said, but if anybody, I thought, it might have been Ada who would do so. I looked to see signs of illness in my sister. Certainly she was pale, but she had always cultivated pallor.

"When he's on tour, I get restless. Since we moved into this estate, I don't travel with him anymore. I'm the wife all year long, but he's becoming a summer husband." She could still turn a phrase on a needle, but where was her fire? Smoldering in the hearth? She seemed listless rather than restless as she spoke.

"Are you happy now with the role of wife?" I couldn't resist taunting her. I wondered at what point being the wife of Caruso had become better than being a star in her own right.

"Now that he can, Rico likes to play the man in this family, and he says it's his job to support us. He's stubborn about it. You may find this hard to believe, Rina, but when we were in New York and Enrico was singing at the Metropolitan Opera House—it's a magnificent theater, all red velvet and gold brocade, it's the La Scala of America—the Australian soprano Nellie Melba, who was the Mimì in their production, got sick. And Gatti, the manager, asked me to fill in for her. But Rico wouldn't let me! I was offered two thousand dollars a night, but he made me say no. Every evening I sat in the audience and had to listen to a lesser soprano, an American woman who didn't know how to open her mouth properly to sing in Italian.

Murder, I say, she murdered the role that could have been mine. It nearly drove me mad. But Rico has to have his way all the time now. He's used to it."

"Was that before you lost the babies, or after?"

"After, but it wasn't a real engagement, it was only to be for a few performances! What would have been the harm in it? I wasn't pregnant with Mimmi yet." Her gaze seemed to turn inward; regret, dismay, played on her face. Then, as she continued the story, she made light of the incident. "Really, Rina, you haven't heard the best part, though. Until Melba recovered and returned to the stage, and for each of the performances that might have been mine, Rico presented me with two thousand dollars—just to keep quiet."

"Rico paid you not to perform?"

"Yes. And who could resist him? His perfumed envelopes stuffed with dollar bills, and the flowers. Not me. I love him. I have to content myself with singing to the boys."

"Lullabies."

"When they're older I'll return to the stage. If we don't have anymore children—well, that could be very soon! Two sons should satisfy any man, but he wants a daughter too."

"He wants more children?" This made me as unhappy as it seemed to make her.

Then Ada turned her face away from me, and she seemed smaller than I remembered. Her head was bent, her eyes once more turned inwards. When she looked up again she said, "Marry if you must, Rina, for the sake of appearances. But whatever you do, don't fall in love with him. And don't have children." Then she noticed the maid, who had been hovering in the background, and ordered her to serve coffee.

PRECISELY ON THE HOUR, at noon, Rico left his study to join us for lunch in the dining hall where we sat at a table that could have easily accommodated fifty. His fingers were black from writing out sheet music. The copying technique that in times of poverty had enabled him to earn a lira or two, now that he had lire in the millions, he continued to use as an aid for study. He hugged me in greeting. He hadn't touched me since our time in London yet his embrace was crisp as the starch in his shirt. Then he sat at the head of the table in a chair that, although it matched the others in design, was larger, more ornate, less a chair than a throne.

"So, what do you think of our new home, Rina?"

"I couldn't have imagined it if I had tried."

"Ah, it doesn't take imagination—what it takes is a lot of money."

"You must be richer than the king himself."

"I'm better known—internationally." We were on the second course of our meal. His hand, as it turned back the grated Parmesan cheese offered by a servant, sparkled with the green fire of a large emerald ring. Jewels and ink stains, the poor man and the rich man, I could see them both in him. But his hands had lost the touch of the sun of Naples. The skin seemed bleached from living in the shade. In New York, I had read, the buildings were so high they blocked the sun. Its rays couldn't reach a man.

"They love him in America."

"At first they laughed at me."

"They adore Rico!"

"Jean de Reske, Jean de Reske—they thought I wasn't good enough to replace him. 'Roly-poly, the Italian peasant,' they called me."

"At the Metropolitan Opera House, Rico is the star! They open the season with him now."

"But they soon forget their aristocrat, that string bean, that bean-polack tenor, because I have the bigger, the better voice. Now the snobs of the Diamond Horseshoe invite me to dinner. Now they jostle to eat out of my hand."

"Rico is paid five thousand dollars a performance! He was offered more by a rival company, but he turned them down!"

"I honor my contracts—nor will I, Enrico Caruso, sing for the lesser house. I make more money than I can spend. I can sing where I choose."

"You're this rich from singing!" I looked around the room, but I meant the entire vast estate.

"It's the records. Nobody knew that it could be anything much more than a curiosity. They were recording farm animals. But the clown in me didn't care and I signed on with Victor because—well, why not if they paid me so well to do it. Now I'm making big American dollars from these records. They are sold all over the country and my fame keeps spreading farther and farther than I could go in a lifetime."

"Is that real singing?"

"It's bel canto, not clucking. It's Caruso, not a chicken. I only have to sing once into the horn, but the royalties keep paying me. If I could only digest diamonds and pearls, with what I earn I could still eat well."

Diamonds and pearls? He must have been eating very well indeed because he'd put on a lot of weight. And though he was at home relaxing with his family, he was dressed up in a finely tailored suit. But then, was this mansion a house to relax in? No, it was a house to play the lord in.

RICO AND I VENTURED out to tour his mammoth estate. The garden was a park, really several parks, replete with clipped hedges, ancient trees, and its own roads. The greens were laid out in geometric lines. Its verdure was that of vistas. Flower beds were set around statues in the style of the empire.

But he had changed in this way too: Rico no longer liked to walk.

"It's too big to see in an afternoon, and you must be tired. It's better that you get some rest now. I have an automobile, you know. Later we'll go for a ride and I'll show you everything—the pastures, the vineyards, the groves of olives—everything."

On a map he pointed out how the roads meandered across the grounds and led into surrounding farmland.

The rose garden was nearby and it appealed to me. Breathing in the fragrance of the flowers, we sat on a stone bench near which a marble Venus offered a marble apple to the unwise. Rico lit a cigarette. If love had a scent, it had become that of burning tobacco.

We hardly spoke. The only sounds were the sounds of silence, of inhaling and exhaling, of bells muted by distance. The ringing was from a monastery on a neighboring hill. The society might have been a brotherhood, not of men, but of sheep, so subdued and intimate was that tinkling call for the Angelus.

WHEN WE RETURNED to the house it seemed deserted and the tour of the building itself led through long and echoing halls. It hardly seemed a place to raise children, for Fofò and Mimmi to run about. Its corridors were dimly lit, designed not for games or shouting, but for hushed reverence.

Our only conversation as we walked was our own footsteps, the clacking of hard heels on marble tile. It was a house apparently uninhabited, yet filled with presence. Were there eyes, painted ones cut out from the oil portraits, through which others, eyes of flesh, peered? Were there shadows, spies, behind the columns, secret doors, and passages?

He led me to a large bedroom. Damask drapes, damask coverlet on the bed, and walls painted the pink that barely blushes in white peonies. A woman's bedroom, I saw Ada in the plush decor. On the vanity, before a mirror which reflected, and so doubled, was a the clutter of pots of creams and powders. He pointed to a chest, stuffed so full of treasure the lid could not be closed. Diamonds spilled out of the dark velvet interior. "Ada's trinkets," Rico called them, that king's ransom of jewels, where a single pin might have purchased the entire street on which he was born.

The bed itself seemed as wide as a field. When I touched it I felt the slippery sheen of satin. The mattress was soft, not firm; I rested my hip on the edge of the bed and sank deeply into it. High-heeled slippers, pink silk ones, were set by one side of the bed; they were trimmed with some feathery substance, so wispy, so delicate, it seemed to have been spun by exotic birds conceived by spiders. On the other side, tucked under the frame of the bed, was a man's pair; they were corduroy so finely ribbed they seemed to be made of velvet rather than cotton. I picked up one of his slippers. It smelled of pungent, sweet herbs, like coriander after rain, muddied in the garden. I sat on the edge of their bed, cradling his slipper.

"A shoe's for the foot—you don't put your nose in it," Rico laughed.

On his side, the night table had an ashtray, on the other side, a book. I reached over and picked up the slim volume to have a look, but the pages were uncut; neither the author nor the title, which was in a foreign language, meant anything to me.

I wanted to forget my sister and my nephews; the place was so big it should have been easy.

"Ada and the children are probably in the nursery, in the north wing. You have yet to see even a quarter of the house."

We left the room by another door than the one we had entered. It led down a passageway the width of a walk-in closet—but what closet runs for fifty feet? He called the other room we entered his bedroom. There, on a dresser, were the familiar portraits of the three Madonnas he worshiped. Everything else was new to me and seemed to belong to royalty, not to the earthy and unaffected man I had known.

His was an antique canopy bed and much smaller than the other. It was a bed built for one, if a regal one, with space enough to stretch. But if two were to lie there, they would have to be lovers to be completely happy about it. Rico untied the gold tassels and spread out the heavy satin panels. Suddenly, we were cloistered in a room within a room. The bed became the whole world and the world was filled with our intensified breathing, our bodies. In the silky darkness of a night in cobalt satin, dressed in all our clothes, we lay together on the bed. His legs disappeared into the billows of my skirt. Very quietly, not speaking, barely breathing, he lightly touched, seeming to explore as the blind read, with the tips of fingers, oh so tenderly, the features of my face.

4

I was resting in a guest room, alone on top of the bedcovers, with a wool blanket wrapped around me. Though my room was filling with shadows, the high square of the window still glowed. The house, each room, had a climate of its own and it was not summer's. Delicious, insatiable hopes for a full life with Rico, onstage and off, were playing out in my mind. I would go to America and become his leading lady at the Metropolitan Opera House. But I needed to throw myself in the way of an American impresario to do that. An English stage had brought Rico and I together again, perhaps an American one might serve to bind us. My sister was an inconvenient detail.

A servant's knocking at the door broke my reverie. He told me that the master would like me to join him at the front of the house.

OUTSIDE IT WAS STILL BRIGHT. The setting sun reflected back from the windows of the house and burnished everything. The horseless carriage was parked on the path leading to the house. My heart quickened with fear; I had agreed to ride in that strange vehicle on a tour of the grounds of the estate. I never knew that something could be painted black yet reflect so much light. The sun blazed back from its polished metal body. Raising my hand to shade my eyes, I squinted as I looked at the vehicle.

Ada was standing on the stairway leading to the main entrance, watching the children. Fofò sat proudly behind the wheel of his new toy, a replica in miniature of his father's automobile. With a whooping cry he picked up his baby brother and plopped him in it. Then he jumped into the driver's seat again and honked the horn to warn me out of his way. I fell back laughing at the danger. As he dipped from side to side to turn the steering wheel, it zigzagged along the drive. He made roaring engine sounds with his mouth as he pedaled.

Rico's automobile looked as if it could have run like the chariot of the sun, on its burning light alone. It shone with the force of a hundred suns, in its mirrors, in its windshields, in the glistening chrome, in the waxed and polished paint of its panels. Touching it, I felt heat, I felt the vibrating pulse of life in the body. The thing sounded like a giant cat, one you could both hear and feel purring under your hand. There had only been horse-drawn carriages at the estate before, so when Rico bought the motor vehicle, he also hired a mechanic. It was the mechanic who cranked the engine.

WHEN RICO JOINED US in the courtyard he was dressed in full costume. As if the vehicle were a kind of horse, he wore riding pants. As if we were about to embark on a run of such high speeds we might lift off from terra firma, he wore the hood and goggles of an aviator.

Ada refused to ride with him. The children kept busy with their own toy and it was running well. Fofò didn't tire of pedaling. But I, who would have willingly, if not without trepidation, entered fire for Rico, didn't hesitate. Like a heroine in an opera, whether for an execution or for a jaunt, I was indifferent to the consequences. I held my head high and straightened my back as I sat beside the leading man in his new role of driver.

"Ready to run!" he exclaimed. It was not posed as a question, but it should have been. Rico lowered his goggles. As if the glasses prevented him from seeing well, he bent his head to peer at the various gauges on the dashboard. As if he had reins in his hands, he sat behind the steering wheel and shook it. Nothing happened. But he knew what a mule was, so he cursed the car.

The mechanic gestured some instructions and Rico groped around the controls and pulled at some levers.

With sputtering, sparking sounds the thing began to shake violently before it bolted forward and back in a jerking motion, in a strange hopping dance.

Now that the vehicle was moving forward, Rico smiled with satisfaction. I tried to smile back.

"What a car needs to make it perfect—riding through the country …" We were fine as long as the road was straight, but when it began to curve, Rico, as if he had studied in the same school as his son, was turning the steering wheel so much that we were reeling from side to side. We veered far to the left and it didn't help when, instead of slowing down, he hit the gas pedal, and we crashed into a row of the large stone planters filled with chrysanthemums that lined the drive on either side. The car toppled onto its side.

Ada's screams brought out the servants who rushed to help Rico and I climb out of the wreckage while the mechanic shut down the engine. Shaken, covered in black potting soil and the remnants of flowers, Rico and I embraced each other. Several of the urns had been shattered. Decapitated chrysanthemums were scattered all around. Ada and the children came running to us. When it was clear that we were not hurt, Ada burst out laughing.

"As a tenor you're the best, the *capo,* but *caro,* believe me, you're no driver!" She tried to restrain her laughter, but it erupted again. She kept laughing until she was breathless and had to bend over gasping, grasping her sides before she could continue speaking. "I think you should get your car modeled on Fofò's, and not the other way around. An engine's no good to you."

Though Rico said nothing, he became very red in the face and his eyes darkened.

"Fofò, darling, you'll let Papa use your car, won't you, now that he's broken his own."

The car was not damaged. When it was righted, the mechanic drove it back into the garage.

"Your papa can sing so that birds listen, but at driving he's hopeless. Be a man—help Papa out. Give him the keys to your car, Fofò, and while you're at it, throw in a few lessons."

"That's enough!" Rico stormed into the house. When he returned, he was dressed for his true role as the successful tenor, in a white silk suit.

Only then did it seem that Ada had had enough fun teasing him. Although the soothing tone she now adopted still had a sardonic edge to it, the kind of tone you might use for a precocious child.

"Who would expect the greatest tenor in the world to drive his own car? It's high time that we hired a chauffeur."

5

Like Rico, I became a seasonal visitor to the estate, returning only in summer with the end of the season at the San Carlo. I had the same excuse as he had to keep me away at other times. Traveling north by train from Napoli was not crossing the Atlantic, but I would linger in the city for about a month until it started to get hot. I knew that Rico would be back at Bellosguardo by then.

The next time I visited the family the Britzia Zust was waiting for me at the station. A uniformed chauffeur emerged from behind the wheel.

"Unmistakable, you are *la patrona*'s sister. And I, I am Cesare, the conductor of this fine automobile, sent here at your service, signorina. For your comfort and for your pleasure!"

His gallant little speech made me look at him again. Before he spoke I had only noticed the uniform, now I saw the man, the grin, the black eyes looking at me as if I couldn't look back. With a flourish and a quick bow he opened the door to the vehicle. Since I was more or less permanently established in one of the rooms at the mansion, I traveled only with the smallest of bags, carrying just a few trifles, mostly toys and treats for the children, but still this handsome man insisted on taking care of it for me and placing it in the back.

HIS BROAD SHOULDERS blocked my view of the road ahead. To my surprise I didn't care, I studied the dark blue serge of his jacket, the sharpness of bones, where it seemed wings were struggling to grow back. The epaulets at his shoulders were gold and tasseled. Though he wore a cap, I could see the hair at his nape was black. The curls looked sculpted, as did his arms, the scalloped lines of his biceps, which I observed when I peeked over his shoulder as if to take in the view of the hills into which we traveled. He turned his head to the side to look back at me.

"Don't worry. I know how to drive this thing." He gave me a wink.

His hands on the steering wheel were broad and bronzed. Such were the proportions of his physique that he might have been one of those statues of the ancient gods in the gardens come alive, an athletic beauty as cultivated by the Greeks and copied by the Romans. And the car was his chariot, responding to his will as if pulled by horses, deployed through the tensing of his wrists.

Those immortals were naked, this man was dressed, but so muscled that it was his body that gave shape to the clothes and not vice versa.

ADA ALWAYS WELCOMED me with a show of enthusiasm, yet every time I came she acted as if it were my first visit—as if it were still a big surprise to see me. I don't know if she suspected me of a liaison with Rico in London, or if such a liaison could continue under her own roof. I was Aunt Rina to the children. I was sister-in-law to Rico. But there was no law to it. Ada was still married to Botti, the Italian way, until death—while Rico was still technically a bachelor. This seemed to increasingly prey on her.

I think that she did not mistrust me or she would not have left me there alone with Rico so often. Perhaps Ada thought she was only leaving me with the children. Or she had other things on her mind.

The more famous Rico became, the more anxious Ada seemed to be about their relationship. She wanted a formal marriage, and if they were to adopt American citizenship, it could be done. For Ada, America was the land where freedom meant divorce. Still Rico refused to become an American. One day I overheard them argue about it.

"I will not renounce my homeland. I am an Italian above all."

"But you live in New York now nine months of the year. You might as well be an American. You've signed your life over to the Metropolitan Opera. We have become a summer family for you since we moved to this estate. A family for when you're on holiday! I am the mother of your children. I have a right to be your wife."

"Botti had that right first. It's not my fault you're already married! You want to come with me to America again? Fine, come. I never stopped you." And then, in a half-pleading and conciliatory tone, "But we have Bellosguardo now. Would you really rather stay in a hotel instead of this palace? You want the servants to be the only ones to enjoy it? This house is where we really live; I just go to America to work."

These frequent arguments were of little concern to me. I was free to spend time with Rico, with his children.

"We're only two Giachetti sisters," I reminded Ada. "I don't mind taking care of Fofò and Mimmi while you go out." As if I was doing her a favor, as if she needed that with the dozens of servants at her command.

In fact, I was more than content to spend time with the children; I was not just waiting to be alone with Rico. Although I gave in to him on several occasions, my love for Rico was never carnal desire first and foremost. My heart had been schooled on Dante. I was just as happy, perhaps more so because there was no guilt, when Rico joined me in playing with the boys.

My brother, my lover—that was not the life I had imagined in what had become a previous century, when I was seventeen and untouched except in my heart by him. This ambiguous life as the affair rather than the wife would have seemed anathema to me then. I blame opera, its reversals and betrayals. And I feared things had become as entangled as in *I Pagliacci*, its play within a play, and the hour might soon arrive when *sangue*, blood, not *sugo*, tomato sauce, would soak my bodice.

6

The children were happy to see me. Even though they had little need for bribes of sweets and playthings when a wing of the mansion called the nursery was overflowing with their toys, they welcomed me—they even welcomed the trifles I brought them. Did Fofò perhaps retain some memory of when I cared for him as a baby in Milan? Did his love spring so freely for me because of that? He treated the marbles I gave him, the brilliant cat's-eyes in green and amber, as if they were precious jewels. They were not to be shared or traded. He kept them in a velvet pouch, separate from the others in his collection, and stored away in the dresser drawer in his bedroom. Every night he had to count them before he could sleep. When I came to kiss him good night, he would pull them out to show them to me again.

"These are dream alleys, *Zia* Rina, with magic powers. I keep a few under my pillow, so when the *strega* comes to catch me, I throw them under her horned feet and she falls and can't eat me like the other one. Mimmi gets gobbled up right away." Fofò shivered as he spoke.

"You have such awful dreams! Every night, sweet boy?"

"No, not every night, but I have to be ready for her when she comes."

And because the children were always happy to see me, Ada began treating my arrival as an excuse to leave them, and the house.

I wasn't unhappy to be left alone with my nephews. I never called on the servants to take over. We spent hours chasing brightly colored balls whose mosaic patterns in the sunlight looked painted. Heat made them soft, released their smell of rubber. Rolling away into the lawn, they gathered the sweetness of the grass—and of the sticky hands that caught them.

They all said I had a way with the boys, but really all I did was play with them. My hands and face showed the wear and tear, scratched by the bushes where I retrieved balls, or glistening wet from plucking them out of the fountains where the startled gold-fish darted about as shimmering orange waves beneath the surface of the water.

WHEN RICO FINISHED his practicing for the day, he joined our games. Then it was the shouts and the laughter of four children playing that rang out in the courtyard. One voice, the deepest, resounded like a golden bell ringing from a church where it was not Christ, but his music, that was divine.

Though it was time for the children to sleep, their mother had not yet returned from her shopping trip. We had eaten supper without her. So we lured them into the nursery with promises of stories and lullabies. And I was the one who sang for them. Rico never sang to his children. He remonstrated with me for asking him to sing to them too. "I'm a professional, an artist, not a whistler." He saved his voice for performance. If his singing didn't soothe his sons, nevertheless it fed them.

Although we had shut the wooden blinds to bring on the night, the dark, without which a child will protest he cannot be expected to sleep—"It's early, it's still light outside, it's unfair"—there was a glow in the room. It seemed to emanate from their skin as a misty aura.

In spite of the coolness of the evening, their cheeks felt hot and moist against my lips when I kissed them. "*Sogni d'oro*, sweet dreams," we soothed their fears of the dark world lying on the other side of their closed eyelids. As we watched the boys settle and drift into sleep we seemed to share the same thought: angels.

Turning away from the children, with a slow smile of pleasure, Rico cocked his head to the side and whispered, "Do you hear that?"

Afraid of disturbing his hushed, rapt attention, I turned my head slowly in the same direction, moved the hair away from my ears to listen fully for what it was Rico was hearing. The rubbing sound of silk running through fingers was all I heard. My hair because of the heat treatments with olive oil made that sound, it had that feel. But surely that was in my ear alone. What did Rico hear? The scratching sound of nails as I attempted to pull my hair away was my own as well; it was also in my ear and not from the room.

"I'm trying to listen, Rico, but I can't hear for the sounds I make myself."

"Stay absolutely still. Movement through air, you know, the swooshing is the sound of speed—but what is the sound of slowness? We need another scale for sound, decibels even for dumbness. Listen, listen very carefully, Rina, listen as hard as you can. Hold your breath if you have to. Now, what do you hear?"

Both children were sleeping face down on their pillows. If there were sounds, it must be their breathing or a current of air, if wind could ease through the wooden slats of the closed shutters. But if there were sounds coming from the boys or from the window, they were imperceptible to me.

"What do you suppose is the sound a spider makes as he spins his silk? His web isn't turned on a wheel, but comes from the depths of his own bowels. A singer should study the spider! It's not enough to hold the note longer. When I dove for *soldini* in the Bay of Naples I learned how to lengthen my breath. Any child can do that for the tourists. That's not special! No genius does, no matter how well, only what has been done before. My ambition for my art is to be like the spider. I want volume and I want power in my voice, but I also want softness, I want a silk in my singing that entangles even silence."

In his kiss then I imagined I heard the sounds of that softness, that silence. Breath when it is held. The closest I ever felt to Rico was in that room of sleeping children. He turned the doorknob when we left so that no grinding sound was made, no clicking of the lock as he closed the door.

THE HOUSE ITSELF seemed to have gone to sleep. Its sounds were a sleeper's sounds, that turning, that murmuring of dreamtime.

There was no excuse, no reason except one, to enter Rico's bedroom. "Come rest with me, Rina."

"But ..."

"Just to lie down. Just to be close for a little while. When I touch you it will be like my sister. Like the first time you visited here."

Which had been innocent enough. But in London Rico had loved me as, in bed, any man loves a woman, with all our clothes removed impatiently, half torn off—that was the first night— then, on subsequent nights, slowly removing an item at a time, lingering on the details, the glissade of buttons of pearl or horn, until I burned with desire, with impatience, and I pulled his head down to my breasts.

But in his bedroom at Bellosguardo, it felt as if we had never been naked together, as if we had never touched that way. When we lay down together there, it had been as if we had entered the hushed, cool air of a cathedral. I had to draw my shawl more closely around me.

"Come, Rina, the children won't wake up. And as for Ada, she's gone, and she won't be back until she's spent all my money. That safely gives us close to an eternity to make love." He took my hand, cupped it in his two, and kissed it.

If I trusted skin, why did I always have to look with my eyes—to keep the lights on when making love? Was I trying to make sure it was really the man I loved and not merely a fantasy? There was no need then for a lamp. It was approaching but not yet dark and the room was illuminated with the slanting radiance of the summer evening, of light as filtered through the trellis of some flowering vine. By wisteria made fragrant and empurpled.

"She never comes into my bedroom. We have an understanding—I go to hers."

"Please, don't draw those panels. I want to see. I want to watch how you touch me."

In the past, I had closed my eyes when he was not there, so that I could see him. I had dreamed about this man for so long, he had seemed still to be a dream; he had moved over me through a decade of dreaming. I knew how to create the sensation of his caress. His way was to come very close but not to actually touch my skin. There was no perceived pressure from his fingertips, which hovered a fraction of a millimeter above my breast. The downy hair on my skin was as grass rising and bending under wind. His fingers rested on the threshold of touching, in that zone where the impalpable dwells. The untouchable in me was what Rico touched with hands as soft as if gloved in a leather of lilies. My skin buzzed, swarmed by bees, honey-filled and without sting.

"It's hot." I removed my bodice, then unpinned my hair. His pale fingers slipped through dark silk, parting and lifting, parting and lifting. The sensation of pins, that nuisance my mind finally went to sleep.

"The skirt is a cloud, a fog, like in London, your legs are lost in it. Let me take it off for you, Rina. I want to see you."

If clothing creates mystery about the body, then why, when the clothes are stripped away, does the mystery remain? It seems the greater mystery is in the skin, in the flesh itself, impenetrable though you fill every orifice. That was how sex was between us; it was not lewd, it was not sport, it was the spirit we sought to embrace. So it was clumsy, frustrating, and even despicable, how, more than our garments, it was our bodies that got in the way. To enter, from head to toe, his body was my desire; but though I clung to him, I remained on the other—on my—side of the bed.

"Just a little, Rina, let me in just a little. I won't make you pregnant. I promise to hold myself back."

HIS SEMEN IS WARM on my belly. It spills as a heart pulses, as an artery bleeds. This life fluid is white. It has the phosphorescence I remember from the sea voyage, lapping at the sides of the ship, the platinum light of the moon.

Rico rolls away from me to light a cigarette. He pats my head and it is ordinary touching again, a gesture that is old between us. It reminds me I am the little sister. I stay very still, the stillness of faked sleep. I let the air do to my body whatever it will. The cooling, the lifting of moisture from skin that is a form of touching almost as subtle as his. It is amphibious, that weaving of water and air.

Rico strikes a match to light another cigarette, but it's blown out instantly. It's a sign, but we don't recognize it. A great wind is coming from within the house, a wind that might be from the rushing of the wings of harpies in flight. I clutch the sheet and cover myself, but it is snatched out of my hands.

At first she doesn't speak, she stands there gasping. When she finally says something, the words come out through short, forced breaths.

"Slut. Sister. Slut. Get out—of this bed! Get out—out of this house! Get out!"

It's as if she doesn't see Rico at all; he is the invisible man. She grabs my arm and yanks me off the bed. Then she picks up my clothes and throws them at me.

"Sister, slut, slut, sister, you slut of a sister. From this day you're dead to me. My children don't know you. My husband, my house—stay away from us!"

7

A secret, a poet wrote, is a worm in the rose. I could not have spoken the truth to my sister, nor to myself—if I knew it. When Rico did not say "stay" to me, when, if he defended me, it was only with silence, my shame was complete.

Ada's fury not exhausted on me, she turned and directed her wrath at Rico, who was nervously butting out his cigarette. Consumed to a stub, as was his member, now shriveled and foolish-looking, it cowered in the shadow of his belly.

"One singer, you said, there could only be one singer in this family! So what is she? Did I give up my career for you so that she could triumph over me, so that she could enjoy what should have been mine—singing onstage—and your love too? Damn you to hell! Damn you both!"

Her rage turned into wailing.

"One singer, Rico, you said one singer! So what am I to you now? What's my role? Am I your wet nurse? Am I your wife? Tell me—tell me what am I to you now."

Then it was I who had become invisible. The recriminations took on the sound of a tiresome quarrel, a quarrel between spouses. The way I left the room I might have been merely embarrassed to be listening in, if slinking away naked, my clothes bunched up in front of me, hadn't testified to so much more. In the corridor outside Rico's room I bumped into Cesare, the chauffeur, whose darting eyes roved over what I, in my distress, failed to hide. Breasts bejeweled by tears.

"I need you. I need you to take me to the station."

"But, signorina, there's not another train until morning. What will you do there?"

"I'll wait. I'll wait as long as I have to."

THAT NIGHT, in silence, Cesare drove me to the station. I imagined then that my life was hell, but it was only purgatory. Don't picture me sitting up all night on some hard bench in a small-town station where there are no benches by the tracks, my neck stiff from holding the sleeping weight of my head as I periodically doze then jerk myself awake. If that is your experience with waiting, it wasn't like that for me. Not that cavernous room of cold slate tiles, its dirty toilet the only refuge from the peering eyes that discover you huddled in a corner, with your mouth wide open and snoring.

Although the building was dark and the door padlocked, I ran up the steps anyway as if I were about to miss my train. I had to escape, and the only way was to run—into a locked door. I tried the handle; I shook it. Then I turned to the stars for counsel, but their glittering offered me nothing as practical as a key.

Beauty is said to be useless, still it was a beautiful night, the dark glistening through my tears. The sky was full of fast-burning stars, the flaring of their brilliant plumes. In comparison, the fixed stars seemed staid in their shining, ambiguous in their light. There was a rose garden near the station, in an ancient villa that had been converted into a public garden. All around, the air was sweet with the fragrance of flowers.

When it is dark, when the senses are sightless and the dazzle of the multipetal rose, the richness of its red, is obscured, its aching perfume rises more acutely. When the eyes go blank, the nose sees farther, deeper than daylight dares.

The shrilling of insects was muted now by the sound of the car's idling engine. In despair I pressed my forehead to the door, more like a child shut into her room than an adult locked out of a station, so when Cesare took my arm to escort me back to the car I gave in like a child, dragging my feet a little but letting myself be led by him. He made a bed for me in the back seat and wrapped me in a blanket that smelled of Ada's perfume, or perhaps it was the scent from the flowers consuming the air. Some jasmine too must have been releasing odor as if it were soul into the night air.

I think I did not sleep that night. Or if I slept, then I dreamed I was awake all those long hours, listening for morning, for bird-song as it breaks out in the darkness before dawn.

8

For three years I brooded in emotional exile from everyone, from everything I loved. Whatever ambitions I had for the stage had been used up in that bed in Bellosguardo. I couldn't fool audiences anymore; my passion was elsewhere. My international bookings began to dwindle and then they dried up. I had foolishly broken with Roberto after my reunion with Rico in London, and now without Roberto to promote or to protect me, even my tenure at the San Carlo was becoming strained. It was the summer of 1909, and after nearly ten years of singing in Naples, I did not expect my contract to be renewed. I was miserable, trying to comfort myself with chocolates and with magnums of champagne.

Rico never contacted me during this time. Did he hope to make amends or to appease Ada by cutting me off without a word? While I was enduring his silence, I heard that my sister left the great Caruso to run off with his chauffeur. The scandal was in all the papers. And still Rico did not contact me.

THE SCANDAL was our family's crisis too. I met with father in Rome to discuss it.

"Every year Rico still sends me that fifty lire he borrowed in 1897, the entire sum having been repaid a dozen times over, but this year there was no note. It was done through a bank."

"He blames the family, do you think?"

"Well, not your mother, nobody would blame the saint. But the rest of us are not so untarnished. But is he himself innocent? What kind of man thinks he can take both sisters and still have peace in his family?"

"You know about that!" I felt so ashamed.

"Yes, Ada told me. She writes to me. I won't point a finger at you except for what it did to your sister. I blame him. Still, it's very foolish to leave Caruso for his chauffeur. But with Ada, you reap what you sow."

"The papers say he's gone to gather the boys together because he's afraid that Ada might come back to take them away."

"It wouldn't be stealing. She's their mother."

"Rico must be very upset."

"Don't cry for him. Cry for the children. He's not going to take time out from his career to care for them himself. Now I'm going to your mother's to try to comfort her for a while, although all that praying gives me a headache. Make your peace with her, Rina, or now she has lost both her daughters."

Ada did not return for the children. She tried instead to sue Caruso for the rest of her jewels, the ones that had been kept in a safe at the bank. But in the Italian courts she had no rights to what was deemed his property. I guessed that when her money ran out, that Cesare might too.

She couldn't just pick up her singing career again in Italy, not with the scandal, and the trial only made it worse. Caruso was untouchable, and she was painted as a pariah in the papers. (Nobody outside the family with the exception of Cesare knew about my affair with Rico.) Nor did she drag my name into her court case. Was that to protect our family? I doubted that she cared to protect me. Still I burned with regret. Hellfire is not brimstone; it needs no chemicals not found in the soul itself.

Reviled and penniless, Ada had to leave Europe in order to work. She found some engagements in South America, where they remembered her from the Chilean tour.

I RETURNED TO NAPLES, but if I had listened to my father that afternoon, if instead of waiting to be fired I had quit the San Carlo, I might have gone back to Firenze with him and made amends with my mother. I might have kissed her lips while she still breathed. I'm sure she would have forgiven my leaving for Naples without her permission. If I had been contrite, she would have relented. If I had taken the time, if I could have more easily masked my shame in front of her about my relationship with Rico. But I thought she would know, that she would see it in my face. When I made my visits to Bellosguardo from Naples, my train stopped in Firenze, but I did not stop then to see my mother. The deadly sins of lust and pride prevented me. Regret and guilt now are both my mother and my sister.

FATHER SENT ME THE TELEGRAM: *Mamma morendo.* Two simple words printed in black ink and on ordinary paper, there was nothing of the gravity of the message in its form. There was no time to worry, no time to cry. I took the first train out of Naples. I didn't even pack; in my distress I left without a nightgown, without so much as a comb.

My heart was racing but the trains were slow. There were always delays on our rail system and that day was no exception. Though I prayed all the way—my mother believed in prayer—I arrived no faster. Looking up from the rosary to glance out the window, I saw the face of my mother, the roundness of her cheek flattened; her lips were moving, but I couldn't make out what she was saying to me. Then she closed her eyes and she became landscape.

After switching trains in Rome, as I traveled north, I welcomed the change in the view, from the spreading umbrella pines of the south to the dark flames of Tuscan cypress trees. The red tile roofs of my region seemed to welcome me home, bringing me closer to my mother. The cypresses seemed to burn for her in a green vigil.

FELICIA ANSWERED MY KNOCK and I walked into a house that imitated an altar with its flowers, candles, and burning incense. I had arrived too late to ask for my mother's forgiveness.

I did not recognize the priest; he looked too young to minister to the dead, to spend his days muttering in Latin. He was seated by the body and praying. He had a holy book open on his lap, but he did not look at its pages.

"Father?"

"I am Father Domenico."

"Father Domenico, please, may I have a few moments alone with my mother?"

"You are Rina, the youngest? She asked for you."

He left the room with a gentle click of the door. Like a child fearing punishment, I approached the body on the bed. But what did I know of punishment from the woman who only knew how to punish herself? If I did anything wrong as a girl, I was never spanked; Mamma would reprimand me with a gesture, a look in her moist dark eyes, so dark—mine like hers—so dark they seemed caverns rather than eyes except for the light in them—and she would raise a finger, point to heaven, and then retreat into her prayers. I lost her to the rosary, not to wrath. And now that she was dead I had lost her entirely to heaven.

I kissed her cheek, now cold and unyielding in death.

ADA COULD NOT RETURN from South America for the funeral—not that it would have been possible to wait for her. Papa showed me her letter:

Caro Papa,

I read your telegram and wept for poor Mamma. But forgive me, there is no sense in my trying to come back now. If I could fly like a bird, I would do so. They say some butterflies here travel as far north as Canada. But if I ever had wings, they've turned into lead. They pin me to the ground, thousands of kilometers from home. Now I will never see Mamma again, not even in death.

My circumstances are pitiable, though I want nobody's pity unless it is yours. At first they remembered me here and I received several bookings because of the Chilean reviews from 1900. But ten years is a long time for a singer not to work. I know that I could get my voice back if I had the chance. But his fame precedes me. I am no longer the soprano, Ada Giachetti, I am that fool of a woman who left the great Caruso for his driver! Scandal shouldn't hurt an opera singer, but because it's Caruso they're afraid—if we anger the great man, one was honest enough to tell me, he'll never sing for us again—so house after house has turned me down. Now I am singing in a cabaret here in Buenos Aires. I sing over the drunken brawling. I sing not arias, but popular tunes, the sad

*ones, where the woman has been made crazy for love, like me,
and has ruined her life.*

*I miss you and mourn with you, my darling Papa. But we don't
have to worry about Mamma. If there's a heaven, her heart's been
there for a long time.*

Love, forever your

Ada

In the end she lost everything; she lost Caruso, she lost her
children, and she lost singing. I don't count Cesare among her
losses. I don't think she was serious about him. If Ada used him
to get revenge, to return one infidelity with another, to make
Caruso a *cornuto* for the whole world to see, well, then she had
what she wanted there. The world loves a scandal. And his fame
made that scandal worldwide. Everywhere he turned the great
Caruso encountered snickers or sympathy, in either case a wound
to his pride.

LESS THAN A MONTH after the funeral, Papa remarried. Nobody
was surprised. He was still a handsome man; a square jaw, with
strong features that age well. His hair had gone gray at the
temples, and that, along with the jaunty, waxed tips of his
mustache, gave him a distinguished air. Though not a faithful
husband to my mother, he acted like an honorable man when he
married his Teresa. It's in the eyes, the quality of his honor; they're
the blue of first light, pure, piercing. And they're Ada's eyes too.

I did not go to the wedding, I heard about it from a neighbor.
He said that my father's bride was dressed in white even though

she had some years before given birth to their son. The boy followed his mother down the aisle, carrying the ring.

I was relieved that my father chose to stay in Rome with his second family. I did not want them in our house. Although I had nothing against Teresa, I loved my mother, her memory. It was too much to accept a stepmother. And so I arranged to have my things sent up from Napoli and stayed on in Firenze, moving into our palazzo, claiming it as my own.

9

Although Rico had not attended the funeral for my mother, he had sent flowers. He must have bought out some florist, so many wreaths had arrived that my mother had been buried in flowers before she was buried in earth. At the time, he was nearby, sequestered at Bellosguardo with the boys, so close, and yet I feared that he had cut us all off, the Giachettis, and that I would never see him again.

Then one afternoon there was a knock at my door. My heart quickened when I looked past a uniformed driver to the Britzia Zust, Rico's car, parked in front of the house. I was invited to visit him and my nephews at the estate. If I consented, the man would drive me there. Balding and stout, he was no Cesare. I asked him to wait and I changed into a lovely dress from my days as a prima donna, a dark one out of respect for my mother, but with the sheen of silk. I powdered my nose and pinched my cheeks.

IT WAS A BEAUTIFUL DAY, sun to warm the face, along with breezes to cool it. Poppies blazed in random spots of coral color in the vibrantly green fields. White bolls, the downy seed kites of poplars, were floating in the air. We drove from Firenze into the countryside. The gently sloped hills, the paler and gold-green of grape vines, the silver-green of olive trees, looked hazy in the distance.

I knew the gate so well, I found myself holding my breath when we came into view of the estate. As we entered and drove along the avenue bordered by cypress, a pheasant strutted along the road. As we neared, it lowered its head and raised its tail to run away into the trees.

In spite of the clement weather, the windows were all shuttered as if the house itself were grieving. The chauffeur opened the front door for me and I walked into the villa.

Rico and the boys were sitting quietly in the reception room. There was an air of mourning I could almost taste, the sour aftertaste of milk coating the tongue. They were dressed formally, all in dark suits, as if I was not Aunt Rina visiting, but a governess about to be interviewed. Or that's how I look back on it now. Then I was only relieved that I had put on one of my better dresses.

As soon as they saw me, the boys came to life. Fofò whooped with excitement and both boys rushed to embrace me. Rico rose slowly from his chair. I could see that he had been seated near a portrait of Ada with the boys. He smiled a smile without mirth. The boys were tugging at my arms to go outside. They wanted to play in the garden. Rico sent them out alone, saying, "Let me talk to your aunt Rina for a little while. Then we'll have ice cream and cookies." Glad to be released, they ran out to play in their good clothes.

"You see how your sister has left us. My boys are motherless now."

"Yes, I know. I'm sorry."

"I should have known better. If a woman will betray one man, she'll betray another. I should have learned from Botti's experience. I was a fool to believe in her." He never acknowledged that he—that we—might have been in part to blame for Ada's actions.

"I always thought she loved you, Rico. I remember that she once told me that other men were just 'desserts' to her. Or was it 'toys'?"

"What other men? She told me that I was all men to her! And I believed her."

I had spoken lightly, to ease the pain with a little joke, albeit a woman's joke, but Caruso was too bitter to see the humor in the idea of men as toys, of men on a menu, not if he thought his name was on it with others.

"The whole world is laughing at me. I no longer play Canio— I am Canio! *Ridi, pagliaccio*—laugh, clown, laugh, because everybody else is laughing at you! And maybe it won't hurt so much!" He turned to the picture by which he had been sitting, and with a sweep of his arm he knocked it to the floor where the glass shattered. That violent gesture, however symbolic, calmed him and he turned to me again.

"Rina, can I count on you? Or are you in every way your sister's sister? The boys love you, their aunt. They need a woman— they need family, not just schoolmasters and governesses. Will you live here with us? You will never need money again. This place will be yours to run as you please. When the season ends at the Metropolitan I will come back on the first boat and we will live the good life here together."

"And will you also leave with the first boat when the season recommences?"

"Don't start on that. Already you're talking like Ada. But you should know what a career demands."

"I'm sorry. Yes, I do know. I'll take care of everything for you."

10

If one summer long ago in Livorno I believed that I would have been happy even as a seamstress if I could have been Rico's seamstress, then I was happy living on his estate, part mistress, part housekeeper, and part governess. I took over the household at Bellosguardo and all the family responsibilities that had been my sister's; in effect, I became my sister. Even the children no longer thought of me as aunt. Fofò, now a boy of eleven, began calling me Mamma.

"You're nicer," he proclaimed. Then he ran out to play in the garden as children do.

Bellosguardo—Rico was the owner, but the true occupants were the servants and I. The money was too good in America; his fee per performance kept going up and up. It was to the Metropolitan Opera House in New York City that Rico was really married. He performed there through the long and cold winters of that northern republic. Then in May, with the end of the opera season, like a tourist, Rico returned to Italy, and like a tourist, he was gone again in September.

Oh, I was happy every summer, and I was even happy in the winter, waiting, keeping house for Rico while he was in New York. Fofò was in military school and only came home for holidays. Mimmi was being educated by an English governess in London, and like his father, he returned only in the summer.

Keeping house required little more than giving a few orders to the servants. During those many months I was alone at the estate, my heart hibernated. Art was that pain I could now do without.

I liked country life well enough even if there was nothing to do except play cards in the evening with neighbors. If I was restless at night, I didn't suffer; I took sleeping potions prescribed for me by the local doctor. He was the only young man among my card-playing companions. The doctor was a good-looking fellow who didn't mind losing at games; in fact, he claimed that he played Scopa just to watch me win.

Those months without Rico, I dined alone at that sumptuous banquet table built for fifty. I had my place set next to his big chair, and I had his place set too as if he was about to join me. I'd watch his portion of food get cold as I ate mine. That chair did not stay empty for so long because of lack of love on his part, or so I persuaded myself. Or so he convinced me. Memory is unreliable. Memory is made of mercury—what stays too long makes everything go black.

Time is made of mercury too. That much I have learned, that much has been confirmed in my days on earth. Time won't stay in the hand; it can't be grasped. What did not poison eluded me. And with age, time speeds up. What was a drip becomes a flow, then a flood. Months, a decade, sped by rapidly when each year was concentrated into three months of summer visits. Rico spent nearly as much time in the voyage on the Atlantic, crossing back and forth from America, as he spent at home with us. But still he returned once a year to touch his native soil, to recuperate his strength, to love those he loved here.

RICO AND I lived together those few months each year, but we were not openly lovers. We behaved discreetly because of the boys. I did not know my true place in his life then. He never invited me to go with him to America. And I pretended not to want to go, not to like the cold, when I would have followed him to the Arctic regions if he had only beckoned. I pressed him to spend more time in Italy instead.

"Why do you spend so much time in America?"

"They love me there."

"We love you here. As does all of Europe!"

"There are many Italians in New York City."

"But surely there are more Italians here!"

"Ah, but then they're not like me. They don't have to roam the earth to make a living."

I thought that, with time, the scandal about my sister would die down, and we could move into a normal life, into a marriage. But his bitterness, his humiliation, did not dissipate with the years. Or seeing me renewed it somehow.

"She left me like shit, not like a cat, an animal that has the sense to cover up with dirt what she dumps, but like a dog, a bitch, the mess all out in the open. The world steps into it and the streets in every city of the world reek of what she's done to me"; "It's too soon to marry. It would make the scandal worse. A man has his pride, Rina"; "It's too soon, Rina, my humiliation is too fresh. I can't act as other men act—not with the eyes of the world on me."

That was what I settled for, for nearly a decade.

Silently, I cursed not him, as perhaps I should have, but my sister, who would never return.

What kept us apart was his great fame. What kept us apart was his pride. With attentive audiences hanging on his every word, his every note, his shame was as public as his success. How could he marry me when I was Ada's sister?

But as for the town, the merchants, the neighbors, I let them think that I was Mrs. Caruso. I wore a gold band on the marriage finger; it was the only item among her portable jewels that Ada had left behind.

IN THE SUMMER of 1918 it was too dangerous to cross the Atlantic. German U-boats were prowling even in American waters. Although Italy was part of the war, in Tuscany it felt like a distant thing. The front was in the far northeast of the country, in the Alpine mountains that bordered on Austria. Our trenches were not made of mud and sandbags but carved out of hard stone or ice. Italian blood didn't flow freely there—it froze up.

As long as we had the harvest from our own fields, the shortages caused by the war did not affect us much at the estate until all the able-bodied men disappeared into the army and we the few, all women, children, and old men, were left to tend to it. That summer American regiments had joined our soldiers on the front while Rico stayed in New York City where the shooting to be done would be without casualties—he was starring in his first film.

His letters to me in those years were all about his performances, his reviews, even matters of his daily toilette, or they contained instructions or questions regarding the estate. They were not letters to read again, or to satisfy a romantic heart like mine. It was as if he had become another person, the great man, the king of tenors, that singing sun king who casts everybody else in his shadow. If my Rico, poor and humble and full of fun, was still alive somewhere inside him, he disappeared when Caruso dictated the letters he sent to me. Those letters were typed, I imagined, by his secretary. Underscored by the printed name Enrico Caruso, the only handwriting was in the signature, and it was barely legible.

II

The most important thing that summer he left out of his letters. I had to find out through newspapers. The war filled every page, and there among the names of the dead was a notice, a name that shocked me, shook me in a way that the list of anonymous names could not. I dropped the paper, but still the faces stared back at me from a photo of Enrico Caruso and his new bride, a young American socialite. The caption read: "A fairy-tale wedding for the king of tenors." All I knew of my rival then was that picture in newsprint, that grainy image. Caruso looked dramatic in black and white, his features and coloring were bold, but the woman was like a ghost in pale and paler shades of gray. I cursed her, wishing to send her back to the netherworld from which she came.

There was a sense of finality in this marriage. How could I explain this one away, even I who had become so good at explaining, at seeing only what I wanted to see? What could I hope for now that I had attached myself to a bigamist? Did I imagine an ocean was enough to separate the marital beds, that a man might have one in the old world and another in the new? Or that if he did not tell me it meant he could not break with me?

I stayed on at Bellosguardo and continued to oversee the estate, still hoping that Rico would come home and explain what I could not.

Io aspetto, io aspetto! Madama Butterfly waited for three years only to be told that her beloved had abandoned her, that he had married another woman. I knew about such waiting. I had sung it on stage, and it had not been cathartic. That was a lie I told myself. It had fed my desire, it had fanned the fire.

The villagers whispered to each other when I came in search of scarce supplies—somehow even scarcer after the war ended. The shopkeepers looked at me with arched brows. And yet I continued to wear his ring, really Ada's ring, until the following spring.

RICO DID NOT KILL ME himself, he sent Giovanni, his brother, to do it. On instructions from Caruso, Giovanni made the trip from Naples to Bellosguardo. I was surprised to see him because Giovanni had never before visited when Rico was not at the estate. I invited him in, asked a maid to make coffee for us. He sat down, but then immediately jumped up again, his hat in his hand.

"I'm sorry, but I did not come for a social visit." He played with the brim of the hat as he spoke, looking at it, not at me. He was not at all like Rico. He was taller, heavier, and slow of speech. Giovanni lived well on an allowance from Rico, but he had none of the polish, none of the refinement, that a life of luxury and leisure can bring. That such a life brought to Rico who became as Caruso a man of high culture, a man who commanded respect. So although Giovanni wore a well-made suit, he didn't wear it as if it belonged to him, it looked rented.

"Is anything wrong? You have news of Rico?"

"I have a telegram with orders from him. You're to leave the estate as soon as possible—and for good. You must clear out all your things. He's on his way back with his American bride. She's expecting his child and he wants to bring her here to live."

I started to weep. Again another woman was having his child, no sister this time, but a stranger—another woman who was not me.

"He said not to pay attention to your tears. He said he has his spies, and he's known about your young doctor all along."

"But there's nothing to that, it's innocent. Did his spy play cards with us, then?" My tears were turning to outrage. "All right then. I'm leaving. If this is how he rewards my love, my loyalty, I'll see him in hell before I see him again!"

When did Rico start buying and selling off people, when did all we who knew and loved him become his servants? Hired, then fired. His fame was a gift like Midas's: everybody he touched turned to gold, and could be easily bought or sold.

The drama that had been my love, my life, had ended for good.

12

A woman, as she approaches forty, either matures or lives out her life as a girl. I chose to retire from that life of drama, of tragedy and unrequited love, first onstage, then off. When I returned to Firenze, and now that I was free, I allowed myself to be consoled by the young doctor. I had learned the value of consolation. He would have married me, but from what I had seen of marriage in my family, I preferred not to.

I traded in happiness for contentment. Content. When I was that young and innocent girl I might have despised this choice, this diminishment to a life of slow days, calm and orderly and unsullied by the highs and lows of passion.

Although it was far less lucrative work than what I had been used to on the stage, I began to offer singing lessons to children. I didn't need to teach. I was comfortable enough financially; I had the palazzo as well as the proceeds from my earnings on the stage, which, thanks to Roberto, had been wisely invested for me.

I think that I would have taught them even without pay, just to listen to the trill of their voices, although sometimes what their mouths produced was less like singing than the squealing chalk makes across a blackboard. Still, I loved those children, their lacquered heads, their ringlets, especially the boys; or I loved the young nephews they reminded me of.

MEMORY IS MADE OF MERCURY. But the memory of Rico in the world is made of shellac. The voice I thought was unforgettable—that the world itself called unforgettable—has been displaced for me by Enrico Caruso's recorded music. What is my mind, my memory, against the millions of recordings? I lose my Rico in a hall of mirrors where there are only reflections of reflections, never the real man, never breath from that voice to cloud the mirrors. All I know of his singing now is what anybody else can know: the recordings of his operatic repertoire, what can be heard on the radio, or perhaps through the open window of some stranger's home, when a Caruso record is playing as you pass by.

But once upon a time there was a man known as Rico—I don't think anybody still knows him as I did, a man who whispered to me one summer afternoon, who whispered my name. He found music in its two syllables and half sang them into my ear. We had eaten good bread under the shining of the Tuscan sun, we had drunk red wine, a whole bottle of it, and we had opened our mouths to each other's tongues. When I try to recall the sound of his murmurings in my ear, the cawing of crows is still much louder. That cawing is like the scratching at the end of the disc, at the end all that remains of the song.

I could never hear the things that he heard, not the slapping of the baker's hand within the bread that we ate, not the drifting into dreams of sleeping children, not the spinning of spiders, but he seemed to reach into those elusive worlds and their ephemeral sounds, and then, as he sang, he made their music resound from his own lips. He told me to listen, and I had listened, I had tried, but in those days all I could truly hear was myself.

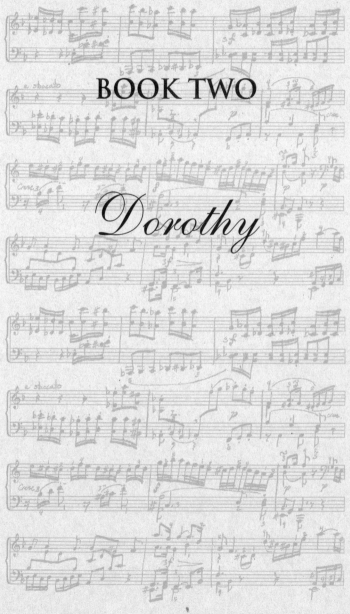

BOOK TWO

Dorothy

An American Fairy Tale

Una volta c'era un re,
Che a star solo,
Che a star solo s'annoio

Once upon a time there was a king,
Who was lonely,
Who was tired of being lonely
—ROSSINI, *LA CENERENTOLA*

I

The dreary rains of November seep into December. Rain or fog in the early morning and a sun, if it shines at all, that sleeps in late and retires early. The year, 1917, was ending. In a few short weeks it would be Christmas. The shops were decorated with holly, their red seeds and green waxy leaves glistened, signaling an end to the bleakness of the season. In spite of the chilling dampness, the rain, I walked along Fifth Avenue, up and down a mile-long stretch of shops and department stores, lingering under the awnings and admiring the window displays. The color, the richness, and the variety of objects offered for sale was astonishing. The rain, just a drizzle really, was turning to snow as I stood in front of a shop specializing in gowns imported from Paris, France, and dreamed before the impossibly thin woman, not a woman at all but a mannequin, dressed in a midnight-blue gown with rhinestones mimicking stars on the form-fitted bodice.

Since noon I had been walking under the endless gray of sky and in the shadow of concrete and steel towers. The farther south I wandered, the higher the buildings and the darker the shadows cast by the skyscrapers. As I approached the core of the city, I was caught up in crowds of other pedestrians. As if I had stepped into a river, I felt overwhelmed by the force of their rushing. I had to make my way against the pull and push of other people.

At Thirty-fourth Street I crossed the road and turned to walk back north where I could breathe more freely again. I was no longer strolling, now like everybody else I was hurrying. Until a door opened from a shop near Forty-second Street, and a beatific singing, *"Glo-ri-a, gloria in excelsis de-e-o,"* floated out into the street and I slowed my pace. The music seemed to have opened up more space on the street, another dimension, and I could breathe again. The voice drew me to the store.

I stopped at the window of a shop specializing in recorded music. Victrolas, known as the amazing talking machines, both the hand crank and electric kind, were displayed in the window along with a number of Victor records in a fan shape around a large photo of the Metropolitan Opera's leading star, Enrico Caruso. The caption read: "Does Caruso thrill you? Buy the RCA

Victrola now and listen to the king of tenors singing in your parlor this Christmas morning!"

I studied the photo trying to see what it was about this man that might thrill anybody. Caruso was dressed all in white, in what looked like silk by its sheen although his costume was that of a clown, an expensive clown. The face was dark yet smiling— the lips were stretched in a smile, but the eyes were very somber. I recognized the image. This was the face of fame; it was everywhere, in newspapers, in magazines, and in newsreels at the picture shows. But it was a full and dimpled face, one that did not much suit a hero, ready to kill or be killed in a musical drama. It was easier to imagine Caruso standing in for Father Christmas.

There was a lineup in the shop. Women and men, all with the latest Caruso disc in their hands, were waiting to pay. Inside I could hear the nuance and richness of the voice, and when the refrain was sung, it filled the room—*"Gloria, gloria, gloria in excelsis de-e-o"*—it was such a full voice, powerful, palpable, I felt embraced by it. The carol warmed me even more than the central heating in the shop. There must have been angels marveling on high that such a voice could be singing here on earth.

Only the crass and repeated ringing of the cash register interfered with the song. The shoppers were patient in their queue, as if waiting to receive Holy Communion. The cash register rang again, the money drawer slammed shut, and the line inched up. But it didn't get any shorter as others joined it. The picture from the window, that face, stared back at me from a stack of postcards. After paying, each customer walked away with a record along with a souvenir picture of the star. I felt that I too must have this Caruso in my living room on Christmas morning. I joined the lineup and, with the last of my pocket money, bought my first disc.

SNOW BEGAN TO FALL more thickly, heavily, with water in its weight. The snow would gradually smooth over the rough edges of the city, cover the soot, tamp down the noise. The wind was blowing white now. It was snowing and it was expected to snow into evening. By morning the gray, the concrete city, would be white, an icy metropolis with its streets voluptuously rounded by the falling, by the fallen snow. And people would wake to a renewed, if constricted, sense of nature and the wild, as if the zoo in Central Park expanded its boundaries overnight and the whole city had turned into a cage for polar bears.

I STEPPED ONTO THE RUBBER MAT in the vestibule and out of my galoshes. The boots were serviceable, they were not the high-heeled, buttoned-up-to-the-ankle, leather ones that other young women were wearing about town. Still, my feet were protected. I appreciated small things like dry warm feet in winter.

As I bent down to pull my shoes out from the boots, snow fell lightly onto the mat. I unbuttoned my coat, the beige camel I had been wearing for the third season then, and slipped out of the sleeves. In the blowing heat of the vent, as the snow quickly melted, I breathed in the musty smell of wet wool. After giving the whole length of the material a vigorous brushing, I hung up the coat to dry. It was a good coat, woven in British mills and cut with craftsmanship, but it was my only coat.

In the parlor the fire was down to a few glowing embers. I went to the window to pull back the drapes a little farther. I wanted light but the luminescence of snow was dimming, lost in the lengthening shadows. As I approached the hearth, I caught sight of my image in the mirror above the mantel. I saw a modern girl, her hair short, bobbed just above the shoulders, and parted on one side. My blonde hair, streaked with snow, looked almost white. It was curling with the humidity released by the melting snow. Would I look like this when I became old, the same square face, the same white-and-red-flushed skin, but with a few wrinkles added on? I was imagining myself old although I had yet to be young. Whatever the twenty-four years of my birth certificate might suggest, in experience I was more like a seventeen-year-old girl than a woman.

Time could not move quickly enough for me; it lagged behind the ticking of the grandfather clock it was my duty to wind. I was bored. I was a comatose patient—not a princess—asleep in my father's house. Or worse, trapped in the cloistered space of the kitchen where it was perpetually morning and my father would be demanding perfectly cooked eggs.

"What was it you used? An hourglass? Is this your idea of a soft-boiled egg? I could bloody well play bloody golf with the yolk!"

My eyes in the mirror and the eyes in the picture on the mantel below it were the same shape, but the look in them was very different. The photograph was a portrait of my mother taken before she was a mother. It was almost lost in the collection of ornamental figurines: Venetian glass and bone china animals formed a kind of menagerie around my mother's serene and glowing face. It was the face of a young woman in love, a fiancée, and it was signed as if by a starlet, dedicated "To Park, with love." My father, Park Benjamin, the second, was already a distinguished man then, a scientific writer, a lawyer, and a veteran of the Civil War.

The pewter frame enhanced the darker tones in the photograph, its grays and shadows, while the whites, the light, appeared murky. I remembered the blue of my mother's eyes, their allure of lapis. But in the photo the eyes were neutral in tone, sky when it is overcast.

My mother was smiling in the photo. I remembered she used to smile a lot, and there were laugh lines around her mouth to prove it. I picked up the picture and ran my fingers tenderly across that mouth. What I touched of course was not flesh, but glass. Closing my eyes, I tried to recall if and when my mother laughed. Certainly not at breakfast when a maid would serve the coffee and eggs and Father sat behind a screen of newsprint. She never laughed then. Father did not like his reading of the paper disturbed. Only the tinkling of a piano from the radio, set at low volume, was permitted.

Father had been forty-five and a widower with three grown children when he married the glamorous young woman my mother was then. He loved Mother very much, but was perhaps not so happy to have young children again. He was jealous of his wife; even of the time she might spend with us. So my older brother and I were sequestered away in the nursery, left in the company of servants for most of the day. We were only allowed to see our parents at breakfast and in the evening at the dinner table.

It was on the once-frequent occasions when Father played host to his colleagues that they laughed. Our home would be transformed then. At these dinner parties Mother's laughter would bubble forth like champagne, precipitously uncorked. The house was festive, almost noisy. And we children were allowed to eat with the guests at the table, although we were sent to bed promptly enough after dessert had been served.

Throughout dinner Father would lavishly pour wine as his guests made witty remarks.

Unlike most of the visitors, there was one, a Professor Pupin, who could more than tolerate children. This rotund little man was a physicist and inventor who kept his sense of wonder at the natural world.

"Consider this, my friends. You think that the cow is a stupid animal, but the greatest scientists in the world have yet to discover how to turn grass into milk."

Dr. Pupin was an immigrant from Serbia. He wasn't fashionable. His clothes looked slept in and smelled of wine-dipped tobacco. His frizzy white hair formed an aura around his head. Whenever the professor came to the house, he stopped at the nursery first with treats for us children. I liked the licorice best, red or black, the long twisted ropes of it. Pulling the bag of candy from an inner pocket of his jacket, he'd shush us to secrecy. Yes, I remembered Mother laughing then at his joke, as they called it, and turning to Father, her eyebrows forming an amused pyramid.

"If we can fly like birds now, Michael, I wouldn't be surprised if one day we manage to turn grass into milk too. Shall we toast the possibilities? To science! To birds! And to all manner of flying machines!"

"To the birds, by golly! I, for one, will not be impressed until we can fly farther than our feathered brethren," Dr. Pupin chuckled. "To the moon even!"

"I agree. But let's see us get across the Atlantic in one of those contraptions first." Father laughed as they all clinked glasses. "You know, Michael, I'm beginning to think those black cattle on your farm in Connecticut are more of a marvel to you than horseless carriages, airships, or wireless communications. I know you talk to your cows, but when you tell me that they're talking back—why, then I'll just have to ask you to resign from the Scientific American Society. As a member I have standards to uphold, you know."

His threats were mock threats then, mock severity, from a mock bully. Dr. Pupin blinked myopically while Father continued to laugh amiably at his friend's expression of dismay.

"It's a joke, old man. It's just a joke. I'm having a little fun— at your expense, of course."

In fact, they were all laughing around the table, all the adults, except for Pupin, that is. But if a joke had been made, then I didn't understand it either. What Dr. Pupin had said about cows made sense to me. I imagined the difference between nature and science as the difference between miracles and magic tricks. Houdini might be able to pull a rabbit out of a hat, and more, but he couldn't feed everybody in the audience with it. But Jesus, the Son of God, pulled miracles out of people, not hats.

I UNDERSTOOD ANALOGIES well enough, I understood relationships, but the thing in itself resisted all the probing of the mind and remained inscrutable. Science didn't have the answer yet, so it required metaphysics to probe beyond the surface. And what about that girl in the mirror, what sort of thing was she—an awkward flightless bird like an ostrich or a dodo? Even my own face was a mystery to me; it seemed as impenetrable as any anonymous lump of matter. Sometimes I felt as if I lived outside my own body, that I was a pair of thick horn-rimmed glasses with warped frames. Not capable of seeing well, nor worth being seen.

THE PHOTOGRAPH IN MY HAND was a poor facsimile of the woman I remembered, it was not really at all like Mother. It was merely the product of a process, silver nitrate reacting to light, to darkness, something like that, a chemical enigma or visual illusion to rival the Old Masters. I didn't understand the physics of it, the workings of the mechanisms that made up the world around me. I knew that there was a switch for light, that there was a measure for time. But even the familiar grandfather clock ticking in front of me was estranging in its operations. Even though I wound it up, I could not know it. No matter how precisely the Swiss springs and wheels operated, the clock would be obscured by an opaque and glutinous substance called Time which gummed up the works. It slowed the thing down. It would stop it eventually, that I did know. But this was not scientific thinking. If Father could overhear thoughts, he would be irritated. He was a man of science, a writer of books on electricity. He knew so much, and he did not tolerate fools—that's what he called most people, particularly those who did not agree with him.

When Father and I would sit together around the fire, I was expected to engage in conversation, to provide the companionship he missed since Mother was gone. Though I listened attentively, I hardly knew how to respond to his rants without infuriating him. Silence seemed safer.

"If you must be so dull, you might at least make yourself pretty." He looked at me hard. "You don't look a bit like your mother. It's hopeless—with those hulking shoulders, you could play Rugby! And what sort of man would ever want to tackle the likes of a teammate in bed?"

I would retreat to my room then, ears burning, and write in my diary. Writing and reading were the acts that saved me. In writing, I could express thoughts freely; in reading, I could commune with other minds, minds more open than that of

Father. The years spent studying at the Convent of the Sacred Heart, if austere, seemed blessedly benign in contrast to life at home with him.

I was only eleven when Mother first became ill. For what my parents believed was a short-term stay, I had been sent to a Catholic boarding school. I remained there until it became clear that Mother would never be able to leave the sanatorium. Father was sick of living alone by then, and embittered by it. He ordered me to return home. But after so many years among the nuns, Father was a stranger to me. Nor did he find in me a satisfactory stand-in for his beautiful wife.

A SOUPÇON OF WARMTH, a soupçon of color, orange-red among the grays of winter light, the beige tones of the walls, the dark oak of the furniture. The fire offered no real light now and barely perceptible heat. As for love, I who had never known it scratched among the cinders while Caruso's *"Gloria"* resounded from the player for the third time. I wasn't going to play the song again just then, afraid of losing the music through overfamiliarity. The mind stops listening to what it thinks it already knows. Instead I added more logs to the fire. The crackling flames seemed an echo of the sound of static at the end of the recording. Using old newspapers as kindling, I watched words blaze up, military words of battles and the deaths of American soldiers, I watched sheets of paper curl into black ash. My cheeks were burning with cold, not warmth. The chill persisted in spite of the fire, in spite of hot air blowing in full force from the vents. The warmth failed to reach me, or failed to penetrate. I felt like tea in a vacuum flask, frozen, where it should have been kept warm. The fire began to heat my skin, the exterior, but inside there was numbness, there was hypothermia, there was a lost child locked away in a dank basement room.

THE GRINDING OF A KEY turning in the lock startled me. In the mirror I saw the nervous flutter in my right eye. My mouth opened, but I was unable to speak. From the mirror a pale young woman looked at me with dread as she clutched an ornately framed photo to her ample bosom.

His voice was the stomping of heavy boots.

"What kind of hell is this? You call this weather!" He raged as he shook the snow from his coat, kicked off his boots. I was bent over, feeding the fire again, when he entered the room and tapped me on the shoulder with his folded newspaper. I turned around but kept my eyes lowered and focused on his tweed jacket, on the braided leather buttons. I could see without looking how his lips curled, his mouth tightened, and his jaw stiffened whenever he spoke to me. He had wanted a sophisticated woman for a daughter, not a bookish girl. When I failed to shine at his side in society, his disappointment in me led to contempt.

"What's for dinner tonight?" He was a tall and very thin man, but he liked his food. He liked his tobacco along with a glass of good cognac, or two.

"Lamb with mint sauce. Rice. Green beans."

"Lamb again! But I wanted steak. You know I prefer steak. Are you trying to starve me?" He stormed to the study with pipe in hand and the newspaper folded under his arm.

"But must we eat steak every day?" My response was not audible over the slamming of the door.

2

Miss B, "Bibi" as Father had dubbed her, returned from shopping on her afternoon off, her plump arms piled with packages. She was a petite woman in her thirties, buxom and bubbly, moving constantly in a flurry of ribbons and laces. Bibi was spontaneous, lively, and confident, pleased with herself and the world; she was everything that I was not. Six years before, she had been a governess in the household of one of Father's colleagues. But Father had lured her away easily enough when he offered her a position as companion to a young adult daughter. Miss B had agreed at once. Such an eminent man—she had declared that it was far more interesting than caring for three small children.

"If I don't get these presents into the mail soon, my family will be very disappointed. Oh, but I'm so cold—and hungry too!" She rubbed her hands before the hearth to warm them. Then she turned her back to the blaze and lifted up her wide skirt a little at the back.

The lamb was still in the icebox. I was dreading another scene. What would incite Father more—no dinner at all or the smell of roasting lamb when he wanted steak?

The sweetness of pipe tobacco was a sign that Father had returned to the parlor. The presence of Miss B always brought out the Master, as I sometimes thought of him—a harsh character from Dickens in a novel about orphans. But with the hired companion, he was someone else; with her, he smiled affably.

"Dorothy is neglecting her duties. It looks like there'll be no dinner on the table tonight." He spoke as if I were not in the room. "Some form of compensation is in order, I should think, and I've been given two tickets to the Met for tonight. Caruso is singing in *Carmen*. But before that we have to eat something. What would you say, Miss B, to dining at the University Club and then accompanying me to the opera this evening?"

"Caruso! They all say his voice is magnificent! They say it's a throat lined in velvet!"

"'The greatest tenor in the world, the voice of the century'— and there's still eighty-three years to go in it. That's a hefty reputation. But can he live up to it?"

Nobody looked at me, not the Master, not my so-called companion, who had usurped my role as the lady of the house and now accompanied Father to the theater and to concerts. The Master loved music and Miss B was a musician of sorts; she studied voice and occasionally sang in amateur productions.

I loved the voice singing the carol, but I had only ever been to the opera once in my life, a matinee production of *Lohengrin* when I was a child. I held Mother's hand as I listened so the music was softened; it was filtered through the lace ruffles at Mother's wrists and scented with the rosewater and glycerin she used to moisturize her hands. Opera needed that to be enjoyed; it needed listening that was like looking from behind a fan. Otherwise it was an assault on the senses; it was a lot of shouting that the world called singing. Only the memory of the warmth of her hand enabled me to recall that day with much pleasure.

In any case, I did not begrudge the favors Father bestowed on Miss B.

"Oh, the joy of it! *So-no for-tu-na-taaa!*" Bibi sang the Italian words in her speech as if they could not be uttered unless sung. She shook out her skirt and smoothed it at the hips. "Oh, look at what I'm wearing! This old thing! I must change at once—and into my finest gown. Although, you know, to see Caruso perform, my best won't be good enough."

As she spoke the former governess did not look at me, her employer's daughter whose wardrobe was more meager, and certainly plainer, than her own. The Master was a man who had to be pried for money. It was not worth the humiliation to ask him. I preferred to make do with what I had. Perhaps Miss B hoped for a Christmas bonus. Hopes made her buoyant, she danced around the room, swirled her ruffled skirt.

"Caruso has a voice that makes you swoon. And he's Italian, like me! Do-re-me-faaaa … do-re-me-fa-la-teeee …"

"Well, that's settled then." Although he had half turned his head to speak to me, he didn't actually look at me. I could not step into such dainty and fashionable shoes.

I sank more deeply into the armchair, as if my blondeness in the wheat-colored brocade of the upholstery might offer camouflage. My eyes stayed focused on my lap, on the embossed words on the binding of my book. My fingers were white in their fierce gripping of the volume.

"As you wish, Father."

IN FAIRY TALES it's the stepmothers, the stepsisters, who are cruel. Fathers are not unkind. If they neglect their daughters, it's because they have died or they must travel on business. And because they are absent, they fail to protect. They are not unkind by nature; they are not unnatural. Not in the versions I was familiar with, and Rossini's *La Cenerentola* was not then among them.

But Bibi was not cruel. She merely enjoyed what was given to her; she didn't question it. And I was glad to have her living with us because she livened up the household. Since the Italian woman moved in with us, music and laughter could be heard in our home again. Now the Master would often play the Pianola to accompany Bibi as she rehearsed her arias. How he would pump and pump for her. Those evenings of music now tempered the ominous gong of the grandfather clock at ten, the tapping of the Master's pipe as he emptied it before switching off all the lights. Since Bibi had joined the household there were more lights, including the best of the beeswax candles, burning past ten.

After the Master and Bibi had gone out for the evening, I returned to tend the hearth. I felt left out of the family party, and very much alone, but fire can be good company. I found solace in that. I stirred the embers, added logs, watched the flames rise higher, licking then engulfing the wood. While Father and Bibi were seated before the stylized sets at the Metropolitan Opera, I attended a private and inchoate concert of crackling, of sputtering, of the heaving and collapsing weight of burning logs. The beauty of sound composed by something rather than someone—music without the burden of lyrics or of melody, music without the burden of interpretation was what I liked best.

3

When the Master and Bibi returned from the opera that night, I was in the kitchen warming up some milk to help me sleep. But if I had been asleep, Bibi's very vocal enthusiasm for Caruso's singing—"Oh, he sings, he sings, and the sound is like a golden light, if light were honey and pouring into your ears"—would have woken me and drawn me from bed to listen to such giddy praise. Bibi seemed drunk on some sort of choral champagne.

And the Master, a man of the most rigorous standards, also extravagantly praised the tenor.

"Tonight's *Carmen* is the first production I've ever seen that wasn't a flop. And it's Caruso that made it work. He's got something more than any other tenor I've ever heard—dramatic power. Others complain that the Met has turned into a circus since he's become the mainstay of the house. But I ask you, why argue with success?"

"Nobody argues with that, Signor Benjamin. They just ask for more and more from him. He has twelve roles to play this season! Do they want to wear him out?"

"You know that's because of the goddamn war. Nobody wants to listen to German sung anymore and that's created huge holes in the programming. Luckily our indomitable tenor is man and voice enough to carry it off."

"Caruso is the greatest. Who needs to listen to Wagner?"

"I hope they don't stop playing Bach or Mozart on the radio. Music is hardly responsible for this war," I protested.

"I suppose you think that our men are dying to listen to the Schubert or some such the Krauts play along with the bullets they send whizzing into their midst. You might think twice before you spoke, Dorothy, if you spent any time in those trenches in Europe. Tell me, are you loyal to this country? If you go into a diner, what do you order? A frankfurter or a hotdog?"

"Why, Father, I would order neither. Perhaps tea and toast, unless tea means I'm being disloyal because of the revolutionary war."

"You're making light of it, Dorothy, but this is a serious matter. We need to purge our language of these German influences."

"Nobody wanted to leave the opera house, Dorothy. Nobody even remembered the war or their suppers. We clapped and clapped. My hands are still red from clapping."

"They wouldn't let the poor bloke leave the stage. The audience demanded encore after encore. And I too found myself standing up and roaring for more along with the crowd. You had to. If you tried to stay seated, your neighbors would poke you until you joined in the clamor!"

"How astonishing. Was he really so wonderful?"

"Not until Caruso sang the Star-Spangled Banner and asked us all to join in did the audience relent. I must say he really has a way with the crowd. He managed to end the evening and keep everybody happy."

4

"It sounds grand. I wish I could have heard him sing too." This lament was addressed to Bibi alone the next morning. I had felt it keenly the night before, but my feelings and wishes were not to be shared with Father.

"But why not, Dorothy, when there are many performances to choose from? Caruso, why, he is married to the Metropolitan! In New York City we are so lucky, so very lucky because there are countless opportunities to hear him."

I BROODED ALL THAT MORNING, playing the Caruso record and listening as I combed through journals and papers looking for reviews of *Carmen*. I found a story in a magazine that declared that the spark was gone from the Caruso and Farrar duo. The article included a large photo of the beautiful soprano who was also a silent-screen star, and on another page a picture of the two singers together onstage. Caruso looked robust next to the fragile-looking Farrar. The writer complained that the current *Carmen* lacked the excitement of an earlier production, an excitement apparently not scripted in the libretto. The soprano had resoundingly slapped Caruso and drawn blood with her nails. Then she had bitten his ear. Protesting that this was an opera and not one of Farrar's movies, Caruso had pushed the soprano to the ground with such force that she had bounced!

Opera, was this what was meant by high art, this Punch and Judy act of knocks and blows? Was this the man that the whole world raved about as "king of tenors"? Was this the man with the velvet throat? Singing the carol, he sounded like an angel, not a thug.

I resolved to judge for myself whether this Caruso was indeed a musical genius or some rowdy prankster. I planned to attend the next afternoon's performance of *Carmen*. The only obstacle was money. My allowance was meager, and besides that, I had already spent it.

THE GRANDFATHER CLOCK STRUCK NOON. Its sound was muffled compared to the tom-tom of my heart, drumbeats in a civil war, as I turned the knob of the door to Father's study. From the bibelot cabinet I selected a silver windmill. After the Master's brief murmurings of satisfaction as he accepted them, such gifts were placed in the display case and forgotten. Although he liked to collect the baubles, he took no active pleasure in them. No touching, no inventory, would uncover my small theft. The biggest risk was in my impulse to confess even as I was about to take the trinket.

At the pawnshop, I found myself clutching the windmill so fiercely that my hand was rigidly locked. I had to pry my fingers apart to show the piece to the clerk. Its edges left a red welt on my palm. The clerk looked up at me from across the rim of his visor, as if he guessed what I had done.

"I'll give you a dollar."

"But …"

"Take it or leave it, miss."

I took the dollar; it was just enough to buy the cheapest of the tickets available for that afternoon's performance of *Carmen*, standing room only at the Met. That placed me in the peanut gallery at the farthest remove from the stage, where I was surrounded by swarthy, restless men smelling of garlic and stale tobacco. They all had their lunches with them, in brown paper bags.

The curtain went up. The setting for the opera was Spain, the city of Seville, staged with a painted backdrop of misty-blue hills, stucco walls, and a large brown door to the far right of the stage to suggest the entrance to a cigarette factory. The music, the singing, had begun but the men kept whispering to each other. They knew the opera very well, or they had seen it many times before. "Caruso," "Caruso" was the name repeated on their lips although the tenor had yet to make his entrance on stage.

The men continued whispering to each other until Caruso entered as Don José near the end of the first scene. He was dressed as a soldier; on stage he was a soldier among soldiers. Gold glinted from his uniform under the spotlights. I was too far from the stage to really make out the features of his face or the details of his costume, but the lights loved the tenor. He was not taller than the others; he was clearly smaller, yet some centrifugal force seemed to emanate from him, and before Caruso so much as sang a note the audience rose in a standing ovation. And those who were already standing around me in the peanut gallery jumped up and down to show their enthusiasm for the tenor. They applauded the reputation before they listened to the singing.

"*Une jolie fille* ... " was the first phrase Caruso sang, posed as a question. It was about the girl in the blue dress, Micaela, who was not played by Farrar, but by Frances Alda. Loving and dutiful, Micaela was not the one in the story who would make Don José go mad for love and jealousy.

Farrar, the screen siren, was singing the role of Carmen, the gypsy beauty. She moved with swaying hips, flicking up the hem of her flaring skirt at the soldiers as she sang to them; her coquetry, her allure was palpable. This was the kind of woman men wanted, I thought, not convent school girls like me who liked to scribble by the fire in their notebooks.

"No wonder Caruso loves her," whispered one man to another, confounding the singer and the role, "it's the cigarettes he wants. Or why pick the tobacco slut over that real sweetheart his mother sends him."

"Yea, who wouldn't rather be first at the trough?" What they said was very crude, though it was reassuring to hear that innocence had its own kind of allure—if these rough men could be an example of all men.

Constantly jostled about by the men, it was hard for me to concentrate on the singing. I had to shrink into myself to avoid their elbows as they clapped and shouted, "Bravo!" Somehow I was as locked out of the experience at the theater as I had been at home the night before, when I listened to Bibi and the Master. I could not add to their accolades for Caruso with a true response of my own. At the back of the hall where I was standing, the clapping, the roaring applause, was louder than the singing.

There were no improvisations that day, no rough stuff—I was relieved about that—but there was also no magic, no luminous moment to make it all worthwhile. Was it guilt that prevented me from enjoying the opera? Or fear that Father might find out? Or the panic, the sudden realization that all I had in the kitchen to prepare for dinner again was the lamb from the night before. While everyone around me was enjoying the opera, I was thinking about recipes, and praying for an alchemical formula to turn lamb into sirloin.

5

Eight days passed without a glimmer of sun, just light snow and freezing rain. Monday becoming Monday as if there were no other day except the bleak beginning of the week, again and again. When I ventured out for groceries, I felt the weight of the sky overhead. The tops of the tallest buildings were lost in gray clouds. The skyscrapers looked more like skewers than scrapers, or like giant hooks dragging the sky down.

As the light seemed so leaden, so weak, I kept the lamps on even in the afternoon. I tended the fire constantly for its light as well as its warmth, read and wrote in my notebook, stared out the window hoping for even the slightest break in the weather so that I might at least take a walk in Central Park, walk in that now white world dreaming of green.

From the slim volume of poetry in German I was reading, I copied some lines I liked into my diary. *"Diese Muhsal, durch noch Ungetanes ..."* The swan's awkwardness was something I could identify with. Stepping from land and into water, the swan turned her waddling into gliding. The transformation was achieved, not by a change in the creature itself, but by a change in its environment. This was the only kind of makeover I could reasonably hope for. No miracle, no dieting, what I needed perhaps was to be transported back in time. Women were heavier at the end of the last century, plump used to be considered pleasing. Then I might have floated through life, perhaps even served as a model for an Impressionist painter. But no, I lived in a photographic era. I was a swan among ducklings. And so I stumbled, a stranger to grace, a stranger to beauty. But in the mercurial waters of my imagination, I moved lithely; in my mind, I soared.

Bibi entered the room humming. "Ah, Dorothy, there you are. I wanted to speak to you—to ask you a very, very special favor."

"Certainly. What is it?" Welcoming the diversion, I shut my book and capped my pen.

"I'm going to a christening for the sweetest baby girl—you should see her! She's got curls, black curls, and she was born with them! The father is my *professore*—the one I take singing lessons from—you know, he's very famous. Everybody knows he's the best. But better than that, if you can imagine the good fortune of this child, Enrico Caruso is to be her godfather! There's no doubt now she'll grow up to be a diva!"

"How exciting ..."

"But what I need to ask you—they asked me—to borrow some spoons for the reception."

"Yes, I'd be glad to. I have a set of silver spoons that were my grandmother's they could use. They're among my dearest treasures. But, Bibi, I'm so bored, it would be good to just get out, to meet some people. May I please attend the reception with you?" There was a warmth in Bibi I loved. I imagined a party of people like her, and felt desperate to go.

"But of course, you'll be most welcome. For a *festa,* the more people, the better we Italians like it. But, Dorothy, I must go to the church service first, so I cannot accompany you. Could you go to the house by yourself and deliver the spoons? I will tell Clara, the *professore*'s wife, to expect you. Now I must hurry to make myself bea-u-ti-ful!"

IMAGINING THE DAY had brightened, I switched off the lamp. A celebration, a new experience, people, people who might receive me with warmth, and something, perhaps even someone, unexpected. I felt a fluttering in my midsection.

Bibi had written out the address for the party, a house in East Harlem, along with instructions on how to get there. I wrote a brief note of explanation for Father and left it on his desk in the library.

And make myself bea-u-ti-ful—transform myself with a dab of toilet water and one or the other of my two good blue dresses. I chose the pastel-colored silk over the wool, and wore a matching hat with a deep brim. I loved the hat. Tilting it to one side, then another, I experimented with the look. Tipped forward, it cast a shadow across my face and suggested mystery. That would be best. I practiced looking around the room, my face half hidden by the hat. At last I was ready for an experience.

Arriving on time and so arriving early, only the catering people were at the house to greet me. They were expecting the spoons.

I lingered by the top of the stairs at the entrance. When Bibi arrived I hoped to feel more at ease.

A jumble of voices, a gabble of syllables, a mush of different languages, as a crowd of people, the party, came in all at once.

I saw the overcoat before I saw the man. It was charcoal colored with a thick fur collar. The coat dwarfed the owner. After a few steps, the coat paused and a face turned and looked up at me. The man took off his hat and kept looking at me, a long unbroken gaze. Strangely, I felt as if I knew him, that somehow I had known him all my life.

As he had paused, so his entourage also paused. The whole party seemed to be waiting to follow him up. Now that his hat was off, I could see his face. It was wide-jawed, and the lips were parted as if he was about to say something. Or was it the beginning of a smile? His eyes were dark, liquid and receptive. His hair was dark too and thinning, his cleft chin full. In the moment, in the suspended movement, one foot on the first of the steps, one hand on the banister, the other holding a black bowler hat, something passed between us—a music without notes, unheard by anybody else.

When suddenly everybody started talking again I realized that I had been holding my breath. Then the man and Bibi both appeared at my side.

"*La signorina è la figlia del mio patrone. Si chiama Dorothy.*"

"Dorothy, it's a great pleasure to meet you."

"I'm charmed, but ..." I stuttered with embarrassment, "s-sorry, I didn't catch your name."

The man laughed merrily. He seemed as amused as he was surprised that I did not know his name.

Bibi knocked at her forehead and whispered in an aside to me, "*Cretina,* this is he!" Then turning to the man in the coat, *"Scusi, signore. Lei non conosce nessuno!"* She seemed to be apologizing.

"My name, my sweet lady, is Enrico"—he tapped his heels lightly and made a quick, half bow—"Enrico Caruso, at your service, signorina." He took my hand and kissed it. His breath was hot, but the kiss made me shiver. He was so gracious as if in not recognizing him I had paid him the most rare, the sincerest of compliments.

I was dumbfounded and tried in my mind to match the face of the man speaking to me with the photo from the music shop, the clown dressed in white silk. What did he think of me, perhaps the only person in the whole of New York City not to recognize him?

"Abito con Lei, nella casa di Suo padre. Sono la Sua compagnia, ma veramente vivo per la musica, per il bel canto."

Caruso was nodding politely to Bibi as she spoke, but he kept turning his attention back to me. Our eyes met. His were brown, a brown so dark they seemed black: they did not reflect back, they did not seem to judge, but they took me in, with warmth, as into an embrace.

"The weather, she is not very fine, Miss Dorothy." A smile played on his lips. He spoke of the weather, but behind the ordinary words there seemed to be so much more, behind ordinary speech I heard a serenade.

"I couldn't agree more. It's dreary, it's completely dreary. I was so happy to hear of this party." When I finally found my voice, all I could do was babble. Yet I was astonished to be talking so naturally to Enrico Caruso.

"I am happy too. I have an automobile for taking fresh air when the weather makes it too ugly for walking. May I call on you and your friend one afternoon to go motoring? If you like, of course, only if you like such things."

"Ma che piacere. Lei è così gentile."

Caruso was so gentle in his manner, so kind—the account I had read about him in the magazine must have been exaggerated, or perhaps some sort of publicity stunt. Caruso did not seem to be the type of man who would knock a woman down. And he would be calling at the house. The star of the Metropolitan Opera, the most eligible bachelor in the county was also a man of such warmth and charm, and he would be calling at the house.

6

"Sono ancora rossa da vergogna. How could you not know him? The world knows him! He is the Caruso!" The key word in Bibi's wailings was *vergogna,* which I began to understand meant "shame." All the way home, Bibi had kept exclaiming incredulously, "But he is the Caruso!"

The morning following the christening party she continued her lament. The Master was gone for the day, and we were lingering over coffee, great steaming bowls of café au lait.

"The Caruso—*che vergogna!* How could you not know him, when everybody—when the whole world knows him!"

Indeed, how could I not have, I kept asking myself as well, when there were pictures of him in the papers almost daily? Near the entrance to the Metropolitan, there had been a life-size representation of the tenor dressed as Don José. I had bumped into it and excused myself to the cardboard figure. Was it because of the distance from the stage, was it due to the effects of makeup and costumes? Could these factors explain my failure to recognize the great man in person at the christening?

"The man and his image—they're not at all the same. He's not really like his photographs—I mean, for one thing, he's not flat, and what's more he's not black and white either, is he?" Then, stammering into apology: "I ... I ... I ... don't know, Bibi, I couldn't really see him because of his coat. He seemed dwarfed by it."

"What must he think of us? What must he think of us! That we're barbarians!" She hid her face in her hands.

"But it was only me! It was always clear that you knew who he was. And he was very polite—no, he was more than polite— he was gracious."

"But yes!" Bibi brightened. "Because he saw my appreciation of his talent we were saved. He gave me his card. What else could that mean?"

"What else?"

"I will ask your father if I may invite the king of tenors to dinner. And I will speak to the *professore* after my lesson. He will tell me about Caruso's favorite dishes. I'll make them all to please him. And then ... and then, who can tell what might happen?"

Bibi left the room singing lines from an opera, *"È la bellezza mia, tutta ricerca in me, ricerca in me da capo a piè ..."* Her eyes were lowered and there was a dreamy expression on her face as she waltzed off, in the arms of an invisible partner.

SOMETHING WAS HAPPENING even if it wasn't going to happen to me. The governess was a pretty and pert Jane Eyre, as

Charlotte Brontë could never have imagined her. The former governess, musical and Italian, was bound to interest the great tenor. What could I possibly have to offer him? How might I draw him? Even though I knew French and so understood the lyrics to *Carmen,* the drama had remained remote. No, it was not on the stage but on the stairs that I felt Caruso's power. Standing alone by the top step, gripping the banister, I was captivated by his eyes, the way they looked directly at me, and by the dark mystery of that look. And when he touched my hand I had felt a jolt. An electric current passed between us yet left no scar, no trace. Could I have entirely imagined it? Was it truly Bibi, and not I, who was the object of his interest? I fervently hoped otherwise. Still, I temporized that even if it were another woman's story, and not really my own, to watch an action unfold was better than no story at all.

7

Garlic, oregano, and olive oil smells wafted through the air. There were pots on every burner. Tomato sauce streaked the wall around the stove, splattered onto the ceiling. Bibi was moving from countertop to stove to sink to countertop—back and forth, again and again. She stopped to chop vegetables. Her apron was stained, her hair was tied back, but a few dark curls escaped from the ribbon and clung damply around her flushed face.

"It all smells so delicious, Bibi. Would you like some help?"

"No—no, there's no time to explain anything. I'm reading and cooking at the same time. It's harder than I thought. These Calabrese dishes are not at all like those from my region."

"So what is it you're cooking?" I inhaled an air rich in aromas. "I recognize some herbs ... thyme? Or is it oregano? There's no mistaking the garlic."

"Spaghetti with tomato sauce. Lentils. *Spezzatino*—that's what we call a stew made of veal with peas. *Melanzane,* eggplant with garlic, fried in olive oil. I bought this round loaf of peasant bread, and spicy olives. And for antipasto, prosciutto, that's Italian ham— sliced paper-thin it's served with melon as an appetizer. I found everything I needed in Little Italy. For dessert I'm making flaky pastry horns filled with ricotta and currants. A feast, Dorothy, I am preparing a feast of all the things I've been told Caruso likes to eat!"

"I'd happily help, you know. I'm good at following recipes."

"But, Dorothy, they're all in Italian! If you really want to help, why don't you set the table? Make sure the candles, the crystal, the silverware, everything, is the best you've got—for Caruso, nothing less than the best will do!"

THE IRISH LINEN and the antique silverware were heirlooms. The touch of linen was always a surprise to me because the look of the weave is coarse, yet the feel of the cloth is so smooth, even soft. Four places at the table, only one more than usual, must be set. For one guest Bibi had spent the entire day cooking—and preparing to cook.

I lingered for a moment where I knew Caruso would be seated and imagined looking through his eyes at me, at the Master's daughter, sitting at the far end of the dark oval table—at the shy young woman always dressed in blue.

HE CAME IN WEARING A CAPE, a blue velvet top hat, a powder blue suit, and black patent-leather shoes. He looked as if he had stepped off the stage from a French opera. I could see from Father's arched brow and thin-lipped smile as he greeted our guest that he had to restrain himself from commenting.

"After singing, what I love best is flowers." Caruso brought a huge mixed bunch of roses and lilies for the "ladies of the house." The white and the red blossoms echoed the lush and vivid drama that is opera.

"*Che bei fiori, sono belli, belli ...*" Trilling her appreciation, Bibi rushed forward to accept the bouquet.

I smiled and, wistfully, with my eyes, followed the flowers as Bibi hurried to place them in a vase with water. I too would have liked to bury my face in the blossoms. I would have welcomed the gold dust of pollen in my nose, and on my skin.

AT THE DINNER TABLE nobody looked at me. I was free to watch Caruso. He must have been used to it from his millions of fans, unaware of my rapt attention. The tenor was engaged in a discussion with the Master, where the Master did most of the talking.

"Wilson is a coward. He dragged his heels about this war. Too busy fighting capital and big business in the country for that. Now we're in this European debacle, but are we ready for it? No—not at all. I tell you it's a bloody farce, his so-called foreign policy! It's been a bloody farce from the start! These Democrats are a bunch of lily-livered do-gooders—and look at the mess they've got us in!"

On the topic of Woodrow Wilson, Father was rabid. Usually he attacked me in his rage. All the sins of the Democrats were somehow attributed to me even though I didn't have the right to vote.

"Might things be different if women had the vote, Father?" I had once ventured to ask, but he had silenced me.

"I won't tolerate that suffragist nonsense. Not in my house!"

Caruso listened attentively, cradling his dimpled chin in his hand, *hmm*ing occasionally and rather ambiguously, whether to show he was paying attention or agreeing politely with Father it was difficult to guess, but there were no arguments between them.

"Are you perhaps not so interested in politics, Mr. Caruso, as you are in the musical theater—in spite of the war and your own Italy in arms?"

"War is hell. I am not a soldier, but an artist. I just sing, and when I do I make a lot of money. I pay my taxes in advance now and I invest every penny of my earnings in Liberty Bonds. That is my war effort, Mr. Benjamin."

"You may call me Park."

"Sometimes I sing for the troops—'Ooooh say can you see …' Money and music, what I can give, I give."

"How about some more wine? Genius mustn't sit before an empty glass."

"It would give me pleasure if you call me Enrico. Park, yours is not a name you can forget in New York City. It is Central, is it not?" Caruso smiled a little smile at his own joke, his eyes crinkling with merriment, while the Master tried to hide his response in his wineglass, drawing in his lips as if the wine had been soured by the pun.

"Are we ready for dessert? I have prepared some Neapolitan pastries," Bibi said.

"Don't you think we've eaten enough?" At that point the Master was unable to contain his irritation, though he instantly struggled to resume an amiable air. "But what I am ready for is coffee and I like my pipe after dinner, if you don't mind, Enrico. Why don't we retire to the drawing room? Shall we?"

Father must have remembered that his guest was a very famous man and that it was a coup to have him come for dinner.

At the end of that evening, as Caruso bid us all good night, I was the one who volunteered to fetch the tenor's things. For the briefest of moments I was alone with his hat and with the matching lush blue velvet cape. I could see he had left his cane in the umbrella stand. The head of the cane was gilded and gleamed in the dim light of the vestibule. Then they all crowded around the door to see Caruso off. The Master nursed his pipe, and Bibi stood beside him, leaning against the wall. They watched while I helped Caruso with his cape, but when he turned to thank me, the others seemed to disappear. He took my hand in his, offered his droll, quick little bow, and then he kissed my upturned palm. The heat of his breath and the moisture from his half-open lips made me quiver. Never before had I sensed such nakedness in my hand.

8

A mulberry tree grew so close to the house that its branches in the wind thrashed against my bedroom window. It was such a tree that van Gogh, the Dutch painter who saw living things as if they were burning themselves up, painted from his room in the asylum at St. Remy. Mornings, it was my habit to watch the small yellow birds that lived high up in the tree's branches. In June the finches got fat on the dark berries it produced. But now it was still winter, it was not yet morning, and in the darkness the birds could not be seen. I pressed my forehead against the icy glass and closed my eyes. All was hushed; only I was awake.

Wrapped in a blanket, I had left my bed to sit on the window ledge and stare into the night. To dream the dreams eluded by sleep, to review the day's events as if through a kaleidoscope. With the light switched off, in the dark, my mind could drift. In emptying itself, my mind filled, as fields fill with snow. In my dreams my body was breath, exhaled breath, vaporous in icy air.

In the sky there was a faint sickle of light, the moon was mostly in shadow, a thin woman undressing behind a rice-paper screen. The stars were diamond chips winking in the ether. The distance of light-years rendered their burning as cold, as brittle as the swirling patterns frost forms on glass. My heartbeat felt like the methodical ticking of the clock, whose function is to measure, not to experience, time.

The house was still but for the sounds of wood, old wood settling on the foundations. The furnace seemed to have shut down. There was a shortage of coal in the city that winter, and it had been unseasonably cold. I shivered even though we had plenty of coal; Father could afford it, but I imagined the cold of those who could not. The only other sound, the Master's snoring, could be heard from the vents through which no warmth, no air now flowed. Soon the furnace would start up again and drown out the snoring.

Though nobody was singing serenades in the garden, I imagined that I heard music. My nerves were string instruments vibrating with inexpressible yearning.

Before going to bed, I had removed a rose from Caruso's bouquet and placed it in a bud vase in my bedroom. Now I held the flower in my hand. I brushed those silky petals with the tips of my fingers, and then I sniffed at the head, delicately, tentatively. "Does he love me?" I asked the rose. But the flower answered as only a flower can, with perfume, heady and ambiguous.

After Caruso left we had lingered together for a while in the drawing room.

"Good show. Jolly good meal, Miss B, you'll sing at the Metropolitan yet!"

Bibi had smiled, but her thoughts had been elsewhere. Perhaps already on the stage, singing a duet with the king of tenors, clutching his hand fervently to her breast in a death scene.

"Next time, Mr. Benjamin, you might offer to play the Pianola and ask me to sing." The glass she held had remained suspended at her lips as she spoke—it had hovered there as if she preferred, for the moment, not to drink but rather to inhale the brandy.

Next time! The tenor would come to our house again. Next time, I resolved to say more. What was so difficult about conversation that it made my throat constrict and my heart thunder? Surely, I needn't say anything particularly clever in order to speak. I didn't dream of impressing him, but only of getting him to turn his head for a moment and look into my eyes again.

Those dark Mediterranean eyes had looked steadily, openly, as the Master lectured on the war, on free enterprise, and trusts. And Caruso had played the role of audience. When he answered his host's few queries, the tenor's speech had been so heavily accented, his English some form of awkward translation, that the voice had faltered in speech in a way it never did in song.

Oh, his accent was sweet. Sweet. If a voice had a texture, it would be that of the flower in my hand. And what would be its scent? Also rose? Or something more complicated, something with depth, something old, prehistoric even, smoldering in notes of amber—but also ethereal, essences of white, climbing flowers, of things airborne—yet velvet, steamy and tropically lush, and impossibly rare, the unfurling of a unique breed of orchid. That was the sound—that was the scent—not of the professional tenor, the famous artist, but of the throaty "signorina" spoken by the stranger I met at the party.

ONE HIP RESTED ON THE WINDOW LEDGE, while the balance of my weight bore down on my standing leg. The blanket trailed to the floor, stirred with the air beginning to blow from the vents. Wind agitated the tree. In the waving action of its branches I imagined the flailing arms of a swimmer drowning in darkness. And I realized that if I didn't call attention to myself, I would sink without a ripple, without a love to call my own.

9

The birds woke me along with the spotlight of sun on my face. I went to the window to wish my avian friends a good morning. But the finches paid me no heed. They hopped about in the branches, chirping all at the same time as in an argument, not as in a chorus. I watched them, smiling, thinking that if I were a cat, they'd be wary. But presenting, as I did, such a familiar, pale day-moon face at the window, I had become invisible to them.

Coffee smells and simultaneously a rapping at the door. "Dorothy, Dorothy, Dorothy, please wake up!"

Clutching my robe, I opened the door a crack. It was enough to allow Bibi to push her way in.

"You will never believe this! Never! Caruso—Caruso himself—has sent round his chauffeur with these. Look, Dorothy, look!" She waved something in the air above her head. "Tickets to *Aida* for this Friday night!"

"How wonderful!" I could see that there were three tickets as Bibi thrust them in my face.

"But that's not all! There's more! There's more! The car will come back this afternoon to pick us up. If we like! If we like!" She took in a deep breath to calm herself. "You may not know this, Dorothy, but in our customs it's not proper for a single woman to go out alone with a man. In Italy there is no such thing as dating. Even after a couple is engaged the family will send the younger sister along to chaperone. So you see, it's important that you come on this outing with us."

"Of course I'll join you. I'd very much like to join you." To be invited to tag along as if I were the chaperone, the hired companion, felt ironic.

BIBI AND I were waiting and watching at the parlor window that faces onto the street when a black limousine, shining like new money, stopped in front of the house. The driver was dressed in uniform, a navy wool jacket with polished brass buttons, a motoring cap in a nautical style. With the engine idling, blowing smoke into the icy air, the chauffeur waited while Caruso came to the door to call on us. He was dressed like a racecar driver, riding pants, beret, and goggles, looking as if he intended to do the driving himself on our outing. We opened the door for the tenor even as he was ringing the bell.

"AFTER YOU," Caruso bowed. He held the car door open for us. First he helped me climb inside. Bibi was about to follow when Caruso stopped her with a light touch on her arm. "Excuse me, but I will sit in the middle so you ladies may both have a window seat."

"Lei è così gentile. Grazie, grazie."

I am not a petite woman. When people are trying to be kind they call me "big-boned." And although Bibi was much shorter, she was buxom and the dress she wore had a double-layered skirt that just added to her girth. We were rather crowded together in the back of that vehicle. Caruso was wedged in between us. Luckily camaraderie came easily to us as we were squeezed into such closeness. In talking, our breaths mingled. Caruso's had a slightly licorice smell.

We drove in sunshine through Central Park. There was no singing as we rode in the car, but there was a lot of joking. As if the automobile were running on laughter rather than gasoline.

"Do you know what is the best fruit?" he asked, and then immediately answered the question himself. "Watermelon is the best fruit. You eat, you drink, and you wash your face at the same time."

Some of the jokes consisted of wordplay in a mix of Italian and English that I had a hard time following.

"I-ce-cream. In my dialect, *i ce creame,* it means 'here we create ourselves.' But don't ask for a cone of that!" He laughed as if he had just heard the pun for the first time. Caruso always translated for me, but there was a gap in the timing of my response; my laughter often trailed after his, after Bibi's. But it was easy enough to laugh even when I didn't quite get the joke because his laughter was so infectious. His smile—the man became a smile the way on stage he became a voice.

That afternoon Caruso was playing the clown for us, whinnying when we passed horse-drawn carriages, bleating as we drove by the Sheep Meadow even though the field was filled with snow, not sheep. We passed lakes that were frozen over; we heard no ducks except for the quacking Caruso. There wasn't a moment of silence. He seemed determined to entertain us.

"Do you know the story of the three *Napoletani?* I can say this joke because I am one!"

"No, tell it, tell it!" Bibi said, while I just shook my head and smiled. He had shifted his weight toward me, and I felt the pressure of his thigh against mine even through the thick wool of my camel coat. I felt a tightness in my throat, in my chest, that I didn't recognize.

"There are three *Napoletani* out for an afternoon walk when a car jumps the curb and kills one of them. 'Poor Alberti, he has a wife and five children,' says the one to the other. 'You know him better than I do, you should go and tell *la vedova,* the widow. But be careful, you must not shock her.' So the other one goes to Alberti's house and knocks. A woman, her belly big with child, comes to the door. He can hear the sound of many children crying and playing in the background. 'Are you *la vedova,* the widow Alberti?' he asks. 'No,' she says, 'I'm Signora Alberti.' 'But I was looking for *la sua vedova,*' he says."

Bibi laughed uproariously, but there was something sad about the joke, and so I found it hard to join in the laughter for that one.

Although it was a sunny day in February, there was a cold snap. It had been minus six for two days in a row then, a record cold for the region. But we didn't mind the frigid temperatures when the sun was so bright, when the day seemed brighter because of the cold.

The sun shone from the dark metal body of the car; it was magnified by the mirrors, multiplied and captured in miniature in the glass windshields; the sun was everywhere, as if we had entered a parallel universe, another solar system, where many yellow stars, instead of just one, burned at the center.

The sky had drawn in its bleached awning of winter white and was blue in every direction. Although it was lovelier, the sky seemed farther away, less accessible, that blue stratosphere. Such happiness, I could taste it. It was sweet, so sweet, but like pastry to a starving woman, it lacked substance, it lacked sustenance, and seemed to awaken a far deeper hunger in me than it satisfied.

WE STOPPED AT A CAFÉ where we drank steaming mugs of hot cocoa. Caruso asked the waiter to add some coffee to his hot chocolate. We ate biscuits.

On the road again, all of us refreshed and relaxed, Caruso expressed his pleasure at spending his day off from the Metropolitan in our "charming company."

"No rehearsing, no scales. Today I'm a free man. Today, ladies, I'm all yours."

"But, signore, can the artist ever truly be free? He lives for music, doesn't he? He lives for singing! I must say, music is in my heart too! Without it, it doesn't beat—without music I might as well be dead!"

"I've heard something like this before, you know, you're not the first singer to sing that tune. But remember this, a performance is for a few hours only, but dead, she is for a very long time. I've been singing on the stage for more than twenty years. A day of rest—well, if God needs one, then so does Caruso."

"But I live for my lessons with the *professore*. He takes me to the heights, he shows me how a voice can open the world like an alpine vista."

"He shows you the high road. I forget there can be no rest for the amateur."

Then Bibi started singing "Un Bel Dì." While she sang, Caruso turned to me and whispered, "Ah, that's Madama Butterfly taking a ride with us. And you, Miss Dorothy, do you also like to sing?"

"No, I'm afraid I can't sing at all. It seems I'm tone deaf. The sisters at my convent school barred me from the choir, and at mass, during hymns, they told me to just mouth the words."

To my astonishment, Caruso smiled happily at my confession.

"Every other woman I meet thinks she is a singer. It makes me so tired." He looked at Bibi for a moment as she continued to sing and then turned back to me.

"The rich ladies in the audience at the Metropolitan, they all think they love opera so much, but they love what they can't understand. If they knew that Giuseppe Verdi is just Joe Green in English, they would not be so impressed by the composer of *Aida*."

Then he sat back, pulling at the soft leather fingers of the gloves resting in his lap as he listened. Strains of tragedy, of suicide, death, and unrequited love, throbbed in the song. I didn't understand the words, but I recognized the yearning in the music.

10

Although I never had anything left over from my personal allowance, I managed to save a little from the household account, the monthly sum the Master allotted me for groceries and running the household. I was not required to do domestic chores; we had servants, but it was my responsibility to manage them. A housekeeper came in every morning and kept the place impeccably clean. A gardener shoveled the snow in winter. But we couldn't keep a cook because of the Master's temper.

Turning his dislikes to advantage, I continued to serve lamb regularly, often the very same cut of lamb Father had refused to eat the day before. I would just put it back in the icebox for the next day. That way the lamb was virtually stretched to serve for several evening meals. There was of course a price to be paid. The Master invariably would go into a rage and then leave to eat at his club. But I didn't care if I had to endure these scenes when I could use the money saved this way to buy more Caruso records.

Our household had the latest in phonographs, an electric Victrola. At a cost of more than three hundred dollars, I could never hope to buy one just by scrimping. My job, if it could be called that, managing the house for Father, was unpaid. But he loved music, and didn't mind spending money on the things he loved, so I could play my own records on the best of these talking machines. Even then, that miracle of sound produced by the Victrola seemed just a technological wonder, a hollow echo of the man I dreamed about.

I hid my growing stack of red-label recordings in my room. When Father wasn't home I would listen to these discs, but I couldn't get what I needed from them. His recorded voice moved, not through lungs, but through the architectural spaces of the great composers, Verdi, Puccini. Yet it seemed as flat as the disc that was spinning on the turntable.

No, it wasn't the singing but the man himself I desired. There was no mold that had captured the puns, the slapstick, that human side of the great singer. Enrico the clown made me feel instantly at ease, but not so Caruso the artistic star.

The sweet and funny man I cherished might be glimpsed in his doodles. Among my treasures I kept one of the self-portraits he scrawled on a paper napkin at the café and gave to me as a souvenir. Yet they too were flat and thin as the material on which they were drawn. The sketches were highly stylized. Although the playfulness in them was evident, something in the bold black strokes of his pen made me shiver—if not unpleasantly.

But where in this recorded music was his mouth? Where in these drawings were his fingers?

II

At Broadway and Thirty-ninth Street we stepped out of the taxi and into a milling crowd in front of the Met. There was always a long line of people hoping for last-minute tickets—I remembered waiting in such a queue for the matinee, the jostling in the line and then the jostling as I stood to watch the performance. This evening I didn't have to wait. We had complimentary tickets from the king of tenors himself.

The Master presented our tickets at the door and we were admitted into the resplendent space that was the opera house, not a house at all really, but a temple built to song. An usher escorted us to our seats. The gold braid on his jacket glowed. Indeed, all the interior of the building seemed to blaze with the same burnished light, as if the walls, the curtains, the huge chandeliers, all were gilded.

Bibi and I decided to wait in our seats for the performance to begin, not that our chairs could contain our excitement. The stage was not so much a dais as a platform projecting into the body of the amphitheater. The stage was horseshoe-shaped with the seating set all around it. The fur coats, the jewels, the silk formal gowns were seated in the three tiers of private boxes above us, the so-called Diamond Horseshoe. If you weren't rich as the Rockefellers or the Vanderbilts, you couldn't afford to sit there.

The Master had gone to the bar for a drink, a gentleman's drink, before the performance; he would drink a few during the intermission as well.

Miss B did a little flutter and dance in her seat. Her full skirt was tulip shaped and made up of several layers. It was in vogue at the time, but too voluminous in the small chair. Even in my slim-fitted dress, I too found it hard to get comfortable. Luckily, we were in the front row, so my rather long legs weren't also cramped. We were seated by the orchestra and behind the drums. When the lights went down, I was relieved to disappear into the darkness with the rest of the audience.

The orchestra had been warming up, making noise, not music, until the conductor stepped onto the rostrum and lifted his baton and the overture began. I had been studying the program with its synopsis of the plot of Verdi's *Aida* and felt prepared to listen—to understand it all.

It was a magnificent set. Ancient Egypt was suggested through a painted backdrop of golden pyramids, and dominating the stage was a sphinx. In the opening scene, the music was bellicose. The chorus was heavy with bass voices, the deep tones of men, priests, and warriors. The priests wore long white robes while the warriors were dressed in knee-length skirts made up of strips of leather studded with metal and draped over white cotton. Caruso played Radames, the leader of the Egyptian army in a war against Ethiopia. When I looked up at the stage I saw his naked calves; I saw Caruso's feet in gold sandals. His legs were muscular-looking and covered with dark hair.

Bibi made little gasping sounds.

"Are you all right?" I whispered.

Bibi nodded, then, opening her mouth like a swimmer coming up for air, she gasped again, "It's my favorite opera!"

I tried to concentrate on the language as much as, if not more than, the music. But that was not an intelligent way to learn Italian, not through that medium where melody is more pronounced than meaning. From the words that were repeated it seemed that the men and women favored different vocabulary; the soldiers bellowed *"invochiamo,"* while the women trilled *"amore."*

"Sanerà il tempo ... " Amneris, the princess, was singing.

Tempo—I knew that meant time, the beat in music. If time heals, it also slays; it corrodes.

"THIS IS MY FAVORITE OPERA." As we sipped sherry in the lobby during intermission Bibi explained the opera to me. "You see, the hero, Radames, he loves the slave girl, not the princess. It means even a servant can dream. In love, anything is possible, Dorothy, anything!"

"But Aida's secretly a princess as well, isn't she? She's only a slave because she was captured."

"Radames loves the slave, not the Pharaoh's daughter. He is Egyptian, that's what counts in the story."

Slave or not, it was Aida for whom Radames ended up sacrificing his life. The princess could have saved him, but he would rather die than marry her.

In the last scene I found myself crying. What I saw was not a hero in ancient Egypt being entombed alive, but Enrico Caruso, the twentieth-century man, the man I knew, about to die. Aida was waiting there in the shadows, waiting for Radames. Death is sweeter in opera when it is shared. It is embellished through song.

From tears to the brio of applause, the audience moved so easily. Sodden handkerchiefs were thrown into the air. As the cast came out one by one to make their bows, the singers were showered with bouquets of flowers. When Caruso stepped back on the stage, the audience rose as one for him. Radames may have died, but he was still expected to give an encore. He sang again, and with tireless ardor, he sang mellifluously, *"Come scordar ..."* And as he sang, cigarette smoke was coming out of his nose and mouth. He was unforgettable, he who could not forget. The audience rose to its feet again and again. We were insatiable. After a dozen encores, Caruso emerged from the wings with a burning cigarette in his hand. He looked all around the house, at all of us, we were still standing, still clapping and expecting more. He waved the hand holding the cigarette, while placing the other on his belly. He patted it. Some laughed, all continued to clap, but this time we sat down because the tenor was hungry.

INVITED TO MEET WITH CARUSO backstage, we became the envy of even those in the Diamond Horseshoe. When we entered his dressing room, he was sitting in a crimson silk robe and smoking.

He used a cigarette holder to smoke; he had several of them on his dressing table. All were ornate, in amber, ivory, and gold, and inlaid with jewels. Although he had just finished smoking a cigarette, he immediately prepared for another, stuffing the tip of the holder with cotton.

"If I cannot smoke, I cannot sing. Smoking is the only thing that calms my nerves. A valet waits for me in the wings with a lighted one so I can smoke as soon as I come off scene. It keeps my throat liquid.

"Stage fright is the price you have to pay for being an artist. Stage fright is the price of perfection. The amateur, the novice, suffers before he makes his reputation, while the artist suffers to surpass it."

He then invited us for a late night supper at a restaurant on Mulberry Street that made "the best squid-ink pasta in the world," but to my disappointment the Master declined for us.

12

In spite of the myriad demands on him, Caruso reserved time to spend with us. When he came by to pick us up in one of his cars, we sometimes went for drives in the country, for a lazy hour or two of landscape and laughter. But more often, the outings were brief, and the three of us would simply go for a few joyous turns through Central Park. Caruso was harried by all the public attention he received. His only other free time he allotted to his tailor. He told us that he needed special fittings to look the part of the great Caruso. He never seemed to wear the same suit twice. And his outfits were, as I had to concede to Father's raised eyebrow, memorable: checkered waistcoats straining at the buttons, yellow leather gloves soft as butter left out in the sun, two-tone shoes, white in winter.

On his only free night, Caruso joined the household for dinner. So it came to pass that our Sunday meal would be served on Mondays, on Caruso's day off.

"I wonder why he comes here? He's obviously not in love with Bibi. Nor does he need to hear me play the Pianola anymore than he needs to hear her sing. You'd think he'd have had his bellyful of screeching with all those rehearsals and performances to have any patience for amateur stuff."

This was a rare instance when something the Master said actually cheered me up. Not that he was attentive enough to my feelings to notice or he would have quickly set me straight. Still, I began to pin my hopes upon this single remark.

Bibi had hopes of her own. Although the woman had not been invited to audition for the Metropolitan, and she had dreamed that Caruso might use his influence to have her there, singing beside him, she continued to hope that he still might soon do so. Meanwhile she busied herself; she dedicated herself as sincerely to appetizers for him as to arias. Caruso's visits continued to set her off in a flurry of cooking and singing, along with hours of primping in front of her mirror.

13

There was proof to support Bibi's belief in Caruso's love for her. She could count the ways his passion, though undeclared, was shown, and she pointed out these signs to me in case I'd missed them. Her conviction produced in me that sense of sudden plunging, as in an elevator whose cables have just been snapped.

Mornings following Caruso's Monday night dinners with us, Bibi would tabulate the evidence of his love for her over breakfast.

"Have you ever asked yourself why he comes to dinner here when he can have his pick of the grandest salons in New York and the best restaurants? To me, it's clear he appreciates home cooking, the Neapolitan dishes I prepare especially for him. Italian folk wisdom says that if you cook like a man's mother, he begins to see you as his wife."

Even though it cut into the household accounts, I was happy enough when Bibi cooked because it meant another evening spent with Caruso. I would have happily hawked all my records at pawnshops to pay for these meals.

Whether in the excitement of anticipation or in the afterglow from Caruso's presence among us, Bibi would start singing. Bibi sang making her toilette in the morning. In a crescendo of notes, she sang in the kitchen in time to the espresso pot's bubbling up. She sang as she stirred spaghetti sauce. After dinner, accompanied by the Master at the Pianola, she offered her repertoire of songs the way some serve brandy or liqueur. But Caruso declined to join in the after-dinner performances. Seated by the fire, he stayed close to me. Smiling affably, he listened. At times he whispered some anecdote from stage productions in his career. I, who knew little of the history of music, began to learn about opera as a biography of Caruso.

"I remember singing this aria with Melba—at the Royal Opera House in Covent Garden. Very cold that lady, even if they say her singing is perfect—perfectly boring is what I say about it.

It was like singing with a fish. So I try to liven things up a little bit. My Rodolfo put something warm and slippery in her hand and I whispered, 'Eengleesh lady no like sausage?'"

He said, "Puccini himself approved me for a role in his opera *La Bohème*. And he was happy to do so—when I went to audition for him, he recognized my name because people had told him about me.

"The high C was a problem for me then, so I joked with Leone—that's what his friends call him. I said, 'You don't need another tenor, you need a soprano to sing the Rodolfo!'"

And, "In Cuba, it was *La Forza del Destino* and the sound for the pistol no work, so what was I to do? Is that a tenor's job, I ask you? I go 'Buuuuuuuum!' and kill Lenora's father with my mouth!"

He told me about sopranos. "They are so serious, they get mad at me if I horse around. Desdemona gets very upset when, after I have suffocated her, I put a squeaky toy in her hand. It spoils her death scene! She's so mad she comes back to life and tries to choke my Otello with the pillow.

"They all know how to die in opera. But it's more important to know how to live." He dropped his voice even lower and said, "Don't tell anyone, but sometimes I think it's more important to laugh than to sing."

"Come join us, Signor Caruso. I need you for the duet," Bibi smiled and coaxed.

"Sorry, I must not. It's my turn to rest, it's my turn to listen." Caruso shook his head and smiled sadly as he spoke. Again he confided: "It's not fun anymore. Singing is serious business. It's my job. Birds sing for pleasure, birdy pleasure. And when I was young in Napoli I sang like that, like a bird—free, when it was for free. But now I am an artist, not an amateur, now I don't sing just to please myself. It has to be perfect. It has to be better each time I do it. And there's the fear, you know, that one day ..."

But really I didn't know. It seemed to me then that he was a painter who didn't care for paint anymore, didn't care for color, except when spread on canvas. He was a Beethoven who could still hear, but whose soul had gone deaf. Deafened perhaps by the crashing applause of so many cash registers.

Bibi must have been too absorbed in her singing to notice him whispering to me during her little after-dinner concerts. She only noticed his notice of her.

"Caruso cannot take his eyes off me at dinner. You see that, don't you? He must be polite to his host, your father, or he might talk only to me the whole evening long."

It was true that he looked at her a lot. We all did. Her animation at those dinners, when Caruso was present, had escalated over the weeks. Nothing was left untold. She recited the recipes, recalled the preparations, her methods of cooking, pinch by dash. She gave homilies on the traditions behind each dish. She recounted her shopping trips, the hunting for the special ingredients, as if they were adventures.

Bibi went on and on with her proofs over the weeks, merging in my mind into one long litany of proofs:

"Though Caruso is fabulously rich now, he knows what it is to be poor. Imagine, at one time, he was forced to pose in a bedspread for photographers because his only shirt was in the wash. That's not the sort of man who'd think less of me because I have to work for a living."

The trajectory from the slums of Naples to New York City and the top of the world was nothing less than meteoric.

Caruso occupied two floors of the Knickerbocker Hotel on Forty-second Street near Broadway. In 1908, when he first moved in, it was one of the highest buildings in Manhattan, higher than the Metropolitan Life. But with all the construction and the competing among the business dynasties and their builders, each year another skyscraper would rise higher than all the others. It was hard for anybody in the city to stay on top for long.

Caruso was as rich as he was world-famous. To have him appear at a party would have been a major coup for any of the socialites from the Diamond Horseshoe. But he declined to be a singing guest. He declined to sing to them for free. The contract for exclusive rights to public performance he had signed with the Met, he told us, was as much to avoid the onslaught of such invitations as to satisfy the manager.

If it was unlikely that Caruso's visits to our home were due to a sudden and unexpected interest in socializing among the old families, so then why did he come? Were the charms of the vivacious singing companion what drew him?

Bibi was convinced of it. "He has fun with me. I make him laugh. I know all the latest *barzellette*. He likes these jokes, and I'm good at telling them. Doesn't he always come back for more?"

In the joking and slapstick, Caruso and Bibi tried to outdo each other. The competition was intense, but nobody lost anything in the fun. I would laugh even though I didn't get the punchline half the time. Laughter itself would make me laugh.

Then Bibi would offer some arguments based on what she perceived, from her experience, to be the nature of men:

"Caruso knows—I'm sure the *professore* has told him— what an attractive woman I am. Giovanni who sings the tenor role in our *La Traviata* is madly in love with me! Just between you and me, the *professore* himself is not above pinching my bottom!"

Desire is instructed by desire. A man wants a woman because other men want her. That was another law of nature according to Bibi. For too many years my society had been limited to the convent school. All my friends from there were girls, Catholic girls who moved in different social circles than I did. My brother was married and living in another city; he couldn't provide me with a link to the world of men. There was not another male I knew who wasn't over sixty, who wasn't an uncle or a cousin. So if this were true, then I was doomed to a life of loneliness.

"For the man, it is the pursuit, the hunt, that excites him. Never show a man your love until he does, that is the cardinal rule, Dorothy. I know how to play that game. I am carefree. There's no guessing if it's love that's in the air, not when you're laughing all the time."

Laughing along with them, was that enough of a shield for me? Since I hardly spoke in his presence, did that give very much away? I loved Caruso. I knew it in the quickening of my pulse at even the mention of his name. And the rest of the time, my whole life, seemed to be one long and drowsy preparation to see him again. I wanted to walk into his arms as into the warmth of a shelter.

Knock and the door shall be slammed in your face—ask for bread and receive a millstone—such were the responses I knew from my "earthly" father. But Caruso shone, oh, though it might have been sacrilege for me to think so, like a heavenly bridegroom! If I dared to ask him for love, would he sneer?

EVERY TIME WE BREAKFASTED TOGETHER after one of those dinners with Caruso, Bibi would either think of a new reason or go over some similar argument:

"He knows the same people I know. He was godfather to the child of my *professore*. Our meeting—it was destiny!"

Was destiny a form of probability? In New York's Little Italy, mightn't they all eventually meet? Could such a commonplace encounter be called a mystery? Was love something predictable? Or was it something more—something unexpected—something perhaps even miraculous?

I met Caruso because of my grandmother's spoons. Might something as simple as a set of silver spoons play a role in the machinations of mystery?

"CARUSO FEELS COMFORTABLE WITH ME—he can speak Italian whenever he wants to. As if he were at home. As if he were still living in his own country. Italian and bel canto—we share the same language."

Bibi spoke Italian constantly to Caruso and her voice would go up several decibels when she did so. Her hands would be equally engaged in what seemed to me, who didn't understand a word the woman was saying then, a mostly one-way dialogue. Bibi touched Caruso constantly as she talked, using touch as if it were some form of orchestration. But Caruso always replied in English. In short, clipped phrases. The more animated Bibi became, the more subdued, the more quiet was his answer.

The heart, mystery that it is, must speak more than one language. Music is said to be the universal language. But what was music to the deaf? Caruso had sung to Helen Keller, her fingers listening at his mouth. What was his singing to her?

Was it sensation, not sound? Was it the surging and heat that is the breath?

"Like will seek like. Italian will love Italian, Catholic, Catholic, singer will love singer. It is a social law. It is the natural order of things. You know that as soon as the season is over at the Met, he goes back to Italy every time. That's where his heart is. With Italy, with Italians."

"I suppose so, Bibi. It seems very important for couples to have things in common. Background, religion, hobbies, etcetera."

In spite of the bitter cold that winter, I no longer wanted it to end. I dreaded to think of him leaving in a few short months.

"'Etcetera'? It takes a Rossini to know how *etcetera* should be sung! Let me tell you that I will be married soon because of your *etcetera*!"

14

Bibi was banking on the general case, on what appeared to be the rule, while I was secretly hoping for the exception. I didn't argue with the evidence she presented for herself. For fear of ridicule, I dared not express my own hopes for the love of Enrico Caruso, whose fortune and fame placed him among the most eligible bachelors in the world, let alone New York City.

What else—what more did I need to know to guess Caruso's intentions? I proceeded by a process of elimination. Following a wavering line of logic, I deduced that what brought him to the house must be an interest in me. There were reasons that he might love me. He might love me because I was young, because I had the golden hair of a princess in a fairy tale, because although I didn't myself sing, I listened attentively to him, and this is the highest virtue in a woman if I were to believe what the sisters of the Sacred Heart had taught me.

Love, that word, floated in an element so volatile that perhaps even to whisper it would render it totally unstable and it would explode, or, more in keeping with my experience, it would simply evaporate.

15

The crocuses, purple and gold, were beginning to bud. They formed startling, glorious spots of color among the gray patches of retreating snow and ice. To fully enjoy a spell of spring weather, we left the car parked in front of the brownstone. The chauffeur didn't seem to mind. He had the window rolled down, he was smoking a cigarette and reading *La Follia di New York,* the city's Italian-language newspaper. Caruso's caricatures were regularly published there, so I had taken to buying the paper myself—not that I could read it.

It was just a few short blocks to Central Park. We entered near Sixty-fifth Street and followed a path that bordered the twenty-two-acre field known as the Sheep Meadow. And there were sheep grazing there that day, lambs frolicking, a bucolic scene, and to be enjoyed near the heart of the most modern metropolis in the world. The park served as an escape, a green and serene center bordered by the gray towers, the bustling to the south.

"Ah, feel the sun on your face. Feel its golden warmth. *Signor Sole,* you are blazing far away in Napoli, but I can see you haven't forgotten Enrico, your native son. Kiss me again." Eyes closed, stretching out his arms as if to embrace the heavens, Caruso stopped to bask in the sun. He had tipped back his hat so that no trace of shadow crossed his face.

We made our way to the mall, a tree-lined esplanade in the European style.

"Che bella giornata! È veramente un sole che mi fa sognare d'Italia." Examining a nearby bench, Bibi added, *"Possiamo accomodarci qui. Non è schifoso."*

"What, sit—when we can walk? Sitting is for the car! Sitting is for the old! It's not for us! We will *marcher* like the French, not march like your *Engleesh* soldier; we will make our promenade in the park, not from a park bench. We will stroll—like this—see." Chaplinesque in his dipping stride from side to side, Caruso slalomed his way along the boulevard.

Although reluctant to leave the bench, Bibi hurried to catch up to him. Her gait was somewhat hobbled, as if her heels were too high or her shoes too tight. Long-legged and wearing flat shoes to diminish my height, I could easily match Caruso's stride. But to allow space for his comic walk, and to avoid being hit by his swinging cane, I kept a discreet distance behind him.

"With good reason," Bibi gasped. "That bench was in the shade. It's not really so warm when you're not walking. You might catch a chill."

"A chill! A singer's nightmare!"

Increasing his pace, as if fear were the incentive, with his gold-headed cane he beat against the invisible. "A chill! A chill!" he exclaimed in mock terror.

WE WANDERED ABOUT in the Ramble for a while and then headed back south through the mall. As we approached the zoo, we saw many children playing and their mothers, or their nannies, gathered in clumps to chat. While the women talked, the youngsters climbed monkey bars, bobbed up and down on the seesaw, or chased each other around trees. Shrill cries of "You're it! You're it!" could be heard from the bushes. One then another of the women turned her head regularly to check on the children. Those pushing or gently rocking prams, pink or blue, were free from such vigilance as their babies napped.

Manic murmurings rose, whispers and sighs, as if bees— hives of them—had been disturbed. Squirrels chattered loudly, to which were added frenetic scratching and slipping sounds as they scurried up and down the trees. It was as if these families, along with all the creatures in the park, had awakened from a hundred years' sleep and were trying to make up for lost time.

When one of the women turned our way and recognized Caruso, she called out his name in surprise. Awareness of his presence then seemed to be conducted through the crowd by a prehistoric form of wireless communication. Some people simply stopped to stare after him. Some, bolder, mostly the few men, greeted him familiarly and insisted on shaking his hand.

"They all think they know me if they hear me sing one time. But what's even funnier than that is they think I know them!" He straightened his hat, lowered the brim, seeking some cover now, not from the sun, but from his admirers.

I stood back when his fans approached, while Bibi nodded to them as if she too were being greeted, as if she had a right to be by his side and share in Caruso's fame.

"Bibi, whatever you do, do not take it into your head to start singing! We're already attracting too much attention. If they hear singing, they will be all over us. Like flies to sugar. You understand I need to rest my voice. A beggar can enjoy the spring sun, but Caruso has to hide or everybody wants to make him work!"

Crestfallen, Bibi assented.

"I don't have to worry about you, Doro," he said in an aside. "You don't act like a prima donna. You don't try to get public attention all the time. I think you understand when I just need some peace."

I felt my face bathed in a golden light. He called me Doro, playing on the sound of the Italian *d'oro,* "of gold." It made me feel precious, transformed, shining as he had named me.

THE LIGHT HAD BEGUN TO SLANT. Burrowing into Caruso's dark eyes, it acquired depth. In the lengthening shadows, the air became cooler. It felt sharp now, so the smell of roasting peanuts was welcome. Caruso bought a large bag to share. We ate as we walked. The crunching sounds of the shells punctuated our conversation. Caruso ate the peanuts with gusto.

"Did you see his poor monkey, the way the animal had to dance faster and faster? Sometimes I feel just like him, jumping around to music. Toscanini—now there was an organ grinder! Good thing I was paid more than peanuts when I worked with him."

Not wanting to litter shells along the way as I ate, I slipped them into my coat pocket.

"You are too good, Doro, you can drop the shells, they're all *naturale.* What comes from earth can go back to earth. What we don't eat, squirrels grab, and birds are happy to peck. The fattest squirrels in the world are here in America. They eat better than me when I was a boy in Napoli."

Although not entirely assured of the natural quality of our garbage, I complied. Self-consciously I opened my fist to drop the shells from my hand. Fragments clung to my damp palm. I had to brush them off.

"In Italy, squirrels and birds are not so lucky. We shoot them for food. It takes a lot of birds to season spaghetti sauce."

"It takes four and twenty to make a pie sing."

"To make a pie sing! I like that—is that poetry?"

"Oh, I didn't make it up! It's from Mother Goose, a nursery rhyme where it's blackbirds that do the singing."

"From the nursery. You know I like babies. You like babies then too, do you, Doro?" He looked up at me from across the brim of his hat, the expression in his eyes hidden in shadow.

"Yes, I do, very much, but I have so little sense of my own life, sometimes I think that I'm still a baby myself."

"*Non ti preoccupare*. Don't worry, Doro. When the time comes, if you like babies, you will know what to do. And you can still be a baby for your husband who'll take good care of you!"

"*Una ragazza di venticinque anni non è una bambina—è una zitella!*"

"I do not like this word, *zitella*," Caruso rebuked Bibi. "It is insulting to call the young woman who waits for the right man an old maid. Doro is too intelligent not to wait. And when the right man finds her, he will get a woman as good as Dante's Beatrice. In Italy, there's no divorce, but nobody waits to make mistakes. It's stupid, so stupid, I can't stand it!" He turned back to me. "You will not regret that you have waited." I felt my face flush with—what should I call it—it was too elevated a comparison to be merely called a compliment.

"If I had my youth to live over again …" But he didn't finish the statement. He checked his watch and lamented having to call an end to our outing.

"It's getting late for me as well. I have a dinner engagement. A friend, one of the girls I know from Sacred Heart, has invited me to dine with her family."

"Will you permit me to take you to your dinner, Doro?"

WE WALKED BACK to the house. The Master greeted us at the door. I ran inside briefly to pick up a gift of chocolates I had purchased for my friend's family. I didn't need to change; I was already wearing one of my good dresses.

Caruso repeated his offer to drop me off at my dinner party to Father.

"That's very kind of you, I'm sure."

Then Caruso and I were seated in the car, alone for the first time. As ever I felt that charge in the air between us, air charged with things unspoken but immediately understood.

Turning to me, his dark eyes shining softly in the dim interior of the vehicle, he whispered. "Now, tell me, Doro, when can we be married?"

16

I could hardly eat at my friend's dinner party and I was quieter, if that's possible. I had to keep the incredible secret of my engagement to myself until Enrico could meet with Father to ask for his blessing on the marriage.

The following morning Enrico called me. His voice over the

telephone, the crackle along with the velvet, had some otherworldly quality—communication as if from deep in the past, or from the distant future. Over the phone, it was harder to understand him; his language, that hybrid of Italian and English words, seemed garbled rather than charming. To fully understand him I needed to see the expression in his eyes, the articulation of his hands, because when he spoke, he did so as he sang, with his whole body.

I wanted him in the body, his arms around me, I wanted the man, not the art, and I wanted him now, and in the room. I was hungry for bread that had not been idealized as wafer and offered communally. I gripped more tightly the receiver, the black polished metal, though it was his hand I needed to hold.

"Father's in the library. He won't be going out until later."

"*Allora, posso venire*—can I come now to ask his blessing?"

"Yes, darling, come, and do hurry. I'm so afraid of his reaction—not … not because he could possibly have any objection to you—not in a million years!—but you see I'm sure, I mean … from things that he's said before, I know he'll be surprised—and my father is not a man who likes surprises."

"Don't worry, Doro. You worry too much. I'll take care of your father for you." This reassurance escaped with a deep exhalation of cigarette smoke. Through this familiar sound I could almost smell the burning, brackish odor of tobacco that had become in part his smell. "I come after lunch."

THAT AFTERNOON the household was hushed as if in anticipation. Bibi had gone for her weekly singing lesson. The Master was sequestered in the library, while I, in feeding the fire, also fed my anxiety, my impatience. It was not cold. I sat by the hearth to read, but I couldn't concentrate. When I wasn't sitting idly with an anthology of English verse in my lap, the page turned to a sonnet, the first line of which I could not move beyond, "How do I love thee ..." I stoked wood, I burned newspaper as kindling, I might as well have torn the poem out of the book and burned that page too—before it burned me.

To my ear the doorbell sounded as a gong, heralding the future. Still holding the book in my hand, forefinger marking the page where the poet, the woman, counted the uncountable, I answered the door.

And there he was, all that I had ever dreamed of, and he greeted me with a gentle smile. Then he took his hat off and lightly touched my free hand. His fingers were as soft as mine, but his nails were more finely manicured, buffed to shining. I could see the half-moons, clearly defined, luminously rising on each nail. Transfixed by the small details, I felt a strange form of vertigo, a sense of drowning, as if I had suddenly plunged from a great height into deep water. I looked to my feet, sinking, not in waves, but into the wool weave of deep blue carpeting.

He was the prince, this man who exuded cigarette smoke and cologne. I was the Cinderella smelling of burnt wood, ash, and china ink. There were smudges on my fingers from copying out lines into my diary.

I took his hat and cane. I closed the door on the waiting car. Its highly polished surface gleamed, a black stallion in its suit of armor, somnolent in the sun.

"I'll tell Father you've arrived. Won't you rest here by the fire? It's cozy, don't you think?" In the role of hostess, I led Enrico Caruso to a chair in the parlor. The formality was essential for me; it helped to check my panic. Then I went to knock at the library door.

"What is it?"

"Mr. Caruso is here to see you, Father." Placing my mouth against the closed door, so close my lips touched the wood.

"All right, show him in—show him in."

After I escorted Enrico into the library, I slipped away. There was a heating vent connecting the library and a guest bedroom. I crouched by the grating to eavesdrop.

"I understand you wish to speak to me concerning some important matter. Well, what in the world could I possibly do for you, Enrico?"

"One favor is what I need, but it's a big one. I wish the hand of your daughter in marriage. Your blessing, signore, I ask for your blessing."

"Well, well, well … I must say … well, well …"

"*Well*—that means 'good,' doesn't it?" Enrico laughed. "*Allora,* you have no objection."

"No, no, not at all, my good man. It's just that it's not every day that someone asks for her, you know. What on earth could I object to? This calls for a drink."

In my mind I could see Father turning to the built-in cabinet behind his desk where Shakespeare shared space with the Scotch.

"To your happiness." He made a toast.

"Let us go to Doro now. She's waiting anxiously for your word."

"Oh, her, yes, I suppose we must."

I entered the parlor on their heels.

"Oh, there you are. Well, I take it this is no surprise to you, Dorothy. You're ready to be married, are you?"

"Yes, Father, I love him."

"You're eager to leave your obligations to me here, to your father, are you?"

"I … I … but …"

"Well, you needn't distress yourself. You're hardly indispensable to this household. I take it that this marriage is no surprise to Bibi either. To be the master and to be in the dark in your own house! It's not a condition to be envied, is it, Enrico? What do you think of that—of your future bride?"

"Please, do not blame her. There is nothing improper. Believe me, she is good, modest and good. My feeling for Doro—it start like music. In the beginning, it is small, almost a whisper, I'm not even sure I hear it. It comes from outside, from the orchestra warming up. But then it grows in my chest, in my heart and head, until I have to burst, and this bursting is my singing. I send you tickets to my performances so I can watch her in the front seat and the passion in the opera is what I am singing to her. The auditorium is full of people, but I have eyes only for my Doro."

17

Later that afternoon, after Enrico's interview with Father, Bibi came home humming. She found Father and me sitting together before the fire, not speaking. But this in itself was not unusual. The Master was drinking heavily, filling and refilling his tumbler with Scotch and ice, while I held dreamily to my lips a cut-crystal sherry glass filled to the brim with the amber-colored liquid.

"Let me pour you a real drink, Bibi, some of this Scotch—tonight we have something well worth celebrating."

"I love a celebration! What are we celebrating?" She made a gleeful little pirouette.

"It seems Dorothy here has bagged herself a big bird. Please, don't pretend that you don't know what it's all about."

"What bird? I don't understand what you're talking about."

"Why, the cock-a-doodle-doo! The singing rooster himself, your Enrico Caruso, has asked to marry Dorothy."

"Caaa-ru-so? *My* Caruso!" The light drained entirely from her face.

"Looks like you need a bit of this yourself. I take it you were also in the dark." The Master handed her a tumbler of the Scotch.

But her fingers failed to close around the glass and it dropped to the floor. The glass did not break but the liquid spilled, a darker pool staining the deep blue of the carpet.

After downing his own glass in a single gulp, he announced, "I'm going to the club for a bit. I'll leave you ladies to clean up the mess."

As I MOPPED at the rug with a wet cloth, Bibi approached me. The standing woman towered over me, the kneeling one.

"You little slut! You evil, evil bitch! You knew I was in love with him! You never said a word when all the time you were secretly making eyes at my man. Meeting him on the sly! I told you about our customs—how it's improper for an unmarried woman to be alone with a man. But you—you sleazy slut—that didn't stop you, did it?"

"No, no, I never … I never …"

"You can fool that old man, your father, but you can't fool me—not for a minute. Anyway, not anymore you won't! You …

you … I tell you, you will be sorry for this. I'll make you pay. I promise you—I'll find a way!"

18

When spring warmth ripened into summer's intense heat, our household, as was our custom, sought to escape it; we would close up the brownstone, move away from the city, and spend July and August at our country place by Spring Lake. That summer I sorely regretted the change that I usually looked forward to because it meant that I would be separated from Enrico. He could only join us on weekends.

The light was beautiful around the lake. Regardless of how hot the day might have been, in the evening cool breezes blew off the water. Wooded trails followed the shore of the lake. All through the week I would walk them alone. The engagement had created a rift between Bibi and me. We hardly spoke anymore. She avoided being alone with me and at the country house she spent all her time with the Master. She seemed to prefer losing at chess, losing at cards, to walking around the lake with Enrico Caruso's fiancée. Although I was sorry to have my former friend so hostile, it was considerably easier to bear than her proofs that Enrico loved her.

DURING THE WEEK, getting out for a hike provided me with an escape from the tension in the house. Outdoors, I was not unhappy. As sentimental as it might seem to someone not young and not in love, in a way I no longer felt alone as I walked the shores of the lake. Without Bibi along, I was freer to dream. In my mind, I was still accompanied by Enrico. Replaying our weekend conversations, I would pause again where together we had paused, at the point where it was possible to walk some distance into the lake without getting your feet wet. Balancing on one of the big boulders, I would rest where together we had rested, where flatter rocks provided a natural, if Spartan, form of seating. When Enrico inhaled the country air, he seemed to breathe in so fully from the chlorophyll atmosphere that a sort of vacuum was created. The suction force of it suddenly pressed me into his arms. As I remembered, I hugged myself and felt again the thrill of his arms around me.

Unlike New York City, with its smells of diesel and burning coal, the air there was fresh. If it smelled, it smelled green. Like the air, the water of the lake was pristine, pure enough to drink. In the shallows I could see right to the brightly colored pebbles on the bottom; I could watch the show of shadow and light made by small fish darting about.

In the evening, I would listen for the loons. Nothing moved me more than the sound they made calling to one another as the light deepened from blue to lavender. When I couldn't see the birds anymore, I could hear them more acutely. One mate cried to the other. It seemed a cry of loss even though the other was nearby. The beauty of the sound as it carried over water made my throat constrict. There was nothing I could compare to its power to move; no duet from opera excited me so.

WEEKENDS BEGAN when Enrico's car pulled up in front of the house. Then there was a more complex and lively music filling the house, a music that was more than exercises at the piano. That music was Enrico's inimitable laughter.

And all week, although he was civil enough to Enrico, his future son-in-law, in his presence, the Master complained:

"That man takes more than his fair share of acoustic space and unfortunately, when he's with us, it's not from singing"; "Why, it's like living with a yapping dog, the way he laughs— and at his own jokes!"; and "A grown man and he play fights using the kindling wood! Obviously the man has never fenced properly in his life."

THE METROPOLITAN WAS CLOSED for the season, but Caruso had another kind of job that summer: he was starring in his first film. It involved a grueling schedule. His day started at six each morning and the work before the cameras often went all day long and well into the evening. On the weekends, he needed to catch up on his sleep and so he stayed in bed well past nine. Although all traces of our breakfast had been cleared by the time Enrico joined us, I would prepare a second breakfast that was for him alone. We would sit together in the cozy break- fast nook and sip coffee; "dishwater," he called our percolated coffee. But he laughed when he said this, and drank it just the same, as he recounted anecdotes about his week on the movie set.

"I'm making my debut in a film called *Cousins*. The story is just like an opera. I play two roles in it: one is a great tenor, and the other is his cousin, a poor artist. Two roles for one man, it's very funny, no? What's funnier is that I get two hundred thou- sand dollars for six weeks' work, and without singing a note! It's incredible! In the picture, when I move my lips, no sound comes out. Can you believe an opera without singing—an opera with a mute, a silent tenor? *È uno scherzo!*"

"Oh, but Enrico, it's wonderful! Only think of it—millions of people, all over the world, will get a chance to watch you. I don't imagine you could, not in a lifetime on the stage, perform in concert before so many people."

"Caruso and his cousin will keep moving his lips even when I have no mouth anymore. It's very *bizzarro*. Watch, yes, they want to watch, but what is it to watch a singer if you can't hear him sing?" He patted his belly. "This is the real *pagliaccio*."

No, he was no Valentino on the screen, the Italian "sheik," who would in a few years make a generation of women swoon. He was only a Valentino in his voice, and film was silent then.

"There is no one like you, Enrico."

"Ah, come to me, my sweet Doro, give a big hug to your *fidanzato*."

The warmth of his embrace was what I wanted. It was as innocent as a man hugging a child. Still, there was intensity in it, a surprising ferocity, as if the child has been a lost child. All week long I had been an invisible woman, ignored by Father, reviled by Bibi, but in Enrico's presence I glowed.

"Can you do something for me, Doro?"

"Anything! What is it?"

"My friend, George Cohan, he wants me to sing a song he wrote for our boys in the war. But it is in English, not like the libretti I know in Italian or French—I learn it faster with your help."

I wrote out the words phonetically for Enrico. Then we spent the afternoon rehearsing the song, with me at the piano with the score and Enrico singing from my transcription of the words, "O-ver d-ere, o-ver d-ere …"

"How can anybody sing with his tongue pressed to his front teeth? It stops the breath—it stops the music!"

By the end of the day, I no longer needed the sheet music and Enrico had made the song his own, rousing and impassioned. Unaware of the passing hours, we were surprised when Bibi called us to the dinner table. She served steak tartare.

19

August was a month of brilliant yellow sun, of intense heat often followed, late in the afternoon, by the indigo of thundering storm clouds and the flash of lightning. I loved watching the clouds roll in over the lake; they came in so low the water turned black. When Enrico was with me we lingered to admire the storm. We lingered by the lake until it was too late and the sky had burst and rain fell in torrents. The thunder was explosive, earsplitting, as if the big guns from the European war were firing from the skies of New England. Only a voice like Enrico's could be heard above the roar.

Lightning was sparking across the surface of the lake. Even then I wasn't frightened with Enrico by my side.

"Doro, Doro, it's time to run!" Alternately screaming and yelping with laughter, we chased each other back towards the house.

The rain was so heavy that lake and sky seemed to form a single fluid sheet unfurling in the dark wind. As we ran we got soaked to the skin. Our clothes seemed to liquefy on us, to flow with the water over our bodies. I was losing my breath. Although Enrico was just a few feet in front of me, I had to shout to try to make myself heard. "There's no sense in running anymore. We couldn't get more wet!" The wind whipped the words away from my mouth, but he heard me, and he stopped and waited until I caught up to him. Then he pulled me into his arms and we kissed. Rain streamed down our faces; I tasted the rain in our kisses.

On the day of my birthday, the sixth of August, Enrico presented me with a formal engagement ring, a huge sapphire surrounded by white diamonds.

"I had to look for a long time to find the blue of your eyes in a stone. This one is maybe almost as beautiful, although it's not so deep, Doro, because no stone can go where your eyes go—to heaven and back!"

"Very nice," Bibi grimaced, inspecting the ring as if it were some kind of insect.

WHENEVER WE PARTED Enrico would kiss me on the lips, the gentlest of kisses. Tender kisses.

"I am lonely for my Doro. In the city, summer is still winter without you. I want you for my bride. I hope you can decide on the date soon," he said to me. But the arrangements were all dependent on Father and he seemed to be in no hurry to set the date.

The following week Bibi had several conferences behind closed doors with my father. One afternoon, after hours sequestered with him in the study, she emerged looking smug.

"Your father would like a few words with you."

MY FATHER WAS SEATED at his desk, clutching a letter.

"You wish to speak to me, Father?"

"Yes. I've written to my lawyer and here's the response. Can't afford to be too trusting of appearances in this matter of your marriage to Caruso, you know. Now read this."

The letter contained information that was widely known about Enrico's past. It ended in praise for his character as well as his patriotic contributions to the war effort. It was laudatory, so much so that it might have been taken from an article in the *Times* written by and for Caruso fans.

"Why, it's wonderful, isn't it? What more could you wish for?"

"No, it's not 'wonderful.' Can't you see, it's black; it's pitch. He's never to darken our door again. Send that bauble of his back." The Master made a waving motion at the ring on my finger, without looking at me, as if shooing a child away. "I withdraw my consent to your marriage."

"But, Father—"

"No buts about it! You need more evidence than your father's judgment, do you? You think I've gone soft in the head like a girl, do you? Well, I haven't. I found out what I needed to know. I hired a private detective." He laid the pictures out flat on the desk for me to examine. "Here's his whore, a fat thing too. Now I can see what he sees in you. And here are his bastards with her in this one. He begat two of them."

I knew about this woman, the scandal had been in all the papers when she abandoned Enrico and their children nearly a decade before. At the time I was still at the convent school, but even the nuns could be heard exchanging shocked whispers about it. Father must have known about it too. So why was he bringing it up at this time, I wondered.

I examined the photos closely but could not bring myself to actually touch them, as if the images had been etched in acids so caustic they would incinerate my fingers. The photograph Father had thrust at me was one of a woman and two children. If this woman was a whore, she was one who dressed immaculately, in white linen with lace. The smaller of the boys was propped on a marble ledge. Grapes and dancing classical figures were carved into the stone on which he sat. I peered more closely at these sculpted figures. There were horns on one and the thighs were shagged. Was evidence of debauchery contained there, in the bacchanal scene on which the child sat? The boy appeared still young enough to look natural dressed as a girl; he was in white like the mother. The intensity of this child's gaze was unsettling. It made me feel as if I were the one being looked at. The older boy was beside the woman, leaning against her. His hair was slicked back and he was wearing a checked suit, a young man's outfit. Both the woman and her older son stayed within the frame of the photograph. They smiled at the baby and ignored the camera.

"When was this photograph taken, Father?"

"It matters to you, does it? Well, his sins, his offspring, now live on his estate in Italy with the sister of that woman, sister of the harlot who left him for his chauffeur."

"It matters to *me,* Father. How old are those boys now? I know Enrico had a life before he met me! And that woman, the mother of his children, where is she now?"

"She lives in Brazil, in Rio, on an allowance from your Caruso. I might add that she lives well on his money. On what ought to be your money!"

"Those boys might be men now, for all I know. But if they're not, then they still need a mother. I'd like to help Enrico raise his sons. He deserves a loving and dependable mother for his children."

"Bah! Sentimental hogwash! And if his bastards inherit everything—then what will you do?"

"I … I'll …"

"That's right. Stop and think for a moment. It's about time you started listening to me. Now remember, you're not to see that man again. And that's my final word on it. At last we'll have some peace around this place. And some real music! I'm sick to death of those brassy Cohan tunes!"

I WENT TO MY ROOM to write to Enrico to warn him, to appease him because he might become angry, justifiably angry, about Father's sudden change of heart. And I had to tell him not to come that weekend, which seemed almost more painful because the consequences were more immediate. Enrico must stay in New York City while I could only continue to dream of him as I walked around the lake.

Although it had never been within my power to persuade Father of anything in the past, I was determined to do so. As I wrote to Enrico, as I tried to explain Father's behavior, I began to suspect what might have gone wrong. Images of Father and Bibi together flickered on my page as figures in film fill a white and silent screen. Bibi was behind this, Bibi must have persuaded Father of something.

In our customs, it is improper for an unmarried woman to be alone with a man. Then living alone with one would be unthinkable. If I married, Bibi, who had been hired as my companion, could no longer—if she valued her reputation, that is—stay on in the household. The Master liked to be taken care of, the Master liked to be amused, and Bibi did the latter more than well enough. The irony was that I was now needed to chaperone the two of them.

Nothing of these conjectures flowed through my pen. My letter was pure lament. My letter was a plea for patience and a vow of undying love. I would reason with Father, I assured Enrico.

Love—the hope of a life with Enrico Caruso—for this I was prepared to fight. The very next day I asked to speak to Father again.

"You won't persuade me with this puppy love of yours for that opera cur, that Italian hound."

"There is logic as well as love in this argument. Please, Father, won't you reconsider, please?"

"Logic, you say." He drew on his pipe for a few moments thoughtfully, then he slowly began to smile. "Well, listen then to this proposal. You know the man has two children by an illicit relationship. What, do you suppose, are the children's and that woman's claims on him?" He cleaned his pipe as he waited several minutes for my response. But I had no idea what they might be outside the natural ones. I remained silent, so he continued.

"You haven't asked yourself this question, I take it, even after I showed you the photos. What about the man himself, are you prepared to ask him?" He waited for a few minutes more for a response he did not seem to anticipate receiving.

"No, I can see that you're not. Well, I've had to think of these unpleasant, very unsavory details for you. So if, after all you know now, you still insist on marrying him, then demand that he settle half a million in cash on you before the wedding and I'll withdraw my objection. It's the only way I can see to protect your interests. Our lawyer tells me Italian law bequeaths everything to the sons. Should Caruso die, you'll be lucky if you get to keep that bauble on your finger. So be practical, Dorothy. No flesh and blood of mine is going to be taken for a ride by some singing wop. Now kindly get out of my study, I've got better things to think about all day long than your feelings."

THE MEETING WITH FATHER left me disheartened. It seemed I had only persuaded him to make it harder. I did not care about the money. What was important to me was that Enrico was not legally married and so was free to marry me. The other woman, although in the photo she looked like a tender and smiling mother, was really a figure of ridicule and scandal, running off with the chauffeur. To blame Enrico, to blame the injured party, was surely too unjust.

What really shamed me in all this was Father's demand that I insist on a financial settlement before the wedding. I who was too embarrassed to ask for a few extra dollars for a new dress from him, my own father, must ask for half a million dollars from my fiancé! I felt a knot tightening in my stomach. I had been brave, but now I must be brazen.

TO MY SURPRISE Bibi offered to accompany me to the city to see Enrico. I didn't ask myself, or the woman, why. Perhaps she hoped to see me humiliated; even then I preferred to face this task with an enemy rather than alone.

Pausing near the entrance to the Knickerbocker Hotel, I marveled at its beauty, its lofty height and its red brick French Renaissance facade. The hotel had been dubbed by *The New York Times* as the "beaux arts tiara of Times Square." My beloved occupied two entire floors of the hotel, where at times he could be heard rehearsing from the balcony; he could be heard over the traffic, over the trolleys and cars and carriages and street hawkers. Bibi and I entered the marble and shining-brass interior of the building and were escorted to the elevator by the doorman. He seemed to be expecting us.

We rode up in silence. It felt like a long way up. I tried not to think of what would happen if the electricity failed, if the cables snapped. I felt unsteady when I stepped off the elevator, my knees buckling. I rested my back for a moment against the wall. Before me was the polished wood of his door and some- where behind it, waiting for me, was the man I loved. Bibi stayed just behind me, a shadow, as I rapped lightly with the knocker. Enrico's valet, Martino, who had been with him for twenty years, opened the door. He was a small thin man with a kindly smile.

"Ah, Miss Dorothy, you make Signor Caruso so happy and me happy too because after you are married at last he will permit me to live with my wife." He offered Bibi a seat in a receiving area and then escorted me to see Enrico.

Taking a deep breath, I walked into another man's study. But this man watched me gently and, except to ask me to sit down, didn't interrupt me until I had finished making the speech I had prepared, explaining, and flushing as I did so, my father's views and his demand.

"Father insists that this be done if he is to consent to our marriage."

"No. Doro, you must tell him no. All my money is invested in war bonds. To cash now would be very foolish—and a betrayal of your country. I lose, America loses, so you lose too if I do it. Believe me, Doro, when I say that I will always take good care of you. What is mine will be yours. Marry me now even without your father's consent. Think it over for tonight. If you say yes, we marry tomorrow. Okay, *dolcezza?*"

"I don't really have to think about it, Enrico—you know how much I love you."

"And I don't want you to think too long—just overnight. Make me happy in the morning. And before you go I will dictate a quick letter to my secretary, apologizing to your father for not being able to meet his demands."

As I turned to leave his study, Enrico touched my arm.

"Doro, I hope I will not lose you for a few dollars. Now that I know what I know about women and goodness—your innocence is worth more to me than money."

In the cab on the way back to the townhouse, Bibi asked, "Well, is he going to give you the money?"

"No, he's not." I said nothing to her about my decision to marry Enrico the next day.

Bibi didn't try to disguise her look of triumph.

ALTHOUGH I DIDN'T NEED THE TIME to think it over, as was proper, I spent the night in the brownstone sleeping in my old room for what would be the last time.

The house had been a ghost house all summer, ever since we had left for the country in July. The furniture was covered in white sheets. The air was so stale we immediately opened windows. But there was not much of a breeze, it was sweltering with city heat, that close, grimy heat. But I would not be rushing back to Spring Lake the next day in spite of the fresh wind that blew there off the water, the marine air that made sleep so comfortable however blistering hot the day might have been. I would stay in my New York sticky skin to marry Enrico Caruso.

After slipping the portrait of my mother into my handbag, I wished Bibi a good night and went to my room. I opened the bedroom window, sat on the ledge, as was my habit, and breathed in what freshness could be gleaned from the garden. There was the perfume of night flowers, the mock orange, intensified by the humidity.

"Tweet, tweet, tweet, *tout de suite,* I will be married little bird. If I wake you, can you help me tell Father? This is not a choice for anyone to lose sleep over. You know my father—he's the one who's sometimes rather loud around here. Who would choose a tyrant—who would choose such a father—over a lover? I choose the laughing, the warm-hearted man—half bird like you, little ones, he's a singer—and what's more, I love him! Still, I'm not unafraid. There are butterflies flitting about in my stomach as when I stole the silver windmill—but it's not some bauble, it's my own life I'm taking this time! What will Father do, do you suppose? I've never openly defied him before. But what can he do when I am Mrs. Caruso? So it is, so it will be, wish me well, dear ones. You may not see me here again very soon. Between us"—I lowered my voice to a whisper—"I'll miss you finches far more than I'll miss Father."

20

I woke with the sun that morning. It was to be my wedding day. I should let the groom know, but I could not decently call him before eight. It was blessedly cooler so early in the morning, but I felt damp and sticky. I ran a bath. I needed to prepare for the marriage ceremony, and what I would wear seemed to be the biggest obstacle. While the bath was filling I went into my mother's bedroom. Of course no dress from my mother's wardrobe would fit me. I found a blue garter in a drawer. *Something borrowed, something blue,* and that it belonged to my mother made it perfect. I had some silk stockings, but there was still the problem of the dress.

The bath was more than full when I returned to the bathroom. The water was starting to slosh over the sides, and the overflow was made worse when I plunged in my hand to pull out the stopper. As I was mopping up the floor I heard Bibi get up. A few minutes later I could smell coffee as I soaked in my bath.

I was getting dressed when she knocked on my bedroom door.

"I'm leaving now before it gets too hot. What shall I tell your father?"

"Would you please take Enrico's letter of apology to him?"

"Sure, but a lot of good that's going to do you. Your father is not about to relent on this matter, you might as well come back with me to Spring Lake this morning."

"No, thank you, I prefer to wait." And that was the very last thing I ever said to her.

I PHONED ENRICO at just past eight. "Yes," I said, "yes, I've decided to marry you after all, despite my father's objections."

"Ah, Doro, you make me so happy." I don't think he had doubted for a moment what my answer would be; a chapel had already been reserved. Our wedding would take place at a little Unitarian church on Madison Avenue at two that afternoon. One of his cars would pick me up shortly before that. He would be waiting for me at the altar.

The next call I made was to my friend from Sacred Heart. She was incredibly excited and happy for me when I explained to her what I needed.

"Oh yes, you absolutely must have something new! What good's marriage if you can't get a new dress out of it!" She didn't mind helping outfit the future Mrs. Caruso. So I went to Bloomingdale's and charged my trousseau to her account there.

I chose a flowing gown, cobalt blue satin, and a matching hat, blue with white wings appliquéd on the side. *Something new, something old,* I wanted so to get it right. I also wore my mother's pearls.

ENRICO WAS STANDING by the altar with Martino and his wife. If Martino was the best man, I suppose then his wife was my maid of honor though she was a complete stranger to me.

The ceremony was over so quickly, even as I blinked in the flash from the photographic powder.

THE MASTER GOT WHAT HE WANTED all along. He couldn't marry Miss B because his wife, my mother, was not dead, and continued to subsist in the sanatorium. Legally, if not insurmountably, Mother presented an obstacle to it.

Without consultation with anyone in the family, the Master adopted Bibi. He never spoke to me again. When he died, he left his considerable fortune to his adopted daughter. To us, his natural children, he bequeathed the sum of one dollar each. There was no challenge to the will. I for one believed that Miss B had earned the money.

21

Fairy tales end with "and they lived happily ever after." You never find out what it was like for the princess to live with her prince, whether they quarreled, whether their love stayed fresh and true. There's no business of daily living to narrate, there's no divorce, there's no sickness or death in them. The sickness and death that came before in the tale is forgotten in the nuptials. But in real life, there is always a limit to that "ever after," and for me it was to last three short years. What I remember of those years is a patchwork quilt of scenes, each square with my beloved's face at the center.

There was no honeymoon period for us because the season at the Met was about to begin again. I entered right into the thick of Enrico Caruso's life and art.

"I will take you to Italy at the end of the season, as soon as we can go," Enrico said. "And you will see how beautiful is our home." But the first home I knew with him was the Knickerbocker Hotel.

After my father's household of silence and dread, I found myself living in one of music and laughter and bustling. I had moved from a quiet brownstone in the Upper East Side into a fashionable hotel in the very heart of the city, its hub. The Knickerbocker was situated on the southeast corner of Forty-second Street and Broadway, right on Times Square in midtown New York. I awoke to the sound, not of birds, but of the rattling roar of the trolleys. The Metropolitan was a short walk away, up Broadway to Thirty-ninth Street, which was very convenient for Enrico, and the New York Public Library was nearby, a little more than a block or so to the east of our building, which was perfect for me. The apartment was immense; it had fourteen rooms, nearly all taken up by the requirements of a single man, Enrico Caruso, the professional singer: an office, a studio, a wardrobe room, a dressing room, and a pressing room among the many.

IT WOULD HAVE BEEN EASY to answer the question as to why I married Caruso, but instead I was asked, "Why did Caruso marry you?" The journalists hounded me and it was always with the same question. This stung me and I did not know how to answer them. I would smile and declare myself lucky.

What is love and how does one choose it? For a woman, some say love is not a choice, but rather the desire to be chosen. What I believe is that love is a discovery, a synchronous discovery, made between two people. To be at home with someone—I think now that it's that simple, and also that surprising, because that someone may be a complete stranger.

Since I did not feel at home living with my own father, I used to wonder what I could possibly hope for in a spouse. Certainly not that miracle my life had become with Enrico Caruso—when I found myself truly at home for the first time and with a man from the other side of the Atlantic.

IN MARRYING CARUSO I had joined an entourage of servants, men the world might view as servants but who were his most cherished intimates. They serviced his every need and were paid very handsomely for it, but at a cost to all personal life. If they had one, Enrico limited it. Though after our marriage Martino was allowed at last to live with his wife, Enrico wagged a finger at him, and said, "Remember now, no children!"

Enrico had so many servants that at first it was hard for me to even remember all their names. I didn't need to remember their responsibilities because all their orders and instructions came directly from Enrico, and he was not undemanding. "Turnip head!" he would shout if they were not followed to the letter.

There didn't seem to be anything for me to do that wasn't already done by the servants. When I wasn't with Enrico, I felt

awkwardly conspicuous and a little lost. Like a character standing around onstage without any lines to speak until the principal,
the hero, re-enters the scene.

All my days began and ended at his side. The bedroom was
the one place where I had Enrico Caruso to myself. In the
morning I would slip out of bed shortly before eight, when it
was time for Enrico to rise. Sometimes this woke him.
Sometimes he would stir and reach for me in his sleep. I would
kiss his hand then, the hand that held me, and ease myself away.
I would go to the kitchen. Martino would be waiting; I never
once had to call for him.

"Good morning, Martino."

"Good morning, Signora. I make the coffee for the Signore
now."

Only Martino knew how to make espresso to satisfy Enrico. I
watched him until I had learned how to make it that way too. He
used bottled water, Italian mineral water. He ground the beans
himself just before making it. They released the odor of roasting
into the air. It was heavenly. Then he filled the filter cone of the
espresso pot. The coffee formed a little mound but he did not
tamp the grounds; he screwed the top of the pot back on, and
placed it on the stove.

When the coffee was done, he poured the thick black brew
into tiny cups. Compared to regular coffee cups they might be
from a child's play china set, they seemed so small to me. But
the coffee was potent; even a small serving could jolt the
nervous system. I carried the miniature cups to the bedroom.
Enrico would be sitting up in bed then, waiting for me. He
said he heard the pot sputtering, that it was his alarm clock,
but it seemed incredible to me that he could hear this through

a closed door when the kitchen was at the other end of the apartment.

"Here's your coffee, darling." I sat on the edge of the bed beside him with my own cup. Then we would talk, and he would tell me all that he had scheduled for the day and I knew how little time alone I would have with him on that and most days. After the first month of this routine, I felt a need to be responsible for more than bringing him his coffee in the morning.

"Enrico, you're always so busy, and the servants do everything. I think I should find a job of some sort."

"You are my wife. If you want a job, well, your job is to love me."

"That's not a job, Enrico, that's my vocation."

"Ah, you are the intelligent one, Doro, with the words."

"I need something to do when you're not around."

"I always see you writing in that book. Why don't you write something?"

My notebook was not a diary of my days but a collection of quotations from my reading: other people's writing, other people's thoughts. A writer needs a subject and I hadn't found mine yet.

Later that morning, before leaving for the Met, Enrico gave me a gold pen and a checkbook with five thousand dollars deposited into my account. I was used to my father's penurious ways with a single dollar. This allowance, then about five times an average man's yearly salary, was astronomical.

"I'll be very careful with this money. I won't spend it foolishly," I promised.

"Spend all you want. I'll give you more when it's gone. It's not for saving. It's for you to have fun!"

"Fun" felt strangely on my lips as if I were speaking a foreign tongue; it was the new way I lived my life with Enrico.

I CAN'T EASILY DESCRIBE what my life was with Enrico Caruso. I must use his full name to try to convey a sense that he carried his public persona wherever he went. Although the quiet moments with him were mine, they were few, they framed days best described as schedules, structured by the rigor and discipline of the performing artist at the top of his field. It was over coffee in the morning and Epsom salts at night that I had him to myself. I lit the first and the last cigarette of the day for him. When I try to recall the routine, the rhythm of my time with him, it comes back with a soundtrack. Those days play back the music of whichever operatic role Enrico was creating at the time. They revolved around his performances at the Met and public appearances. Each hour was parceled out in advance, much of it in minutes.

Opening night for the Metropolitan's season of 1918, the event during which I made my debut as Enrico Caruso's wife—why, everyone made way for me! My entrance caused a ripple of whispers and movement through the crowded salon of the theater, and as I approached, a sudden silence descended on the throng that parted miraculously, like the Red Sea for the Israelites, to let me pass. Men and women, they all watched me as I walked by. Though I wasn't used to being looked at or admired, being Enrico Caruso's wife gave me courage. Perhaps it was like acting; my role became clearer to me that night, and it was social: to shine for my husband in public. Then I found myself smiling into strangers' faces. And if I didn't focus my eyes and really look at them it wasn't so difficult. I felt very pretty in my white velvet gown, white chinchilla wrapped around my bare shoulders. And if I also borrowed beauty from the tiara and magnificent necklace I wore, both set in white gold and studded with diamonds in the garland style—well, the diamonds were dazzling. They seemed to catch and reflect back every light in the theater. I shimmered as I walked. Dressed this way, my height was not hulking, but regal. I could hold my head high. His love made me beautiful.

Still I was relieved when an usher found me and led me to the private box Enrico had now permanently reserved for me in the first balcony. Heads turned up to look at me from the mezzanine as well, but only if I leaned forward could they really see me, so I sat back in my chair and relaxed into my fur wrap as I waited for the opera to begin.

"How do you like the opera, Mrs. Caruso?"

"It was splendid, Mr. Caruso! When the lights are on, I sit in my box and all heads turn, all eyes are watching me. Then, when the house lights go down, I get to watch you!"

He chuckled, he chortled, he laughed as a child laughs, openly; he laughed as a Neapolitan laughs, with his whole body.

"I didn't know you were funny too. I know you are good from the first moment I saw you. Good like the Madonna herself, good like what you know all your life and can trust. But funny—that's a bonus!"

Married life agreed with me. Even his preferences became my preferences. I did not know I liked my coffee black until I drank it in the mornings with Enrico. I was good at the supporting role of wife. I had no other ambitions.

Now that I was Mrs. Caruso I could be seen at his side in photos in the daily papers. At the Met I sat in the audience every night and basked in their adulation for him. And the shy young woman I was changed, grew confident with his confidence in me.

Still, our life together was not without its misunderstandings, the worst incident triggered by his jealousy. It wasn't as if I hadn't been warned that he was jealous, but I could never have guessed the extent of it. When he was away from home on a tour, he would caution me in his letters. His fears sometimes even triggered threats, the violence of which seemed to come straight out of Opera: I could not take them seriously:

I lay down for a while because my head gave me a bad pain, I think perhaps one day you will leave me! Oh no! you don't do such a terrible thing or I will kill you! Remember that I am geloso, and you must hope to never see me that way.

Enrico had told me that he was a one-woman man, but one who had been betrayed to heartbreak and scandal by his first love, Ada.

"The chauffeur, the chauffeur, she left me for my driver. That's what she thought I was worth, or that's what, by her actions, she told the world!"

There were no young men among his servants now. The men who stayed on in the household had all been tested for loyalty through years of service.

"Dorothy, you must not speak, you must not be seen with any man but me. Not even to say hello on the street. You understand?"

"Not even a relative? Not even a cousin, if I should meet him by chance?"

"Not even a cousin. People who see you don't understand if he is your cousin."

There were no male friends I had to give up; he was so good to me I would have readily complied anyway. I took it to be something of those customs of Naples I didn't understand, so I was prepared to humor him.

Then one day I was made to understand the seriousness of the problem. It happened at one of those parties he hated but felt obliged to attend, though I was actually rather pleased to be there. The band was playing when we arrived and Enrico wanted to dance right away, but I told him no, that I wanted to just sit comfortably at a table with him. The truth was there was no one yet on the dance floor, and the very thought of all eyes turned on me as I danced with Enrico Caruso—well, I wasn't quite that confident yet.

I remember that it was a spring evening and the hall was near a lake. One side of the building was entirely composed of sliding-glass doors and they were all left open. A singer joined the band onstage and they started playing a dreamy new song I loved, called *Apple Blossom Time*. Branches blushing with pink blossoms filled my eyes as he crooned that song of love and courtship. The dance floor began to fill with couples then. There was a breeze, a rather cool one, coming in through the open doors. It made me draw my stole a little closer around my shoulders; it picked up the hems of the fuller skirts among the women dancing, who, with every turn, risked exposing more leg.

The dance floor was a sunken one and tables were set all around it. It felt a bit like a stage even though I was seated in my usual role as audience. It was a privilege to have such a view. The moon was rising over the lake, its silver glow lighting up the landscape both from above and from below. Inside the ball-room, the tables were in darkness except for the flickering tea lights. Shining over the dance floor, there was a rival moon, a sphere of cut glass, diamond bright and shimmering with a fractured light.

I was content to stay on the sidelines, to observe all the dancers and note the lovely gowns. Enrico went to get us drinks, and while I waited for him a colonel in dress uniform, a friend of my father's, greeted me and asked me to dance. It would not have been polite to refuse him. We were waltzing on the dance floor when Enrico stopped us. He took my arm firmly and insisted on going home immediately. As I protested feebly, he became brusquer. Our host was alarmed to see us leaving so soon.

"No, no, we must go. My wife has a headache." He spoke through curled lips, with barely controlled rage. The poor man looked baffled, as was I.

The way Enrico did not speak to me throughout the drive home, the way he avoided looking at me, and the way he spat out orders at the driver and at me was familiar—like my father, not my husband.

Behind the closed doors of our bedroom he began to shout at me.

"Why do you dance with that man when you refuse me? Is he better than your husband?"

I apologized, with all my heart I tried to explain, but it was impossible to reason with him. I had unwittingly hit that deep nerve, that source of furious anger and pain in him. The humil-iation of Ada's leaving him was that scar that would not heal. He did not forgive me—not that night anyway. After that I became guarded in the presence of other men, careful not to arouse his doubts in any way.

ALL THAT ANGER towards Ada, all that hurt and yet he continued to support her financially. Most men would not have been so generous. I was very surprised when Enrico gave me the task of going to the bank to arrange to have her monthly allowance forwarded.

"I still feel responsible for her," he explained. "She is the mother of my children."

I took it as a sign of his basic trust in me, as well as his openness about his relationship with her—that I had nothing to fear from his former love.

22

What man is perfect? I learned to live with Enrico's jealousy. It seemed ironic to me. He was the star—anyone would expect me to be the jealous one! With days as organized as those in our household, time passed quickly, almost imperceptibly. The season at the Met was near its end. It was another year, 1919, spring and the anniversary of his marriage proposal, when feelings of nausea in the morning led me to consult a doctor. In my naivety I hadn't considered the obvious, that I was pregnant. After the doctor confirmed it, I waited until Enrico and I could be alone to tell him. Perhaps this was one of the few days I actually found myself annoyed with the umpteen people, the colleagues, the barbers and the tailors and the journalists, who had to be satisfied before I could have a moment alone with him. Even at dinner that night

I knew we would not be alone. When Enrico was performing, dinners were late at night, after the show at the Met, in some restaurant along with his friends from the cast. Among them Antonio Scotti, the baritone, and Enrico's dearest friend, who lived at the Knickerbocker as well, in an apartment below us. Even the ride home would be in company, most likely listening to another tale of Scotti's latest heartbreak. He was a ladies' man though he always presented himself as the injured party. But by that point in the evening I could listen patiently because the day was drawing to a close and Enrico and I would soon be home. And at last I would have my husband to myself.

While Enrico was changing for bed, I rehearsed in my mind how I would tell him about the baby. I remembered how he said he liked babies, and this one would be the fruit of our love. But when he walked into our bedroom, I could not hold back my good news any longer, and I just blurted it out.

"Enrico, I'm pregnant. Isn't it wonderful!"

At first he seemed stunned. He was dressed for bed in his striped silk pajamas; he didn't say anything, just slipped his hands into his pockets and grew thoughtful. I had expected a more open, a warmer response. I had expected fireworks as on the Fourth of July, but there was barely the cool spark from a sparkler in his eye.

"What God sends we keep," was all he said.

IN MAY we made our first trip to Italy together. While I thought of it as the delayed honeymoon, it was much more than that to Enrico. For him, these voyages were not holidays, but rather like the seasonal migrations of birds, a return to native and nesting grounds. He talked about it as taking me home. I had not known until then that we were not at "home" in New York.

When we docked at Naples, Enrico ran excitedly along the deck, waving his hat to the waiting crowd. It was a nautical cap that might have caused him to be mistaken for the captain, except that there was no mistaking him. And it was not the captain of the ship that the milling crowd was hoping to catch sight of, but the great Caruso himself. Banners and signs with his name were held aloft, paper confetti was thrown. It was blowing about in the sea winds. A multicolored snow cascading under the blazing Neapolitan sun! Though New York is on the same latitude as Naples, there the similarity ends.

"This is the city where I was born. The sun knows me here. Everybody knows me here, Doro."

"They all know you in New York too, Enrico."

"Ah yes, that's true, but this is my native land."

From naples we made our way slowly up the coast by car to Enrico's estate at Signa. Nothing had prepared me for the luxuriance of the Italian landscape, the vibrant colors, the heat, and the sun shining as if upon another planet. As we approached the massive gates of the estate I thought a king must live there, not Enrico and I. Then we drove a long way along an avenue bordered by cypress trees, such tall and stately trees it seemed we were passing through a procession of green Roman columns.

At the villa Enrico's sons were waiting to be introduced to me. Fofò, his first son, was a young man with very erect posture, inculcated through a lifetime of military school. He didn't look at all like Enrico; he was taller and blue-eyed. Fofò was formal, offering me a clipped bow as we were introduced. At twenty-one, he wasn't much younger than myself, and I felt uncomfortable with him. Then I was introduced to Mimmi, the younger son. The boy had Enrico's dark eyes, but his face was not squared like his father's, instead it was long and oval with that quality of contemplative grace you see in the tilt of the head of figures in the painting of Botticelli. These qualities and the fact that he spoke English made me feel close to him right away.

"I am very pleased to meet you." He spoke with a refined British accent.

The salon was enormous and seemed designed for display rather than living, but we gathered in an area where the furniture had been arranged around the fireplace and that felt homier. Enrico rang a service bell and a maid came with a tray laden with coffee and cake, a delicious country pear cake, not too sweet.

His sons sat on either side of Enrico on a couch while I was on my own in a rather stiff antique chair. The conversation was a little stiff too at first, but the cake was very good. We ate and drank more than we spoke. By the time we finished the cake, it seemed we had all relaxed a little.

Then, smiling rather wistfully, Mimmi pulled up a chair beside me and asked, "May I call you Mother?" If I could be a mother other than to the child I carried, I thought it would be to this boy.

OUR LIFE AT BELLOSGUARDO was idyllic. When we first arrived the air was thick with poplar seeds blowing about in the air, so thick it seemed like a snowfall. They accumulated on the ground, looking like eiderdown, as if a god had torn open an enormous pillow and the feathers scattered everywhere. It was still cool then, but as the summer progressed the days got hotter. These were days of open clear sky, of resplendent weather. The heat of the sun was undercut by the coolness of the breezes. The air was perfumed with the sweetness of flowers and the tang of chlorophyll. No noise disturbed the tranquility of the place, unless the birds could be called noisy, but their clamor was musical and not the roar of traffic in New York. I could understand why Enrico wanted to spend each and every summer on his estate. I loved it too. If I had some difficulties being a foreigner there, I thought I might overcome them by learning to speak Italian, and Mimmi gladly began teaching me words and phrases.

In the mornings, Enrico would be occupied with rehearsing songs for the next season's repertoire. His accompanist would drive into the estate from Florence at nine in the morning, and for three hours each day music would resound from the villa. Fofò was a young man and off with his friends in town; I didn't see him much except at meals. But while his father was rehearsing, Mimmi and I would go exploring around the grounds. Sometimes then we would hear the Caruso voice escape through an open window, the harmonious strains of his song rising over the dissonance of the birds of many species calling all at once.

Mimmi was a charming boy and he delighted in many of the things I delighted in. We would read English poetry to one another when we sought to idle away the hours while Enrico rehearsed. We would also watch for birds, and revel in their Latin names, as we tried to identify them from descriptions in field guides. The boldest of the birds on the estate was the *pica pica*, or, as it is called in English, the black-billed magpie. They had long iridescent black tails, white bellies, and bands of white that flashed from their dark wings when they opened in flight. They were bold birds. One afternoon, a magpie hopped onto the fountain right by where we were sitting and drank from its spray.

On more active days we would visit the farmlands on the estate to see the animals there. One kept poultry, and there was a white peahen setting on twelve eggs that summer. We were curious to see them hatch. I was pregnant and awash in motherly feelings that extended to all creatures, but most powerfully to Mimmi, Enrico's motherless boy.

We whiled away the hours of a whole summer together with bird-watching and poetry until it was time to return to New York for the new season of opera at the Metropolitan. That Mimmi should return to America with us was my idea. I told Enrico that the boy, who would be turning fifteen in the fall, was getting too old to live with a governess in England, that he would benefit from going to school in the States and living with us. This pleased Enrico, and I wondered why he never thought of it himself, of having his children living with him when there were more than enough servants to see to their needs. Martino did not return with us. After nearly a quarter-century of personal service, he was promoted to majordomo and left in charge of the estate.

23

Back in New York, the pregnancy gave me for the first time during my marriage to Enrico Caruso a schedule of my own, one that was not based on his. But he seemed happiest with me then, when I was at my fattest, his fears and jealousy subsided.

I spent whole days shopping for the baby and furnishing and preparing the room that would be the nursery. Enrico never questioned any of my purchases, he only worried that I might not have enough money in my account, and so my bank balance never dwindled, but rather seemed to grow the more I spent. The baby's room was to be right next to our bedroom, adjoined by a walk-through closet, and across from Mimmi's room. When I asked the boy if that suited him, he said that he had no fears about the baby crying.

"He'll be a Caruso, his cry will be a song. It won't keep me awake, it'll put me to sleep."

They all thought I would give birth to a boy. They saw it in the shape of my belly, I carried high, and that meant it would be a boy. They saw it in the way the baby kicked so energetically, the napkin I had on my lap moving with a life of its own meant that it would be a boy. All the signs in Italian folk wisdom said that it would be a boy. But there was no science in these signs. I would have been happy with either gender except that I knew that Enrico already had two sons, and that he wished for a daughter.

I said that I followed more of a schedule of my own when I was pregnant and that's true, but I never stopped going to Enrico's performances. I had my own box, a little balcony close to the stage where I could see him and he could see me. I never missed a show even though I never fully appreciated opera. It was too unnatural for me. I only went to hear Enrico sing, his voice made even the most artificial of poses and dramas warm and alive.

It was very close to Christmas. Enrico had already left for the theater. He needed more time to get into the costume and the makeup that aged him by many years for the part of Eleazar in *La Juive*. My due date was at the end of December, but Enrico hardly had time then to worry about me and the baby to come. That day I left for one of my by then weekly checkups with the doctor. I felt fine so I didn't go in one of our cars. I walked the few blocks it was to the doctor's office. But when the doctor examined me, he had me admitted into hospital right away. I was already in labor though I had felt nothing yet. The baby was born on the evening of December 19, while Enrico was performing. The doctor phoned the Met to tell him. After Enrico took his bows that night he passed out cigars with pink ribbons all around. Old Saint Nick came by a little early for him that year. Enrico called the baby his Christmas *presente*. He wanted to name her Gloria. I thought of the hymn, of the first time I had heard his voice coming from the music shop on Fifth Avenue, and happily agreed.

24

The other side of birth is death. The other side of the wedding is the funeral. We don't see the symbolism and the symmetry in these things as we're experiencing them, not when they're separated by the luxury of years. We don't feel the inversions as irony except perhaps when one follows so closely on the other.

The end of the fairy tale approached soon and very quickly although I could not recognize the signs at the time. I remember Gloria was about four months old then, just a baby. It started in the spring as Enrico complained of headaches. It was so unseasonably cold that spring of 1920 that I thought the extreme temperatures might be in part to blame. The headaches worried Enrico, adding to the tension he always felt before a performance. The pain also made him feel disoriented and interfered with his concentration. As the headaches persisted he went to see a number of doctors, but received no satisfactory medical explanation or treatment for them. I think that made him desperate or perhaps he would never have gone to a practitioner like Dr. H. I don't know where Enrico got his name, from some Italian acquaintance no doubt.

Dr. H's treatments consisted of laying Enrico on a metal table, and running an electric current through some zinc plates that had been placed on his stomach and weighed down with sandbags. After that ordeal Enrico was then shut into a sort of electric sauna.

He could hardly speak after those sessions, how were they supposed to help him sing? I thought Dr. H was a quack, but I couldn't prevent Enrico from seeing him. Enrico was the best of men, open-hearted and generous, but once he had made up his mind about something there could be no discussion. Still, I wish I could have found a way then of questioning the doctor's credentials without seeming to question Enrico's judgment.

ENRICO CONTINUED with these treatments until we left for Italy again in May. Mimmi did not come with us that year; he had quite taken to America. He had joined the Boy Scouts and signed up for a camp that summer, but Enrico was dubious about the organization.

"Mimmi, I made my brother take my place in the army, while you volunteer for it! I really don't understand." But he agreed to let him go.

Blessedly Enrico's headaches seemed to be forgotten while we were at Bellosguardo. Although he still rehearsed every morning, he allowed himself to rest for the remainder of the day. It was a more relaxed schedule that he followed in Italy. Though I didn't have Mimmi that summer, I had the baby, and she kept me busy.

But with the end of summer and our return to New York, Enrico's health would once again deteriorate. We were barely home and settled again that fall when he left for a six-week tour that included Canada, the South in the U.S., and Havana. And Enrico came back from that tour exhausted. Still he would take no time to recover. It was by then the end of October and he had to restudy *La Juive* for the November 15 opening of the season at the Met.

Perhaps his exhaustion that fall made him more susceptible, or perhaps it was the susceptibility of singers, their fear of colds that sensitizes them and makes them more prone to infection, I don't know. We were taking a drive in Central Park. It was early in December, there was no snow on the ground, but temperatures were frigid and there was a sharply cold and penetrating wind. But it was a day so bright, it fooled you, it looked milder than it was. Enrico had rolled his window down to smoke a cigarette, flicking the ashes outside as he smoked. I didn't complain about the icy draft created, I just hugged my coat closer to me. It was a lush and very warm fur, a mink coat, and nothing like the worn camel hair one from my days living with Father. Now I had several of these sumptuous furs to choose from.

Enrico had hardly finished rolling the window back up when he started coughing, an uncontrollable and rasping cough. I asked our driver to pull over to the side of the road. When Enrico finally caught his breath, he instructed the driver to take him to Dr. H's office, while I was dropped off at home to return to our Gloria.

I knew what Dr. H would do for him; he only used one treatment for all ailments and it would be useless. All I could do was hope that it would not be harmful. Enrico would always return buoyant from these sessions, thinking he had been cured. But the effect of those treatments never lasted.

Later that evening, the cough started up again and Enrico also began to complain then of a pain in his left side. He coughed throughout the night.

The next day Enrico was scheduled to sing *I Pagliacci,* and in spite of his illness he would not cancel his performance. Enrico would never willingly let an audience down, but clearly he was afraid that he might do so this time. Before he left for the theater he said, "Doro, be on time and pray for me." Before I had Gloria I was never late for a performance, but a small child will sometimes panic and start to cry when she sees her mother go out the door, even though her nanny is there to tuck her in and keep her safe. Though I never missed any of his performances, more than once since her birth I had been late because of her cries when I tried to leave the apartment. But that day, to compensate for any possible delays, I left earlier than usual. I did not want to risk disappointing Enrico.

At the Met I sat as usual in my crimson velvet box, waiting for the performance to begin, worrying about Enrico the whole time. My nerves echoed the discord of instruments in the orchestra tuning up, harsh and crashing. Not that I felt much better when the opera began. After the prologue, when Enrico made his entrance onstage, I could tell that he was in pain by his posture, the way he held himself, and the carefulness in his movements, as if he were nursing some wounded creature against his chest. As I watched him dressed as Canio, the clown, the whiteface only added to my sense of foreboding. Still I had to sit through the opera smiling. I knew the public image Enrico wanted to present and I was not about to let him down. As the spouse of the star, that was the kind of acting that was required of me.

That night Enrico sang bravely, he sang beautifully, he did not cough once, but as he began the aria "Vesti la giubba," his voice broke and he stumbled into the wings. From my vantage point, I saw him fall into the waiting arms of his secretary, Zirato.

The curtain came down as I rushed to the dressing room where I found Enrico stretched out on a divan and lifeless-looking. I knelt down by his side and touched his lips, reassured by their warmth, the soft breath on my fingers. He opened his eyes then. "Doro, it was the pain. Please go back to the box so everybody thinks I am all right."

"But, Enrico, you're not all right. You must rest, darling. Surely you're not thinking of going back on the stage tonight!"

Just then Dr. H entered the room with his doctor's bag that I imagined filled with vials of snake oil. He examined Enrico in what seemed a perfunctory manner to me. Then he strapped Enrico's side and declared that it was nothing serious and that he could go on with the performance. Dr. H called it "intercostal neuralgia," something else I supposed that he could treat with electrodes.

So I went back to my seat where I had to smile and lie to the concerned in the boxes nearby. "Oh, he stumbled"—Enrico had entrusted me to say this. "It's nothing at all really. Don't worry, the show will go on." And so it did, to applause and calls for encores.

THERE WERE A FEW DAYS, but only three, until Enrico's next performance at the Met. He was supposed to rest, but Enrico's idea of a rest was not bed, but to spend a lot of money Christmas shopping. Those three days passed quickly and festively, but the dull pain in Enrico's side did not dissipate. Still Dr. H insisted that it was nothing serious. He just strapped more and more bandages around Enrico's chest, tighter and tighter. I wondered how he could breathe, how he could sing, bound up as he was.

Then it was Christmas Eve, and Gloria's first Christmas. The resinous scent of the Christmas tree filled the salon, producing an air of the country in our city dwelling. Gloria sat in her high chair near the tree while Enrico and I decorated it. She was chortling with delight at all the colorful decorations, the twinkling star-shaped lights and the shimmering garlands of tinsel. She waved her arms about and made as if to grasp one of the dangling ornaments. Enrico laughed at that and took the blue ball he had in his hand to show her. He bent down to her and held the glass ball aloft so that she could see both their faces reflected back from its convex and shining surface, as if their faces were suspended together in that midnight blue heaven. Where is that image now? The light left no trace. The ball is stored in tissue paper, in the darkness, in a box among all the other ornaments once touched by him. It was such a happy moment, it would have been perfect if he hadn't been ill, if he had only agreed to rest, to stay with us, his family, and let someone else stand in and sing for him on Christmas Eve.

That night when Enrico made his routine preparations for the performance, brushing his teeth then gargling and prepping his throat, he spat up blood into the sink. But when I expressed alarm, he insisted that it was from brushing his teeth too hard. That explanation did not calm my fears; I remembered how he had told me once that a tenor could die from hemorrhage onstage after singing a high note in full voice. Still I had to watch him go.

AT THE MET that night I didn't feel up to my part as Mrs. Caruso. Though I had learned to accept the watching eyes of the audience before Enrico came onstage—as I have said, it was his wife who was on show at those times—that evening I avoided meeting any of their eyes, and instead pretended to study the libretto.

In spite of the heavy makeup, the full beard, and dark grease-paint that Enrico used for the role of Eleazar, I thought I could detect the pallor of his face. Again he held himself stiffly, not that it was surprising bound as he was in that straitjacket of bandages. But whatever pain he felt then, it did not detract from his performance. In the audience, many of us were weeping when suddenly tears turned to horror as blood started to come out of his mouth. Still Enrico ignored the bleeding and kept singing to the end of the aria. Then he could hold himself upright no longer, and he dropped to the floor.

I had been paralyzed with shock and fear, but when he fell, I rose instantly, and as the curtain came down, I rushed backstage. I found Enrico lying unconscious in the dressing room. And this time he did not respond when I knelt by his side. Zirato was about to call Dr. H again, but I stopped him and called another doctor, a real physician. Once the doctor examined Enrico, his diagnosis was acute pleurisy, verging on pneumonia. There was no question of Enrico going back on the stage, although in his delirium he began murmuring of doing so. I took Enrico home to bed immediately, and hired a nurse as the doctor had recommended. I thought he would recover now with proper care, but I did not realize how serious pleurisy was, or the complications that could arise from it, the pressure on the heart as well as on the lungs. A few days later the salon had to be turned into a hospital ward so that the doctors, the best surgeons in the field, could operate to drain the pleural cavities. Thankfully, the operation went well.

Enrico didn't like being an invalid, but this time there was a team of doctors to insist that he rest. Then to my consternation Dr. H started visiting again and acting as if he were in charge of Enrico's treatment. When he began ministering to Enrico without consulting the other doctors, I knew I had to put a stop to it somehow. Late one night he came to see Enrico. I pulled myself up to my full height and stood in his way. I wasn't afraid of Dr. H; he was a small toad of a man and I towered over him. I don't know what enabled me to do what I did, I am not by nature a violent person, but I was furious, and months of watching helplessly as he endangered Enrico's life only fueled my fury. Dr. H tried to ignore me and push past me to Enrico's door, but I firmly blocked the entrance.

"You see that window," I said. "It's fifteen stories down. Come here again and I'll push you out of it." Never in my life have I been so angry or so ruthless. And that was the last we saw of Dr. H.

SHORTLY AFTERWARDS Enrico had a relapse. Fluid had once more built up in the pleural cavities to a dangerous degree and the doctors had to operate again. This time when the surgeons reopened the incision they found viscid fluid in the deepest parts of the cavities. It was a matter of life and death. The doctors told me that they would have to remove four inches of rib bone. Though that would mean the end of Enrico's singing career, I had to consent.

"Don't tell him, please don't tell him," I begged the doctors. If Enrico knew he wouldn't be able to sing again, I feared he would never recover.

My worst fears seemed to be confirmed when Enrico did not come out of the anesthetic after the operation. We all tried to rouse him. Mimmi came to his side but could get no response. Then I brought Gloria, but she started to cry when she saw that her father didn't move.

"Hush, darling, your daddy's fine, he's just sleeping. Mamma made a mistake, because I can see now that he's still too tired. We'll try to wake him up again later after he's had a bit more rest."

They called it a coma. The prognosis was bleak; it did not look as if Enrico would recover. Days passed and his face was turning into a death mask, shrunken and drained of all color and expression. He lay in bed without moving, it seemed that he was scarcely breathing. Those were dark winter days with skies as bleak as our hopes. The windows iced up; the sun itself, a winter sun, seemed cold, white with frostbite. I never left the apartment during this time; I stayed by his side.

It was on the tenth day of the coma, when I was starting to lose hope, that we had a visit from the Italian ambassador.

"Signora, I know Enrico would never turn away the ambassador of Italy," Zirato advised me before showing him in.

The ambassador wore a pink carnation in his gray-striped suit. I don't remember his face, I remember the flower, the color; it looked so fresh, so alive against the drab gray of his suit. It seemed to be blooming from the wool. It was such a tender shade of pink; it seemed to flush with hope where there was none. The ambassador kissed my hand silently before turning to Enrico on the bed. Then he bent over him and spoke into his ear, not in a whisper, but with a voice in the imperative.

"Caruso, your country and your king order you to live." He pulled the carnation out of his lapel and placed it in Enrico's hand, and then patiently waited for a response. Of course the ambassador hadn't any idea how many days we'd been pleading with Enrico to wake up, and to no avail. I was about to explain it to him when, though very faintly, I heard Enrico speak.

"Let me die in my country," he said as his fingers opened and then closed around the flower.

Come Back to Sorrento

*Of course these details are not important enough for history, and
you will read them without any idea of recording them.*
—PLINY THE YOUNGER, A.D. 79

I

In the early morning hours, from the distant shore of Sorrento,
the volcano was indigo ink smudged on the horizon. And barely
perceptible, in that crepuscular light, smoke was curling from its
summit. That day, in the first quarter of the twentieth century, as
the sun rose I saw the sky brighten. But not so in Roman times,
the sky stayed black then, the day after Vesuvius erupted and
destroyed the port city that was Pompeii.

From his estate at Misenum at the northern arm of the bay of
Naples (now called Capo Miseno), Pliny the Elder, the renowned
scholar, saw an immense cloud rising like an umbrella pine from
the mountain. When the great man realized the danger, he led
the fleet of ships under his command in an attempt to rescue

those in the path of the volcano. His nephew, Pliny the Younger, who stayed behind, survived to write about the disaster.

Countless lives were snuffed out that night along with the life of his dear uncle. But they were all in danger, even those not directly in the path of the volcano, from the falling pumice stones and ash. "As protection against objects they put pillows on their heads tied down with cloths." The history is preserved in the details he conveyed in letters to a friend: "I looked round: a dense black cloud was coming up behind us, spreading over the earth like a flood." And the ghastly fear: "We had scarcely sat down to rest when darkness fell, not the dark of a moonless or cloudy night, but as if the lamp had been put out in a closed room.

"I … derived some poor consolation in my mortal lot from the belief that the whole world was dying with me and I with it." (Although my world too seemed to be dying around me, at least it was not the whole city and its people in mortal danger!) "Then there was genuine daylight, and the sun actually shone out, but yellowish as it is during an eclipse. We were terrified to see everything changed, buried in ashes like snowdrifts."

Pliny's world had become an earth where ice was fire, and where snow was black and burning. What I was confronting now, in Italy, in the summer of 1921, was not such a conflagration. What I feared was the death of one man, Enrico Caruso, my husband. Though gravely ill since Christmas, though still too weak to travel, Enrico had insisted on leaving New York and going back to Italy. If he were to die, there was only one city in the world where he wished to rest for eternity—his *bella* Napoli. His illness made even the blue of the bay look black to me.

OUR JOURNEY BY CAR from Sorrento to Pompeii posed no such seismic dangers. We were modern pilgrims traveling in style. It was July and the weather was so dry even the roses we saw along the way were white with dust. Only the green tops of orange trees rising above walled estates seemed to offer some freshness—at least for the birds. Our destination was a Catholic church, the Madonna of Pompeii, erected on the site of the ruins of what had once been a temple to Apollo.

LITTLE LIGHT FILTERED THROUGH the stained-glass windows of the cathedral. While Enrico visited the priest in the sacristy, I waited and watched votive candles as their flames wavered, sputtered, and smoked. I stood by a Jesus whose heart was exposed and crowned with thorns. Half recognizing the unsmiling face, and how even the eyes of the Son of God were darkened with a premonition of mortality, I lit a candle. As I watched the flickering flames in their melting pools, the black wicks, and breathed in the smell of wax, of burning, it might have looked like prayer, although I was standing, not kneeling. When Enrico touched my arm, it startled me.

"It's okay now—I thanked the Madonna. No need to worry anymore, Doro."

He was no longer a sick man but his beaming and confident self again. His fears had evaporated and he was ready and enthusiastic to visit the archaeological site that had once been the ancient city, Pompeii. Although you couldn't argue with Enrico, you could plead for yourself.

"Silly, wait for some real heat, Doro, just wait. In *agosto,* the *solleone* burns everything up. In Napoli we call the sun a lion, and it makes you wish it was a real lion so you might find a little shade—even if only in its mouth!" Then he laughed. It was good to hear him laugh again.

Although I was flushed with heat, Enrico looked cool enough, his suit almost crisp. I wanted desperately to just go back to our hotel and take a cool bath, but I wasn't prepared for the consequences if I insisted. Once Enrico had made up his mind to do something, he took any reluctance on your part as betrayal.

TO OUR SURPRISE, there was a formal party to greet us at the gates of the ancient site. Endless speeches and presentations preceded us wherever we went. But in this case, to make such elaborate preparations, the flowers, the ribbons, the mayor and his councilors dressed in full gala, they must have known we would visit Pompeii even before we did ourselves. Then Enrico, who had bowed and smiled graciously throughout the ceremonies, and without any sign of fatigue, also waved away the sedan offered to visiting dignitaries. No matter that he was Enrico Caruso, the greatest tenor in the world, he was going to walk. He marched ahead of our party, the Giovanni-Giuseppes of his innumerable acquaintance, who, after gorging themselves at lunch, ambled sluggishly behind us. For if the maestro walks, the disciples know that they must follow—and also on foot. Muttering about the sun and the heat, they put handkerchiefs on their heads.

I kept well ahead of those slovenly men, but I was also careful not to catch up to Enrico until he wanted me to, until he would half turn and gesture with two crooked fingers, the way you might coax a child, to come along.

WHEN IN THE EIGHTEENTH CENTURY the site for Pompeii was rediscovered, the buried city was found to be curiously intact. Its inhabitants had been preserved in a ghastly game of statues. We were walking the streets where many of them had continued about their business as usual, making love, exchanging money, to the end—even as the earth shook and fire hailed down from above. What for? So that in the future anthropologists would have something to study, the textures of everyday life in antiquity? And I, what was I doing? Acting as if everything was fine, was I pretending to be a tourist and ignoring the end that was to come? Did fate put me beside Enrico Caruso so that I might record the small details, the intimate gestures of his last moments?

POMPEII WAS A CITY full of ghosts, of shadows. The stone structures of the buildings seemed to be crumbling before our eyes. The soil was dust, clinging to our shoes, rising in small puffs around our feet as we walked. The air itself seemed arid and the atmosphere was breathless. Villas, temples, shops, the vinery, the bathhouse, these walls remained intact, but the roofs were all gone. They might have been dollhouses for the offspring of the Roman gods. I imagined the faces of those divinities, childish yet severe, looking down at us, and then their huge fingers entering the buildings from above.

The names of the owners of the villas were still engraved or had been reproduced at the entrances of the estates, but those once-illustrious men were now cataloged inventory at the natural history museum in Naples itself.

There were murals in the bathhouse and in the temple, images with the color and obscured light of tarnished yet precious metal. The aqueduct and the drains, what the Roman Empire produced in lieu of philosophy, were dry. What remained of the water system were trenches, really traps now that must be negotiated as we walked on slabs of broken stone whose hardness and heat penetrated the soft leather soles of our shoes.

At least my sandals, although perhaps not pretty enough to be seen on Caruso's wife, were sensible. But Enrico, who only ever bought the best in things, did not own a single pair of comfortable shoes. In his closet you could find at least fifty pairs of the finest quality leather and design, but they were all too tight. Fortunately his usual idea of a hike was about two blocks. He never used the car to go to the Met; he would stroll from the Knickerbocker on Forty-second Street, where we used to live, to the opera house nearby on Broadway. Fifty pairs! When Enrico, the barefoot boy, had saved enough from singing in choirs to buy his first pair of shoes to wear to an interview, he found that, as he walked in the rain to his appointment, their cardboard soles simply melted away.

To walk the streets of Pompeii is to enter the rarefied air of a museum display. No tree, no green thing, mediated the light and extreme heat of the sun as it bore down on us.

Enrico paused and I caught up to him. He had placed his head against a wall, not as in fatigue, but as in listening. He seemed entranced by a silhouette, an animal and a human figure, of what might have been a child and his dog. Had the bodies grown into the walls? Had the pair stepped into the stucco for safety, and then stepped out again, leaving their shadows behind?

"Doro, do you think he was running away—it's a boy, isn't it—or was he just walking his dog?"

I shook my head, biting back, with my lips, alarm.

"It doesn't matter why—when the end is the same. When fate comes for you, she comes." He paused, then added, as if suddenly very short of breath, "He—was—running—away."

I looked again at the figures on the wall but could see no signs of motion.

Enrico touched his midsection and unbuttoned his waistcoat, the material straining at his stomach. The gown I wore was free flowing, loose at the waist, skimming my body, the best thing I found to wear in that climate. But all Enrico's suits seemed cut too small, as if his or his tailor's notion of fit was that of pigskin gloves.

Earlier that day, at lunch, when a huge platter of preserved meats and cheese had been placed on our table, Enrico was adamant that we couldn't eat that and ordered chicken and salad for us instead. His friends, however, half devoured the antipasto before we were even served. Why was Enrico bloated when he hadn't eaten, when he had merely poked at his chicken breast with a fork and declared that it smelled? Mine seemed all right, and I would rather eat it myself than watch flies do so.

With a fan of white shredded material, a half-naked boy with Caravaggio curls was trying to shoo the pests away, but to no avail. The child was the only thing besides our forks and the insects moving in the noon heat. Enrico only nibbled on some fresh fruit, a peach, very fuzzy and bruised-looking in the shade of the trattoria's awning. Then he dipped his fingers in rosewater to rid himself of the sticky juices, like coagulated sunlight, drying his hands with the linen napkin.

THE DUST OF CENTURIES, millennia, blanched our shoes. Licking my lips because of the dryness, I tasted its chalky grit. As if I'd stepped into the wind after a cremation, after the emptying of an urn. White ash, bits of bone, I imagined earthly remains coating my tongue.

"IT IS NOT FAR NOW to the temple. The Romans worshiped Venus and Apollo. But the gods didn't save them," Enrico said.

We walked on and Enrico seemed to know where he was going although his friends had the maps and they were somewhere far behind us. I very quietly stayed close to him. Few knew his need for serenity, for silence. For the world, he was always the artist and sometimes the clown, but with me, he didn't have to perform. Back in New York, when it was known that he had purchased tickets for the circus, the show would completely sell out. The box where he sat became the fourth ring. He would mimic and engage the troupe. His body became a hand signing in slapstick. The clowns had their grins painted on, but Enrico's smile was real.

ALTHOUGH HIS CLOTHES HAD WILTED, Enrico's face wasn't flushed; rather it was pale-looking as he removed his hat to mop his brow with a large silk handkerchief. As if the sun had suddenly bleached instead of bronzed him. He supported himself against a nearby wall, breathing heavily.

I felt helpless when, out of the blue, a sedan approached us. As a native New Yorker, I knew how to hail a cab. I hoped for rescue, but it was already occupied. The Emperor Hirohito of Japan, a small dark man with a little mustache, to whom we'd been introduced at the welcoming ceremonies, made quick bobbing motions to us from his seat.

Enrico was clearly ill, but the great Caruso rose to the occasion and responded by taking off his hat again, this time with a flourish as he made an exaggerated bow to the emperor. In spite of his bravado, in rising from the bow, he stumbled forward. I rushed to keep him from falling, arms open, as one moves into an embrace.

"I bow like a *gentiluomo* in an opera buffa. Then I faint like a prima donna—*quel vergogna!*"

He removed my arms from about his waist, but not without first giving them a little squeeze of affection; then he pulled out his handkerchief again, spread it out on a raised slab of stone, and sat on it.

"The lord of this villa will not mind if I sit on his front stoop. His dogs are asleep for eternity and will not disturb his siesta by barking at me."

I kept praying another sedan would come.

"If I could still sing ... if ... Doro, in an instant, the world would rush here!" He touched the side of his chest where the doctors had removed a rib to drain the pleurisy. To save his life, they had, Enrico lamented, sacrificed his living.

"The doctor said, 'I save you!' *Stronzo*. Without singing, who is Caruso? Tell me, who and what is he?"

MUMBLING IS ENGLISH. Whereas vowels in Italian explode, English makes mush of them. There was suddenly a lot more of my language. A party of tourists was walking nearby. I leapt into the street to ask for help, but the group was already turning the corner away from us. I raced after them, calling out all the while. The tour guide heard me first.

"Caruso, please," and *"sedia"*—I was uncertain which language to use.

The guide immediately went in search of a sedan for us while his group followed me back to where Enrico was sitting. They

were all Americans from the Midwest, I guessed, and not about
to restrain their curiosity—not that I've known much restraint
even from New Yorkers as far as Caruso was concerned.

"Mr. Caruso … sir … please, for my mother—for my aunt …"
Enrico autographed all their admission passes. Such souvenirs
could not be bought.

When, at last, the sedan arrived, Enrico's friends were sitting
in it. They were eating spiced olives and spitting out the pits over
the side. I could smell the garlic, the spice. It made me feel
queasy.

Enrico needed support to stand up. With him leaning on my
arm, we made our way through the tourists to get to the vehicle.

"Please, he's been very ill …" I started to say, but Enrico
stopped me with a look. "Kindly excuse us, please … kindly …"
And the crowd parted for us, let us pass with only a few daring
to touch his sleeve.

I made the friends climb out of the sedan. I asked for their
water bottle and offered it to Enrico, who took a few sips.

"What kind of sun is this? Doro, it makes me see stars!"

THE CAR WAS AN INFERNO. I had all the windows rolled down
and then I placed a light cotton throw on the hot leather seats
before helping Enrico inside. With the turning of the ignition
key, he fell into a doze.

We kept the windows open, but only a crack, because of the
dust. The drive back to Sorrento was into the setting sun. Small
mercies to be blinded without fear; the chauffeur wore dark
glasses. Blinded by the beauty of the sky turning scarlet and the
flashes of the blue, blue water of the bay. It would have been
paradise if not for the heat. It would have been paradise if not

for Enrico's boorish companions, and their influence over him. If he had heeded my plea and not insisted on going on that superstitious pilgrimage to his Madonna's church in the first place, and if we weren't all already half dead from our visit to the city of the dead.

Another small mercy, Enrico slept the whole way back to our hotel while I listened to a kind of duet made by the cicadas shrilling and the humming of the engine. The Giovanni-Giuseppes had squeezed into the front with the driver. Their talk was indistinguishable to me from the general droning sound of our travel. But I didn't have to listen to them, nor try to understand their rough dialect.

2

"I go on no more excursions—it's enough now!"

But that didn't stop excursions from coming to Enrico. A young man, perhaps still adolescent, his face had the softness of skin that has yet to be scraped by a razor, came to our hotel in Sorrento to meet Caruso. The boy had a letter of introduction; he begged for an audition.

"Signor Caruso, if you say I am a singer, then I am—then I will be one for sure!"

Enrico sat down at the white piano—it traveled with us wherever we went—to accompany the would-be tenor. Perspiration gleamed from Enrico's brow; he mopped at it with his handkerchief. The boy stood at his side, clutching the lyrics, waiting to be cued. Enrico's pale face worried me. I left the room; I could not stand watching him tire himself out for a stranger.

I went to check on Gloria, who was sleeping in the room adjoining our bedroom in the hotel suite. The makeshift nursery was down a long hall from the sitting room and well away from the piano, not that music or singing was likely to wake her. That was so familiar that opera, like lullabies, put her right to sleep.

A few notes and the music stopped, a few notes again, then I heard: "No, no, no." The boy was trying to sing Rodolfo's aria from *La Bohème*, "Che gelida manina," but his singing was feeble and colder than the hand the song eulogized.

"No, no, no ..." again, and then a miracle of transformation—the boy's tin flute rose as a golden horn and a voice of such richness and tenderness sounded that it could only have been one voice in the world. The piano had stopped. It was not a recording. The voice was all there was of music and all that there needed to be. I ran to the salon and found Enrico standing, his arms flung out as he sang with joy and with the kind of open pleasure that spoke more to life than to artistry.

"Doro, Doro, I can sing again! I have not lost my voice. I can sing! Listen darling, just listen to me."

Then Enrico moved onto the balcony and repeated the song. A man with a herd of goats, and a fruit vendor, these were his audience that afternoon. Unmoved, the goats kept bleating, but the men stopped. The vendor took off his cap. Leaning on his cart, he looked up and listened.

Even though the young man, the would-be tenor, obviously had no talent, Enrico sent him off with a check to help him with his studies, as if the young singer had healed him. He thanked the boy, and for the remainder of that day Enrico planned his next season at the Met—as if he had never been ill, as if he were not still ailing. He was preparing to resume his career.

"Remember, Doro, my art will always come first, even before you."

And he could never say no to his art.

3

The sky, its blue had begun to look bruised. There was no more singing at the Vittoria, our hotel in Sorrento; blood came out of his mouth when he tried.

So much color—that's what beauty is, display, that's what tragedy is as well, high drama. The great Caruso was dying. Unable to get good doctors in Sorrento, I ordered everything packed and shipped while we traveled by car to Naples and moved into the Vesuvio, the grand hotel by the waterfront there.

In Naples we got the attention we needed. The doctors came in teams. Every expert in the area was consulted. They came late at night; they came at all hours. They huddled in circles; they argued about the diagnosis, they argued about the treatment. One recommended that Caruso's kidney be taken out. For that Enrico would have to be moved again, and this time by train to an infirmary in Rome. I would have complied in spite of his fever, I would have ordered a private train if such a thing could be had, but the proponents of the operation, the doctors Bastinelli, they were brothers, said that it would take two weeks just to arrange it at the hospital.

"He could be dead in two weeks!" I hissed at them. I did not want Enrico to overhear. The doctors just shrugged and turned away.

Useless, they were all worse than useless, with their offers of faint and false hope. Except for their drugs, these at least helped Enrico to rest.

I KNEW WHAT I SHOULD BE FEELING, but the shrieking of Enrico's relatives was grating on my nerves. My in-laws and their cronies, when they weren't crying or drinking, they were whispering about me. *"Anglo-sassone,"* they called me. They said that I was cold because I didn't cry. Not in front of them, I didn't. Not alone either. I was numb, I suppose. Or I was just Dorothy, that little girl Dorothy of the convent school who had lost her mother and didn't know what to feel. But my mother had not been dying; she had been confined indefinitely in a sanatorium in the country. When I was still a child, on holidays at school, Father had taken me to see her, but Mother would just look past me to some spot over my head, or, on her good days, she might smile and nod at me, but as if to a grown-up and a stranger. Mother was not dead, so how could I mourn for her? If I had cried, it would have been for myself, it would have been self-indulgent.

The Mrs. Caruso I had become stayed out on the balcony; I could stay there when Gloria, our darling girl, was sleeping in her room. If Enrico were to pass away now, how would she, I worried, a two-year-old child, live a lifetime without her father?

I remember his words: "I don't care so much to die, Doro, but I will miss you and my Gloria when I am gone. I will not see her when she's big enough to reach the door handle."

I stayed out on the balcony, but not because of the heat; it was really more comfortable inside the hotel where the marble-tile floors and marble walls kept it cool. Inside you were reminded what Mediterranean winters could be—that dampness, that chilling dampness. I stayed on the balcony because the view calmed me, that spectacle of purple sky and purple horizon with volcano smoking, that vista that was older, older than anything I knew in Manhattan.

4

At the Vesuvio we were sleeping separately because of his illness. He needed to rest, he needed to be tended to by physicians and nurses throughout the night, but as ever I was there by his side in the morning. But when I came to him in his illness, Enrico would often still be drowsy because of the drugs. I brought not coffee for him then, but cups of steaming chamomile tea. He was still asleep that morning. I placed the cup on the night table, sat on the edge of the bed, and watched him. Even in sleep his face seemed tense with pain. He groaned. I touched his hand; it was cold and clammy. Had the fever abated? Would he recover now? His eyes opened, and he turned to me.

"Ah, my Doro …"

"Everything's going to be just fine. This is the worst of it, darling, I promise, it'll all be over soon!"

"It's the pain, Doro, it doesn't go away. It stays awake by my side even when I am asleep."

"I'll call the doctors for more drugs. You shouldn't be feeling any pain now, Enrico. It's important that you rest if you are to get well."

"No more drugs. They make me stupid."

"Oh, but darling, they seem to be helping. Your fever is down this morning." I bent over and kissed his brow; it too seemed cold and clammy. "Why, by tomorrow morning you'll be all better. You'll turn away the cup of chamomile tea and ask for your coffee as usual. And it will taste good again. That acrid taste in your mouth will be gone, and you'll drink your coffee to the last drop, yes, drink and savor good espresso again. Won't that be grand! Then you'll get back your strength; you'll see." I gently squeezed his hand. Then I picked up the cup from the night table and brought it to his lips, and he took a few sips of the tea.

"But will I sing again, Doro?" he whispered.

"Yes, of course, you'll sing again. You'll get out of bed and go to the balcony. All Naples will be waiting to hear you sing just for the joy of it in the morning, the joy you've missed—the joy that has missed you. And here in Naples, Enrico darling, you'll be able to make out their faces, the adoring faces of your fans. Here you won't be singing from the balcony of a high-rise. The people below won't look like moving dots to you. You'll see their smiles as well as hear their cheers."

"I want to sing but I can't even ..." gasping, he clutched the sheet at his chest, "I can't get my breath ... Doro, Doro ..."

5

The grief of the Italian relatives was canine. Giovanni, Enrico's brother, and the innumerable cousins and their spouses, as they took turns going into the dead man's room, each howled louder as if to outdo the others.

Enrico's own sons were not so melodramatic. Tears glistened, sometimes dropped, from their eyes, but their grieving was almost soundless. Almost as soundless as my own. They spoke softly to one another. Fofò had his arm around his younger brother Mimmi's shoulder half the time. Rodolfo, or Fofò, was twenty-three, and Mimmi, Enrico Junior, was just seventeen, still a boy really. With their heads bowed, the brothers rested against one another. The waiting was over, that vigil without sleep, now the wake had begun.

THE WAILING WAS NOT SO UNBEARABLE as the smell of death that began to insinuate itself from the sickroom.

We all believed that Enrico was a saint; we expected the scent of roses, not decay. That his body should begin to decompose so quickly, that unmistakable odor, was shocking. The smell moved with the stealth of a cat, circling the bed, rubbing itself around your ankles; subtle until it jumped onto your face like a large and slobbering dog. You couldn't get away from it.

What bitter irony for the man of such impeccable grooming. He used to bathe twice a day, long hot baths soaking in verbena salts. Carnation by Roger Gallet was his favorite soap and his skin smelled of that, of sweetness, of flowers.

He used to change his shirt on the hour.

He doused in eau de cologne; carrying huge atomizers of Caron perfumes, he sprayed each room in the suite with it. The smells of his origins, the smells from the slums of Naples where the sewers contaminated the drinking water, that odor of death by cholera and the guilt of surviving fifteen siblings, must have haunted him all his life.

ARRANGEMENTS HAD TO BE MADE, but I felt paralysed. I leaned for support on Martino who was now overseer of Enrico's estate and had traveled down from Bellosguardo to be by Enrico's side.

"Because of this heat, signora, the funeral should be soon. But it will also take time to prepare everything. He was no ordinary man, the signore. All of Napoli will want to see him buried in state."

6

I was awake the whole of that night. I was afraid to sleep, afraid of what I might forget, even overnight. I wanted to recall, to record while I still could, every word that had passed through his lips. The unsung syllables, the ones he whispered to me alone. I kept switching on the bedside lamp and scribbling in my notebook his words, his witticisms. When it was still dark, as the birds began their clamor, I gave up on sleep. I rose and dressed or was already dressed and had slept in my clothes. Forgetting small details is natural as despair and exhaustion clouded my mind at the time.

My husband's room was only a few short steps from mine. I made my way in the dark to see him and stopped before a circle of darker mounds blocking the door to his room. Enrico's relatives, his stepmother, his brother, his two sons, were asleep in chairs lined up around his bedroom door and it seemed I had to pass a gauntlet, a snoring gauntlet, to reach him. As I hesitated I heard voices at the other end of the hall, but I couldn't see who was there. A single lamp was lit near the entrance to the suite. Its feeble and orange light seemed a halo, a hellish halo though. It offered not light to see by, but like a star of the stage, not the sky, it served only to illuminate itself, throwing all else into shadow. As I approached I could make out two figures, their forms, not their features.

A woman was speaking in hushed tones—"... *agosto* ... *amaro*"—that's all I could make out. I must translate from Italian, I cannot think in it. I must translate what I hear before I can speak. This makes me slow, this makes me anything but the warm and spontaneous person that my in-laws need me to be to understand me. I recognized the other voice as Martino's. He was whispering in response to the woman, to this visitor arriving with the first light on the day of Enrico's funeral. So Martino did not notice me as I approached them until I was in front of him. I saw her face then. Or what I could make out of it; she had a veil wrapped around her head.

"Martino, who is this visitor, and why didn't you call me?"

"*Scusi,* signora, I thought you were sleeping."

"Well, you can see that I'm not, so why don't you introduce her to me?"

Before responding, Martino looked to the woman as if for permission to name her. "Signora, this is ..." But the woman interrupted him, and turning to me, she demanded to see the body. "Rico" she called my husband, as if she knew him intimately, as if she knew him better than me.

"Enrico's sons are sleeping just outside the door to his room. Who are you to intrude on a family's mourning?"

In the glow from that single and shaded table lamp in the vestibule, I don't think I could have clearly made out her face even without the veil. But instinctively I knew who she was, and with that realization came a wave of nausea, of senseless panic, as if even now Ada Giachetti could just show up and take my Enrico away from me. If she had a right to be there, at his deathbed, I didn't want to acknowledge it. But what would Enrico have wanted? And even as I wondered, I knew. He hadn't punished Ada for abandoning him; all his life he continued to support her with a monthly allowance. And so I let Signora Giachetti go to him and beg for his forgiveness now that it was too late.

$\mathcal{R}$EQUIEM

col tuo nome nell'anima
col nome tuo nell'labbra

with your name in my heart
with your name on my lips
—PUCCINI, *TURANDOT*

I

These are the facts, what I knew of my husband after three years of marriage. He was five feet nine inches tall, taller than me by a good half-inch. Those photos where he seems shorter distort the truth. If not in height, Enrico was a giant in stature. He weighed 175 pounds, and his body was hard, if not muscular. His complexion was cream-colored, with no ruddiness in his cheek. His hair was black, coarse, and straight. His hands were broad and his fingers squared. His feet were small and wide. His mouth was so large he could hide an egg in it. His smile was ready, genuine, and warm. His eyes were soulful. They had the color and warmth of wood, alive in the tree, reaching for the heavens. He never ate five plates of spaghetti for lunch! He ate lightly then, chicken vegetable soup and a salad. His favorite vegetable was raw fennel. His breath would smell of that, like licorice, like sweet anise. He smoked two packages of cigarettes a day, always using a cigarette holder. He drank mineral water, not highballs. He owned many cars and was often photographed in them, but he never learned to drive. He would have no pets in the city. He allowed no caged birds at the villa. He prohibited the shooting of songbirds on the property. Though he always kept his Italian citizenship, above all other countries in the world he preferred to sing in America.

If I tally the days we were together in three years of marriage, it might explain why I still felt like a newlywed.

2

The sun shone brightly that third day in August 1921, but Naples was dressed in black. Banners with *"Lutto per Caruso"* were hanging from the windows of shops; the owners had closed up for the day and joined the line of mourners. They had moved the body to the main floor of the hotel, and the city made its way through the doors to view the great Caruso for the last time. From the balcony I watched the queue snaking around the building and beyond, never seeming to get shorter, but rather longer by the minute.

I could not make myself go to the salon and see him dead and among so many strangers, although my brother-in-law, Giovanni, begged me to. He dubbed me *"sangue freddo"* because I would not; he accused me of having no heart, of not loving Enrico. He feared the scandal of what people might think. *"Anglo-sassone,"* that word again—Giovanni never let me forget that I wasn't Italian.

Now that Enrico was dead and I found myself surrounded by Italian relatives, by bankers, and by lawyers, I hated that difference between us. All the arrangements were in their hands; I had to trust them to know what to do, to be honest, and to be fair. They gave me papers and I would sign, *Dorothy Caruso*.

Because I hadn't even thought about what I would wear to the funeral, not about what I needed to wear, Martino ordered a long and heavy crepe veil for me to drape over one of my dark blue dresses, and so it became a widow's garb. I had no black dresses. I liked my blues. Although I would be only twenty-eight in a few days, I knew that the country would expect to see me in black for the rest of my life. The veil was makeshift, but effective; it covered me from head to foot.

The king of Italy himself sent a telegram offering the royal basilica for the ceremony. I should have felt honored; my husband, as if he were a member of the royal family, would proceed in state to the Royal Basilica of San Francesco di Paola. I should have felt honored, but I was too depressed. I would have foregone each and every honor to have him alive, to be back by his side.

RIDING IN A CLOSED CARRIAGE, we followed the coffin to the basilica. Giovanni was weeping uncontrollably; he was red-faced with weeping. His handkerchief soaked, he tried to dry his face with the inside of his hat. I sat by one window while his stepmother was wedged between us. On her head she wore a black lace kerchief, tied under her chin. Wisps of white hair escaped from the sides. Although her eyes were filled with tears, her grief was restrained. She muttered prayers. Ave Marias. The beads of her rosary clinked as her fingers moved over them.

There was a mass of people in the piazza, but they seemed not so loud as Giovanni. As our carriage pulled up in front of the cathedral the crowd became restless, murmuring. Yet when I stepped out of the carriage they all made way for me. A few voices rose higher and greeted me with cries of *"la vedova,"* the widow!

Soldiers dressed in their colors escorted us up the steps and then rapped with the butts of their rifles on the church door. It opened slowly as in a dream. And as in a dream I walked down the long dark aisle to my seat, the royal pew, within the sanctuary. The exalted music of the high requiem mass accompanied my steps. The faces of the congregation turned as one face to look at me as I made my way down the aisle. In front of the altar rail, on a high catafalque covered with flowers, in a glass coffin, lay the body of my beloved husband.

There were prayers and the burning of incense followed by speeches, but no word, no song, no kiss could make my dead man rise again.

THE FUNERAL PROCESSION led to the Del Pianto cemetery on the outskirts of Naples. It was green and flowering and so beautiful that it might have been a garden, not a graveyard, except for the many chapels in white stone built for the dead. Enrico Caruso rests inside one of those white marble chapels. Cypress trees shade his resting place. A stone Madonna watches over him.

3

After the funeral, Gloria and I stayed on at Bellosguardo for a while, and for the last time. There was no way I could keep the estate, not from New York anyway, and Enrico's sons wanted it.

Although Mimmi was barely of age to take on such a responsibility, he, Fofò, and his uncle Giovanni agreed to settle for the estate.

It was strange staying at the mansion without him, the only place he had called *"la casa mia."* Enrico had been so proud when he showed me around on my first visit there. Yes, I thought the place magnificent, but I slept fitfully at the villa. To me, it always seemed haunted by his love for Ada.

I STILL COULD NOT CRY. I felt numb, cold, guarded and numb, numb more than anything. And it was not until more than a month had passed that I found the courage to play one of his Victor recordings again.

At times Enrico would invite friends to listen to what he called concerts of his recordings. They always clapped and cheered for him as if at a live performance. Once Enrico tested them and played a recording by another tenor as his own. He was disappointed when his friends clapped and cheered all the same. Some even praised the singing as Caruso's best yet.

"Fame, it makes people deaf," he confided. "Only you, Doro, hear my real voice because you are not listening to something called Caruso."

Strains from "Vesti La Giubba" played to the end of the disc. *"Ridi pagliaccio,"* the clown sings though he is broken-hearted. He orders himself to laugh.

I had had enough of tragedy. I decided to play something other than opera, something from among the canzone he would sometimes sing. I chose a light tune, "Luna d'Estate," a love song with a rousing tempo. It caught the nature of young love, love when it's in a hurry. Turning up the volume until I could listen with more than my ears, until I could feel the sound as a physical force, its pressure against my skin, and so truly hear with my whole body, I played disc after disc. The day was hot, but his singing made me shiver. Then Gloria, who had been playing in the garden, came running in—"Papa, Papa!"—expecting to see him.

It was impossible to console her, only her father could have comforted her then. I took her to bed for her afternoon nap and pulled out one of the many letters written to me when he was away on tour. I read one to Gloria as other mothers might have read a fairy story.

"This is the voice of your father. Listen, he says he loves you, listen, stop crying, darling, he says to dream of him. He dreams of you, darling, even now that he is in heaven."

This Montreal is a cold place like the St. Petersburg I remember from my Russian tour a long time ago. Outside is freezing, but in the hotel the heat makes me sweat. I turn on the light. On one side of my bed I see your smiling face and our Gloria, and on the other side is my mama, and the Madonna. When I kiss you all, I feel safe, as safe as sleeping on an altar, but so sad because like the Madonna you are all here only in spirito. What I need most now is to hug my Doro, my sweet wife, who is sweet like cake, but also very good like good bread. Do not be restless all night like me. It is sad I am far away, but dream, my darling, I be home sooner that way.

The record was still turning when I came back into the room; it was spinning silently except for the crackle of static, those scratching sounds at the end of recorded music. I couldn't bear to lift up the needle again, to crank the recorder, to listen to my husband perform again. I was never one to prefer the songs of a golden toy to the living, to the breathing bird, the nightingale.

AUGUST 3, 1921

All the windows are shuttered. The hall is dim, lit only by a small
shaded lamp near the entrance to the suite. It might be the
darkest night although it is dawn. It might be death, not sleep,
that keeps all in the household from stirring.

A repeated knocking rouses Martino. He has been sleeping
in his clothes on top of the bed, denying himself comfort
because his master is dead. Wearily he gets up, wearily he
smoothes down his clothes before presenting himself to answer
the door. Assuming his duties as a servant has its comfort,
small comfort.

The knocking continues intermittently, a light knock, a nervous
tapping. Martino's not sure what to expect, who might be calling
in the dark of night. When he opens the door he is startled.

"Signora." He bows formally.

"Amaro," Rina whispers. Bitter. They do not exchange condo-
lences. Words of condolence seem trite to them now. All words
seem trite.

Martino signals to her with two crooked fingers to follow him.
Everybody in the household is sleeping now, so he can take Rina
to see the body of Caruso. She will have her chance to grieve and
the current signora, Dorothy, need never know. But when he

turns into the hall he sees her coming, her pale face and blonde hair seem to radiate a light of their own.

Martino tries hurrying Rina, but Dorothy Caruso blocks their way.

"Martino, who is this woman?" Dorothy trusts him, but she doesn't understand why he is trying to sneak this stranger into the suite.

"*Scusi,* signora, I thought you were sleeping."

Rina cuts him off: "*Voglio baciare il corpo del mi' amore.*"

Rina is speaking, not in the Neapolitan dialect, but in Italian, so it is easier for Dorothy to understand what she is saying. As she studies Rina's face, Dorothy thinks she recognizes it.

"Are you Ada Giachetti, then?"

Rina does not respond to the question. She doesn't understand English, but the naming of her sister makes her afraid that she will now lose her chance to say goodbye to her Rico. Rina wails, "*Per carità, vorrei vedere Rico.*"

"Who is Rico?" Dorothy asks.

"Signora, she just wants to pay her respects to the signore. If you would only allow her a few moments with him, I know she will not bother you no more after that." Martino addresses Dorothy Caruso haltingly but respectfully in English. He tries with his tone to soothe the mistrust he senses in Mrs. Caruso.

"Martino!" Her voice rises in pitch as she angrily insists, "Tell her that I know who she is, that I've seen her photo, the one taken at the estate, with her sons when they were little. She abandoned Enrico, and the children as well. Ask her what she thinks she's doing here now that he is dead."

Mrs. Caruso is too upset to speak in Italian. Martino seems to be translating for her. "*Lei pensa che sia Sua sorella ...*" As he does so, Dorothy looks at "Ada" closely. She seems to be already dressed as the widow, while Dorothy herself has yet to change her clothes. The full skirt of her gown, the mantilla of midnight lace draped around her face and shoulders make her look as if she has just arrived from another century.

THE YOUNG MEN, two of the sleepers in the hall, wake to the sound of the voices. Whatever stiffness is in their joints from sleeping in chairs, they easily shake out. They yawn and stretch, look at the closed door to their father's room, then at each other. They remember that he is dead behind that door, but the commotion down the hall must be investigated.

"Mammina!" Fofò cries out when he sees Rina.

"Zia!" Mimmi cries out at the same time.

Rina breaks down sobbing when she sees them.

Mother and aunt, how could this woman be both? Dorothy wonders. As the young men kiss and embrace Rina, Dorothy looks to Martino for an explanation.

"Signora, she is the sister of their mother, she is Rina Giachetti." Martino shakes his head sadly. He feels helpless to explain the complexity of the relationship to his mistress.

Overcome by emotion, Rina collapses into her nephews' arms. They take her to a chair. Fofò stays by her while Mimmi goes for some smelling salts. That, along with a little vinegar doused in a handkerchief, helps Rina recover. She turns away from the young men ministering to her to plead to Dorothy who is standing by silently watching. Rina keeps her tone sweet and low as she begs to see the body, to kiss his cheek, to say goodbye. Martino and the boys all look at Dorothy, waiting for her to respond.

She addresses Martino, not the woman: "Tell her that the body is about to be moved downstairs and that she can see him there."

The hotel's salon was to be Caruso's death chapel; half the city would soon be waiting to pay their respects to him.

As Martino translates for her, Rina starts crying again. She turns to Dorothy, half angry now, but still pleading that she *must* see Rico—just a quiet moment before the mobs descend on him.

Dorothy is somewhat shamed by the woman's pleading; it is a small enough thing for her to ask. Dorothy relents and nods yes.

Anxious to see her Rico, Rina breaks away from her nephews. Martino leads the way to open the door. They are careful not to disturb the two remaining sleepers on the chairs. Rina slows her step to a near halt. Before entering the room she must brace herself for what she is about to see. She takes a deep breath before stepping inside. Dorothy follows closely behind her.

"Not alone. I must be in the room with you." Dorothy says it in English and then she says it in Italian, as Rina turns to protest, *"No! No!"*

Dorothy switches back to English and turns to Martino, who is still holding the door open, to translate the order. "Tell her that she has no other choice. He's my husband and I insist on being there."

Rina clenches her hands in anger, in frustration. But she has no choice, she must submit to the American woman's will. Bowing her head, she pulls the mantilla across her face.

CANDLES ARE BURNING all around the bed. The sacramental odor of incense from the extreme unction mingles with and sweetens that other smell. The atmosphere in the room is that of a church, very still and charged with a sense of both absence and presence. But there is no god on the bed, only a dead man lying in state where once he slept. The servants have removed his sweat-soaked pajamas and dressed him in a tuxedo. Caruso looks to be decked out for a gala, not for a funeral, not for his own funeral.

Rina kneels by the bed and whispers to the body. Then she takes his hand and kisses it; she kisses his fingers one by one. She kisses what Dorothy can no longer even bear to touch and this makes Dorothy feel somewhat ashamed at her own squeamish fears. But more than that she marvels at the purity of the woman's love, in the vision that can see beyond the dead body to what was the beloved, the living person.

Dorothy whispers, *"Pace,"* and leaves the room.

OUTSIDE, THE DOORMAN TAKES UP HIS STATION at the entrance of the hotel. He's still tired from the day before, from handling the press of the crowds all hoping to view the body of the tenor. Coffee bars are opening their doors and setting out tables and chairs on the terraces. The scraping of chairs, shutters being thrown open, the racket of business and breakfast, and mixed with all these sounds he begins to hear words, words crackling, followed by music, and then the voice, the singing voice of Enrico Caruso that seems to proclaim that he is still alive. The man steps back from the door and looks up at the hotel, searching out the balcony of the royal suite, where you might have expected Caruso at any moment to step out and sing. A figure dressed in dark blue is leaning against the railing, looking out to the larger horizon, at the vista of the bay.

In her grief, Dorothy seeks solitude on the balcony, she seeks silence, but hearing the voice of her husband makes her close her eyes to better listen. This voice will be in time all that remains of him on earth.

As the doorman steps back to his station he bumps into a woman rushing out of the hotel. Because of the old-fashioned clothes, she might be a peasant except for the elegance of the cut of the gown and the luxurious sheen of the cloth. When the woman notices the voice she stops suddenly on the street and turns to look back at the hotel, then up to Caruso's suite. She shakes her head, no. As if it were cold on that hot August day, or as if to block her ears, to hide her eyes, she winds her mantilla closely about her face. Then she walks quickly away from the Vesuvio, from the singing. But the voice is not coming from the hotel. Wherever she turns the voice surrounds her. It seems to come from many different directions all at once as more shutters are thrown open, and radios and records play in honor of the great Caruso.

Acknowledgments

The inspiration for this book was Lucio Dalla's beautiful and haunting song "Caruso." While the characters in this novel are real historical persons, and basic facts are honored, this book is literary fiction and not biography. To echo Emily Dickinson, if it tells the truth, it tells it slant. The letters within the text are not actual documents although Caruso's letters to Dorothy in the novel are based on letters in Dorothy Caruso's biography of her husband, *Enrico Caruso, His Life and Death,* published by Simon and Schuster in 1945. I have also used in the dialogue some of her direct quotations of Caruso, including some of his jokes, his marriage proposal, and his dying words. Another major source for this novel is *Enrico Caruso, My Father and My Family,* by Enrico Caruso Jr. and Andrew Farkas, published by Amadeus Press in 1990. In reading these books I became very interested in the women in Caruso's life and their influence on him. In his memoir, Enrico Caruso Jr. laments the exclusion of his mother and his aunt from the official story: "Most books about Enrico Caruso devote a negligible amount of space to the two women around whom the better part of his adult life revolved. These were the Giachetti sisters: Ada and Rina."

Also of great use to me have been two picture books: *Caruso: His Life in Pictures,* by Francis Robinson, Bramhall House, U.S.A., 1957; and *Caruso: an Illustrated Life,* by Howard S. Greenfield, Collins and Brown, Great Britain, 1991.

Other sources include: Dante, *La Vita Nuova; The Letters of the Younger Pliny*, translated by Betty Radice; and Rainer Maria Rilke's poem "Der Schwan," or "The Swan." I have translated a line from Fitzgerald's *Rubáiyát of Omar Khayyám* into Italian, and quoted from one of the quatrains as an epigraph. I have also quoted phrases from the poetry of d'Annunzio and translated them from the Italian. Operatic sources include the following libretti: Bizet's *Carmen*, Gluck's *Euridice ed Orfeo*, Leoncavallo's *I Pagliacci*, Puccini's *La Bohème, Madame Butterfly, Turandot*, Rossini's *La Cenerentola*, and Verdi's *Aida*, as well as the video *Pavarotti at Julliard*.

Livorno is known as Leghorn in English.

AND FOR THE MANY THANKS to the people essential to my life in general and this book in particular, thanks to Cameron Hayne who acted as my first reader (and out loud at that) and also gave me technical support and assistance with my Internet research. The following websites may be of particular interest: www.metopera.org and www.grandi–tenori.com.

I am deeply indebted to the two women who both loved and believed in this book: my agent Jackie Kaiser, of Westwood Creative Artists, and my editor Barbara Berson, at Penguin. You would not be reading this novel were it not for their faith in it, their work with the book, and their guidance of the author. Thanks also to my American editor, Trish Todd, at Touchstone/Simon & Schuster for her enthusiasm for the novel and for pushing me further. I would like to thank Bernice Eisenstein for the fine ear she added to the task of copyediting the manuscript, and Catherine Dorton for a beautiful job on the production.

Thanks to Rosemary Sullivan who recommended me to Jackie. And special thanks to Bob Amussen for offering his critical insights and editorial experience. Thanks also to other friends and family who have read the story and shared their impressions: Jane Munro, Jan Conn, and Susan Glickman, my sister Lisa, and my daughter Emily.

I'd also like to thank Bryan Newson who lent me the picture books as well as the Dorothy Caruso book. Thanks to Terence Byrnes for the author photos.

Thanks also to Concordia University for sabbatical travel leave and an equipment grant. Thanks to the Institute of Advanced Studies of the University of Bologna for a poet-in-residence position. Drafts of this novel were written at their Villa Gandolfi Pallavicini in summer 2003.

Tenor of Love

1. *Tenor of Love* is told from the points of view of two of Enrico Caruso's three loves: Rina Giachetti and Dorothy Caruso. How do you think the story might have been different if the author chose Ada Giachetti as its narrator? What differences would there have been if Caruso had told his own story?

2. Rina suffers in her innocence, afraid to acknowledge and accept the truth of her sister Ada's affair with Rico, Rina's own love. Have you ever been so blinded by love that you could not, or would not, acknowledge the truth of some matter?

3. Why does Rina give up Rico to Ada, finally, in Fiume? Why does she stay when she learns Ada is pregnant with Enrico's child?

4. Rico promises Rina that he will marry her when he has achieved success, but instead he chooses a life of sin with Ada, who is already married. Do you think Rico ever had real feelings for Rina? He pretends to shoot himself with a stage prop at the very idea of having to choose between Rina and Ada—is this all for show? Why do you think he refuses to marry Rina, even after Ada leaves him?

5. Do you feel sympathy for Ada's downfall and poverty as a cabaret singer in South America? Did you expect such an ending for a woman who enters the novel as a goddess worshipped by her family, her lovers, and her audiences?

6. Dorothy and Rina have much in common, particularly their innocent upbringing and role as late bloomers. What other similarities do you see between them?

7. What is it about each of the three women (Ada, Rina, and Dorothy) that Enrico Caruso seems to have needed in his life? Why is Dorothy the only one he chooses to marry?

8. "Caruso, the artist" seems a wholly different man than "Rico, the amateur tenor." How do you think fame and fortune change people? How do they change Rico?

9. If you have never heard Enrico Caruso perform, does *Tenor of Love* make you want to do so? Why or why not? How do you feel about the great tenor after reading this fictionalized version of his life?

Q&A with Mary Di Michele

1. *You are an award-winning poet and author of eight books of poetry. What made you decide to write a novel?*

   I love the novel as a form, the sweep of the story across time. Because it takes time to read the novel (as well as to write it!) you live in the world of the story, you get to know the characters, and you remember along with them what's happened before. The effect is haunting. Both the writing and the reading of a novel is an intimate process. E. M. Forster, the great British novelist from early in the last century, said that novels are about the interior life. Poetry is, too, but the novel is about the interior life in relationships, in a social and historical context, and that fascinates me.

2. *How do you think writing poetry has affected your fiction writing?*

   As a poet I am aware of both the meaning and the music, or sounds, of the words I choose. This was very useful I think in writing a novel about singers. The language itself wants to sing.

   The poet loves language but is at the same time perplexed by its limitations. It's somewhat ironic that often what the poet really wants to express is what can't be said, what has no words for it, even silence itself. That's very close to the struggle of my characters when they try to describe a voice that is gone, when they struggle to recall what couldn't be recorded on disks. In my attempts to imagine Caruso and the power of his voice, I had an inspiration. I imagined one of the sources of the magic of his singing was in his extraordinary ability to listen, that he could hear sounds imperceptible to most human ears. As if he were able to tap silence and so add mystery to the incredible beauty and richness of his voice.

3. *How closely does* **Tenor of Love** *follow the historical facts of Enrico Caruso's life? Did you contact any of his living relatives while writing the book? Did you visit the locations you describe so beautifully?*

   I followed the recorded facts of his life closely. But the interior life is not found in the facts. The interior life, the feelings, the motivations in the book are all imagined. Historical novels are about what the facts leave out.

   I did not contact any of his living relatives; the facts of the book are mainly garnered from two memoirs: a book written by his son,

Enrico, Jr., and one written by his American wife, Dorothy. The people who knew him intimately are all dead. Really I was seeking to conjure the myth, the legend rather than represent the real man.

Yes, I did visit these places. A sense of place is very important to me in the process of writing, I need to experience it, see the landscape, the quality of the light, feel the weather, smell the air, the trees. I think that writing fiction is part intellectual, part instinctual; the research for a book is better if the body takes part in it, too.

4. *You say in your Acknowledgments that Lucio Dalla's song "Caruso" was the inspiration for this novel. What about the song made you want to research and then write about Enrico Caruso's life?*

I found that the song's themes of love, loss, the artist, and shifting identity, along with its images of the sea and the beckoning lights of America, resonated deeply. The song was the first spark. It got me thinking about Caruso, recalling how my father spoke of him always with such reverence. (Opera is my father's great passion.) The way Caruso is caught between two countries—Italy, his native land, and America that made him a superstar—his restlessness I recognize through my father's inability ever to be truly at home again, not in Canada nor in Italy.

5. *The majority of* Tenor of Love *is about Enrico Caruso's life before he came to America and became a star here. What made you choose to narrate the scope of his entire life, rather than detail the adventures of his stardom?*

I wasn't interested in detailing his stardom, his career—I see that more as the biographer's job. I wanted the impossible, I wanted to hear his speaking voice, and so I searched for the beginning of his story.